SOPHIA MINETOS

Sons of Vagrants and Lords

BOOK 2 OF THE DRIFTERS' SAGA

Cover by Franziska Haase, www.coverdungeon.com
Edited by Cameron Heyliger

ISBN: 978-1-7355933-4-0 (paperback)
ISBN: 978-1-7355933-5-7 (hardback)
ISBN: 978-1-7355933-6-4 (epub ebook)
ISBN: 978-1-7355933-7-1 (mobi ebook)

www.sophiaminetos.com

For Christina and Sia

Prologue

At the bow of the ship stood the would-be lord of a wasteland. The figurehead cut through the air, mist kissing her carved lips, her wooden arms held out in a permanent gesture of triumph and freedom. Most of the vyrships—as they were called proper—lacked such embellishments, but an artisan had crafted this one. He'd named the vessel the *Floriana,* after his wife.

The sleek, narrow ships could stay afloat in waters calm or tumultuous, and move swiftly without the help of wind to any location their captain willed. They still had sails, though, merely for the sake of tradition. A vyrship's magic worked whether or not a warlock was on board, but most of the captains and admirals preferred to have one anyway. In the Second Realm, folks with magic in their veins were few in number, and the hearts of all the captains had grown heavy with superstition in these bleak times.

Lothar was the warlock on the *Floriana.* He had been by Lord Dain Harney's side for years now, on land and at sea.

Lothar glanced over the railing. It was overcast and foggy, but he could still see his reflection on the gray waters. The weathered face staring back still hadn't ceased to shock him. He looked so much older than forty. The recent years had worn on him more than decades of sun or labor ever could.

"How much further?" Lord Dain Harney's stern voice easily drowned out the sound of the sloshing waters and the humdrum chatter of the soldiers on board. He spoke without looking at Lothar directly.

Dain Harney was a slim but sturdy man, with ashy brown hair and a beard that was always so neatly trimmed that Lothar wasn't sure where the lord found time for such frivolities. He was pale and tall, and his neck was always stiff, his chin jutting out. The only feature he shared with Joad were his large, blue-gray eyes.

Lothar frowned. "Very close." He closed his eyes to concentrate on the essence they were following. It was difficult to focus with the tireless cacophony of the ship and sea—the best way to trace it was to lie still in pure silence—but he could still make out the being's energy. Lothar's location powers had not failed Lord Harney yet, and he needed to remain in his good graces.

Every being had a distinct essence, a thread in the web of all living things. It had taken years for Lothar to master his craft—gleaning an essence from a target's hair or skin or blood, familiarizing himself with it, expanding the scope of his consciousness to reaches far beyond the horizon. Identifying the precise location of an individual was still challenging for him, but years of dedication to his craft had enabled him to do so. The further away they were, the more difficult it was, but the threads of this being were prominent. Lothar felt them easily as a powerful gust of wind.

Lothar had come to know this essence from a shredded old garment Dain's soldiers had found on a nearby isle—an artifact belonging to the fabled warlock they sought.

As much as Lothar had dreaded this journey, he knew it would not compare to the one that came next. As soon as *this* was over, his powers would be turned to the hunt for Joad Harney's sons.

They'd wasted months trying to find his daughter, to no avail. Lothar had taken her essence from one of her hairbrushes, and as he'd exhausted his spirit to probe he webs of his realm, he found nothing. If Lia Harney was still in this world, she was nothing more than a corpse, or perhaps she *had* followed her brothers to the adjacent realm after all.

The portal behind the Harneys' palace had shut years ago, and no one knew why. Joad's sons escaping through it had been an act of desperation. It wasn't like the manufactured portals that the early settlers had fashioned. The portal on the Harneys' land had been there as long as this world itself. It was something primal, something ancient. The only reason nobody had bothered using it to escape this realm was because nobody knew what they might encounter passing through it. They knew it would take them to the First Realm, but nobody dared to face what might be lurking in that strange spot in-between worlds.

Part of Lothar hoped that Lia had fled this realm, but he was not optimistic.

Her face flashed briefly in Lothar's memory, and Lothar struggled to blot the image away. It was too much. Lia had been his daughter's dearest friend. How many nights had he spent watching Ingrid and Lia playing on the shore?

Secretly, he hoped that she was already gone. If they *had* discovered and sacrificed her, Ingrid's spirit would never forgive him.

The memories of Ingrid drew up thoughts of his wife, Alva. When he'd left with Dain on this expedition, he'd found her waiting by the window as she often did, resting her chin on her pale knuckles. He'd kissed her temple, then she'd murmured something unintelligible. Her gaze was vacant. She'd been this way ever since they found Ingrid's body on the hillside—there wasn't much left of their daughter to bury. Her coffin was almost empty.

But that was why Lothar was here. To end the slaughters after many long and bloody years.

At last, the shape of an island appeared on the horizon. It was as bleak as the silver sky, and dark as the sea that cradled it. The ship carried them to its shore, a wide strip of land abundant in rocks and shells.

It took a good while for the crew to file into the longboats and row to the island. The dull creak of the oars pushing against the waves was the only sound splitting through the air. Lothar scanned the faces of their soldiers. Most had their heads tilted down, gazes aimed at their boots and the layer of seawater darkening the belly of the boat. Lothar couldn't blame them. This place felt oppressive as slabs of stone weighing on his shoulders.

They filed out onto the gravelly shore. The land climbed up-ward—a vast tract of steep, rocky earth. As they began to scale the sloping beach, Lothar felt the presence they'd been tracking grow-ing stronger, looming close ahead. He shuddered beneath the folds of his cloak. It was an essence unlike any other he'd tracked: rotten, vile, steeped in malice.

Dain walked with his chin raised, poised as if he'd faced worse before. And he *had* faced worse, but so had Lothar. He'd been on the expedition that had brought them to that monstrous god, had heard that deathless voice making its demands. Joad had been there, too.

Joad Harney. The only lord Lothar had ever wished to follow. There were nights he swore he felt the ghost of Joad craning over him, and he wondered if the spirit would kill him in his sleep. He'd deserve it.

Now, he only followed Dain Harney, Joad's brother, for the sake of their world. There were days Lothar wished that he was a man with nothing left to lose, just so he could have the courage to tell Lord Dain Harney what he truly was.

A traitor. A coward.

When they'd laid Joad's body to rest, Dain had whispered clearly, *'We should have told him.'*

Joad's gruff exterior had always hidden a trusting heart. He never would have expected his brother to turn against him, to orchestrate his death. And Dain *had* planned for Joad to die, just not the way it happened.

The ground tilted precariously. The travelers spent another hour mounting boulders and climbing down the dips in the land, weaving around the trunks of trees that looked dead but weren't, watching the shadows flicker and change. How anything managed to grow in this stony landscape seemed like a work of sorcery in itself. The air was damp, the mist unpleasantly cold on their faces. As they marched toward the island's center, Lothar swore he could feel watchful eyes boring into them from a sliver of nearby darkness. A time or two, he could have sworn he glimpsed flitting motion off to his side, but every time he looked, all that stared back was a stretch of ancient stone.

Lothar closed his eyes to focus on the essence.

"It's coming," he said.

The presence drew closer, its thread growing more and more powerful, swelling until he almost couldn't bear it. The energy was prominent, the thread bright. Lothar felt it looming nearer and nearer.

The mist parted to make way for a shadow.

They'd reached him at last.

The warlock.

The figure was motionless on the slope, standing several yards ahead of them. A hat dotted with holes shadowed its face. The being—Lothar was no longer certain it was human—was impossibly thin, with a tattered coat hanging from limbs so narrow it looked as if the slightest breeze would tear it apart. Unwavering. Agonizingly still. Like it had waved its gloved hand and stopped time itself.

Its face forced a gnawing despair to grow inside Lothar, but a moment later, he realized that it was a mask. Formed of lusterless metal, it was banded and bolted across its width, and almost featureless save for two rectangular slits for the eyes. But there was nothing behind those slits. No human eyes to meet, to reveal that it was a man like himself and not some foul thing unearthed from a barren and forgotten realm.

It waited a moment, and it must have finally occurred to Dain that the being was waiting for him to speak. "We've traveled many miles to find you," he said to the entity. "And we have sought you for many years. If what they've said is true, you are a warlock of unmatched ability, one who can travel between realms as he pleases."

For a moment, the entity was silent. "That is true." It wasn't the voice of an ageless being, not the cadence of some vengeful god. It was, simply, the voice of a man.

"There are others who have said that you can raise the bodies of those you have killed," Dain went on. "And move the hills themselves, if you choose."

"I can," the being replied matter-of-factly.

Lothar looked back to the vyrship. It tantalized him. He entertained the thought of betraying his lord, of fleeing back to his isle and doing what Joad had wanted all along. But doing such a thing would mean death, if not condemnation to live out the rest of his days in chains. And if that happened, then all of this—Ingrid, Joad, each mission, his desperate fealty to Dain, the remorse that threatened to drive him deep into the earth—all of it would be for nothing.

A chill spiraled down Lothar's spine.

Dain's lips curled into a joyless grin. "I've come to bargain with you. There are three young men I'm seeking—my kin. Around six years ago, they escaped into the First Realm. We've come to ask you to bring one of them back to me. Any of them will do, but he must come to me *alive*. Name your price."

Lothar swallowed. Locating one of Joad's sons would not have been a problem for him—plenty of their belongings remained in their father's old halls, from which Lothar could fetch hairs and trace their essences in the tangle of threads spanning their new world. Lia had been the only one of Joad's children he'd ever known well, but from a distance, he'd watched those boys grow up. How would he gaze upon their faces and see anything but Joad's blood? How could he lead *Joad's boys* to their deaths?

Perhaps they weren't even alive. Maybe they'd died trekking from this world to the next one, or maybe the portal had spit them out into the sea or some other perilous place. It might be a mercy if so.

If Joad hadn't jumped, he would have been the one they'd given up for the Rite. Dain had wanted it to be painless. It was under his orders that Halfdan, a warlock with the power to put entire armies to sleep, had cast the swathe of darkness that covered Joad's home. They were supposed to take Joad, unconscious, to the monstrous god who demanded it. Lothar hadn't known of these plans until after Joad's death, but by then, he'd had no choice but to swear fealty to his new lord.

When Dain and his men entered the fortress, Joad's wife and several of their guards were the only ones asleep. Their children were nowhere to be found—escaped through the one-way portal behind their palace, no doubt. It didn't take them long to find Joad's body splattered on the rocks. He had ended his life on his own terms.

He had known nothing of Dain's plot. Lothar had spent many nights wondering what had driven Joad to take that final leap, and his only conclusion was that Joad had assumed that the darkness was some new terror, some penultimate doom for them all, and leaping to his death after saving his children seemed a better fate. If Joad had known that Dain's treachery was inevitable, had known that Dain would make a sacrifice out of him no matter the cost . . . perhaps he would have surrendered himself. Dain wouldn't have had to bother with spells at all.

But it was too late for that, now.

The entity's head turned in the direction of the *Floriana.* "For your ship."

Dain's brow creased. "My ship?"

"Yes."

"Why?"

The entity answered without hesitation. "I seek the ore."

Lothar exhaled. The ore was the reason many of the early First Realm settlers had come here in the first place, though some had stumbled upon this world by accident, entering through one of the vastly improbable spots where the veil was so thin that portals opened without silver or conduits. There were the Alfirians, the Suryans, the Quierrans . . . and just half a century ago, there had been the Marchant expedition from Hespyria, with Joad and Lothar's grandfathers amongst the party.

Few of the voyagers had actually found what they sought: ores of magic—raw magic, that could be wielded and shaped into whatever its founder desired. It was the ore that had allowed the settlers to create the vyrships, and the floating beds of fertile land for their crops. A brutal war that had concluded with the formation of the

Order of the Second Realm, to keep blood from raining so liberally upon the sea once more, had also been fought over the ore.

Lothar wondered sometimes if a common enemy would have eventually united the settlers anyway, regardless of the Order. For around a decade, every one of the settlements and their lords had united to search for the Source of the monsters plaguing their world.

Now, they'd found the Source, and one of Joad's sons would pay for it with his life.

Dain answered with a weighty nod. "Very well. If you bring me back one of the boys, I will give you my ship."

It took all of Lothar's willpower to keep from cursing at him. It had to be a lie. Lothar wouldn't let a deathless warlock take away his ship.

Would he?

One wasn't simply gifted a vyrship. Captains took an oath to their ships, one that bound them to their vessel and gave them magical control over it. Traditionally, when their sons came of age, captains relinquished the oath unto them.

For years, Lothar had had no choice but to trust Dain Harney. Now, he was Lothar's lord and captain. With or without trust, Lothar had sworn fealty to him. All for Ingrid's memory, and the memory of every soul the monsters had claimed.

Dain was silent for a minute, and his throat caught when he spoke again. "Whichever boy you bring to me . . . do not let him suffer."

"I cannot promise that. I will do what I must to bring him to you alive."

Regret flashed in Dain's eyes. Just a flicker. Certainly not enough to make him turn around, to reconsider.

"Very well, then." Dain motioned to Lothar. "My own warlock is gifted with the ability to track any living soul. If you bring him to the First Realm, he will guide you to them."

The entity lifted its head slightly. Lothar guessed it was a nod. The emaciated being approached him, and a sickening, almost mad feeling rushed through his veins.

This was his duty.

One of the entity's long, gloved hands reached for something hanging from its neck. Lothar squinted and saw that it was a talisman—a strange stone glimmering from a binding of knotted twine.

The entity noticed Lothar staring at it. "This is called the timestone. It enables me to pass from world to world without crossing through Median."

A rarity indeed.

When its other hand reached for Lothar's, he was ready to take it. He had prepared for this. He had spent days waiting for this moment, for the entity to guide him into the next realm. But nothing could have braced him for its touch, firm and cold and unforgiving.

"Wait!" Dain demanded.

The being turned to face Dain and the throng of somber-faced soldiers. "What?"

"How long will it take?"

"It will take me as long as I require to find them. As soon as it is done, I'll return to you," said the entity.

Dain hesitated. "What is your name?"

There were several different rumors of this being's origins. Some said that he was a former lord, banished from his island by his own people. Others said that he had come with the Marchant expedition and strayed from the party to explore the realm and earn his powers. A few people believed that he was old as the Realm itself . . . but Lothar thought that was unlikely, considering that the scrap of cloth holding his essence hadn't crumbled entirely to dust.

"You may call me the Vagrant," said the entity. "I need no other name."

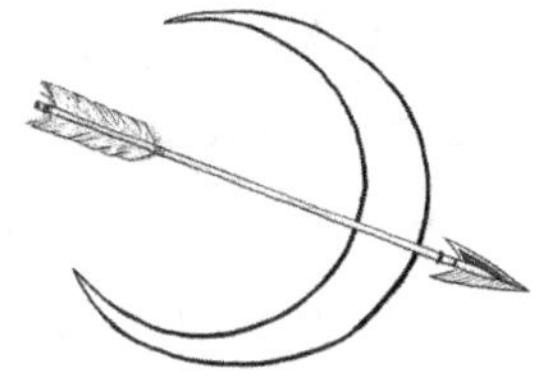

Chapter 1

"I'll describe it to you once more . . . it's half a knife. No handle, just the point of the blade. It got broken, and—"

"*Sir.*" The undertaker frowning at him from across the front desk wasn't even *trying* to hide his exasperation. It was only midmorning, and he looked ready to go home and sleep. This discussion should have been over nearly as soon as it began.

But Halston kept it going, as if maybe just the right amount of wishful thinking and desperation could make the blade—the other half of their conduit—materialize in the undertaker's office.

Halston and the undertaker wasted a few more moments staring at each other in silence. Morning light seeped in through the dusty blinds, casting a faint glow on the undertaker's stubbled cheeks. He had rough hands—tanned and brawny. Halston wondered if it was these hands that had hewn up the earth and rolled Sterling Byrd into an unmarked grave. Did gravediggers think about the lives of the men they buried? Or did they swat the thoughts aside like gnats?

The undertaker ran a hand down his blunt chin. "Look, son—I

ain't supposed to give up the dead's possessions. Not to anyone who ain't family . . . He *wasn't* your family, was he?"

"No." *No.* "Is there any chance we could . . . *check?*"

The undertaker furrowed his brow with a hint of disgust. "No, son. My job is to put bodies in the ground. I ain't in the business of digging them up again. But between you and me . . . and the Wandering God . . . we chose to cremate the corpses after the massacre. Nobody wanted those killers buried in our town."

That meant there was no trace of Sterling left. He'd been made into ashes, scattered across the earth.

Seeing the disappointment on Halston's face, the undertaker continued. "But even so, I'd remember coming across something like that. Half of a knife? I pat 'em all down. Check their pockets every time. Didn't feel or see a knife."

For a moment, Halston was suspicious. He hadn't mentioned that the blade was adamite, and he could only hope that nobody who'd come across the bodies had figured it out. If they had, they'd probably sold it as soon as they were able, and were now well on their way to making good use of that money.

But there wasn't a hint of deception in the undertaker's eyes. Besides, Halston hadn't really been expecting the blade to be here, anyway. Sterling had probably found another place for it . . . somewhere it would be safe, and hard to find. His powers enabled him to do what Halston and his brothers had spent years working toward, no conduit required. For Sterling, that blade was merely a piece of bait to dangle over their heads. Job after job, year after year.

The undertaker was still frowning at him. Halston hoped he hadn't been too rude. He knew he couldn't wait for this to be done with, so he just tipped his hat and started moving toward the door. "Thank you, sir. I appreciate it. Have a nice morning."

"You too, son," the undertaker said flatly.

Halston made it to the exit in two strides and stepped back out into the daylight.

Already, the morning heat was thick, but the fresh air helped Halston to steady his breathing as he started making his way down the dirt road. It had been unbearably stuffy inside the undertaker's.

The office was at the edge of the little town, along a dirt road passing by a church of the Wandering God and a cemetery where headstones basked in the sun. A split-rail fence ran along the other side of the road and divided the edge of town from the great forest beyond. Cicadas hummed in the trees. Apart from that, the town of Dolorosa was quiet and motionless. The townsfolk were likely cooped up inside, fending off the heat and grappling with the events of the previous week.

One week.

For seven days, Sterling had been dead. And for seven mornings, Halston had woken up and murmured the word *'free'* under his breath, only to find that it still hadn't set in.

Gryff and Hodge were waiting for him, leaning against the fence about twenty yards away. Gryff stood with his brawny arms folded, snakelike face raised to the sun. The Azmarian's expressions were always subtle, but there was a look of something that might have been contentment in his golden eyes. For once, he didn't look like a rattlesnake braced to strike.

Hodge was scuffling around the wooden fence alongside the path, kicking a pebble across the ground. His shoulders slumped when he spied Halston coming their way. "No luck?"

"No luck."

Hodge snorted and ran a hand through his unkempt black hair. "Figures."

"Ain't surprised." Gryff adjusted his rifle sling and knapsack. "Reckon maybe we should've left one of 'em alive. Could've badgered it out of 'em at gunpoint. Least we wouldn't be entirely in the dark."

Halston shook his head. The conduit had been the last thing on any of their minds the night Sterling's men came for them; they'd been concerned with nothing but staying alive. Besides, he was grateful that they'd taken out his entire gang on that fiery night. Even if it meant a lead on the whereabouts of their conduit, Halston knew he'd spend all his days feeling like prey if any of those men were still breathing.

In regards to the other half of the blade, fortune had failed them so far. But the girls would return soon, and then it was on to their second plan.

The girls had gone to Vega this morning to cash in the last of their bounty for silver. They were supposed to meet Halston and the others at the end of the town, where this road snaked further into the forest. Once they'd decided to move on, they'd sold the horses to a nearby rancher, and that would give them enough money for train passage to Banderra. From there, they'd find a Nefilium Pass and cross into the Outlands. As hard as it had been to part with his palomino, Halston knew that the poor steed deserved better than a precarious trek through the Outlands.

Halston had to count his blessings—there were plenty of them. Their wounds from their last battle with Sterling had healed, and when the girls returned, enough silver would line their pockets—or Gryff's knapsack, rather—to open their portal. To get them home.

They'd paid for that silver with Sterling's bounty. In a way, Sterling had finally kept his promise that someday, Halston would earn all the silver he needed to find his way home.

Of course, they still had half a conduit to find. Without it, the silver was no good . . . just extra weight, and a windfall for any robbers they might run into on the road.

If everything went smoothly from here, there would be no need to return to Dolorosa. Halston didn't spare a moment to take it all in, bid it no quiet goodbye. If Dolorosa's people knew the truth, he doubted they would return any fond farewell from him.

They walked along the fence, passing by the boxy wooden buildings. Some of them were charred. Halston could think of little but the flames that had seized the town just days ago, and the blood watering the earth beneath the smoke.

"You look mighty troubled, kid," said Gryff.

"How did he do it?" Halston asked, looking away from the scorched buildings and then to the ground. "Sterling. Men like him that burn down everything that crosses them. How do they go on living?"

"They ain't like you, kid. They don't *think* about it."

Gryff was right. If Sterling had survived that night, Dolorosa likely would have never crossed his mind again, even the plunder soon forgotten. Halston doubted Sterling had ever thought of the screams, the terror in the townsfolk's eyes. To no avail, Halston had sometimes tried to understand how Sterling's mind worked.

But it made no difference: he was gone now. Impossible as it seemed, Halston had to remind himself of that. *He's gone.*

The girls were waiting for them on the outskirts of town, lingering by the fence. Tsashin sat cross-legged on the ground, toying with the flowers growing by the fence posts, her raven-black hair draped evenly over both shoulders. Lorelin was pacing back and forth, while she tossed a coin into the air and caught it on the back of her hand. And Jae sat on the fence, watching the mountains as if they were whispering to her in a language that no one else could speak. Under the shade of her hat brim, Halston could just barely make out the glint in her stormy, blue-gray eyes.

Lorelin pocketed the coin, then adjusted the ribbon binding her thick blonde curls. "We ought to have a toast tonight. We got four more bars of silver. Does Gryff want to carry them, or should I pawn them off on you, Hodge?"

"I'll take 'em," Gryff said. He unslung the pack from his back as swiftly as if it weighed no more than cheesecloth.

"You sure?" Lorelin asked, surrendering the hefty silver bars into the bag. "Doesn't Hodge need the exercise? He looks like he could use some meat on his shoulders."

Hodge narrowed his eyes at her. "Too far."

Lorelin pointed to one of her black lace gloves. "You know, if you hadn't used my gloves as a napkin last night, I might've kept that thought to myself. Let this be a lesson to you."

Hodge rolled his eyes, scratching at the back of his neck. "Guess we've gotta go find Argus, then?"

Halston thought he saw Jae shudder before she hopped off the fence and broke into a surefooted walk. "This way," she said.

Halston looked after her with a raised eyebrow. She was moving too fast, too readily.

"Do you remember *exactly* where it is?" Halston asked, taking the first step after her.

Jae nodded, though she didn't turn back at him. "I ain't gonna forget a place like that."

In the few peaceful days since Sterling's death, Halston had started to notice more about Jae. How narrow her frame was beneath her baggy clothes and freckled, sun-roughened skin. She had lots of scars—little ones, marks she probably couldn't recall the origins of. Her real smile was smaller than her false one—subtle. Hardly a smile at all. But the joy in it was brighter than stars burning out in the black of night.

There was so much she hadn't told him, and so much he longed to know. Questions roiled through his mind, and uncertainty crashed through him like the rapids of some perilous river. But Halston knew that once he'd found himself racing down a trail at Jae Oldridge's side, nothing could make him turn back.

And so, without speaking, he followed her into the woods.

———

Jae had accidentally hurried too far in front of the others. She leaned against a sweet-smelling ponderosa so they could catch up, and lifted her shirt so she could peek at the burn. The flesh wasn't half as red as before, and still tender, but the once-broken skin had mostly healed.

Jae had Lorelin to thank for her recovery. Lorelin had given her some sort of paste made out of crushed leaves, and when Jae had spread it on the burn, the rush of cool relief was enough to make her start laughing.

Still, she tensed at the memory of Argus branding her skin. It had ruled over her dreams these past few nights—the ghosts had to compete with the searing hot metal on her side, Sterling and his burning scowl.

They'd strayed from the marked trail, and now they were venturing down a path cut by Jae's memory. Summer had taken its first breaths by now, and the sun threw heaps of its light through the overstory. It awakened her senses. She felt sharp. Grounded.

The pines rose up around them like giants, casting thick shadows over the forest floor, blanketed with twigs and needles. The trees seemed endless. After she'd escaped Argus, Dolorosa had been Jae's beacon, and the woods were restless waters she'd had to tread, half-drowned and trembling.

Maybe she'd been wrong when she'd said she remembered exactly where Sterling's camp had been. Her mind might have blotted out parts of that night—perhaps to keep her from losing it. Still . . . couldn't she at least lead them back to the bluff where Argus had died?

"Are you sure we're going the right way?" Hodge called.

Jae broke into a stride once more, looking over her shoulder at the Harney brothers. They were far enough away that they looked even more alike than usual. Inside, they were night and day, but outside, they had the same light brown skin, dark eyes, and surprisingly wry smiles.

"I think so," Jae called back through the trees, and that was as optimistic as she could be right now.

They kept walking. Soon, Jae's calves began to ache. That was a good sign. "It's steeper here," she announced, tapping the ground with her heel. "Evia chased me uphill around here."

"Think there'll be tracks?" asked Hodge. There was a trace of impatience in his voice.

"No," Tsashin said, her dark eyes flicking across the earth. "The weather would have erased those by now."

"*Any* of this look familiar?" asked Gryff.

Jae sighed. "Not just yet."

She hoped they would find *some* trace of Sterling's men. Her easiest bounty had been two robbers who had left their dinner scraps on the side of the road. At first, she'd been wary, thinking she might've stumbled into a trap. Then she caught them snoring in a clearing not half a mile away. One of them had dozed off on his watch. But Sterling had been too clever to leave such an obvious trace of his presence.

They continued on their way. Jae hooted when she spied a dead juniper with bark blackened by a lightning strike. "I remember this tree."

An unruly bush rustled to their right. Jae sprang back, but the culprit was only a hare. He stopped to wrinkle his nose at the group, then hopped away on his long legs. Jae strode in the direction he took.

"Why this way?" Lorelin asked.

"He's gotta drink something," Jae said, though it wasn't much more than a baseless guess. "And I caught Evia watching me by the brook."

And to the brook they came. It was fuller than it had been a week ago—it had rained a few nights back—and the water trickled over the rocks in a sweet, rhythmic babble. Jae led them up the slope, opposite the water's flow, marching over thick water plants and slippery stones.

"There!" Jae cried at last. She pointed to the stone bluff half-hidden by the trees. The shadows masked the shelf of rock where Sterling had stranded her. Her legs itched with the memory of her muscles straining.

They headed in the direction of the bluff. Closer, closer, trudging up to a point where the trees thickened.

Tsashin and Jae slipped through the thicket first and came to the drop-off point beneath the bluff.

Tsashin screamed.

"Shh." Jae raised a hand, trying not to frighten Tsashin any more. She could make out the dark shape of the body in her periphery, but she didn't look directly at it just yet. "He's dead. Can't . . . can't hurt us."

When Jae *did* look down at the body of Argus Byrd, her stomach flipped and shrank in on itself. She'd seen plenty of dead men before. Had a hand in some of their deaths, too. But whenever she looked last upon their faces they'd been boxed up in a coffin, no more than a day or two gone. Now, Argus, once a warlock powerful enough to give a body to a ghost . . . wasn't much more than bones. It clearly hadn't taken long for the beasts in the woods to find him.

Tsashin had turned her back to what was left of Argus. Her somber brown eyes stayed rooted to the ground. Halston and Hodge came to Jae's side, Gryff and Lorelin trailing close behind them. They all looked at the body like a locked chest—one they had no key to open.

Beyond her own experiences with them, Jae still knew so little about ghosts. She'd heard about unburied souls returning to haunt the living. Was the spirit of Argus lurking in the trees, watching them? Waiting to carry them off like Pa? The thought hadn't crossed her mind till now. At once, she felt miserably stupid.

"Jae?" Halston's voice was soft as the touch that found her shoulder.

She couldn't answer him. She had no words yet.

"Hey, look."

Hodge's voice pulled her back to her senses. He was standing over Argus with an outstretched hand. In his palm was a gold brooch with a blue stone in the center, one coin, and an envelope. Water had creased and yellowed the paper, and in the center was a lump of hardened wax. "Look here. Not bad."

Jae's legs stiffened as Hodge tore into the envelope and took out the paper inside. "Dammit," he muttered, holding it close to his face. "Can't read this."

"Jae," Halston said again.

She couldn't stop the words that came—stupid and desperate and cowardly as they were. "We can't *take* from the dead."

Hodge raised an eyebrow. "What?"

"Put it back. *Now.* He'll haunt us." She almost winced—her words had come out far more venomous than she'd meant them to.

"What are you *talking* about?"

Jae threw up her hands. "I said we can't take from the dead! Ain't you heard of hauntings?"

Hodge just rolled his eyes. "Jae, even if he *did* come back and haunt us, I doubt he'd care about a stupid letter."

Jae barely heard him. Had there been this many shadows a minute ago? Her blood was roaring through her. The land seemed to be whispering. It was a hollow, bitter sound—the sound of anger. Wicked men had stopped here. And then one of them died. The earth remembered.

If Argus was here, he remembered, too.

"Jae, there's nobody here." Halston kept his hand steady on the small of her back.

Vengeance.

Was that the only reason ghosts stuck around? *She* hadn't killed Argus. Neither had the gang. But Jae hadn't a clue why Pa's ghosts had wanted *him,* and there wasn't a shred of doubt in her mind that if Pa hadn't hidden her away, they'd have taken her as well.

Had Pierce left a ghost? Sterling?

Hodge crammed the paper, coin, and brooch into his pocket. "If he was gonna come back and haunt us, I think the bastard would've shown up by now. Ain't like any of 'em *had* souls, anyway."

A fragile calm found Jae, then. The panic wasn't gone, but the world turned clearer, stable as a peg in hard-packed dirt. Warmth spread across her cheeks.

Halston was right. There were no ghosts here. What was she so afraid of? She'd killed before, and the fear of being haunted had never scared her so much—at least not more than the thought of Pa being gone for good.

As they turned to leave, she realized what she was really afraid of, though she didn't dare say so out loud. If ghosts came again . . . and carried off her gang this time around . . .

A brand-new fear had taken root in her heart.

She didn't want to remember what it was like to be alone again.

———

That night, they set up camp in a small clearing by the brook. After they'd built a fire and started to lay out their bedrolls, Jae excused herself and found a lonesome spot by the water. She was sitting just close enough that Halston could make out her faint shape in the growing darkness. *Leave her be,* he told himself.

Now, they were quietly feasting on roasted roots and basking in the campfire's warmth. Halston stirred the bed of coals with a stick, watching the flames lick at the dry, brittle wood. Smoke swirled in the air like a battalion of ghosts. Halston snorted.

In one hand, he held the crumpled letter. Water had turned the script into a sea of murky clouds. Still, he hoped that maybe he could make out a word or two, a signature . . . *something.*

"Can I see it again?" Hodge asked, though he must have also known that it was futile.

Halston passed it to his brother. "Be my guest."

Hodge had barely skimmed it once before he grunted and moved to toss the paper into the fire.

"Don't!" Lorelin cried.

"Why not? It's useless."

"It can't hurt to hang onto it. Where did you put the envelope, anyway?"

Hodge took the envelope from his pocket and passed it to Lorelin. She ran a finger along the shorn edges. When her thumb encircled the wax circle, her face lit up.

"I can't believe I didn't take a closer look at it. I recognize this seal!" she said in a hushed voice. "Red wax. A rose stamp."

Tsashin and Hodge perked up. Gryff leaned in Lorelin's direction, and Halston almost sprung to his feet. "What? Where . . . Who . . ."

"*The Dusty Rose*," Lorelin said confidently. "It's in Bloomsburrow, just north of the Monvallea-Mesca border. The . . . procurer always sealed his letters with a red rose while I was there."

Procurer? "So it's a . . ."

"Pleasure house?" Lorelin said matter-of-factly. "Yes. It is."

Hodge looked at Lorelin, eyes wide with an air of mischief. Halston would have flicked him on the noggin for it if he'd been sitting closer. "So did you—"

"Did I *what*, Hodge?" Lorelin asked sweetly, as if the end of his question couldn't possibly be anything but innocuous.

Hodge's cheeks flushed. "I mean, did you . . ."

"*Sell* myself? Not that it's any of your business, but no, I didn't," she said with haughty irritation. "It's a trick I learned from a gal I met on the road. You go to a pleasure house and sign a deal with the procurer or the madam. Then you take on chores from the other girls to get them to take the clients for you. It's a soft bed and three warm meals a day until you get caught. Works like an absolute dream for maybe a month or two." She wriggled her fingers in midair. "And you'd be surprised how many fellas don't pay attention to their back pockets."

Hodge patted his pants down.

"What's the procurer's name?" asked Halston.

"Randall Dupont." Lorelin tugged uncomfortably at her lace collar. "Could be someone different, now. But . . . I didn't exactly leave the place on good terms. He's not . . . *fond* of me."

"So you're sayin' we'll be hard-pressed to get his help?" said Gryff.

Hodge snickered, sounding just like he had when he was thirteen and Vince Emberhill taught him a pack of new curse words. "Son of a gun, Lor. What'd you do, steal? How much did you take?"

"Nothing. I mean, nothing he noticed." She flicked a speck of ash off her shoulder. "I smashed a bottle over a client's head. He called me something I won't dare repeat. Randall told me I could either apologize to him or leave. So I left."

Halston didn't comment on that. There was no doubt in his mind that the man must have deserved it, but in their present circumstances, he did wish that Lorelin had left the place on better terms.

Lorelin moved over to Halston just to pat him on the shoulder. "No need to look so glum. It's not all lost. Mr. Dupont might act like a gentleman, but he can't say no to an old-fashioned bribe."

"That's the plan, then?" Gryff said with a loud snort of doubt. "Bribe him?"

"Bribe first, shoot second," Lorelin said plainly.

"Are we *possibly* shooting him if bribing him doesn't work, or are we *definitely* shooting him to get the money back?" asked Hodge.

"The first one," said Lorelin. "We've got plenty left over from the bounty."

"Well, I wouldn't say we have *plenty*. And *no shooting*," said Halston. Gods, he'd had enough shootouts for one lifetime. "What kind of bribe are we talking?" He braced himself for the worst.

Lorelin pursed her lips. "I don't think forty crowns would be unreasonable."

Halston sighed. They needed that money to get to Banderra. "Offer him thirty, first."

"Alright, thirty."

Hodge tilted his head. "Think you could sweet talk him down to ten?"

Lorelin batted her eyes. "I'll try my best, dearest."

Even if Lorelin had bad blood with the owner, she had a talent for smoothing things over with a gentle word and a coy smile. Halston just hoped that Dupont wouldn't be the exception.

The sun had set completely, and weariness was settling comfortably over all of them. Halston decided that they'd sort out the rest of their plan in the morning. He took the first watch and tried to stay present, to focus on the woods and listen for any disturbances.

But his gaze was untethered, roaming from Jae's languid silhouette to the sleeping faces of his companions. Even unconscious, they all looked more at ease than they had in weeks. Halston was glad to see it. He was glad for this night.

Soon, things would change.

He started to imagine the coming weeks, months, maybe years. Gryff would come to the Second Realm with them. He'd been trying to get away from the Hespyrian law for years. When Halston had first told Lorelin where he was from, she'd acted as if he'd told her he lived in a world where gold grew on trees and gems sprouted from the bushes. *Anything* to get away from her bounty and Adwell Fisk's thirst for vengeance. She'd like the ocean, and air that wouldn't dry out her skin.

Then again, she'd been acting . . . different since they'd left Luna. Quieter, to Halston's surprise. Before this, he hadn't realized that *quieter* was a possibility for Lorelin.

They'd have to get Tsashin back to the Yunah nation on the way too—somehow. Halston just hoped that her memories would reappear.

And Jae . . .

No, he wasn't going to think about that just yet.

She was still sitting a comfortable distance away from them all. Halston wanted to talk to her.

She should have heard him coming, but the shining water must have had quite a hold on her. A twig was in her hand, and she let its end skim the brook's surface, making faint, circular strokes on the water.

He stopped on the gravelly banks a few inches shy of the water. There was enough moonlight for him to make a shadow. "You look tired," was all Halston could think to say.

"I ain't tired. I'm just . . . thinking."

Halston figured Jae had spent more time inside her own head than anyone else he knew. Whenever she was quiet, she seemed a whole world away. "Do you want to talk about it?" He slid his hands into his pockets, colder all of a sudden.

"Not really."

Some unfamiliar feeling touched him, then. The need to let her be was grappling with his longing to stay near her. Jae had been conjuring things inside him—things he'd never felt before that first night outside Murietta's Rock.

She looked small, sitting there. "May I kiss you?" he asked. The thrill of speaking such a phrase hadn't waned. He suspected it never would.

She looked up from the stream. "That would be alright." Her eyes were shining like the purest ore.

He kissed her once—quickly, and left her by the brook. Maybe he should have said something more. A promise to protect her?

'Argus won't haunt us?'

'Everything will be fine?'

But whether or not he said anything, he knew all too well that she would be alright.

———————

Jae figured that folks who weren't scared of ghosts had never actually seen one.

They hadn't felt the frigid air that followed spirits, heard their hollow, raspy voices, or seen the way their wispy bodies moved like shadows over the earth.

A part of Jae envied their ignorance, but scared or not, she'd met plenty of folks who at least believed in them. How was it that so little was known about spirits?

When Jae dug through her memories, when she turned over every stone of the past in search of something Pa had said about the spirits of the dead, she found nothing.

There were times when he spoke about Ma, and the dozy look in his eyes used to make Jae wonder if that was what people really meant when they said they were haunted. No screeching spirits in their attic to wake them up at night. Just the invisible presence of grief, always lurking somewhere nearby.

He'd told her about dangerous men and dangerous beasts. He'd told her about the Nefilium, how some looked like men and others looked like monsters—though they were all keener than humans and far more powerful. He'd told her to always carry flint or matches with her, as shifters were scared of fire. He'd told her to stay away from any creatures who lived in lakes or rivers as many of them liked to drown passersby for fun. He'd told her that if a suspicious gift showed up for her in the woods—a steaming loaf of bread, a new pair of boots, a box of ammo—not to pick it up, no matter how desperate she was.

But he'd never said a thing about ghosts.

Jae had asked about them a time or two during her travels. It was strange; she could mention the Nefilium, or monsters—shifters, lycans, even river serpents—and fellow travelers mostly knew what she was talking about. But ghosts?

If they'd seen one, it had been fleeting. When she asked about them, most folks looked at her like she was mad, but she'd never *cared* whether they thought she was mad. All she cared about was finding the truth.

Jae tossed a pebble into the brook. Droplets rained on her, making her skin tingle. A chill traced down her neck. Her nerves shifted slightly.

A presence had crept up behind her. She turned around, ready to tell Halston to go back to the camp, that she was fine, that she'd get some rest when she was ready.

Instead, she gasped.

"Jem?"

The ghost who had saved her life waited at the treeline, watching her with faint, curious eyes. His wispy, bluish form stood out in the darkness, and through him, Jae could see the blurred shapes of the trees. Though his features were faint, Jae could still make out most of them. He looked like a young man, twenty-five or so, but his disposition made him look weathered beyond his years. Stubbled cheeks, baggy clothes. He looked exactly as he had the last time she'd seen him.

"Been lookin' for you." Jem glided closer to her. "Can't stay long. I was wondering if you—"

Before he could finish speaking, Jem blinked out of sight. Jae squinted.

After a long stretch of silence, he reappeared several paces away. "Dammit," he said, then edged closer to her.

Jae could only stare. "You alright?" Perhaps it was a strange thing to ask a ghost, but he was glaring at the ground and muttering in frustration.

"It's like I'm a damn *fish* or something!" Jem's arms flailed above his head. "Hook in my lip. Nothing I can do about it. Pulling me back to the damned mine."

"Mine?"

Jem's reflection shone on the surface of the brook. "I hope I ain't bothering you, but you're only person I could come to—who's seen me like this, I mean . . . I don't want to scare some poor soul half to death. But I came to ask you if you knew of any warlocks. Like Argus, I mean. Who could . . . who could . . ." He pointed to himself. "Who could do what Argus did. Give me a . . ."

"Body?"

"Yes. Do you know one?"

Jae's heart knotted up when she had to tell him, "No, I'm afraid I don't. I could ask Halston, though." But she doubted any of them could do Jem a bit of good. A warlock who could give bodies to the dead? Panning for gold in this brook seemed like a better test of their luck.

Jem hung his head. "Alright. I figured it couldn't hurt to ask." The ghost's form was snuffed out again, but he reappeared a minute later in the treetops before floating back to Jae's side.

"What's happening to you?" she asked.

"It's pulling me back. To the mines," he murmured. "I died in a shootout there. Sterling had Argus—never mind. It's a long story. Ain't a fun story, either."

She couldn't blame him. A curious part of her wanted to pry, but she couldn't make a ghost relive the night of his death, especially when he seemed so desperate to reverse it.

Jem stayed hovering there for a few moments before he slipped away again, then reappeared once more. The poor fella must have been trying with all his might to stay near her place. Jae wasn't quite sure why he was sticking around, but she didn't mind his company in the slightest.

The mines, she thought with dawning realization.

In death, Jem had to fight to keep his spirit from being tugged back to the place he'd died.

That meant . . .

"Jem," she said. "If . . . let's say Sterling and his men wanted to haunt us. Avenge themselves, or . . . I don't know what. Would they be able to?"

Jem tilted his head. "Have they shown up yet?"

"No." She swallowed. "We came across Argus in the forest today, and it scared me half to death. I felt like his ghost would pop out of the bushes."

"We can't show ourselves in the daylight," Jem said. "When the sun comes up, we just . . . stop. It's like falling asleep. But if you ain't seen his spirit yet, I reckon you'll be just fine. He probably went on to what's next."

"What *is* next?"

Jem smiled sadly. "Can't tell you that. But I saw it and turned back. Wasn't ready yet. I wasn't . . . I wasn't *done*. I tried to get back into my body, but . . . I guess I waited too long, or I was too badly hurt or something. So . . . now I'm just stuck like this."

"But . . . was it nice?" asked Jae. "What you saw?"

Jem was there a moment, gone, back again a moment later. "Oh, sure. It was real nice."

That *look* he gave her. It was really something. Like stumbling over a cabin's threshold and toward the hearth—simple and certain and warm. It wasn't quite enough to make her believe that everything would be alright, but it washed away some of her fear. Right now, that was more than she could have asked for.

Jem was looking at all of the trees with a faintly sad expression. Jae couldn't fight the curiosity that overcame her, then. "What's keeping you here, Jem?"

He answered very plainly. "A couple hundred regrets."

With that, Jem vanished one last time. Jae waited for him to pop up, to rise from the brook like a geyser once or twice more, but he was gone for good, now. Well, for the night, at least.

Jae gazed at the reflection staring back from the world inside the waters. Her face was lighter, less weathered than before, somehow.

Jem was fighting—pushing against the pull of the place he'd died. The mines, wherever they were, had a hold on him.

And that gave her two pieces of wonderful, wonderful news.

The first was that the further they got from Dolorosa, the less likely it was they would run into the spirits of Sterling and his men.

The second was that if she could figure out where those ghosts had died . . .

She might have a lucky shot at finding Pa.

Chapter 2

Lorelin woke from a dream about winter. She'd been lying in the snow, clothes soaking, and crying—deep, heavy sobs made powerful by the state of dreaming. When she rose at last, her cheeks were wet and warm. The tears had fought their way out of her nightmare.

Lorelin breathed in as deeply as she could, reminding herself that she was awake and that it was summer. That brought her some comfort.

She'd been raised on silk pillowcases and ever-roaring fireplaces. Her first winter in the wilderness had nearly killed her, and every once in a while, the memories returned to her at night. Lorelin had been one of the lucky ones. She'd met folks who had lost fingers, toes, limbs to frostbite. Even now, she could recall shivering in the snow, forgetting what warmth itself felt like. When the winter had passed, she'd expected that she would feel stronger, like she'd conquered some gauntlet. But she hadn't felt stronger. There was nothing left in her but anger. Anger that lurked beneath forced laughter among a thousand strangers under a hundred roofs.

Luna and Martina had calmed the storm. For a time. And now, she was just good at distracting herself from it, smothering it however she could: through motion, healing, a good meal when she could find it, a pretty jewel when she could snatch it up.

But she was getting tired of the storm. And now, with the Dusty Rose and Randall Dupont on the horizon, it seemed that it wasn't fading anytime soon.

Still, fretting about it wouldn't do her a bit of good. The more she longed for Luna, the less she could focus on the matter at hand: helping her gang.

Hodge was still awake from his watch, and Lorelin offered to refill the water supply while he got a fire going. Lorelin gathered up the canteens and waterskins and started following the brook, only to find Jae sleeping on the shore. No bedroll. Her braids were sprawled out over her shoulders, and the daybreak light caught in the gold tones in her chestnut hair. Lorelin nudged her on the shoulder. When Jae didn't stir, Lorelin flicked water onto her face. Jae scrambled upright.

"You've got mud on your face," Lorelin said, tapping the apple of her own cheek. She passed Jae two of the canteens. "Think you could help me refill these?"

Jae wiped the mud off in one sloppy, exaggerated swipe of her sleeve, then picked up the canteens and uncorked them. Without a word, she lowered the spouts into the brook.

Lorelin had watched Jae with Halston the night before. It was hard to keep from teasing them. She was happy for them . . . especially Halston. The boy hadn't had much to smile about these past few years, and she was glad that he'd found someone who might soften his heart . . . and maybe it would all work out for them in the end. Lorelin hoped it would. She'd very much like to see them happy.

But now, Jae was quiet and stony, in a way that even fatigue couldn't explain. "Is the mud more comfortable than the ground over there?" asked Lorelin. "I ought to try it."

Jae's eyes were unseeing. "No."

Lorelin tried not to take offense at her unappreciated jape.

Jae was silent for a moment. There was something haunting the space behind her eyes. Lorelin felt that she had to speak. She was all too familiar with how unspoken words could burn. Those candle-flames could turn to wildfire far too easily.

"You don't have to worry about yesterday," Lorelin said gently. She hoped Jae wasn't embarrassed. "I know about the ghosts. I understand why you got scared. I mean, I'm—"

"It ain't that, Lorelin. I . . . I saw him last night. Jem."

Lorelin blinked. "*Who?*"

Then Jae told her the full story of the ghost that had saved her from Argus, and how he'd visited her the night before.

Jae wasn't speaking to her, really. It was like she was talking to somebody six feet under, a lost loved one whose grave she was visiting.

This was good news, certainly. If this ghost had spent some time in Sterling's presence . . . could he help them find the other half of the conduit? Lorelin held back from asking. She didn't want to work Jae into a lather again.

Still, maybe he could help them. "I'd hate to be too pragmatic here, but do you think there's a chance he'll reappear tonight? Before we ride out to the Dusty Rose?"

"To where?"

Oh, right. Jae hadn't been there to listen to the plan last night. "Never mind. I'll tell you over breakfast."

Jae rubbed at her chin thoughtfully. "Jem was kind to me. I'm starting to wonder if maybe ghosts ain't so bad. There are scarier things in this world."

"Living men are scarier than ghosts," Lorelin said plainly.

What was a ghost, really? Just a man. A man who couldn't age or grow weary or sleep and have nightmares. Just *drift*. Lorelin thought she might like to try that, for a while. To float around untethered.

"Maybe it's foolish to hope," Jae said slowly, "but I'm wondering if I could learn something from him. Figure out where those ghosts took my Pa. I thought about it all night and . . . I don't know. Sometimes I feel like if I think about something long enough, it'll start makin' sense. The answers will come to me. Guess that works for smart people. But it doesn't work for me so much."

That coaxed a small laugh out of Lorelin. "Smarter than you give yourself credit for, that's for sure."

She shrugged. "Just when I need to be. I feel like I'd be sharper if I didn't have a million things flying around inside my head." She peered back down at the shallow waters bubbling over the stones, still with an unsettled look in her blue-gray eyes.

"You still look a bit . . . flustered, Jae," said Lorelin. "Need someone to listen?"

"I don't think so, no. Thanks, though."

The morning was bright and new. They sat in silence for a good while, watching the waters flow over the stones, and Lorelin imagined them washing away her savage dreams.

Lorelin would take them to the pleasure house. It was certainly a half-desperate lead, but it was far better than none at all. If luck was on their side, they'd figure out a way to the other half of their conduit. And then . . .

Then . . .

Then what?

Where would Lorelin go?

She'd always imagined that she'd go with the Harney boys to the Second Realm. But that was before she'd returned to Luna. For the past few weeks, she kept imagining herself stumbling upon two paths. One led to Luna, the other to Halston's home. One was a whole world away from Adwell Fisk, from the handbills printed with her face, from the Rangers and the Hespyrian law. Surely, she could find some peace there.

But Martina was waiting somewhere down the other.

She tried to let the thought pass. To let it rush past her like a stray gust of wind, here a moment, then off to somewhere else. But the thought of her healer kept circling back twice as strong.

Chapter 3

The Drifter thought about counting the stars.

Why not? It might help him to pass the time. He'd been days or hours into this journey, pacing down this path, and there wasn't much to look at besides the stars out here. The rolling dunes stretched far and wide around him, expanding well into the horizon. Like sleeping gods, they were. Dormant and almighty.

He hadn't felt wind on his skin since before his journey began, and he missed it. He longed for it to return, to feel it gather and swell and stir up the untouched sands. He wanted *motion*. There must be wind here, sometimes. Or there had been, long ago. Something must have created these sand mountains, so soft and delicately sloped compared to the snow-capped, rocky peaks he remembered.

Mountains, forests . . . miles of pine. Shadows, branches, thickets, and places to hide. There was nothing but wide-open space here. Sand and sky and stars.

The path was almost unnaturally straight. Hewn from flat stone, it ran on and on, smooth and unblemished as glass. His boots made soft thuds as he walked at a comfortable, rhythmic pace. He pulled his jacket more tightly around his shoulders. He considered humming or singing . . . something to do with his mouth.

Speak your name at the gates.

It was the only instruction he had, and with every step he took, he wondered what it could mean.

He only hoped that he would know the gates when he saw them.

On and on, the Drifter moved. He was growing fond of the sky above. It wasn't quite black—it had a blue tint to it, like deep water, and so many stars that it made him keenly aware of his size. For a time, he felt sure of himself. Almost secure.

Then, beside the path, there was the growl.

It was a thought. A fragment of a memory of a dream. It couldn't be real—nothing here could be *real.*

The wretched shape rose into his line of vision. Briefly, the Drifter sensed its hunger—a deep emptiness that no amount of flesh could sate. It was smaller than the Drifter, about half his size. But it waited for him on lithe, sinewy legs with talons sharp as spearheads. Its muscles stretched and flexed beneath rough, scaly skin the color of ash. For the first time since he'd come here, the Drifter remembered horned toads.

Then, it bared its teeth.

When the creature's eyes met his, fear did not seize him. Instead, there was a strange, faint longing—a slight comfort to know that something else with a beating heart existed in this place. Could it speak?

The beast only stared back. Its tongue flicked over its lips. The Drifter instinctively reached to his hip, and his hand fell hopelessly upon nothing.

No gun.

No merciful blade.

He hadn't been allowed to bring a weapon with him on this journey. All he had were his hands and the clothes on his back.

The beast leapt for the Drifter with open jaws.

The Drifter stumbled backward, and the beast followed him across the path and into the sand. Scampering, pausing, scampering again. It let out a growl, then leapt to claim its prey.

They danced in circles. Their feet struck the sand and sent clouds of grit spewing upward and out. The Drifter dodged the snapping teeth and swiping claws, twisting left, right, backward, silently reciting some half-forgotten prayer. The fangs nipped at his calves. Its teeth ripped a gash in his pants, then slid across his skin. Wetness budded from the graze. He shuffled backward, nearly tumbling to the ground.

The beast rose on its hindlegs. One of its claws slashed at the Drifter's hand. He cried out as blood blossomed from the cut.

He used to be able to speak to his enemies, to use words to divert his opponent's mind. But this was only an animal. If he were to die here, he'd die nameless and unmourned. The beast would leave his bones behind, and he would rest under a billion nameless stars. The notion of dying alone shouldn't have scared him more than the jaws snapping inches from his heart. But it did.

The creature's whiplike tail slashed his ankle. The Drifter fumbled, and he crashed down into the sand. The grit stung his eyes. He fell limp. A fire-hot rush traveled to his head and braced him for the end; all he knew was that it would be easier than to keep fighting.

The gates.

A vision of the gates occupied that endless stretch of time as he waited for the teeth to start mangling his chest. He pictured his hand on the latch, the metal cold beneath his palm. Softly, he would speak his name. And like the last bird to swoop up to its flock, he would leave this place.

With a burst of newfound strength, he kicked. His heel struck the beast's nose.

Its burbling croak assaulted the Drifter's ears, but it was enough. Just enough time on his end.

He took off his jacket as fast as he could. Before the monster could lunge again, he looped the cloth beneath its jaw and yanked.

It screeched, scrabbled, then wheezed. The Drifter listened closely. Its breathing ceased. Its feet stopped twitching. No more wheezing.

Perhaps he should have looked at it. The weight hung from his arms, this dead thing, suspended from his jacket sleeves. This opponent. Fallen.

But he was no winner.

Not yet.

The fire in his chest drove him onward.

He stepped back onto the path. The Drifter ignored the light grazes on his leg, the fresh wound on his hand. Part of him had been worried that the path might disappear if he left it—he'd been warned that things were different here.

But here it was. And in spite of himself, he was glad.

The Drifter journeyed on. He forgot about the blood on his clothes entirely.

Chapter 4

The journey to Bloomsburrow took them most of the day. The forest succumbed to a rolling stretch of prairie, where the golden grass grew almost as high as their knees. Lorelin's legs were aching, and she started to miss her horse terribly.

They arrived at the town at dusk. In the fading light, Lorelin could make out the dim outlines of the buildings against an orange-colored sky. Bloomsburrow was small . . . bigger than Dolorosa, but not by much. The line of structures blended seamlessly together into a single boxy shape, save for the pleasure house. It was a single, solitary edifice sitting about a quarter mile from the rest of the town.

The Dusty Rose was a white, two-story house with a pointed roof and a balcony looming over the front porch. Lorelin wasn't sure what the point of a balcony was. There wasn't much to look at out here but a dirt road and grass. Appropriately, rosebushes swaddled the outer walls. Inappropriately, a sign reading *The Dusty Rose: Boarding House* dangled from the porch's rafters. Lorelin snorted.

They made their way to the entrance, and Lorelin did her best to swallow her apprehension and let her nerves go still. Dignified, composed. A lady, molded into demure perfection, just as she'd been before her betrothed, Adwell, had forced her to break her chains.

It had been ages since she'd set foot inside a pleasure house. At least, not one that she'd known was a pleasure house outright. Occasionally, she'd glimpse a serving girl in a saloon sneak a wink at some nearby cowhand, and she knew what it'd meant. She'd listened to plenty of men boast about their favorite whores. Rarely were their words spoken with love. They spoke about them as they would a prized gun or a stack of gold . . . except they never said that their guns or gold were stupid or filthy, or any of the other thousands of foul words they had for the women whose bodies they bought.

Lorelin returned the favor when she could, if she'd gauged whether she could call these men 'pigheaded bastards' without getting shot.

They entered the house, and the smell of tobacco made her stomach lurch. So bitter, so rank. It was far stronger than Lorelin remembered. The air was tinged with the smell of something sweet, too, but it wasn't pleasant. It was sweet like rotting fruit.

Jubilant piano music filled the sprawling room. A garish red and violet carpet covered most of the floor, and mismatched tables and chairs dotted the open area. The wallpaper looked like it could use some paste around the corners. A small chandelier bathed the room in a faint glow, and off to the side a stairway spiraled upstairs to the bedrooms. Lorelin wondered what her old room looked like now.

On one side of the room was a grimy bar, and on the other side, there was a small stage. On it, a trio of girls with thick curls and delicate frames swayed and sang to an audience of wide-eyed men. Lorelin didn't recognize any of the performers.

There wasn't a single onlooker in that crowd who wasn't dazzled. All were men, and most of them looked at least twice as old as the dancing girls. They would laugh and whoop every time one of the dancers spun. A flock of crazed birds could have swooped over the audience, cawing and squawking, and not a soul would notice.

Tsashin and Jae were looking pointedly at the carpet, while Gryff and Halston surveyed the crowd. Hodge was staring approvingly at the dancers, and Lorelin thought about pulling him back to the matter at hand when she caught the eye of the baby-faced youth tending the bar.

Oh no.

The poor boy's face began to glow with recognition. "Mara!" he cried.

One of Lorelin's many fake names in circulation. It was a good thing he'd used it; it was easy to forget which names she'd used in different towns. She forced a grin and hoped the boy would think that it was genuine. "Pleasure to see you, Leonard. I'm surprised you remember me."

"Why wouldn't I?" The boy looked like a kitten amongst cougars in this smoky dump. He took his eyes off her for a moment to take in the rest of them—and Gryff with a slight but unsubtle glare— then returned his gaze to her at once.

Lorelin glanced at the floor, trying to ignore Leonard's infuriating ignorance and pantomime bashfulness instead. "That's true. I *am* quite memorable."

"Did you change your mind? Are you . . ." He got quiet. ". . . *coming back to work here?*"

Gods, it was pathetic. She'd always suspected that Leonard only worked here to gawk at the girls. "Afraid not. I came to ask Dupont for a favor. Where is he?"

Leonard raised one soft-looking hand and motioned to a stiff figure off to the side of the stage, standing with his hands behind his back.

Lorelin wasn't sure how she'd missed the procurer to begin with. Mr. Dupont was tall and sleek, with a thin mustache and paper-pale skin—like he hadn't ever spent more than a minute out in the sun. It was hard to say how old he was. There were no furrows around his eyes or forehead, but his skin seemed almost unnaturally smooth, like over-polished wood. Clean face, pristine clothes without lint or wrinkles, and hair so slick it resembled a wig. A man wearing several masks and a very thick coat of paint.

The way he stood and watched the dancers was strange. His stare wasn't hateful, but it wasn't warm, either. It was like an iron weight hanging from a fraying rope—harmless. Until it snapped.

Now was as good a time as any.

Dupont's countenance didn't shift when he spotted them approaching. Nobody in the audience paid them any mind, save for two cowhands in dirty shirts who tittered at Lorelin. She ignored them. The dancers were singing a song about meeting a lover by a river or something and twirling like their lives depended on it. Their ruffled skirts floated on the air, and the billowing fabric reminded Lorelin of blossoms catching in an April breeze.

"Mara." Mr. Dupont seemed ready to bite on the imaginary name—catch it in his teeth and crush it. "A face I never thought I'd see again. Excluding the handbills, of course."

It was a game. He wanted to see Lorelin stumble, wince, cower. But she refused to let him win.

"Yes. That photograph of me is horrendous. I'm much lovelier in person, aren't I?"

"Certainly," said Dupont. "A girl like you is worth every penny. I've heard the lawmen *and* the Fisks are offering a hefty reward for your capture."

Lorelin made a point of drawing circles with her thumb just above her holster. "That won't be necessary. I'd hate to make a scene. But speaking of rewards, I *do* have an offer for you."

She'd leave it at that. She couldn't let him know how desperate they actually were.

Mr. Dupont shook his head at Lorelin in a dismissive, pitiful way. "You didn't like it here, did you, Mara?"

"No, sir. I didn't like it here."

"I don't see why not. The food here was better than what you've been eating, surely. You've gotten thinner since I saw you last." He paused, then regarded the others with a slight curl of his lip. "I see you've found new company."

"I certainly have, sir."

Mr. Dupont began looking over them as if they were cattle at an auction. Lorelin wished she could sink through the floorboards. Then, Dupont glanced downward. It took Lorelin a moment to realize that he was staring right at Tsashin. "What's a little thing like you doing amongst the ruffians?"

"Don't speak to her," Hodge snapped.

"*Hodge,*" Halston hissed through his teeth.

Mr. Dupont drifted closer to Tsashin. "How old are you?"

Tsashin let out a short, fluttery breath. She was so much shorter than Dupont that she had to lift her chin to look back at him. "Sixteen." Slowly, she shrank away from the procurer.

"Ah. I'd have guessed thirteen." Slowly, he looked her up and down, from her cascade of shining black hair, to her delicate hands, to the soft moccasins on her feet. "Hmm. Very pretty."

The fantasy of smashing his nose in with her fist lit up in Lorelin's mind, but after that her thoughts became a whirlpool. She had to speak, act, *something,* but Dupont had caused every part of her to harden. She couldn't budge.

Hodge raised his voice, making it reign over the rest of the room's cacophony. "I told you to stop talking to her." Anger dripped like blood from his words. Some of the men in the audience turned to look at him.

Dupont smirked. "What for? Is it a sin to speak kindly to a beautiful girl?"

Hodge curled one rough hand into a fist, then took a stride in Dupont's direction. "Don't think I don't know exactly what—"

Before Lorelin could act, Halston slapped a steady hand on Hodge's chest, halting him. "*Don't.*"

Hodge's hand crept closer to the knife at his belt. "I ain't repeating myself again, so let me say it one more time: if you say *anything* to her again, I'll—"

"Sorry, my boy. This establishment strictly prohibits knife fights," Dupont said coolly, allowing his hand to travel to the elegant holster cradling a pistol at his hip.

This surely wasn't the first time Dupont had been threatened, and it certainly wouldn't be the last. *Hold off,* Lorelin silently spoke to Hodge, willing her words to somehow enter his mind. *Just a little longer. Just until we can get a lead from him.*

"Alright." Hodge moved his hand away from the knife. "Perfect. I shoot even better than I stab."

Halston stared daggers at his brother. "Go outside and wait for us if you can't behave yourself."

Without a moment's hesitation, Hodge obeyed, knocking down a few chairs in the process. The dancers had left the stage, and the pianist had stopped playing. The audience was still there, and about half of them were craning their necks to get a better look at Dupont and the gang.

Mr. Dupont waved a hand at the pianist to signal for him to pick up the music again, that there was nothing to see here. The keys tingled tentatively once more. "Are your other companions pre-pared to be civil?"

Everyone nodded. For Lorelin, it was not a lie. She would be civil. But she wouldn't, couldn't, be *kind* to this man.

Mr. Dupont extended an arm toward a nearby hallway. "Excellent. In that case, I hope you'll join me for supper, and we can discuss your proposition."

Chapter 5

$\mathcal{L}$orelin prayed that they weren't just wasting time.

Dupont had led them upstairs to a cramped dining hall, where two scruffy, broad-shouldered men were standing like they'd been waiting for them the whole time. Dupont had greeted the men with a terse nod, then commanded the gang to leave their guns in a cabinet outside the room. The men stood there stoically, each of them keeping one hand firm on a gun handle, and the only movement they made was to lower their brows into a glare each time somebody made eye contact with them.

Everything in this dining room was as shiny as Lorelin's old life had been, from the flatware and the glossy plates to the chandelier covering the table in its gilded light. But it was *too* pristine to enthrall her, to make her marvel and gape. It sickened her.

A dim-eyed serving girl had brought out the food, and now, plates of leafy greens, boiled potatoes, and dark roast beef sat before each of them, steaming and dripping with gravy. Nobody dared touch it.

Mr. Dupont was eating, though. He sawed carelessly at his

meat—making a big show out of being the only one with a knife. The sound of the utensils grating on his plate sent waves of vexation through Lorelin's veins. He didn't seem to mind the unwavering stares from the surrounding company, but he didn't say a word.

They were waiting—floating in the sea of silence until he threw them a line by speaking. When men like Dupont believed they had the upper hand, nothing could destroy that belief. Lorelin decided to break the silence at last. She wouldn't let him think he was in control here.

"Argus Byrd," Lorelin said. "We know he's been here." She almost flinched—she'd spoken carelessly, and done nothing to mask her biting tone. Usually, delivering a line with syrupy sweetness was easy for her. Maybe she was getting rusty.

Dupont dabbed his mouth with his napkin. "Sure. He wasn't quite a regular, but he came here often enough. Though I read in the paper that he died with his men in a shootout." His dark eyes glowed with understanding.

"Did you ever write to him?" asked Lorelin.

"No. Why?"

"We found one of your letters in his pocket, though we couldn't read it. He'd been . . . out in the rain."

Dupont snorted. "*Stealing* from corpses? I'm surprised you were alright with getting your hands dirty."

Lorelin ignored the comment. "Do you know who the letter could have been from?"

"One of the girls, I'd imagine."

"Who did he . . ." She cursed herself for not being able to force the words out. "Which girl?"

The corners of Dupont's mouth lifted into a satisfied grin. "You mentioned a reward."

"We can pay you thirty crowns. If you let us speak with her."

"Fifty," said Dupont.

"We—"

"Take it or leave it."

Bribery, then threats. That was what they'd agreed upon. They were unarmed, but he was also outnumbered, even with his bodyguards.

Lorelin loosed a breath. "Alright. Fifty crowns."

Dupont stood and pushed in his chair. His movements were steady, almost graceful. "I'll go fetch Ella. I'm fairly certain she was Argus' favorite. Wait here, please."

He slipped into the hallway. When the sound of his footsteps faded, Lorelin reached for the neglected fork on the table and slid it into her waistband. It wasn't much, but a fork was better than her bare hands. She prodded the tines with her fingertip. They were pathetically dull.

Gryff was sitting next to Lorelin. He leaned closer to her and whispered, "Fifty crowns? That's cuttin' it close, Lorelin."

"We don't have a choice," she hissed back, then glanced at Dupont's hired guns to make sure they weren't listening. The men were glaring at the two of them, but they hadn't crept closer to eavesdrop.

"Sure we do," said Gryff, lowering his voice even more. "We twist his arm and—"

Suddenly, the door hinges whined, making them all jump. Dupont entered with a tall, flaxen-haired girl in a sapphire dress. She held her chin up in a bold sort of way that Lorelin couldn't help but admire. Everything about her seemed to glimmer—from her glossy curls to the dewy circles of rouge on her cheeks. She wasn't shivering, and there wasn't a trace of cowardice in her wide set blue eyes. If anything, she just looked bored.

The girl folded her arms across her chest. "Is this gonna take long?"

Lorelin tried not to smile. "You've spent some time with Argus Byrd recently, yes?"

"Well, sure."

"When?"

"Eh . . . a month or two ago. I don't like Argus that much, but he pays well. He's sweaty as all hell."

Lorelin tried not to choke.

Ella looked at Dupont bemusedly. He motioned to the others to keep talking—permission to question her, but his stern, furrowed brow foreboded that they were working on borrowed time.

"Did you write him a letter?" asked Halston.

"No. Well, I gave him a letter, it wasn't for him. I was asking him to take it to my sister in Copperton. I needed money. The post is too slow. Or they keep losing the letters I send her. I said I'd let him book me for the whole night the next time he was here if he got it to her."

Lorelin forced a polite smile. For gods' sake, they were going to be here all night.

"Argus has a brother called Sterling. He has a lot of . . . employees," Halston said quickly. "Did he ever meet with any of them here?"

"You mean his friends?"

"Yes. His . . . friends."

"Oh, yes, often."

"Did Argus ever mention any . . ." Halston waved a hand. ". . . places that they were headed on business? People they were working with? Hideouts? Somewhere nearby, maybe?"

"Not really. He would complain a lot of the time. I usually just pretended to listen. He would get angry sometimes. Once he yelled at me, and it scared me something awful. But that wasn't bad as the time . . . well . . ." Her gaze trailed downward and settled on the floor.

Jae tilted her head. "Well what?"

"It was a strange night. Carmen started knocking on our door just after we'd gone in, saying that some fellow was outside and that he needed to see Argus right away. Argus started cursing, and that scared me, so I was crying. And then Argus slipped her a coin to leave us alone. Then somebody else started knocking on the door and said that he needed Argus to come outside and meet with him, and that he had what Argus asked for. I'd never seen Argus looking so angry before, but he stepped outside. Argus started yelling at the fella for interrupting us, asking why he couldn't just wait another half hour and all that. I just laid in bed and listened to them yelling in the hall. The other man kept saying that he didn't understand why Argus was so angry, that all he wanted was to give him what he owed him right away, but Argus just kept cursing at him."

A man paying off a debt to somebody like Argus was far from unusual, but this piqued Lorelin's interest. "Did you hear the man's name?"

"I think he was called Sylmare. I remember the name because it sounded so nice."

Then, a scream put the conversation to an end.

Fools, they all were.

While Ella was speaking, they'd all let their focus stray. Dupont and his hired guns loomed behind Tsashin like keepers at the gates of death. Tsashin was slumped over the table with her cheek pressed to the cloth, her delicate face frozen unnaturally.

Lorelin and the others sprang from their seats. The bastard . . .

Tsashin held up a trembling hand. Blood trickled from her

fingertip. A knife—barely large enough to open an envelope— glinted in Dupont's grip.

"Settle down," he said dully, as if the gang leaping to act was a mere inconvenience. Then, he looked down fondly at Tsashin. "Just a cut, little one. In a minute, you won't feel a thing."

Lorelin's fingers wrapped around the handle of her fork. The fury ripping through her was so swift and hot, she hardly cared how stupid, how measly she must have looked with it. "You get the hell away from her. Right. *Now.*"

"Oh, hush. She'll be perfectly fine. Just motionless for an hour or two. I dipped my blade in meabane solution. " He pinched one of Tsashin's tear-streaked cheeks. "Then I'll have the other girls make you pretty."

Plunging a fork into Randall's windpipe suddenly seemed too kind a fate for him.

He gave Lorelin a wry smirk and dismissively drew his pistol. "There's no need for a fuss. Here is my bargain." He nodded at Tsashin, whose eyes were growing wider with fright. "*Her.* You may keep your fifty crowns."

"*She* ain't *yours* to take, dammit!" Jae roared.

"Steady, now." Dupont's finger drifted toward the trigger. "Ella told you what she knows, as agreed. I'm taking this one in exchange for that information. *That* is my price. Cross me, and I'll shoot."

"Bastard," snapped Lorelin.

Then, a six-shooter's hammer clicked.

But it was not Dupont's.

Two figures slid into the room. One was a waifish girl, golden-haired and swathed in scarlet cloth. She looked like a ruby plated with gold. The barrel of a gun kissed her temple, gripped by . . .

By . . .

"Hodge," Halston whispered.

Hodge made no reply. His eyes were pure venom. "Heard every word you said, Dupont."

"Weren't," Dupont's breath hitched, "you outside?" His fingers began to shake, if only slightly. His hired guns exchanged a dumbfounded glance with one another, but hesitantly pointed their muzzles in Hodge's direction.

"Hell no." Hodge jostled the girl in the crook of his arm. "But if you touch Tsashin again, your prize girl goes down."

"*Please*," the golden-haired girl moaned. Hodge pressed the gun to the side of her head again, and she whimpered.

Dupont's body went tense, and he began to stammer. Men *always* stammered when they knew they'd lost.

"Drop the gun," Hodge said coolly.

The weapon hit the floor. Evidently, the prospect of acquiring a new girl didn't outweigh the loss of Dupont's best girl.

"Now kick it far away from you."

Dupont did as he was told.

Hodge motioned to the two gunmen. "Them, too. Kick 'em under the table."

The men didn't budge, though one whispered something to the other. Dupont whirled around and hissed, "*Drop them*."

The men let the weapons fall, then dejectedly kicked them under the table.

Hodge released the girl, then immediately snatched up Dupont's fallen gun and passed it to Halston. As Halston grabbed the gun, he gaped at his brother with a strange look that was part confusion, part shame, then joined his brother in aiming at Dupont's body. The girl hurried to Ella, who took her in an eager embrace and stared at Hodge like he was something vile.

Lorelin bit her lip. It was all she could do to keep from sputtering.

Desperate as they were, she'd never expected this from Hodge—fiery, golden-hearted Hodge, holding an innocent girl at gunpoint.

"You're—" Dupont started.

He never got to finish his sentence. Without warning, Gryff seized him from behind. Dupont's cry was brief. With a hefty grunt, Gryff threw the flailing procurer through the dinner table.

The sound of cracking wood stung Lorelin's ears. Shattered porcelain tinkled as it slid down the table's slanted fragments, piling onto Dupont's chest. The procurer moaned, then went still. He lay like an empty, forgotten sack, draped over the wreckage. Blood streamed from a fresh gash on his face, and Lorelin hoped that it would scar.

Chaos erupted. Dupont's aides tried to dive for their guns, but they were already buried beneath the pile of split wood and broken dishes.

"Hands in the air! Sit down!" Hodge bellowed, aiming at the men's heads.

The two men got to their knees and raised their arms, trembling in Gryff's shadow.

The two girls had turned to statues, their mouths stiff and perfectly round. Lorelin wondered if they were going to help Dupont, or if had they been counting down the days until something like this happened, when all their silent wishes came true.

Hodge flipped a pair of crowns to Ella and the red-garbed blonde. "These should feed you for a month. Get yourselves out of here. For good."

The girls each caught one coin, shared a befuddled look, then bolted out of the room, their glossy hair flying behind them.

Gryff took Tsashin—who seemed more paralyzed from fright than from the meabane—up in his arms and started for the door. The others followed close behind.

Lorelin took one last look at Dupont, still splayed like a rag-doll in the ruins of his perfect dinner table. He moaned softly. If they'd had time, she would've made an even bigger mess of his face. But there was no time to spare. They had to get Tsashin somewhere safe.

They slammed the door behind them, threw open the cabinet, and gathered up their belongings. With that, they sped through the now-empty house and out into the night, sprinting down the road that cut through the prairie. Lorelin didn't look back. Her world turned to a blur—the patter of her running feet, her gang hustling at her sides.

She should've been thankful that they'd made it out. But on nights like this, sometimes all she could do was curse.

Curse Sterling. Curse Dupont. Curse the life she'd fled and the one she'd denied herself, time and time again. Curse not knowing, *never* knowing, what came next around the bend.

And she left the Dusty Rose behind, cursing like a madwoman.

Chapter 6

All Hodge wanted to do was shout, to curse their foolish-ness till he ran out of breath.

How could they have been so stupid? It would have been one thing for the gang to head inside. But Tsashin?

He should have said something. Stopped it when he'd had the chance. They'd failed to protect her.

They ran for at least an hour, tearing down the dirt road cutting through the grassy hills. Hodge hated the open space. It made him feel like all of their backs had glaring targets on them. If Dupont and his men came after them on horseback, they were goners. Nobody said a word, but Hodge's brother cast him a couple of scathing looks.

Hodge paid them no mind. On the run, he kept glancing back, and each time he did the road was empty. Maybe Dupont was in no condition to chase after them.

When Hodge's chest felt ready to burst, the road began to snake through a lightly wooded area. The trees were short and sparse, but the scanty coverage was certainly better than nothing.

When they all felt safe enough to slow down into a brisk walk, they ventured into the cover of trees, still within sight of the road but deep enough in the shadows that any passersby wouldn't take notice of them. Halston had started rambling—something about how they didn't need to create more enemies for themselves—but Hodge wasn't listening. He wasn't paying much attention to *anything* besides Tsashin, who was locked in Gryff's arms. Her legs were stiff, held at an odd angle, and they weren't the only part of her that was petrified. Her face had frozen into a blood-curdling look of shock.

Together, they circled up inside a small ring of aspens. Hodge stood there panting like a dog, desperately trying to catch his breath. With more gentleness than Hodge had ever seen in him, Gryff laid Tsashin down.

Lorelin bent over her, already arms-deep in her knapsack. "Can you move?"

Tsashin struggled to lift a hand and flexed her fingers. "My arms. A little."

"And your legs?" asked Lorelin.

"No. Nothing there."

There was a bloodstain on her deerskin tunic from where she'd pressed her wounded finger. Lorelin swabbed the cut with water, then liquor, and wrapped it in a thin strip of cloth. "Don't worry. Meabane is harmless once absorbed. You may feel a little tingly tomorrow, but after that . . . good as new."

Hodge breathed in, long and deep, thinking about how Dupont might look with a few dozen bullet holes in his body.

"I didn't think he'd do this," Lorelin said, then released a heavy breath. "I'm so sorry, Tsashin. I never expected *this* sort of thing from him. I—"

"Well, he did it anyway," Hodge spat out. He was too tired to bother with coddling anyone's feelings right now.

Lorelin didn't speak. She just shot him an indecent look, then returned to tending to Tsashin.

Halston joined them, kneeling beside Tsashin. "How do you feel?"

Tsashin's throat bobbed with a swallow. "I'll be alright."

Halston nodded, then got to his feet. Hodge had already braced himself for what Halston said next, but it still didn't soften the blow. "Are you out of your *mind?* What were you *thinking?*"

"I did—"

"You held that poor girl at *gunpoint!*"

"No, I didn't!"

"What are you even talking about?"

"I mean, I held her at gunpoint, but she said that she was glad to do it!"

Halston just gaped at him. "*What?*"

"I paid her off, damn it! I found her in the hall and gave her a crown to help me out!"

Everyone was gawking. Hodge hardly cared.

He'd only stepped outside so Dupont would shut up and get off his back, then he'd snuck back into the house. When he found that they were in the dining hall, he'd pressed an ear to the door to eavesdrop. The second Dupont threatened Tsashin, his mind had sped down some sort of unmarked trail. He'd been thinking just straight enough to sprint down the hall, find the girl with the nicest dress, and pay her to help him get Tsashin away from Dupont.

Hodge swallowed. "She would've been fine either way. I pulled the round out of the first chamber."

Heat rose to his face. Hodge glanced over Gryff and Jae's addled glowers, Halston's confusion, Lorelin's sheer surprise.

"Alright," Halston said at last with heavy relief. "Alright."

Had he not expected this? Had he really thought Hodge had wandered off and actually threatened to take that girl's life?

That's what y'all think of me, huh?

It shouldn't have stung so much.

He hadn't been himself in those few minutes. Something had overcome him, steered him into a stupor. Hodge hadn't *really* threatened the girl. But if it was the price he'd had to pay for *anyone* in his gang's safety, he would have done it. He would let them all think him a monster if it meant leaving that place unharmed.

It was the truth, and the truth of it—of the person he'd come to be—terrified him.

He looked to the sky. The stars suddenly seemed unfamiliar, like a massive hand had reached up and stirred them around, scattering them into a brand-new arrangement. He felt lost, the way he had when he'd first seen the desert of Mesca. During his boyhood, he'd been surrounded by nothing but misty air, swelling waves and damp sand, and he'd fallen into a world of bone-dry dust. Perhaps the heat and grit had turned him into someone else. Some reckless tearaway. A stranger to the child he'd been back home.

Had this realm left stains on his heart? If it had, he wanted to wash them out. He wanted to be different. Gods. What did *different* even look like?

"This ain't good," Jae muttered as she started to pace back and forth. "We don't need someone else coming after us."

"I don't think he'll be any trouble," said Lorelin. She was seeing if Tsashin could still flex her elbows. "I think Gryff struck enough fear in him that he'll stay in his house till dawn, at least."

"You never know." Jae turned her head in the direction of the road. "Should we keep going?"

"Not now," said Halston. "We won't get much further if we don't rest."

Hodge took the first watch. An hour or two passed. An invisible heaviness was weighing him down. The scene from the pleasure house kept rolling in his mind, and in it, he was watching himself, like he was seeing the whole thing through the eyes of a god. And he wasn't sure what to think about that angry boy standing there with a gun pressed to a pretty girl's head.

Tsashin slept soundly. Hodge had been gazing at her for a while, fearing that she'd be too shaken to really rest, but she hadn't stirred in the slightest. Was it exhaustion, or had the meabane sapped all the energy out of her? He couldn't look at her for long. Not without guilt barreling down on him like a train.

Lorelin had laid her bedroll out next to Tsashin. She checked Tsashin's bandage once more, then sat on her blankets. "Are you alright?"

"Sort of," said Hodge.

The memory of the day he'd opened Tsashin's strange, crudely built coffin sprang to the forefront of his mind. The glimpse he'd caught of her sleeping face before her eyelids flew open. Frozen in a dreaming state, sealed in darkness. For . . . for who knew how long?

Hodge snorted. Tsashin was braver than all of them.

"Hodge." Lorelin's voice was gentle, in that sisterly way he knew too well, when she was trying to soften the blow she was about to deliver. She paced over and sat down beside him. "She doesn't even know who she is."

"What do you mean?"

"We're all she has." Lorelin laid a hand on Hodge's lap. "But you can't take advantage of that. Promise me you won't."

Heat coursed through his veins. "I don't know what you're talking about."

Lorelin shrugged. "Maybe I'm misreading things, but . . . I've seen how you look at her, and . . . Just be careful, alright?"

Hodge frowned. "You think I'd hurt her or something?"

"Of course not," said Lorelin. "But she can't give you what you want, Hodge. You must know that."

Hodge said nothing to that. He wasn't going to think about this a minute longer. Instead, he just waited while Lorelin walked to her bedroll, laid down, and drifted off. Hodge sat there for a while, fiddling with his jacket buttons, willing himself to quiet his mind.

The night got colder. Hodge looked back to Tsashin. She was beginning to shiver. He took the jacket from his shoulders and tiptoed to her, draped it over her chest, and without looking at her face, he marched back off to his resting spot.

He hoped that dawn would come, soon. He couldn't wait for this night to be over.

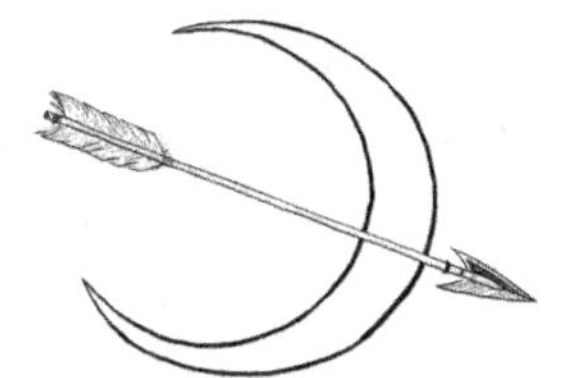

Chapter 7

*V*yrships didn't need sails to work, but for tradition's sake, most had them anyway. Hodge had always liked looking at the sails of his father's ship. They reminded him of summer clouds.

Hodge waited with Halston and Elias on the beach. They all had their sleeves pushed up to their elbows, and water glinted off their brown forearms. His brothers were talking about something he figured was probably very boring, so Hodge was amusing himself by tossing pebbles into the waves. The air smelled clean and new.

The other lords liked to joke about his family's island. They said that there was nothing on it but rocks, and their father was a lord of stones. But they'd clearly never seen this beach. There were brightly colored shells, if you knew where to look, silvery fish in the coves, and crabs with sweet white meat. Hodge's prized seashell lived on a stand beside his bed. It was curled like a horn, sunset-colored.

Their father was supposed to leave on another mission today. Over time, Hodge had gotten used to it. The first voyage he could remember was when he was three. They'd had to pry him, wailing, from his father's shoulders. But

Hodge had lost count of the journeys now. They were lumped together in his mind, like the barnacles he sometimes saw covering the rocks. The sting wasn't so bad anymore. It was there. But he knew how to handle it.

The brothers were quiet, now, watching their father's vyrship bobbing on the waters. Elias pointed to it. "Maybe he'll take me next time."

"He's not going to," Hodge said, tossing another rock into the waves. He wasn't trying to be cruel. He just couldn't stand the thought of his father and brother being away at the same time.

"He'll have to take me soon," Elias said. "I'm going to inherit that ship one day. It's time I started learning the ropes."

Elias was looking less like a boy and more like a man each day. In the past year, he'd grown far taller than both his brothers, and his once narrow limbs now showed the beginnings of muscle.

"Not if you die first," Hodge joked. Halston glared at him. Never could take a joke, could he? But Elias could, and he just laughed.

"If they find the Source," Halston said slowly, "will you still get the ship?"

Hodge was surprised that Halston had asked it. There was no doubt that they'd both wondered that often, but Halston was the first one who'd wondered it aloud.

Elias shrugged. "In that case, I imagine it'll be my duty to explore. Like they did . . . before." He held out one long arm and swept it across the line of the horizon, the ocean leading to a world unknown.

Before the monsters came, of course, the admirals had once used their vyrships to explore this realm. In the grand scheme of things, their world was still relatively new. The blood of voyagers and pioneers ran through their veins.

Hodge liked the thought of exploring, but he couldn't imagine what it would be like to be stuck on a ship for months at a time. He'd get sick of the tight space. There'd be nothing to look at but blue water and a slightly lighter blue sky while he paced over damp wood, wind stinging his cheeks. He needed motion: he needed to be running on the shoreline, seeing the world unfold around him, doing all he could.

They stood on the shore until the ship became a dot on the horizon, then disappeared entirely.

They spent the rest of the afternoon swimming in the cool waves until their fingers were wrinkled. Hodge was trying to get the others to dare him to swim out to what they called the Tower: a spire of brick rising from the waves a few miles off the shore. It had been there forever, long before the Suryans, Quierrans, Alfirians, and Hespyrians had arrived in this new world. Halston believed that it had been built by gods. But every time Hodge brought it up, they begged him not to go. For all he knew, there was a creature waiting for him at the bottom—one that would swallow him whole if he got too close.

That was one of their father's rules: Don't swim out too far. Keep the windows shut at night. Never remain outside after sunset. That was when the monsters came.

But it had been a good time for the islanders. 'Prosperous', their father called it. Nobody had fallen to any of the monsters in at least a year, and they were thriving. The fruit crops were plentiful, and their father's men had discovered a new archipelago only sixty miles away. They said that the soil was rich.

But the day drew to a wretched close.

When they got back to the castle, they heard sobbing coming from Lia's room. They found their sister leaning over her bed, face buried in her hands.

"What's the matter?" Elias rushed to her side and took her in his arms.

"Ingrid," she wailed, digging her fingertips into her hair. Her shoulders heaved with each labored breath. "They found her this morning. It took them hours to figure out it was her. She . . . she . . . was in pieces. Something . . . something got her."

"Hodge?"

Hodge woke up with a start. Dammit, he'd dozed off during his watch. Halston was going to kill him.

"Hmph," he murmured, stretching out his arms. His back was sore. "What time is it?"

"Midmorning," said Tsashin. She seemed to have more energy

this morning, shifting her weight from one foot to the other. Somehow, she was looking even more lithe than usual. "Want to go find roots with me?"

"Sure."

They ventured out into the trees, scanning the ground for daylilies or wild onion sprouts. There was an even mixture of pines and leafy trees here, and large stretches of grasses and wildflowers between them.

It was good to see Tsashin moving. There was a faint half-smile on her full lips, and the sun brought out the copper tones in her brown skin. He could see that she'd made a full recovery from the meabane. She was missing that brightness she usually had, though, and that hurt to see.

Hodge rubbed his neck. There was a dull pain nagging at him there; he'd been sleeping at an uncomfortable angle. "Don't, uh . . . tell Hal I dozed off."

She gave him a quick grin. "I'd never."

She meant it. If there was anyone Hodge would bet had never lied in their lifetime, it was Tsashin. Promises were sacred to her. She saw the good in all of them. She'd stuck around, helped them where she could, for no good reason at all.

He didn't deserve her.

None of them did.

"We're in Monvallea now." He wasn't sure why he'd said that, but now that he'd started, he felt like he had to keep going. "And . . . the Yunah nation ain't too far, right?"

Tsashin's dark eyes looked to the ground. "I don't know."

Right. No memory of it. He was pretty sure it was in . . . northern Monvallea? Southern Banderra, maybe? It was a large tribe—he knew that much—and he'd heard rumors that some of them lived in this region. Even if they brought her there, the odds of them finding her family were slim if she didn't have her memories back.

"Well, Jae's got her map. With her, there's nothing we can't find. And then we'll find your family, and . . ." He'd said something like this to her before, and he still wasn't sure if she believed him. He wanted it to be true, to say it and find a way to make it real . . . *and I won't let anything like what happened at Dupont's happen again.*

Should he say sorry? There was nothing he could say to make it better, nothing that could make it okay, no matter how many times she tried to brush it off.

"I don't know how long I was underground, Hodge." She spoke the next part so softly that he almost didn't hear her at all. "I don't even know if they're still alive."

She could have been buried in one world, then woken in a brand new one. Decades could have come and gone.

"I'll bet they are," said Hodge. "I'll bet they're waiting for you."

"It's the strangest thing," Tsashin mused. There was a distant, somber look in her eyes. "I can feel the empty space in my chest. Where they're supposed to fit. But I don't know their names. Their faces. I don't remember what home looks like."

Hodge tried to picture the Yunah nation. Did they live in wooded lands, or grassy ones?

He hoped that the views were nice—with good high points to watch the sunrise. Tsashin always seemed to enjoy watching the dawn turn to day.

They walked in silence for a while, continuing to study the ground. No roots yet. Hodge scratched his neck and brushed a few strands of his hair behind his ears. It was almost down to his shoulders, now. He'd have to hack some of it off with his knife, soon.

"I realized I forgot to thank you. For saving me," Tsashin said at last. "I . . . I was scared. When you came in with that girl. But I knew there had to be an explanation. I knew she had to be pretending."

"You did?"

"I did."

His own brother had doubted his honor for a moment that night, and Tsashin—a girl who had seen him with his hands bloody on more than one occasion—had not.

He wasn't thinking right, when he spoke next. But part of him knew he had to tell her. "Tsashin. I keep thinking. And . . ."

"And what?"

"That can't happen again. I can't let you get hurt. I mean that . . ." He had to pause for a second. It was all he could do not to curse Dupont's name. "I don't know. I keep thinking we should . . . find you someone else? Someone to take you back to the Yunah nation. Someone . . . someone safe."

Tsashin frowned. "Safe? Is anybody *safe* out here, Hodge?"

Hodge lowered his head. She was right. In the Hespyrian West, any stranger was a gamble. One was just as likely to find a blade at their throat as they were to find someone with a generous heart. He was stupid for suggesting otherwise. Tsashin was no fool.

"I'm as safe with you as anyone," Tsashin said. "And Hodge . . . do you really think I'd walk away from you?"

"What do you mean?"

"I don't think I could leave. At least, not now. I'd spend the rest of my life lying awake at night wondering what happened to you."

Before he could even understand what was happening, sparks came to life in Hodge's chest.

Oh, no.

Dammit, Lorelin.

Hodge opened his mouth to speak, but his mind had gone blank. Hodge had always known exactly what to say to the dozens of girls he'd met in inns and bars and even on cattle drives. But right now, he couldn't figure it out with Tsashin.

She doesn't know who she is.

"Thanks," he said, then silently cursed himself. *Thanks? What the hell?*

Tsashin merely smiled. "Of course."

At last, they found a patch of daylilies and got to harvesting the roots. They were flimsy and narrow, but gathered and roasted, they would make for a decent, hearty breakfast.

"It's been a while since you've told us a story," Hodge said as he bundled up an armload of the plants. "Think you could tell me one? Something with a good ending."

She didn't just tell him a story. In the half hour they spent gathering roots and walking back to their camp, she told him several: one where a hero traveled to the edge of the sky and brought back the sun, a story where an antelope tricked a pack of coyotes into eating a mound of sand and escaped his own death, one where a weaver created all sorts of flowers for her children, weaving their petals with colors she'd gathered from the rainbow. Hodge liked the stories well enough, but what he liked the most was that telling them always seemed to raise Tsashin's spirit. She seemed happiest when her voice was spinning a story.

He hoped that luck would lead the way from then on. Somehow, he had a hunch that a deeper part of her remembered her home and she was spinning the stories for those she missed the most.

———

Sylmare.

They'd spent the entire day trekking north up the road, tossing that name back and forth, whispering it swiftly and slowly, stretching out the word as though they would hear some clue within its sound. When they weren't scattering their tracks and looking over their shoulders for anyone Dupont might have sent after them, the name was on their lips. *Sylmare.*

At sundown, they circled up for the night in a small clearing shaded by a short but stony bluff, then started fishing for a new approach. There was no one else the boys knew of who would have a lead on any living folks who had ties to Sterling. The other half of the dagger felt impossibly out of reach.

"We could go to Coy's again," Lorelin suggested.

"Not after Gryff threw him against the wall," said Hodge. "I sure as hell ain't going back to the shooting pit."

Lorelin crossed her arms over her chest. "Do you have a better idea?"

"We could go back to his hideout," offered Jae. "Or the Lawrence Mine, maybe. See if he left anything there."

Gryff shook his head. "Sterling was always careful about not leavin' a trail behind. If there was anything useful there, he likely burned it right after we left."

There were too many knots to untie. Even if they did figure out a way to locate the other half of the conduit, they also still had to find a Nefilium Pass to cut through. How they'd do that, Jae still wasn't sure. Beyond the Cannocs, the Outlands waited for them.

And Jae didn't dare mention it, but she imagined that once they reached the other side of the mountains, she'd have to separate from them and continue her search for Pa alone. But she didn't want to think about what that would be like just yet.

When the moon came out, Jae joined Halston to listen to the crickets sing. They sat on a flat-topped boulder overlooking the clearing, with a perfect view of a nearly endless treeline. Starlight spilled over the pines. She was grateful for the view, for the quiet of the night. The day before had crushed her, between the guilt from Tsashin getting roped into this mess, and the regret of leaving the Dusty Rose with almost nothing to show for it. They were headed north, but now it seemed more a way to put distance between themselves and the pleasure house than to reach the Outlands. There was no point in going there without the conduit.

Jae breathed in the wintery-smelling tang of the trees. Despite the restlessness in her mind and bones, the silent company of the pines was exactly what she needed. It was like the spirit of Hemaera herself was speaking whispers of comfort to them. Jae pictured the half-goddess wandering through the trees, bow in hand, on the lookout. Some folks said that Hemaera granted wishes to weary or desperate travelers. They could certainly use *her,* right now.

Halston was staring into the night with a dull, empty stare. He looked half-asleep and a quarter dead.

Jae pulled her knees up to her chest. "Wanna talk about it?"

"Not really," Halston murmured. "I don't think we're going to fix our conduit. Maybe we'll have better luck if we just head toward the Outlands anyway. Maybe we could even find another conduit up there. It seems just as likely as anything else."

She knew he was just rambling. If they cut their losses and searched for a new conduit, then all the years Halston had spent with Sterling would've been for nothing.

"And the Nefilium Pass?" All the man-made passes through the Cannocs were heavily patrolled by Rangers. If an ordinary man—or a pack of wanted criminals—wanted a way in, they needed to take one of the ancient passes that the magical folk guarded jealously.

Halston shrugged. "I always imagined we'd pay Sterling to give us a lead on one."

Jae bit her lip. "Wish we'd wrung that outta him before I gunned him down."

Halston snorted. "No. We're better off this way, I promise you."

Halston took his half of the blade out of his pack and placed it on the stony earth. Above him, the sky rippled into a soft-edged circle. The center was opaque.

"Veil too thick here?" asked Jae.

Halston nodded, then put the broken knife away. "We'd be crossing through Median for ages if we opened it here." The circle disappeared, making way for the starlight once more. "I think Sterling might've just gotten rid of it. Tossed the other half into the river or something."

Jae hated that he might be right. She wondered if Sterling's rotten spirit was somehow watching them, doubled-over laughing. "I doubt he'd just throw it away. If anything, he sold it."

"The only thing he loved more than money was causing others pain," said Halston. "Wouldn't shock me if he just . . . destroyed it."

In the clearing, Hodge, Tsashin, and Lorelin were laughing while Gryff polished his rifle. They were playing some game with pebbles and sticks. Jae wasn't sure what the rules were. Maybe they were making them up as they went along. It seemed a trifle foolish. There was no reason to be having a good time. Then again, maybe there didn't need to be a reason.

There was a faint smile on Halston's lips. Jae was tempted to kiss it off of him, then thought better of it, realizing she wasn't feeling quite so bold. "We'll figure it out," she said, as if it were a matter of fact.

There was something about Halston that made her want to make promises about things she couldn't control. Things that were impossible, even. She didn't understand it, but trying to explain it would likely take a lot of work and time, so she was trying not to think about it too much.

Tsashin tossed a stone in Hodge's direction. He swatted it with his stick, and the stone flew up into the sky and landed somewhere far away. He threw up his arms, hooting like a miner who'd just struck it rich, and spun around toward Halston. "Did you see the distance on that one?"

"Can you knock it off?" Halston called down. "We're getting closer to the Outlands. Who knows what you could awaken in the woods?"

Hodge rolled his eyes. "I'm not going to *awaken* anything."

Then, at the foot of the boulder, a smoky mass of blue knit together into the form of Jem.

Tsashin screamed. Lorelin fell over, and Gryff sprang to his feet. Everyone began hollering, flailing, jumping. Jae leapt from her resting place and regretted it at once. She tripped and landed on all fours, nearly losing her breath. After regaining her footing, it took nearly a minute of her yelling at everybody to calm down before they listened.

"It's Jem!" When the shouting stopped, she caught her breath and explained. "He's the one who saved me."

"Dammit!" Hodge lowered his gun. The poor boy was panting like he'd just sprinted up the steepest summit in the Cannocs. "Why'd you have to scare us half to death?" he demanded.

Though he had no blood, Jae could have sworn she saw a blush creep into Jem's face. "Sorry. I didn't mean to scare y'all."

Gryff snorted. "What are *you* doing here?" Harsh as it came off, Jae couldn't blame him. If it weren't for what Jem had done for her, she would've been hesitant to trust anyone who'd been in Sterling's company for so long—living or dead.

Jem gave a little shrug. "Ain't sure where else to go. I've been trying to follow y'all, but it's been tough." And he explained to them everything he'd told Jae several nights before, from his untimely death at the mines to his deal with Argus. A pact he'd sacrificed for

Jae. He told them about the mines and how the further he was from his death spot, the harder it was to stay in one place.

Hodge arched an eyebrow. "You've been *following* us?"

"Yes, but listen here. I've been thinking, and . . . I reckon I can be of some use to y'all. I'm searching for a warlock. One who can give me back my life. And I thought maybe I could help y'all out if you help me look."

"Hate to be so frank," Hodge muttered, exchanging a dark look with Gryff, "but I don't think any of us want help from one of Sterling's men."

Jem's face sank into a glower. "Didn't *you* work for Sterling?"

Hodge hesitated, then began studying the ground. "Fair enough."

"I think you'd be better off somewhere else," said Gryff. He paused, his long, reptilian nose twitching slightly. "Might you know where Sterling put half an adamite knife?"

"I remember him using it to bargain with y'all," Jem said grimly, "but I ain't sure where it is."

Halston sighed.

"What do y'all need it for?" Jem asked.

"To open a portal," said Halston. "We were hoping to find a Nefilium Pass, then get to a spot in the Outlands where the veil is thin."

Jem's head perked up. "Nefilium Pass? There's one I can take you to. Nestor's Caverns."

"Where's that?" asked Jae.

"At the edge of the Cannocs. It's a big ole cave, running miles under the mountains. Day's journey through 'em. Guarded by Nefilium. Mountain men. Safe enough as far as the passes go, if you can pay the tithe."

"How can we pay them?" Halston asked.

"We paid them in spears and knives last time," said Jem. "But they love silver and gold trinkets, from what I remember."

Lorelin's face lit up. "Think a gold brooch would suffice?"

Jae had almost forgotten about the frippery they'd discovered in Argus' pocket.

"I reckon it would," said Jem.

Jae had heard of the Nefilium tithes from Pa. He'd told her that some preferred crops or livestock, others loved gold, and the strangest ones asked for payment in the form of memories and dreams. But even if they were rich in food, gold, and dreams, they still didn't have the conduit. Without it, there was no opening the portal.

Jae slid the map out of her pocket. "Nestor's Caverns," she whispered. Sure enough, the pathway to the caverns spread out on the paper like a bloodstain.

They might not need Jem to take them there after all, but perhaps there was more he could tell them.

"Jem," Jae said slowly. "You wouldn't happen to know a fella by the name of Sylmare? Someone Argus might've worked with?"

"Sylmare, you say?"

"Yeah."

"Well, if that ain't just it," Jem said with a coy smile.

"What do you mean?"

"Sylmare ain't a fella. Sylmare is a *place*. Small town up in the Outlands, couple miles from the Glenn River. But nobody calls it that anymore," Jem said. "That was its old name, I think. Before everybody there died. Now they call it *the Shroud*."

"What for?" asked Jae.

"Trying for a joke, I reckon. It's a town full of spirits, and it's cursed. Something came and killed everyone there several years ago.

And for some reason, they can't cross over to what comes after this world. They're just . . . stuck."

Jae whispered to her map, "Sylmare." Nothing. "The Shroud." Again, nothing.

She cursed under her breath. Maybe the map only worked for towns full of living people.

The tug of the mines dragged Jem away for a minute, then he popped up behind Hodge again.

Lorelin tilted her head. "What would Sterling want in a place like that?"

"We never went *into* the town. Just passed it by—Sterling had some business with a man who lived there. The only living one. Treasure hunter called Flint . . . Barrow, I think it was?"

"*Treasure hunter*," repeated Halston. His brown eyes lit up like a hearth.

If they were to bet on anyone having the other half of the knife . . .

Jem's face glowed with understanding. "If he doesn't have it, I reckon he might know where it is . . . but the townsfolk might chase you away."

"What do you mean?" asked Hodge.

"Every time we were on business there, Sterling made us keep our distance from the town. Flint said that the spirits there didn't trust the living—guess he was the exception. Said they do their best to chase any travelers off. They're worried about folks finding out about their town. Maybe they think people will come and gawk at them like a circus or something. Gotta do their best to protect their peace."

The sole living man in a town full of ghosts. *That* was something else. It felt like a song that folks sang around the fire year after year, age after age.

But now, Jae almost wished she could throw her arms around

Jem. From the looks of the others, they were feeling the same way. Everyone looked like they'd just stumbled upon a forgotten treasure, relieved after they'd been hollering in shock just a few minutes ago.

Gryff shifted in place, looking more than a little uncomfortable. "I think I know a way we could stave off the ghosts."

"Well say it, won't you?" said Hodge.

"Settle down." Gryff waved a dismissive hand. "There's a Nefili man I used to know. A brewer. Zeph is his name. Used to make potions of all sorts . . . Bummed a thing or two off him, back in the day. If I ain't rememberin' it all wrong, he could put together a brew that could make someone look like a ghost. Skin that looked like sheer cloth, blood still flowin' underneath."

Jae whistled under her breath.

"One of the *Nefilium?*" Hodge went off. "You've been friends with a Nefili man this whole time? One with *magic?*"

"We ain't *friends,*" Gryff grumbled. "As a matter of fact, he won't be thrilled to see me. But if this town of ghosts is our only shot, then it's worth a try."

"But how are we going to get to Sylmare?" asked Jae. "My map won't show it."

Jem was glowing like a child seeing snow for the first time. "I'll guide you there!" he said, voice speeding a mile a minute. "If you take me to the Nefili man. He could—"

"I don't think his specialty is . . ." Gryff paused. ". . . giving new bodies to the dead."

"But he might know somebody who can. I ain't got nothin' to lose," Jem went on. "Besides, if you lead me to him, I'll be your guide. To Nestor's Caverns, then to the Shroud. I can—" He vanished at the peak of his excitement, then reappeared after a few moments of uneasy silence.

So sure of himself. Jae was trying hard not to envy him. Then again, maybe there was a thing or two they could learn from this odd spirit.

"I hate to say it, partner," Hodge said slowly, "but something tells me you won't be much of a guide."

Jem frowned. "Better than nothing, ain't I?"

"You're *dead*."

"I've been trailing y'all for days anyway," Jem argued. "Tough as it's been. Besides, the further north we go, the easier it'll be for me to keep from fading. I died in Banderra."

"Can you meet us at Smith's Creek?" asked Halston. "In . . . five night's time?"

After they found the first half of the knife, their initial plan had been to take the train to the end of the railroad, which was just south of Banderra's northernmost border. The station was in a small town called Smith's Creek. From there, they planned to travel north to the Cannoc Mountains and find a Nefilium Pass. Perhaps they'd be taking the train sooner than they'd first expected.

"I certainly can," Jem said simply. "Smith's Creek. Five nights from now." And he vanished quicker than a blink.

Halston released a drawn-out sigh. "Well . . . it's a gamble, but it's far better than the *nothing* we've been working with."

"Hope we find him," murmured Gryff.

"And if we *do* find him," Lorelin said slowly, "and he *does* have the knife, how do we get it from him?"

Nobody spoke. An adamite knife was practically priceless. Even if they were still bounty-rich, no amount of money would get any man with half a right mind to give up a piece of adamite . . . especially a treasure hunter, who would almost certainly know its value.

Hodge said it at last. "Force him, I reckon."

"No," Halston broke in.

"Hal—"

"I'm tired of fighting."

"I don't think it *matters* if you're tired of it," Hodge said grimly. "If he's got it, we take it from him. If he sold it, we make him tell us who has it. I don't see another way."

Lorelin stepped in between them. "Come on. We don't have to argue about this now."

They left it at that, but Jae could tell that all of them had some picture of confronting Flint Barrow forming inside their heads. Whatever it came to, they could only hope that there wouldn't be blood.

Before they settled for the night, they mapped out their course for the next few weeks. They would take the train to the roots of the Cannoc Mountains. Gryff would lead them to the Nefili man for the potions, then Jem would take them to Nestor's Caverns and the Outlands. And after that, they'd find Sylmare, Flint, and the other half of the conduit.

When Jae lay down to sleep, she whispered a little prayer to Hemaera. *If you bless any travelers today . . . bless us.*

Chapter 8

They spent the next several days trekking to the train station in Clovercrest, a small town in the green Monvallea hills. There, Halston caught himself humming an old voyaging song he'd learned from his father. He couldn't remember the last time he'd felt like whistling, humming, singing . . . Maybe there was something in the northern air. Something lively filling his chest.

I took my heart to the sea
Wandered round beneath its sky
Took my soul and turned it gold
Took my love and let it fly.

Purchasing the tickets had been simple enough. They'd been ready to flee on the off chance that anyone recognized them, but this far north, settlers and lawmen were sparse. The middle-aged man at the ticket booth hadn't batted an eye at them when they'd bought their tickets, and the conductor paid them no mind when they boarded the car.

The car was warm and well-lit, and as they shuffled to their seats, any second thoughts Halston had had about spending so much money on their tickets disappeared. They were saving time, and a night of genuine, uninterrupted sleep would do them wonders.

Apart from two tired-looking cowhands and a fast-asleep old man, they had the car to themselves. The sun had faded the walls, and the floor looked like it could use a good scrubbing. But the car was decent-smelling, dry, and perfectly quiet, and that was more than enough for them all.

There was something pleasant but strange about boarding. Halston remembered his first train ride, when he'd gone on business for Gus. He'd spent the entire journey with his forehead pressed to the windowpane. Outside, the world flew by. Haslton had watched with wide eyes as the sky darkened and the bursts of green woods faded into a soft, blurry black. It was the first time since entering this world that he'd felt full of wonder instead of like he was balancing on the edge of a bridge, bracing himself to fall at any moment.

They sat two to a seat—Halston and Jae, Hodge and Gryff, Lorelin and Tsashin. Without saying anything, Halston gave Jae the window spot. He knew that she'd prefer it. When she'd adjusted herself, he sat and sank back into the plush red velvet. He'd almost forgotten what it was like to rest on something soft.

For a good while, they sat in companionable silence as the train rocked them, climbing over dry land that would turn colder and greener as they traveled north. Gus used to joke that you could see the line between Mesca and Monvallea where the brown turned to green. They'd crossed that line on many cattle drives.

Sometimes, Halston wondered if his life would still look like that if Elias hadn't gone and avenged Gus. Cattle drives, nights by the fire, laughing with the other cowhands all along the way. Often, he missed it. But there was no use in grieving it. This was the life he had now.

For the first time, though . . . he was beginning to see that there was some good in it.

Jae was slouching in her seat, facing the world flying past them outside. And despite his weary muscles, part of Halston wanted to talk to her all night, if she'd let him.

"I have to ask, Jae . . ."

She turned to face him. "Ask me what?"

"We're going to a town full of ghosts. I've been thinking back to the day we found Argus, and . . . I don't know."

She quirked an eyebrow. "Don't know what?"

"Are you sure about this?"

"Are you?"

"Yes, but—"

"Then that's all I need, Hal," she said with a grin.

When they'd first come to this world, it had helped Halston to know that he was not alone. If his brothers hadn't been at his side, he'd have gone crazy.

So he knotted his fingers through Jae's and whispered, "You won't be alone."

She grinned again, rolled her eyes, and playfully swatted at his shoulder. "I don't need a bodyguard, Hal."

Well, alright. He'd been foolish to expect any other response from her. Still, he swore he could see the tiny coals of fear smoldering behind her eyes. No wonder she made a habit of hiding them under the brim of her overlarge hat.

"I know you don't," he said.

They didn't speak for a while. Outside, Halston watched a flock of jackdaws take to the twilight sky. He wondered where they were headed. "Have you ever felt invincible?"

Jae snorted. "*That's* a question."

Halston couldn't help but smile. "Well, have you?"

"A time or two. Never in the heat of a moment, though. The feeling always comes after I've made it out of something wild. But it never lasts long. Reckon I'd die if it did." She squeezed his hand. "What about you?"

"My father and I were walking along an inlet, once. When the hydrells were migrating. Thousands of them."

"Hydrells?"

"They don't have them here," he said. "But they're the most beautiful birds I've ever seen. Their feathers shine like spun gold."

"I'd like to see those."

"You'd love them, Jae." He caught himself smiling wider. "Every time I saw one . . . I felt like the world was mine. Like I'd never grow old. Never die. I'd just . . . *last.* On and on."

"Were they magic?"

"They sure looked like magic."

She nodded. "You ought to see them with your pa again, then. When you get home."

Halston swallowed. Now was as good a time as any to tell her. "I won't be seeing him again. He's dead."

Jae's face blanched, and her grip on his hand tightened. "Gods, Hal. I'm so sorry. I didn't kno—I mean, I don't know what—"

"It's alright. You don't have to say anything. There's nothing to say." And the truth was, Halston didn't want her to say anything. There were some things he struggled to speak about.

Instead, she wrapped an arm around his waist and nestled closer to him. Her warmth sent a wave of calm through his body—one so unfamiliar that it almost frightened him. He'd never known this feeling before—never noticed anyone quite like he noticed her, never had somebody gracing nearly all his dreams at night, never found himself craving so much time with another, even if it was borrowed.

Was it borrowed? The thought sparked blurry pictures of the future in his mind, of Jae leaving, of Jae coming with him, of Jae lying dead in a pool of blood while he stood by, powerless.

"You alright?" she asked, studying his face.

No. He wasn't. "I'm fine."

Speak to her about it.

But what could he say? Ask her to come with him through the portal? To abandon the search for her father—one she'd pursued with the same fierce fidelity he'd had for his journey? Her life was here. His was elsewhere. He could be the master of all words, some god with a divine power for language, and nothing he said would alter their course from the fork that would inevitably split their path down the middle.

It was then Jae removed her hat with her free hand and set it on her lap. She placed her head on his shoulder and squirmed for a moment, getting comfortable. "Mind if I rest here?" she asked with a grin.

Halston leaned into her. "I never mind."

"Good."

From across the aisle, he caught Lorelin flashing him a devilish, self-satisfied smirk. And for the first time, he didn't feel like dismissing it. He just smiled and rested a hand on Jae's lap before he drifted into the soundest sleep he'd had in months.

Chapter 9

The Drifter's hand wouldn't stop bleeding.

He'd wrapped the wound with a scrap from his jacket and unwound it periodically to check if it was healing. The slash the monster had given him stayed red and wet, refusing to scab or fade. He just mopped up the blood with his shirt and continued onward. He'd slept some, but been wary as he'd drifted off, wondering if he'd bleed out during the night. It hadn't happened yet.

He was beginning to wonder if death was at all possible in this world, but he was in no rush to find out.

Some time during the long night, he came upon a house sitting by the path at the foot of a sand dune.

It was a two-story house, fairly large, with a pointed roof and few windows. The Drifter thought of the little homes he'd seen while riding through the desert years ago, and wondered to himself if anyone still lived in them. Some had been ramshackle, built out of wooden planks and weathered by years of wind and sun. This house appeared to be made of the same stuff.

If not for the circle of footprints looping toward the front door in the sand, he would have passed it by.

The Drifter dared to tread closer. Yes, definitely footprints. He wasn't sure if the thought of having company out here was comforting or frightening.

When he raised his head and glimpsed a moss-green eye watching from the window, he felt no instinct to fight or run. There was only a faint, amiable curiosity inside him.

The front door swung open, the hinges screeching like a wounded animal. A man stood in the doorway. He was old, but he had young eyes, round and wide with childlike wonder. His clothes were strange: a shirt and trousers made of scraps of mismatched cloth crudely stitched together and scratched-up boots that had surely seen better days. The man regarded him with a reproachful look, arching one silver brow.

"Did *she* send you?" asked the man. He sounded ill, as though he'd been coughing up dust moments earlier.

The Drifter nodded.

He waited for the man to shoo him away, but instead, he motioned for the Drifter to come inside. The Drifter saw no reason to turn away. Nothing out here seemed safer or more dangerous than anything else.

Hard-packed dirt formed the floor, and the walls were whitewashed and sturdy. In the corner was a pile of furs, and in the center of the wall was a fireplace stacked high with unburnt wood. Two identical chairs sat on either side of the hearth. The ceiling was low enough that the Drifter had to stoop slightly.

The Drifter sat in one chair, and the man sat in the other. He was not looking at the Drifter. There was a worn leather book in his hands. He stared at the open pages, but his eyes weren't moving. Looking, but not seeing. Not reading. Not understanding.

"How long have you been here?" the old man asked without looking up.

"I'm not sure." How was he supposed to measure that here? With no rising sun, no changing seasons, no scraping hunger or parching thirst to tell him that time was passing at all?

"Hmm." The man pointed out the window. "Did you notice the grave on your way in?"

"No."

"Have a look."

The Drifter rose from his seat, nearly smacking his head on the ceiling beams, and ventured to the window. Outside, a lopsided cross protruded from the sand. He narrowed his eyes, searching for an inscription on the marker, but it was blank.

"I can't recall his name," the old man continued. "But I do believe he was decent company. Stayed here a while. Never did tell me why he came here. But I found him dead out back one day. Took me ages to bury him. Can't say how it happened. Perhaps he killed himself, but I wasn't able to figure it out."

Killed himself. Was that even possible, here?

The Drifter couldn't bring himself to look away, though he tried. He suddenly felt very aware of his bones and teeth, the blood and soft flesh surrounding them, how fragile he really was. How quickly he could cease to *be* if he wasn't careful. He readjusted the cloth binding his hand again.

"Do you remember why you're here?" asked the old man.

"Yes. I'm supposed to find the gates and speak my name."

"What gates?"

"I don't know. But I'm sure I'll know them when I see them."

"It's a good thing you remember why you're here, I suppose. I don't."

"I'm sorry."

The old man motioned to his book. A journal, the Drifter now realized, glimpsing the slanted handwriting filling the pages. "I brought this with me. Reckon I was here for someone named Kate. I sure wrote about her a lot in here, some time ago. But I don't remember her. Don't remember who this man who wrote these pages was. He must've been me. In some other time. But I'm not me anymore. I don't remember when I stopped."

The old man laughed softly. The sound was brittle, full of pain. The Drifter had never heard a laugh like that.

"I sure must've loved her," he mused, riffling the pages with his thumb. They fluttered like the beating wings of a moth.

The Drifter's stomach clenched. Would he start to lose his memories, too? He closed his eyes and begged himself to remember. *Remember, remember.*

He willed the memory to resurface in his mind. The task he'd been given. The faces of the people waiting for him.

Illusions brought themselves to life, the offspring of the marriage of his imagination to his will. Roads crawling across the planes of this world. Himself, walking across them, guided by some force unseen, which he had no choice but to trust. And the pathways would bring him to the *gates,* and then he would be gone.

This place would be gone.

He would return.

Exhaustion claimed the Drifter. He felt himself sinking back into the chair, eyelids growing heavier by the moment.

"You're welcome to stay here," said the old man without looking up from his journal.

The Drifter said nothing, but after checking his wound again— still not scabbed—he gave in to his fatigue and fell into a dreamless sleep.

Chapter 10

After the train ride and several days of hiking through ragged forests and sprawling grasslands, they reached the border of Banderra. When Jae finally looked upon the peaks of the Cannocs rising to the heavens, the strangest feeling settled over her. Part of her had expected she'd cry—that the memory of the last time she'd stared at these mountains would catch her like a flash flood and sweep her away. But the glittering silver ridges and crests filled her with a sharp sense of anticipation. It wasn't peaceful, but it didn't scare her either. A challenge waited for her, something that might bring her to her knees, but not to her death. She wasn't afraid. And that was more than enough.

Gryff had been even quieter than usual these past few days. Jem had popped up every now and again to assure them they were headed in the right direction, but it was just a formality as of now. Jem didn't *really* need to guide them until they got closer to the Shroud. No one had bothered asking Gryff more about this Zeph fellow. They'd learned quickly that Gryff's answers were vague at best and defensive at worst.

All day, they'd been passing over a long stretch of grassland. For miles and miles, the wavering grass stretched on, with few shrubs or trees to mark the rolling green. Jae disliked these plains. She longed for the forest they'd spent several days weaving through, for the cloak of pines and shadows. Out here, she felt like a target. Anyone—anything—could turn up on this flat land and strike them down. She'd been here many times before on her trips south with Pa, but he'd always made her feel as safe as she could be.

Hell, she was probably *safer* now with the gang. But she didn't feel it, and she was starting to miss the unwavering bravery that only seemed to exist in childhood.

It was nighttime, now, and they all took to setting up camp. Jae had just finished helping Lorelin get the fire going, and Hodge and Halston were scrubbing the roots they'd gathered with water from their canteens. Tsashin was smoothing out the bedrolls. Jem had appeared a few minutes ago, and was hovering next to Gryff, asking him about Zeph.

"I ain't sure he can help you, Jem." It was at least the fourth time Gryff had reminded the poor ghost.

"Why's that?" Jem asked, sounding polite as pie.

Gryff glanced at the others, who all had turned their focus to him. He snorted, realizing perhaps that he might as well just tell everyone the truth.

After a long moment of glowering silence, he said, "I lost a bet to him."

"What's wrong with that?"

"He was mad about losin' his prize. I reckon he didn't think I'd actually win. Then he accused me of cheatin'."

"Well, did you?" asked Jem. He didn't seem to be trying to get a rise out of Gryff. His eyes glimmered with sincere curiosity.

Gryff just glared at him. "Don'tcha have somewhere else to be?"

"No."

"Can't you . . ." Gryff waved a hand. "What are you still floatin' around here for?"

"Got nothing else to do." Jem sighed. "I didn't say this before, but . . . being dead is dull. I've been bored out of my skull for years now."

"You don't *have* a skull," Hodge pointed out.

Jae covered her mouth to hide her laughter.

Jem pointed a finger at Hodge. "Well, you've got me there, but I—" And the mines tugged him back before he could finish his thought.

Jae just kept smiling at the space he'd disappeared from. She liked having the ghost around.

They all finished eating and sat silently in their circle for a while. Jae felt fuller than she had in months, and she was braced for a night of restful sleep.

Hodge looked up from the fire, then whistled at the night sky. "Would you look at that?"

Jae joined him in peering at the stars. She hadn't been paying much attention to the sky until now . . . There was so *much* of it. There was little out here to cover the deep blue. And there were so many stars turning in the dark, more than one could count in a thousand lifetimes.

Tsashin pointed to something in the distance. "What's that over there?"

Everyone but Gryff craned their necks, then started moving to get a better look at it. It was a dark, still shape looming out in the fields about twenty yards away. At first, Jae reckoned that it was a boulder, but as they crept closer, they saw that it was too square. Forgotten items lay strewn around it—a hand mirror, a cigar box, cloth sacks stained brown by muck and sleet. In the center of the trash heap was a piano.

"Hmm." Jae nudged the instrument with the toe of her boot.

"Who chucks a piano into the middle of the Banderra plains?" Hodge mused.

"Folks moving north, I reckon," said Jae. "Lightening the load before the trail got too steep." Often she and Pa had come across piles of trash like this. They'd always had a grand time leafing through them whenever they'd had a few minutes to spare.

Hodge strolled up to the piano looking very sure of himself, then took a seat at the splintering bench. He pressed a finger down on the keys. Slightly out of tune, but not enough to make anybody wince.

"Still works," Hodge said flatly. He pretended to stretch out his fingers, then he started pressing the keys as if he were poking holes for seeds in the earth. His song—if anyone could call it that—was like Hodge himself: loud and brisk and all over the place.

"Oh, you're going to drive me *mad*," Lorelin broke in. She slid onto the bench next to Hodge and gave him a playful but powerful shove to get him out of her way.

"*You* know how to play?" Hodge asked with a mockingly doubtful sneer.

"I was a well-brought-up girl," Lorelin said, sounding so self-important it was a wonder she didn't burst into laughter at her own voice. "Of course I can."

Lorelin played a scale, which turned into a song. Jae didn't recognize the tune. It was something slow and silvery. Despite the instrument's age, Lorelin managed to make it sound nice. It was like a cup of lukewarm, bitter tea on the road; imperfect—but somehow, just what they'd needed.

The notes quickened into something cheerier. "Anyone know '*View from our Canoe*?'"

Of course Jae knew it; it was one of the first songs she remembered Pa singing.

"An old favorite," Halston said with a light laugh. "We used to sing that one on cattle drives all the time." The spark in his eye made Jae's heart skip two beats, and she hoped he wouldn't notice the blush that crept into her cheeks.

"Good." Lorelin softened the song for a moment. "Now, if you don't sing, I'm throwing you into the nearest river."

Lorelin's voice wasn't beautiful. It was a far cry from it, in fact. But the bravado she put into it was as bright and as buoyant as she was, and somehow that made it better than a voice that was really and truly lovely.

"There are waters pure as aether
In the view from my canoe
There are mountains shining pearly
With a snow that gleams like dew
There's a moon that glows relentless
In a sky of deepest blue
But there's nothing that my eyes have seen that
Could ever outshine you."

Jae was no singer, either. As it turned out, neither were the Harney boys. But Hodge sang with almost as much gusto as when he started to dance like a madman and spin Tsashin under his arm until she sounded dizzy with laughter. Gryff stayed back by the camp, sitting there in silence. Still, Jae would have bet her life that there was the ghost of a smile on his face as he tended to sharpening his ax.

They stayed like that for hours. Lorelin played and sang, and they joined in, harmonizing best they could with their tired, untaught voices. Laughter and song were good medicine. Jae hadn't realized how badly she'd needed some of it. So they sang until they got tired, and then a little longer after that.

And during the last chorus of their final song, Jae sat down to catch her breath, her chest sore from laughing so hard, and a blunt and almost scary thought struck her. *I've missed this.*

How was it possible to miss something that she'd never had before?

Hodge tapped her on the shoulder. "Are you alright?"

She blinked twice. This one-time stranger, this boy, this friend of hers . . . was asking if she was alright, even though she wasn't hurt. "Sure."

Though part of her felt close to crying, she started to laugh as they retired back to their makeshift beds. How could she not? Who in their right mind could keep from laughing at a feeling so wonderful and strange?

When they finally settled for the night, Jae was beginning to reckon that things might turn out alright.

Chapter 11

The next few days carried them north through the Banderra plains, and gradually the plains became the Cannoc foothills. There were more trees here than in the plains, but the surrounding land was mostly made up of flowering hills. The grass was greener, the air crisper and cooler, and in the near distance, the snow-capped Cannocs rose like giants over the horizon.

Hodge woke before it was warm. He found himself walking alone and thinking of how for the first time in years . . . he didn't feel as if he were desperately grasping for something out of his reach. He'd learned a lesson or two about getting his hopes too high. But an *end* . . . an end to years of feeling chased . . . was it in sight? Even if it wasn't, he felt he could at least picture it.

Hodge drifted away from their camp and started downhill. Around him, the world was lush and inviting. Everything in Mesca, even the forests, felt dry, like there was a fine layer of dust on everything, living or dead. Banderra felt more alive. Greener. The hills themselves seemed to glow under the sun. Hodge felt as if he were treading over the green velvet cape of a giant from one of Halston's old books, one who was wise and powerful but never cruel.

Hodge stopped when a cluster of something bright caught his eye. A bush covered in red bulbs. Raspberries! It was going to be a good day.

He hurried to the bush and set to stripping the branches of the plump, sweet fruits. He'd wake Tsashin first. Maybe she'd—

Mid-thought, something struck him on the back of the head.

Hodge fell to his knees with a short yelp, losing hold of the berries. Stars swarmed across his vision like startled birds. Some part of him demanded he grab his gun, but his hand couldn't fight against his dizziness.

The voice that followed just confused him even more. "Damn beggars! Who the hell do you think you are, boy?"

"The victim of an unprovoked attack?" murmured Hodge, which earned him another smack across the small of his back.

"Wise cracking one, eh?" his aggressor boomed.

A bit of clarity returned to Hodge's brain, and he finally got a look at his opponent. On any other day, he would have laughed at what he saw.

The man stooping over him was the shortest man he'd ever seen—even shorter than Tsashin. Despite that, he was stocky, walking on a pair of legs thick as tree trunks. His clothes were a sight . . . a heap of furs and leathers stitched up with cords of all different thicknesses. On his head was some type of hat resembling the gnarled top of a dead tree. His gray hair stuck out from the brim, scraggly across his forehead, framing two wild, tawny eyes. He brandished a large, knobby branch like a sword, and Hodge reckoned that was what had whacked him upside the head and back.

Hodge found that his hat had been knocked off his head, and

now, it was sitting a couple yards away. He reached for it, and the short man smacked him on the back again.

Hodge had enough strength this time to whirl around on him. "What was that for?!"

"Thought you were trying to pull something."

"I was reaching for my *hat*, you son of a—"

A force hammered into Hodge's chest, throwing him backwards. He cried out as he landed hard, dirt and leaves scattering around him. He pushed himself back up to his knees, coughing.

What was *that?* It was as if a burst of wind had shot him out of thin air.

The man smugly waved his knobby staff. "Watch that mouth of yours or I'll blow you twenty miles away."

It was too damn early for this.

Just then, Gryff's giant shadow appeared on the ground before Hodge.

"Damn it, Zeph, what did you do to him?" Gryff roared.

If it weren't for his throbbing head, Hodge would have lost it with laughter. Of course. *This* was Zeph.

Zeph's eyes widened. "Well, now. It's been a while, Gryff. Come back to boast? I reckon you never found the wind demon."

"*Wind demon?*" murmured Hodge. He was still seeing stars, so neither Gryff nor Zeph seemed to hear his slurred words.

"I ain't here for that. There's . . . there's something *they* need." Gryff gestured to Hodge with his knuckles, then over his shoulder in the direction where the others slept, not knowing how good they had it—none of them were getting cuffed on the heads with a big stick.

"Well, are you going to be their messenger, or are they going to ask me themselves?" Zeph prodded Hodge in the shoulder with the stump of his staff. Hodge was tempted to snatch it and snap it over his lap, but if this fella was their ticket to getting them home, he'd better keep his hands to himself. "Go round up your friends, then follow me. And like I said—watch that mouth of yours."

———————

"Wake up, loons. Gryff's friend just smacked me upside the head and he ain't happy, so we'd better go *make* him happy if we want whatever the hell it is we came for."

Of all the things to wake up to.

Jae tried not to grumble as she rose. The morning light stung her eyes. She sat up, taking in their surroundings—her stirring companions, the grassy hillside on which they'd slept, the white and yellow wildflowers dotting the ground.

Hodge hadn't explained himself further when they packed up camp, but it'd been a while since she'd seen him looking so worked up. His expression wasn't quite a pout, but it was still damn funny, and she might've laughed if it weren't for her confusion.

Hodge led them to the foot of another hill, where Gryff was waiting with someone who could only be Zeph. A Nefili man. Apart from Grove, he was the only one she'd ever seen.

The sight of him struck her with some odd mix of surprise and curiosity, like when she spied trees growing at odd angles out of hillsides, or horses with mismatched eyes. Things that weren't impossible, but odd enough that she couldn't help but stare for a moment. He looked like someone had just dug him out from beneath the roots of a tree and he'd stepped into the open air with mites and dirt clods tumbling from his limbs.

Zeph slogged forward to greet them. "This way," he ordered gruffly, turning his back to them and starting in a new direction. His voice was everything Jae expected—deep and gravelly as upturned earth.

As they followed him through the winding hills, nobody spoke. The silence became uncomfortably heavy, and Jae kept looking at Gryff, waiting for him to speak. But he was quiet as always. No surprise there. Jae wondered what sort of 'prize' Zeph had been forced to surrender to Gryff after he'd lost that bet all those years ago. Just by listening to his grunting, she reckoned it must have been something he hadn't expected to give up.

She hated not having the faintest clue what waited for them at the end of this trek. They might as well be walking blindfolded.

Jae had often wondered where the Nefilium lived. She'd always imagined that they didn't need to sleep much and likely had little need for houses. If she had a few thousand years to live, the last thing she'd want to do was waste any of it sleeping. She'd spent her younger years picturing them wandering aimlessly, maybe taking up a spot high in a tree or some silent cave if they ever needed a moment to lie still and watch the world pass them by. So it was hard not to let her mouth drop open like a trap door when Zeph led them to what could only be his house.

Zeph had brought them to an enormous meadow rimmed by a silvery-clear brook, and at once, they were overcome by the sound of birdsong. A rainbow of wildflowers covered the entire area. In the center of the meadow was an ash tree so large and craggy that no force of nature could have grown it—this was magic, plain and simple. The tree's trunk was as wide as a cabin, and in its center was a stubby little door. A series of smaller houses were built here and there throughout the branches, linked by dozens of nets and ropes and ladders wound with ivy and moss.

Zeph opened the front door, stepped inside, then turned around and stared at the lot of them like they'd just appeared out of thin air. "Well? Are you coming inside or not?"

Halston took the leap of faith and went in first. Jae hurried after him.

If any part of her had been tired, the smells inside the house woke her at once. There were the scents that any passerby could expect from a small cabin—smoking wood, baking bread, and a trace of dust. But there were also smells she'd never dreamed a little forest house would harbor—rain, sweet rosiness, and a hint of something coppery.

Zeph trudged past them, ducking beneath a row of potted plants dangling from the ceiling on frayed lengths of twine. The wooden floor creaked beneath his uneven footsteps.

But unlike a cabin, the room was humongous. There was a pot cooking over flames roaring in a stone fireplace. Jae looked over the dozens of shelves that lined every inch of the walls, all covered in treasures—silverware and stones and balls of string and stacks of paper, books and cloth and bottles and jars and things Jae couldn't even name. A rope ladder led to an opening in the far-up ceiling, through which a shaft of sunlight streamed down, striking the room in a beam of yellow.

Zeph rummaged through a pile of dishes for a minute, then emerged with an armload of differently colored bowls. He set them on the floor in a misshapen circle and said, "Sit down and eat. We'll discuss our deal while we do."

They all hesitated. Jae wished she'd remembered to tell them beforehand that one never refused hospitality from the Nefilium—Pa had told her that doing so would often invite disaster. "Much obliged, sir," she said to Zeph, taking a seat. The others followed suit . . . except Gryff, who remained stuck to the wall.

Jae picked up her bowl. It was stone, and shaped like a leaf with its tip torn off. Zeph worked his way around the circle with a kettle. The unidentifiable soup sloshed out of it with each step he took, trickling down its sides and raining steaming droplets onto the floor. Zeph spooned the soup into the bowls as he moved. Jae thanked him as he stomped away from her, and he answered with a short grunt.

They ate quietly for a quarter of an hour. The soup was thin and very hot. Jae swallowed it in small, careful sips to keep it from scorching her throat. It tasted like bark. She kept hoping that somebody would pipe up and break the silence already, but nobody dared, herself included.

Zeph had no bowl. He ate from the kettle itself, scooping soup to his lips with the ladle. "What do you want, Gryff?" he said at long last.

"A potion," Gryff said without looking away from the floor. "Spirium."

"Spirium, eh? You gonna waste it like you did my rope?"

"*Waste it?* I *won* it."

"You told me that you never found the wind demon. Just let that monster run free, eh? What happened to your quest for vengeance? I recall you told me you'd stop at nothing for it. Didn't realize you meant that literally. You did *nothing* with the treasure I gave you."

"Drop it, Zeph." There was a hint of a growl in Gryff's voice, now.

"I'll drop it if you admit you cheated."

"I didn't cheat, and you shouldn't have made the bet in the first place if you weren't prepared to part with it. That ain't *my* fault."

"What's holding you back from finding the wind demon, then? Cowardice?"

"*Watch it.*" Gryff's eyes narrowed.

Zeph lifted a hand dismissively. "Sorry to rile you up. Just doesn't make sense to me why you wouldn't use the lasso, considering you were so desperate to win it from me all those years ago."

"Listen, do you want it back? If so, it's yours." Gryff reached into his pack, pulled out the strange gold lasso he'd used to wrangle Argus a month or so ago, and threw it on the floor. "There. Just take it."

They all stared at it for a few moments.

This was the prize Zeph was so flustered about? Jae had never thought that there was anything special about the lasso beyond its strange color.

"I *can't* take it back," said Zeph. "Even if I wanted to. It's bound to you, now. The power won't work for me anymore."

Gryff snorted, then picked the lasso back up and shoved it into his knapsack.

"Are you ever gonna use it?" asked Zeph.

"*Maybe.*"

Nobody else said a word. Jae's soup was getting lukewarm. She was thinking about slinking out the door and letting Zeph and Gryff sort this out themselves, and by the way the others all seemed to be uncomfortably inspecting their bowls, she reckoned they were thinking the same thing.

Still, a restless part of her was itching to ask about this *wind demon,* whatever it was.

Zeph was eyeballing Gryff's pack, now, looking a little less flustered. "You were really ready to give it back to me?"

"The offer still stands, if you think it's at all possible," Gryff said with a terse nod.

Zeph cleared his throat. "It ain't. Well then. Spirium. Whatever for?" His voice was level, now. Mild.

Gryff didn't beat around the bush. "To get to the Shroud.

But we sure as hell ain't gettin' in as livin' folk. We've gotta pass for ghosts."

"Why on the gods' green earth do you want to go *there?*" Zeph asked. "It's cursed for a reason. Dripping with devilry."

"We're going one way or another," Gryff said, firm as a stake in the ground. "Name your price."

Zeph shot Gryff a baleful glare. "Did you bring your *kids* here? To decide this for them? Why aren't *they* telling me what *they* want?"

"They ain't my—good question. Why don't you ask 'em?"

Zeph eyed them all with suspicion, which gave Jae the hankering to step outside again. "Thievery?"

Jae caught a flash of embarrassment on Halston's face before he summoned that perfect rigidness that he'd worn the night they met. "No. What we seek is ours. It was stolen from us."

"Stolen from you?" Zeph's nostrils flared. "What is it, then? Listen. If you're here for gold, you might as well leave now. I'll have no hand in any of that."

His words could have cut through stone. Jae could almost see a thousand stories lurking behind his pale eyes, with a thousand bursts of bloodshed staining troves of gold. How many travelers had come begging for Zeph's hand in winning it?

For a while, nobody said a thing. Then finally, a soft voice offered up an answer. "It's love," said Tsashin.

Zeph blinked in surprise and glanced at Tsashin, who was sitting across from him with her hands folded.

Zeph murmured something Jae couldn't hear, then said, "Love?"

"Yes," Tsashin said. "All of us seek . . . a reunion. With those we've lost."

Jae's heart began to sting. There was truth when Tsashin spoke, the untarnished kind.

Zeph's eyes were wide. His lip quivered under his scraggly beard, and for a moment, Jae thought he might weep. But his face broke into a smile, and a laugh erupted from somewhere deep inside him, a real roar that seemed to shake the walls and silence the birds outside. Nobody else laughed with him. Jae wasn't sure if she wanted to chuckle or slink back into a corner.

"Love!" he hooted. "*Love!* Dear girl, do you want to know how many travelers have knocked on my door? How many of them have asked—*begged*—me to grant their wishes?"

Tsashin hesitated, looking puzzled. "No?"

"*Hundreds,*" Zeph cried. "And no more than a handful of them have ever told me that it was for *love*. But I remember each one of them." Gone was his hard-worn shell. It was like Tsashin had chipped off his winter frost, and now they could see the ground thawing underneath.

And so Zeph stood before them at last, and he made his offer in the sort of tone that let them all know that there was no bargaining: they could take it or leave it. But it was brief, and it was fair.

"You will stay with me for a week," he said. "You may use the fire and cookpot, but you're responsible for feeding yourselves. The earth is your bed. I will give each of you your tasks daily. I haven't had enough hands to tend to my land in years. While you work, I'll brew the potion. Mind you, it'll take me the week."

He waved a hand. "Eat. Finish. I'll be back in a while."

Zeph stumbled out of the door, murmuring and laughing to himself. "Love," he whistled as he stepped across the threshold. "Of all the damned things. Love."

Chapter 12

As Tsashin stepped out into the dawn-touched world, all she could think about was how nice it was to *move*.

They'd spent the past couple days completing tasks for Zeph. Truly, she hadn't minded any of them—the chores had kept her busy, been something to occupy her mind. He'd left most of the garden work to her. She was becoming familiar with the flowers and the crops, and beginning to recognize the plants in the garden rows as easily as old friends. The bees hummed and danced with the plants. There was just the right amount of sun and shade tangling together into a sweet blanket of warm and cool. She only wished she'd found a better way to keep herself busy earlier on.

She tried to fight the impulse, but often, she dwelled on her fears and frustrations . . . the dangers looming ahead of them, the uncertainty of what each day would bring, and the ever-present frustration of being unable to remember exactly who she was.

It could be worse. If it weren't for the others, Sterling would have hauled her away, and she didn't want to think about what he'd had in mind for her. But some part of her—one she was too ashamed to give a voice to—wished that he had lived a little longer, just enough for her to learn where she'd come from. Who had put her to sleep and buried her, and why? What sort of magic had kept her alive under the soil? And how long had she been dormant in that darkness?

Sometimes, it felt impossible not to dwell on such things until her heart raced. She rarely spoke of these thoughts, fearing she'd burden the others. If she mulled it over too long, she seemed to conjure a monster to join the pack of beasts already chasing after her through the dark parts inside herself. And she ran and ran, but she couldn't help but look over her shoulder every couple of steps to face the creatures' wide mouths. *Speak. Tell me what you want.* But the mouths didn't speak—they just gnashed their teeth and roared.

It was the third day of their stay with Zeph. He'd been doling out jobs to them each morning. Chopping wood, patching cracks in the gnarled foundations of his treehouse, ridding the meadows of weeds that Zeph said were choking out the native plants.

A couple times, Tsashin had seen Gryff and Zeph talking. Neither of them looked especially thrilled, but they weren't tense, either. Whatever the fuss about that strange lasso was . . . it seemed they'd found a way to put it behind them.

That morning, Tsashin had assumed he'd put her in his garden again, but instead, he'd handed her a cloth sack bulging with seeds. "Go to the sanctuary," he said, motioning to the sky. "It's the top-most room. Refill the feeders."

Tsashin crossed the platform surrounding the center of the tree-house. She squinted at the strange, circular structure atop the tree. From its roof, a pair of doves emerged and took to the sky. Yes, that had to be it.

She sucked in a breath. She hadn't had to climb any of the ladders yet.

Tsashin stuffed the feed sack into her belt and began scaling a rope ladder toward the topmost house. The ladder swayed each time she jammed a foot into one of the loops. She couldn't recall the last time she'd climbed anything.

She climbed and climbed, trying not to look down, and her muscles trembled more with each breath. She didn't dare look down. If she did, the fear might cause her to surrender her grip on the ropes.

But as she neared the sanctuary, the sunlight wrapped its arms around her. Just like that, she wasn't tired. She couldn't tell if it was magic or sheer relief or both, but she welcomed it wholeheartedly.

The sanctuary resembled a cabin that had somehow been lifted off the ground and tacked to the tree, peeking just above the forest's canopy and surrounded by a circular platform atop a too-thin branch. Tsashin wondered how much magic it took to keep it aloft. The wooden walls were full of windows—no glass—and there was an enormous, gaping hole on one side of the delicately sloping roof.

Tsashin pushed the sack of seeds onto the platform, then hoisted herself up from the ladder. The wood was warm through her shirt. She got to her feet, and when she gazed out over the world below, amazement made her fall still.

The forest stretched past the horizon, like an ocean of pure green. From inside the sanctuary, birdsong mingled with the sound of . . . Were those bells?

Tsashin stepped into the sanctuary. Moss and grass carpeted the floor, and flowers of every color bloomed on the walls. The air was heavy with their dizzying, honey-sweet scent.

And then there were the birds. Dozens and dozens of birds.

A small jungle of ropes, bells, and baubles covered the ceiling and walls. From them, the birds leapt and fluttered and sang to each other. Night-dark larks and day-bright blue jays, finches with crests of gold and wrens speckled like the riverbanks. *'Welcome!'* they seemed to call to her. *'Oh, food! Do stay a while, please!'*

This was the sort of place she could easily spend a few hours. Or several days.

Tsashin poured the seeds into the feeders—knobby bowls carved of wood and stone dangling from thin ropes—and the birds hurried down for their feast, calling out to each other like old friends. She laughed along with them—laughed like she never had before. At least, in the short span she could remember.

When the sack was empty, Tsashin sat down cross-legged on the floor. She rested her chin on her hand and watched the birds, a dance of hundreds of fluttering wings and brightly crested heads. They moved so carelessly, so freely—like children. Their spirits were beaming behind their eyes, made-bold in their music, and she listened until numbness prickled at her calves.

She was finished here, and she knew she should probably head down sometime for her next task. But would Zeph mind, really, if she spent a while longer up here? How could someone enter a place like this and then leave so soon?

"A fine place, isn't it?"

Tsashin glanced backward. Zeph had walked into the sanctuary, but his heavy steps hardly made a sound on the soft, mossy floor.

Tsashin smiled. "It's beautiful."

"I reckoned you might like it up here." Zeph peered up at the rafters, where a flock of finches were cavorting in a patch of flowers amongst dangling bronze bells.

"Did you build this place?"

"Certainly did." Zeph's eyes crinkled at the corners when he grinned. "The birds bring me stories. News from the world."

"Is it good news?"

"Not always, no. And some of them come here to get away from it."

A strange, heavy calm fell over Tsashin. "I've wondered that before. If they could understand us."

"They can. And sometimes, they have things to say to us. But most people don't care to listen. Mortal folk have little time and even less interest in such things."

"I could do it. I have all the time in the world," Tsashin said. She almost winced at the trace of bitterness lacing her words. "I'd like to hear their stories."

"Gryff mentioned you were a storyteller," Zeph said.

Tsashin nodded. "Do *you* have a favorite story?"

"Sure. Have you heard of Zuya? Old Konohe legend."

"No." Tsashin leaned in his direction. "But I'd like to."

"Starts the way most legends do. Strife. Pain. Fear. There was a restless spirit terrorizing Zuya's village. Tearing up the earth, setting fire to everything they'd grown. The spirit killed anyone who dared to try and stop it. They said it turned the dawn itself blood red.

"At last, they stopped trying to fight it, and instead asked the spirit what it wanted. Imagine how much simpler things would be, if we all spoke before we fought, 'stead of the other way around. Anyway, the spirit told them that all it wanted was to be *heard*. And if someone sat still for three days, and listened to all of its stories, without sleeping, without eating, without wandering off . . . then it would leave them be.

"A few of them tried, but restlessness claimed them all, and in retribution, the spirit took their lives. Zuya was different. She listened to the spirit's stories, and she lasted through the three days.

"She'd succeeded, and so the spirit told her this: the stories it had given her would have the power to break curses, whenever they were retold. Till the day she died, she repeated those powerful tales to all she knew."

Tsashin tilted her head. "Do you know the stories?"

Zeph smiled sheepishly. "I'm afraid I don't."

Tsashin hoped her disappointment wasn't plain to see. There was something wonderfully exciting about a story with the power to break a curse.

"I'd imagine the stories of a spirit are elusive," Zeph continued. "Though I'm sure they find their way to exactly who needs them."

"Is the story true?" asked Tsashin.

"You're a storyteller," said Zeph. "I'd imagine you know that the strangest tales are often truer than we might think."

Tsashin couldn't argue with that. She'd been unearthed from a coffin alive and well—save for her banished memories. Nothing strange would ever surprise her again.

They were quiet for a while. Tsashin watched Zeph wave his staff, and at his motions, feathers, dirt, and leaves gathered into a pile on the floor. With a burst of air, Zeph whisked the debris out the window.

Tsashin began to wonder about the limits of Zeph's power, if there were things he could do besides control the wind. Would it be selfish to . . .

No. She was going to ask him. She'd work a hundred nights—a thousand—if that was what it took. Despite her stomach starting to pitch like a leaf caught in a current, she began her plea. "Did Gryff tell you how they found me?"

"He did indeed."

She breathed in. "Would you be able to—"

"I can't give a girl her memories back," he said, not unkindly. "That's a power outside my own."

Tsashin glanced toward the floor. "I'd imagined so. I . . . I only thought I'd ask."

"Right," Zeph said. The glint of pity in his eyes embarrassed her, and she hoped he couldn't tell. She was beginning to loathe feeling so helpless.

"You don't gotta go with 'em, y'know." He spoke kindly but firmly, the way Tsashin imagined a father might speak. "Trouble seems to follow Gryff wherever he goes. Seems like the others suffer from the same affliction."

"They're my friends," Tsashin said. "They're all I have in the world, right now. Them, and my stories."

Maybe she wasn't safe with the Harney gang, but until she knew who she was, she wasn't safe *anywhere*. They'd protected her this long.

Besides, danger or not . . . she couldn't bring herself to imagine turning away from them now.

Zeph only looked mystified. But after a moment, something shifted in his expression, although only slightly. A granule of understanding. Tsashin imagined that he'd been alone for so long, he was hazy on what it was like to partner up with another—to depend on another soul, or five.

"You keep that gentle heart of yours, Tsashin." With that, Zeph retreated into the newborn day. "It's rarer than gold."

Chapter 13

Jae lay on top of her bedroll, listening to the crickets singing in the hills. They'd circled up in a patch of soft grass and larkspurs near the edge of Zeph's clearing, and the smell was so sweet that Jae had started to breathe a little easier. Still, sleep hadn't found her yet.

She had a knife in one hand, a chunk of wood in the other. For the past half hour or so, she'd been trying to whittle it into the shape of a bird.

She kept thinking about the hydrells Halston had told her about. Though she hadn't a clue what a hydrell looked like, she figured they couldn't be much different from ordinary birds in this realm.

When her hands felt stiff and raw from carving the wood, she took Pa's compass from her pack. She flipped it open and watched the needle settle in the direction of the Cannocs, the Outlands. North. She liked to think that it was pointing in Pa's direction, too.

Just looking at Pa's compass had always brought her some

comfort, helped her feel more at ease. She felt that perhaps Halston could use something similar . . . if she could get the wooden bird to look decent enough. Because soon, they'd need all the comfort they could get.

Thoughts of the storm ahead began clouding her mind. Monsters in the Outlands, Nefilium who didn't take kindly to mortal travelers, unlike Zeph, and the looming northern winter that always seemed to arrive sooner than anyone could brace themselves for. And then there were the Rangers . . .

No. She wouldn't think about the Rangers.

Jae looked at Halston, who was sleeping soundly a couple yards away, and she smiled. Dawn was close. She could tell by the smell of the air. It was fresh and almost sweet in that near-morning way. Halston murmured something in his sleep. She thought about nestling up to him.

It was then Jae overheard Zeph speaking from around the bend of his treehouse—she was just close enough to make out what he said.

"I told you already. There's nothing I can do."

Jae sat bolt upright, brushed herself off, and stood. She snuck around the corner and saw Zeph and Jem facing one another behind the house. Jem floated dismally under one of the rope ladders.

"Do you know any warlocks who *could?*" Jem asked. The pitch of his voice rose with a note of desperation.

"No. Mind you, no two Nefilium or warlocks are entirely alike. It's . . . rare that one finds the same power in two of them," Zeph explained, with a hint more gentleness than his first remark.

Jae was familiar with that tone. She'd heard it most often from sheriffs who had enough regard to treat her half-decently, but not enough to take her seriously.

"You may as well follow this gang, Jem. Maybe you'll find some help at Sylmare. Perhaps the ghosts there will know of someone who could help you. I can't say for sure. But I'll be no use to you."

Jae had come to know that dim but hopeful look on Jem's face all too well. "Thanks anyway," he said.

Just as Jem slipped away, she stepped around the corner to take his place. Zeph's mouth firmed into a straight, hardened line. "You fancy yourself the fox of the bunch, don't you?"

"No," said Jae.

"You seem to enjoy sticking your nose in everything."

"Sure do." There was no point in denying it.

Zeph blinked in surprise. If Jae didn't know better, she'd have thought that he was holding back a gravelly laugh. "Refreshing honesty." He squinted at the space where Jem had been a moment earlier. "Ain't every day you see a ghost hanging around living folk."

"We ain't an everyday bunch."

Zeph snorted. "That's for sure. Been a while since I've spoken to a spirit. I'd almost forgotten how flighty they can be."

Jae thought of Jem haunting the mines where he'd died, then another thought crossed her mind. Zeph was surely as knowledgeable as any of the other magic folk out here. "Can I ask you something?"

"I imagine you're going to ask me anyway, even if I say no."

Well, that was true. "What do you know about ghosts?"

Zeph motioned for her to follow him with his staff. "This isn't something I can answer simply. You may as well come with me. I have a lot of potions to bottle, but I could use an extra pair of hands. That can be your final task."

Zeph led her to the room where they'd had his earthy soup when they first arrived. Steam rose from the liquid in his cookpot, but it wasn't bubbling. The silver potion sat in the cauldron like a vat of cool mud.

Jae breathed in what might have been a whiff of the brew.

For a second, she forgot herself. It smelled just like the air after a thunderstorm.

Zeph handed her a funnel and several glass vials, then instructed her to begin ladling the potion into it. Jae got to work, careful not to touch the liquid. Even though she'd be swallowing it in good time, something about that silver, syrupy goo set her on edge. Still, she'd bite the bullet and drink it when the time came.

"So," Zeph said, pushing up one of his sleeves. "What would you like to know?"

"Can ghosts kill people?"

She'd asked this before, mainly posing the question to drifters she'd met on her travels. Every time, she'd held her breath. But those who'd seen and even spoken to ghosts always said they weren't sure. And part of her was glad, because if there was a chance those ghosts had forced Pa to join them in death . . .

No.

But Zeph seemed to know. "It's possible for them to kill, but rare. It takes a great amount of willpower for a ghost to touch something."

So taking Pa away had been no easy task for those ghosts. Lifting him off the ground and riding off on their spectral horses had taken concentration and grit.

Could he have escaped? And if he had, why hadn't he come back to her? Or was he lying in some unmarked grave, mourned only by the wind?

She'd entertained such possibilities before, but never for long. If she did, she'd break, and if she broke, she couldn't keep going. And she *had* to keep going. It was all she knew how to do. At least she had an answer.

Now for her second question. "Can ghosts be killed?"

She was beginning to wonder if Zeph had forgotten her question entirely when at last, he spoke up. "They can't be *killed* the way that mortals can. But they can be vanquished. One can send their souls to the next world, never to return."

"How?"

"God-ore," he replied.

"I ain't heard of that."

Zeph stuck a hefty spoon into the cauldron and gave the potion a quick stir. "Mortals have other names for it. White iron, earthmarrow, adamite—"

"Adamite!" The glass vial in her hand almost fell to the floor. She tightened her grip on the thing. "But how?"

Already, her heart was doing somersaults. Adamite! Her answer—Pa's gods-damn salvation—had been within her reach ever since she'd met the Harney boys. Surely their half of the knife could cut down a ghost or two.

"It only has to touch them. I've met Outlanders who carry god-ore arrows or bullets to fend off ghosts and revenants . . . rare as it is, just a trace amount of it will do the job."

Jae shivered at the mention of revenants. Word was that there were some warlocks and Neflium who could raise men from the dead to do their bidding, but the life they regained wasn't even close to the real thing. Like machines, they were. Thoughtless, moving, but not *feeling*.

"So if I got my hands on an adamite bullet," Jae started, hoping she didn't sound too eager, "I could take out a ghost?"

"Sure. But it ain't easy to hit one," Zeph warned, as if he'd stared through her eyes and into her thoughts. It made Jae wonder if reading minds was another magical ability he kept up his furry sleeve.

"Why not?"

"They're elusive, as you might've noticed. In the corner one moment, out the window the next. Solid space doesn't faze them the way it does us."

Jae looked out the window to the barely lightening sky and the rolling hills beneath, and she knew that she would leave this place knowing that what Zeph had told her was more valuable than any bounty she'd ever claimed.

They finished bottling up the potions. Jae felt she ought to say something. They'd paid for these brews in labor, but Jae knew that it couldn't possibly be enough to repay him for this.

"Thanks," she said. "Thanks an awful lot."

Zeph looked her up and down. "Been a while since I've had such a . . . curious visitor."

Jae tilted her head. "Do you remember everybody that comes here?"

"Sure. At least vaguely. But there are some who couldn't leave my mind even if I tried my damnedest to force them out."

She wanted to ask if Gryff was one of them . . . but there'd be no point in that. She already knew.

"I still have to remind myself that mortal folks are . . . intricate," he muttered. He wasn't looking at Jae. "And that every man who passes me by is a couple thousand shards held together by . . . something that only humans seem to have. Something that the magic folk don't."

Something.

Whatever it was, she hoped she had lots of it.

Chapter 14

That morning, they left Zeph's place with vials of the potion. "Mind you," he'd warned. "A sip of the potion will give you the appearance of a ghost for about ten hours. Use the spirium sparingly, if you can."

They'd all thanked Zeph tremendously, then went on their way. As they returned to the trail, Jae looked over her shoulder to find that Zeph was watching them. He sat upright on a boulder shrouded in moss, the strange king of his own small territory.

Would they ever see him again? Jae hoped she'd made the weight of her gratitude clear to him—not only for the potions, but for telling her what he knew about ghosts.

Now, they were bound for the Nefilium Pass. Nestor's Caverns.

Jae checked her map shortly after they left Zeph's meadow. The Pass wasn't far, and Lorelin had the brooch to pay the tithe.

The day's journey brought them to a lily pond at the side of the trail, and Jae was sure that it was the finest campsite they'd ever found. The air was deliciously cool, the smells sweet, and the water tasted better than certain meals Jae had eaten on the road before. When the others retired to rest, Jae and Halston took the first watch.

Nobody had given them permission to walk in circles round the pond, but both of them figured that it'd be just fine. They finally felt as though they weren't on the run . . . and they had the whole world to themselves.

This was the largest pond Jae had ever seen—almost the size of a lake. Its ripples sparkled like jewels in the moonlight, and the blue reflection of the Cannoc peaks glinted on the surface. The grass and water plants sprouted high and tickled their legs as they strolled. Jae certainly wouldn't mind languishing here another night or two.

"I'll miss all this green," Jae said, "when we're crossing the caverns. Gods. I ain't been to Banderra in years. Pa and I had a cabin here. The mountains were lovely in the summer, but miserable to cross in the cold."

"You seem like you're built for that sort of thing," said Halston. "I think it'd take more than the cold to snuff out a fire like yours."

The fire came rushing to her cheeks right about then. "I think we ought to rethink this whole thing," she said.

"What do you mean?"

"Why bother? Crossing the mountains, braving the Nefilium Pass and . . . who knows what else?" At once, any control she'd had over her laughter disappeared. "Why don't we join a circus or something?"

Halston raised a hand. "Gods, no. I'd freeze up in front of a crowd."

Ah, leave it to Halston Harney: he could brave gunfire from a band of outlaws, but the thought of putting on a performance made his blood run cold.

"You don't *have* to be in front of the crowd," Jae said, leaning in his direction. "You can keep the books for us. Dole out the funds."

"Hmm. I'll consider it. What about you?"

"I can . . . I don't know . . . sing."

"Oh, *sing?* I heard your performance the other night," he said with a wry grin.

Jae shrugged. "I ain't good at it. That doesn't mean I can't do it. And Lorelin can play the piano. Tsashin's got her stories. Gryff could . . . break things in half."

"Hodge could do trick shots." Halston's smile was wicked, almost unlike him.

"He certainly could. See? We've already got a plan."

She wanted to tell him how much she liked this—making outlandish plans they didn't believe. If she could be twelve again and have faith in such things wholeheartedly . . . what a wonder that would be.

Would they have been friends, if they'd met as children? Sword fought with sticks, climbed trees, wasted summer afternoons together? It was nonsense to long for it. But she longed for it anyway.

Eventually, they sat down in the grass. Feeling bolder than usual, she rested her head on his shoulder. Halston wrapped an arm around her and held her close as a treasure to his chest.

The stars were numerous and fire-bright. What did the stars look like in Halston's world? Were they as magnificent as these, or were they even brighter, even more wondrous? Did they name the constellations and weave tales out of them, too?

"Do you tell stories about the stars? Back where you're from?"

"Of course," said Halston. "See that one, there? With the three bright stars in the middle? The Suryans call that one Ishwar. And there's another constellation that bears a . . . striking resemblance back home. My mother told me that Ishwar wanders from world to world, watching over his people wherever they go. She said that he followed the Suryan voyagers when they left the First Realm and came to the Second."

Like the Wandering God. "Hmm. Ishwar."

"Yes. He's the hero of a lot of the old Suryan stories. I read all about him when I was younger. He was *my* hero, too. Knew how to use his wits as well as a sword."

"You read a lot of fancy books, didn't you?"

Halston faced the ground with a half-embarrassed grin, then scratched the back of his neck. "Every lord insisted on educating his sons. Hodge and Elias couldn't have cared less about literature, but . . ." He whistled. "I miss my books. Spending the day reading on the shore."

Jae nearly jumped. "You *lived* by the ocean?"

"Yes—"

"You're kidding me!" she said through shaky laughter. "You lived by the *ocean* and you never even told me?"

Halston blinked in surprise. "I didn't realize you had such a . . . fondness for the sea."

Her cheeks got warm. "Well, I've never been, but Pa would always talk about it." She looked to the moonlit glow of the pond's waters, imagining them instead crashing over a glimmering shore, stretching far beyond the reach of her sight. "He went to the coast of Kalstira a few times. And . . . he told me he'd never felt a peace like that before, when he was standing in the shallows. Like he understood the world all at once, and nothing felt scary to him at all."

"I know what he means," Halston said. "I think you'd love the sea, Jae. I'll have to take y—"

And there he stopped.

Jae bit her lip so hard she braced herself to taste blood. *Not a* word, she told herself. Don't *make him say anything else.*

The silence lingered for a time, then she remembered why she'd gotten him alone in the first place. There was something she had to give him.

She took the finished wooden bird out of her pocket. "This is for you."

Halston took it. "A bird?"

"Yes!" She clapped her hands. Part of her had been worried that he wouldn't see what it was. "Glad to know I ain't useless at whittling. I . . . I thought back to you talking on the train. About those hydrell birds back home. Brought you some peace of mind, didn't it? Thought I could remind you of that bird again, somehow. Though I doubt this one's half as pretty."

And Halston gave her the most honest smile she'd ever seen— one that lit up his entire face. She wanted to catch that smile like a firefly.

"Thank you." He ran a finger over the bird's dull beak. And then he kissed her. Out of the blue, it was, and then it turned slow. Wonderfully, marvelously slow.

He hadn't kissed her since that night they'd left Dolorosa. She'd been wondering if it would be the last time.

She hadn't wanted it to be the last time. She didn't want this to be the last time, either.

"Ha-hem."

Halston pulled away from her first—a part of Jae knew that nothing short of a lightning strike would've gotten her to part from him. But when his mouth had left hers, she made herself turn. Gryff was standing behind them. He didn't look displeased, but Jae still felt like she ought to shrink away. She hadn't wanted an audi- ence that night.

Gryff's look could have startled a rugged mountaineer. "Keepin' watch, eh?"

"Yes," Halston said, though Jae scarcely heard it at all.

Gryff snorted. "Get to bed then, both of you. I ain't trustin' y'all to be awake at the same time. We're in unknown territory now, and we need someone who will actually keep an eye out."

"We—" Halston started.

"*Go.*"

Halston cleared his throat, then offered Jae a small, sheepish grin. "Goodnight, Jae." There was a sweetness to his goodbye, so gentle that she could hardly stand it. Halston started back in the direction of the camp, but Jae couldn't bring herself to follow him just yet. Something about Gryff's firm stare and the way he was facing her told her he wasn't finished.

Jae should've just started walking, but maybe it was better to get this out of the way now than face it in the morning. "What?"

"Listen here." Gryff's tone turned her insides to tar. All at once, she felt like sinking away. "The two of you are young. Have your fun. But you'd best be careful."

"What do you mean 'careful'?" There was no such thing as *careful* out here. They were about to march into the thick of the wilds—a country of monsters, hard-worn and lawless men, and nature's freezing touch.

"Be careful with *him*," said Gryff. There was a warning in his voice, and Jae didn't like it. "He's a good young man, and he's fond of you. His spirit is strong. But it ain't unbreakable. Don't toy with him."

Her chest was heating up, and anger began budding on her tongue. "Why would I *toy* with him?"

"I ain't sayin' you are, but you can't act like this'll go on forever."

"I—"

"What're you gonna do? Drop everything and walk through the portal with him?"

'*Are you?*' she wanted to spit. She was tempted to tell Gryff that this was none of his damn business, that he hadn't a single clue about what was stirring in her head or heart.

"If not," Gryff went on, "then don't let him think you will."

She couldn't speak, because a deeper part of her knew he was right, and it was making her sicker by the second.

Jae turned her back to him. A wave of nausea began churning in her stomach, but it wasn't quite as bad as the white-hot rage inside her skull. She couldn't bear to let him see her face; she was getting embarrassed with her own anger, but she couldn't shake it away. She looked to the north. North. There—to the wilds. There—to the Outlands. There—to the place the ghosts had taken Pa.

She could do it, she thought. Leave now. March off and finish the rest of the night on her own, then keep walking into the rest of her life. One without the gang. Without Halston.

It'd have to come sooner or later. She could get it over with right now. Soften the blow. Make it out with cracks in her heart, but fewer than there'd be if she put it off.

But she couldn't.

Fragile, weak, glass-hearted girl . . . she couldn't.

Jae started back to her bedroll. Sleep seemed like a fine reprieve. "I won't toy with his heart, Gryff," she said, trying with all her might to keep her voice from quivering. She thanked her lucky stars she'd turned her back in time, before her first tear fell. "I won't."

Chapter 15

Halston had never liked this part of the mountains. He'd gone on a cattle drive to the roots of the Cannocs before. Passing into their shadow made him feel impossibly small, like a lone fish darting through a vast, dark sea. The snow-capped peaks seemed left over from a time before, an age where the years passed more slowly, before people, before languages were sounds.

And on the other side of these mountains, the Outlands waited for them.

They'd been hiking up a trail rimmed with boulders, scattered pines, and steep, craggy cliffs for the better part of the day. Now, the sun had set, and Halston decided to check the thickness of the veil here. He placed his knife on the ground and watched the circle open in the air. Opaque, perfectly black. He drew in a breath. Still thick, here, but Sterling had sworn that the Outlands were a gold-mine of weak points in the veil.

Maybe there was no point in checking now. The other half of

the conduit was still beyond their reach. Still, he had enough hope inside of him to be a little bold.

It was then Jem appeared, with an unusually merry look on his face. "We're close! The caverns are only a couple miles from here!"

Halston turned to address the others. "Should we set up camp?"

"Why bother?" said Hodge. "The sooner we get to the Pass, the better, I say."

So they marched on, slogging quietly down the twisting path. Halston thought of the Rangers who patrolled these routes day and night. He couldn't help but admire them for it. It would be easy to forget oneself in a place like this. A man's body might surrender to the slopes and winds, his mind to the mountain's spirit.

Before long, the party reached the summit of a steady incline, and when they peered over the far side of the slope, Hodge whistled. "Damn. What happened here?"

Before them, the trail ran downward into a valley, and the land within it was in shambles. Uprooted pines lay piled together atop mounds of scattered soil and stone. Although it was only upturned earth and the wreckage of the trees, it made Halston think of the way battlefields were described in the Suryan epics he'd always loved, the stillness, so chilling that to disturb it seemed a vice.

"You sure we're heading in the right direction?" asked Halston.

"Sure as the sun—" Jem disappeared before he could finish.

The gang started downhill without him, hiking over the earthy debris. Unease formed in Halston's chest. Was whatever had done this still nearby? He could smell the freshness of the sap, and the loam might have still been damp.

Less than a minute later, Jem reappeared. "—rises."

They continued moving over the trail, downhill, then to the flat stretch cutting through the valley. The mess of earthy rubble continued well into the valley, though there were more trees still standing down here. Jem and the moon became their lanterns.

"What do you think happened there?" Halston wondered aloud, surveying the scattered earth and logs. He doubted that this wreckage had been the work of men.

"Ain't sure," said Jem. "If you like, I could scout the area out for a bit. See if I find anything."

"That would be—"

Halston's reply was cut short by the sound of sliding gravel.

He froze, then one hand jumped to his hip. He faced the direction of the sound, searching for motion in the trees, but he saw nothing.

Then, something slammed into the tree behind Halston.

Before the projectile hit the ground, Halston drew his gun.

Stones flew through the air like a flock of startled birds. Nobody shot back—they were too busy dodging rocks.

They could only run so fast. There was nowhere to move without running into a tree or exposing themselves the relentless barrage of stones. One struck Halston's shoulder, and the jolt of pain nearly made him lose his footing. Another hit Gryff in the chest, and he cursed aloud. Tsashin had her hands clasped against her head, trying to dodge the stones and sprint forward at the same time.

They kept hustling down the trail, but their attackers were just as swift to follow them. Through the treeline, Halston glimpsed them. Shaped like humans, but with slate-gray skin. Broad shoulders, well-muscled arms.

Jae cried out as a rock struck her hip, then she spilled to her knees. Halston skidded to a stop and bent down to offer her his hand. She took it, and another stone whistled just above their heads before they rose. A hair closer and it might have been fatal, or at least knocked one of them out.

Were they aiming to kill? If so, Halston knew they'd have to find a way to start shooting soon . . . but he didn't know if that was a fight they could win. Though their attackers were moving too swiftly for him to gauge exactly how many there were, he guessed they were outnumbered by at least ten.

"Stop, stop!" Jem called out. He was hovering far above the chaos. "We mean no harm!"

"Hold!" a voice boomed. "*Hold!*"

The last volley of slingstones hit the ground. The attack came to a lull, and for a moment, there was silence. Then, heavy footsteps rustled the undergrowth, and with them, a massive silhouette emerged from the bulwark of trees.

Before them stood a god.

Surely he was a god, if not something close to one. The being stood a head taller than Gryff. Like the others, his entire body was deep gray, and the scanty starlight brought out the metallic flecks of his skin and shone off the blade of the spear he clutched. Though there were fingers on his hands, each leg ended in a cloven hoof. He had eyes large and bright as the harvest moon. Halston couldn't bring himself to look away from the goat-like horns sprouting from either temple amid thick, dark, tangled hair. They shone like volcanic glass.

Halston recalled Jem mentioning the Nefilium who guarded the caverns: the mountain men, he'd called them. There was no mistaking this clan for anything else.

The being was unclothed, save for some sort of cloak draped over one shoulder and fastened at his hip with an iron clasp. "Not Rangers," he said, revealing broad, jagged teeth as he spoke. "Here for passage, then?"

"Yes," Halston said. He'd almost forgotten himself.

One of the others—a second-in-command, maybe—said

something to the leader in their own tongue. Their language sounded surprisingly smooth and wispy—not at all guttural, like Halston might have expected. The word 'Delgon' came up more than once. *Delgon,* the stony-skinned lieutenant said with an air of firm reverence. *Delgon.* That was the god's name.

Delgon was no longer paying the gang any mind. Instead, he was facing Jem with an unfriendly stare. *"You."*

"Sir?"

"I remember you. You were with the Byrds." A snarl tugged at his lip. "Though you were alive, then."

Jem stammered for a moment. "I . . . I—"

The mountain men began murmuring to one another. Delgon remained firm and sullen in his spot, but Halston sensed the anger lurking behind his shell of stony skin, ready to break loose at any moment.

Delgon spoke some command to the rest of the mountain-folk, then motioned to them with a flick of his spear.

None of the gang could even *think* about running off before around two dozen spearheads were inches from their skin.

Jem yelled at the stone men to stop once or twice, then his voice abruptly cut off. When Halston raised his head, he found that Jem had vanished.

Now, of all times.

"We've got gold for you!" Jae yelled as two stone men pulled the pack off her back and pried the gun from her hand.

"It's true!" Three more soldiers snatched all of Lorelin's weapons. "Check my pack! We've got crowns, too!"

None of the mountain men bothered to look for the treasures. They just shuffled to each one of them, stripping them of their weapons and knapsacks. "No more bargaining, no more speaking. You will follow us and remain silent until you are questioned. Ignore my orders and you will be *speared.* Understood?" Delgon ordered.

They answered with obedient silence.

Halston fought against the pounding terror in his chest. He *had* to remain steady. Surely, Delgon planned on letting them live. If he didn't, he'd simply skewer them all now. But what did he want from them, especially if he'd snubbed the gold?

Halston exchanged a look with Jae, and for once, her fear was blatant. He'd never seen her eyes so wide before. Whatever Delgon wanted, Halston hoped they could find a way to talk themselves out of this, and fast.

They began marching after Delgon, surrounded by the spears of about ten mountain men. The other fighters shuffled back into the woods, taking refuge up in the trees or down in the bushes, blending almost seamlessly into the landscape. What were they bracing themselves for? An attack? Was that why they'd started hurling stones at the gang unprovoked?

The fighters led them to a pile of stone slabs pitched together like a tent. From far off, it looked inconspicuous enough, but as they came closer, a stairway hewn from stone revealed itself beneath the slabs, trailing deep into the darkness below.

The climb down was lengthy. The stairs were wide enough for a dozen men to walk side by side. Mounted torches decked the rough stone walls, illuminating every nick and crevice along the hewn walls.

At last, they reached the end of the steps. Halston paused for a moment. It was all he could do to catch his breath at the sight before them.

The stairway had brought them to a cavernous hall. Directly across from them, a pair of enormous gates barricaded what lay ahead. The gates rose as high as the ceiling itself. A tunnel for giants.

And, in the darkness lurking past the gates, were Nestor's Caverns. Their passage, their way into the Outlands, their portal, their home . . . was just yards away. Yet, it couldn't be further from their reach.

Halston studied the fierce eyes of the surrounding Nefilium. This made no sense. These mountain men guarded Nestor's Caverns, collected the tithes of travelers . . . surely, they were used to travelers entering their valley. Why on earth had they ambushed them?

They should have been passing the gold brooch to Delgon, waiting as he inspected it, seeing how the torchlight caught on the facets of the stone in the middle. Instead, they were his prisoners.

The others were caught up in a trance similar to Halston's, scanning their surroundings with half-dazed stares. As they came closer to the gates, a stairway off to the side of the entrance revealed itself, trailing somewhere further underground. The Nefilium hustled them toward it, and a long climb down brought them to a deep basin of stone the size of a meadow. An enormous metal candelabra dangled from the far-off ceiling, bathing the pit in yellow light. The pit was smooth, with walls about eight feet high, and entirely empty.

The soldiers lowered the party one by one into the pit. Halston fought to keep what was hopefully a stoic expression as they seized him by the torso and half-dropped him into the basin. Perhaps this was how roosters felt before they were thrown into a cockfighting ring.

Halston took in the others. Hodge, Jae, and Gryff looked ready to kill every single one of Delgon's soldiers. Lorelin's face was vacant . . . It was as if she hadn't even noticed them lowering her into the pit. Tsashin had her eyes shut tight.

Delgon loosed a snort. In the firelight, Halston could make out the muscled planes of his chest, the flecks in his eyes—they glimmered like the inside of a split stone. "You came for passage, didn't you?"

"Yes," Halston coughed out.

"Are you working for Sterling Byrd?"

"Sterling Byrd is *dead*," Jae announced forthrightly.

"Even if you could somehow return all he stole from my people, it would make no difference." There was a paper-thin barrier over his tone, barely shielding them from untamed fury. Halston recognized it from the way Sterling himself used to speak, just before his temper broke loose on everyone in the room. "The last I saw him, he and his men left two of my people dead before they took all we had. No trove of jewels, no ocean of gold, will *ever* pay for their lives."

Halston could picture the scene perfectly. The corpses of the two mountain men lay splayed out in his mind as if he'd been there himself. Mouths agape, gray skin bloodied, frightened eyes glazed over. He wondered if Sterling had finished them off quickly, or if he'd found some reason to draw out the mountain men's deaths.

He wanted to apologize, to offer Delgon some solace. Halston understood him. But some shadowy part of him felt that he'd had a hand in it himself. It was a portion of his silver, his earnings, that had helped Sterling run wild all those years.

I wish you knew. Halston wished he could plant the thought into Delgon's mind. *He stole from us, too.*

It was then that Tsashin spoke with the bravery Halston could not summon. "They didn't deserve to die," she said quietly. "We're sorry."

Something softened in Delgon's expression at that, but just barely. He began pacing near the wall, then started muttering, sounding more as if he were speaking to himself than to the travelers in his hall. "Perhaps you *can* be of some use," he muttered. "He's already demanded an offering from me."

"*Who* has?" asked Gryff.

"*Fengor,*" Delgon almost growled the word. "One of the wolf lords. He is angry with me—accused me of creating a landslide that destroyed a part of his abode. His wrath is untamable. He has sent a wolf to run rampant through my valley, destroying everything in its wake, terrorizing my people until I send forth two offerings. I refuse to surrender the lives of my people. We've been trying to kill it, but it evades us every time."

Without warning, Hodge stepped forward. Only Hodge could face an ancient mountain entity with his shoulders back and his mouth fixed in a half-smug curve. "Reckon I could shoot it."

Delgon ceased pacing. He looked over the band of disheveled wanderers and thieves in front of him, and with a hint of pained disbelief said, "You *what?*"

"You heard me," Hodge went on. "I'll be one of the sacrifices, but I'll bet you I can shoot it down. If I kill the wolf, will you let us pass through Nestor's Caverns?"

"My *warriors* have not been able to slay the wolf. You're only a *child.*"

"I can do it," Hodge said. "You're sending us to our deaths any-way, so what do we have to lose?"

Halston opened his mouth. He had to say something, but what was there to do? Delgon needed two offerings, and he had an entire pool of captives to choose from. No amount of talking or begging would sway him.

Especially now that he had a volunteer.

Delgon drifted closer to the ledge. Delgon was the only being Halston had ever seen who could cast a shadow over Gryff.

"You'd offer yourself up?" Delgon asked. If he was trying

to keep the sheer disbelief from leaching into his voice, he was failing.

"Sure," Hodge said plainly. "I'll be the first course. As long as you let me bring a gun."

"No."

"Why not? If I go down fighting it, the wolf still gets to eat me and your troubles are gone."

Halston almost wanted to shout at Hodge for trying to negotiate with a being who was already sending him into the maw of a wolf, but he kept quiet. Maybe, just maybe, it was worth asking for. Whether or not he decided to kill them all, Halston doubted Delgon planned to let them go free.

Delgon was quiet. Halston wished that he could hear the Nefili man's thoughts. He was quiet for so long that Halston half-expected him to walk away and spend the whole night mulling it over.

But at long last, Delgon made his demand. "If you flee, and the wolf returns within the next few nights, I will choose two of the others to take your place," Delgon said at last, gesturing to Gryff and the girls. "But if you slay the wolf, I will grant you passage through the caverns."

"Deal," said Hodge.

Delgon's eyes were motionless. Had the eons taught him how to look so vacant? "Does anyone wish to be the second sacrifice?"

Never in his life had Halston ever answered such an absurd question so quickly.

"Me."

A thousand threads of fear wound their way through Halston's body, but he couldn't let them tie him down. His brother needed him.

He braced himself for Delgon to explain things to them, perhaps to paint a picture of what their execution would be like. But the next few moments unfolded in a blur. Delgon spoke an order to his soldiers in his own tongue, and without a second to spare, they leapt into the pit and hastened to grab Halston and Hodge.

Halston jumped in Jae's direction.

He was too late. Rough arms looped around him and dragged him back, quicker than a whip. His fingers almost touched Jae's. She had her arm outstretched.

He'd have burned, bled, starved, done *anything* to kiss her then and there, but they tore him away from her too quickly.

They knew of no other Nefilium Pass. *This* was their best chance of getting under the Cannocs, and if they didn't take this mad gamble, their chance was about to fly away from them, perhaps forever. Halston had to get it for them.

Hope had made a madman out of him, but there was no time to pass it on to the others.

An uproar came from them as the mountain men seized Halston and Hodge's arms. Jae screamed Halston's name. Lorelin and Tsashin were crying. Gryff shouted something that might have been *'Are you crazy?'*

As the soldiers ushered them out of the pit and back into the cavernous halls, Halston gave one final cry.

"We'll come back!"

Chapter 16

For the second time that night, Halston and Hodge were led at spearpoint through the woods, but this time, they came to a towering pine.

It was the largest tree Halston had ever seen. It stood out amongst the ordinary firs and spruces—its canopy could almost kiss the clouds. Strange runes and hastily hacked markings flecked its golden-brown trunk.

Perhaps the panic had started playing tricks on his mind, but Halston thought he heard a low hum coming from the tree.

Beside it, a trio of stone slabs formed a crooked table, or perhaps an altar. Dark stains marred its surface. Halston wasn't sure if it was a comfort to know that they weren't the first sacrifices here.

"Are we in the right place?" one of Delgon's soldiers asked.

"Yes, Fengor demanded I bring the offerings to the Genia Tree."

Delgon's soldiers unslung coils of rope from their shoulders.

"The hell?" Hodge blurted. Halston didn't have it in him to try and get his brother to quiet down. "You're gonna *bind* us?"

The mountain men said nothing. Perhaps they shouldn't have been surprised that Delgon and his soldiers didn't trust them not to run.

Ropes, not chains. It was madness to be thankful for such a thing, but Halston was thankful nonetheless.

There they bound the brothers, one on either side of the trunk. Tall as the tree was, the trunk wasn't impressively wide. Had their arms not been tethered, Halston could have reached backwards and touched his brother's shoulder.

"This ain't fair!" Hodge cried. "I need my shooting arm!"

Delgon didn't say anything. Maybe he'd never intended to let Hodge try at all.

Then, Delgon tossed something on the ground. In his periphery, Halston could make out Hodge's gun lying on the earth a few paces away.

"I told you that you could bring your gun, but I never said your arms would be unbound," Delgon said.

Of course. The sooner the wolf stopped plaguing his people, the better. Why put all his faith into Hodge killing the beast when his death would sooner pay the debt?

"I'm *going* to kill it! Why don't you believe me, dammit?" Hodge cried.

"You may try," was all Delgon left them with. The Nefili lord and his companions retreated back to the path, then disappeared into the night, whispering amongst themselves.

Afterward . . . it was eerily silent. There was hardly any wind, and the quiet was almost suffocating. Halston wondered if the mountain folk were near them, close enough to watch.

Delgon had mentioned that the creature was a servant of the 'wolf lord'. What on earth could that mean? Was this wolf intelligent? Would it relish destroying them, delighting in the act of tearing them apart for the sake of it, or were they only another mouthful of meat to satisfy its hunger?

Hodge's whisper caught Halston off guard. "Maybe it's better this way."

"Don't say that." Halston wished he could reach for his brother's hand.

"All this." Hodge's throat caught for a moment. "Jumping through hoops, trying to get home. And the others . . . all they've done for us . . ."

"They *wanted* to come with us."

"Can't see why. Maybe they'd be better off without us."

Halston couldn't tell Hodge that he was wrong. He had spent his share of time wondering the same thing.

"They've stayed, Hodge." In spite of it all, they'd stayed.

Because it had never just been about the portal. It had become far more than that, on the nights that Sterling had beaten them, dangled their freedom over their heads . . .

Through it all, they stayed together.

Halston continued, "Well, whether or not they're better off without us, they want us to come back. Don't you think we owe that to them?"

A deflated sigh left Hodge's lips. "I can't even reach my gun, Hal."

Halston tried to relax his muscles, to steady his mind as well. Maybe there was an answer here. Then, he remembered that they'd been in a pinch like this before—before they'd even had a gang.

"Remember that time we got stuck in the cave?"

Hodge let out a mirthless laugh. "How could I forget?"

Halston doubted he'd forget that day even if he lived to be a thousand years old. The two of them had just been boys. They'd gone exploring without Elias, who'd neglected one of his mathematics lessons and been forced to stay home and make it up. They'd found a cave while they were swimming and climbed eagerly inside.

Exploring it was fun while it lasted. The underwater cave was enormous, shimmering with shells and caked with barnacles.

But then the tide began to rise, lapping at the walls of the cave. Halston and Hodge had confined themselves to the narrow strip of stone at its edge and prayed that it wouldn't rise further and cover their heads in seawater. The whole time, they'd held onto one another. Fortunately, as the hours had passed, the tide had ebbed, and they'd managed to swim out. How their mother cried when they returned home that night. She'd forbidden them from leaving their tower's grounds for two months. That was a few years before the monsters started to appear. After that, they hardly left the fortress at all.

"I think about that night," Hodge said. "I think about it all the time."

Halston remembered how small his brother had felt in his arms. *It'll be alright, Hodge. It's okay.*

I love you.

He'd been just a child, but after they'd escaped, he'd almost wanted to fling himself into the sea to escape the shame of leading his brother into danger like that.

"If we got out of that," Halston said slowly, "then we can get out of this, too."

"Need some help, there?"

Halston looked to the sky. There, descending toward them slowly, was Jem.

"Great," Hodge muttered. "Look who decided to show up."

Jem hung his head. "I'm sorry. I did my best. I got . . . overwhelmed. The mines pulled me back."

Hodge grunted. "S'alright. I ain't exactly in a good mood right now."

Halston wasn't angry with the ghost. It wasn't his fault that Delgon had recognized him, and he hadn't been there for Sterling's massacre of the mountain folk.

"I reckon I can help you," Jem said. "Just hold still a moment. I'll get you out of these bonds."

"*You* can touch the ropes?" asked Halston.

"I can if I concentrate. Just quiet down, please."

Halston held still as possible. He released his breaths in steady, shallow exhales, trying best he could not to challenge Jem's concentration. Jem reached for the ropes once, twice, three times, and on every try, his hands passed through the fibers.

Then, at last, Halston felt Jem take hold of the bonds. Slowly, just a fraction of space at a time, the ropes began to loosen. Jem kept picking at the knots, and little by little, the tension eased.

They could do this.

As soon as they were free, Hodge would take up his gun. Maybe they could scale a nearby tree and surprise the wolf from above.

The ropes were getting looser, looser—

A howl came from the distance.

The ropes stopped slipping away.

"Jem?" Halston asked the empty darkness. The ghost was gone. *Damn it.*

The howl came once again, closer this time. Halston cursed under his breath. Part of him was praying Jem would reappear, but it would do them no good. It was time to *move*.

"I think I can get my arm free!" Hodge gasped. "Hang on."

Halston and Hodge both began squirming and jostling at the ropes, desperately trying to free their arms. The howl echoed through the night once more, and this time, Halston turned his head, fully expecting to see the wolf pacing straight toward them. It wasn't there, but it must have been just out of their sight.

At last, the ropes slipped from their bodies and landed in a heap at their feet.

Halston was in a daze as he spun around, joined Hodge's side, and watched his brother snatch his gun up off the ground.

They hurried toward a nearby pine, this one with branches hanging low enough for them to scale. "Climb!" Halston hissed through clenched teeth.

They took to the tree. The pine needles pricked at their skin, and the thick sap clung to their palms and the soles of their boots. Behind them came huffs of hefty, low breathing. Halston climbed behind Hodge, grabbing for the branches and placing his feet down as fast as he dared. He put too much confidence in a step, and his heel skidded on the branch. His heart skipped a beat. He lost his footing, but caught another branch at the last second. *Thank the gods.* He kept on climbing.

When they were about halfway up the tree, they each chose a sturdy enough branch to plant themselves. Hodge braced himself with his gun at the ready, and Halston looked down to the woods, waiting for the wolf to find them.

And find them it did.

The creature came stalking across the land slowly, flanked by the army of shadows, mingling with the surrounding darkness.

Halston's breath went still at the sight of the thing.

He'd seen wolves before—he'd even had to shoot one on a cattle drive a few years ago. His blood had run cold at the sight of its bared teeth, but in death, he'd pitied it. It didn't look large at all when it lay limp on the ground.

This wolf was larger than a horse. Its muscles clenched and rippled as it moved, and Halston sensed all of the power they could unleash . . . more than enough to crush his bones. They'd snap like kindling. The wet smack of its jaws sent icy chills down Halston's spine.

Go, he urged it silently to take a few steps forward, closer to Hodge's range of fire. Just a nudge thataway, then this could all be over.

The wolf lifted its nose toward the moon. It jerked sharply to the left, then began stalking in their direction.

It knew they were here.

Before Hodge could shoot, the wolf leapt toward the tree.

The creature's growl almost shook the ground. It lifted itself onto its hind legs and slammed its front paws against the trunk. The tree shifted under the wolf's weight, groaning as the beast started to bark. Halston clung to a branch with one hand, grasping with all his might.

The wolf jostled the trunk again. Hodge lost his grip on his branch, then teetered before he fell. He cried aloud, and Halston reached out with his free hand.

"I've got you!"

He caught his brother's wrist, and yanked him back, giving Hodge's wrist just enough of a pull upward for him to regain a spot on a lower branch.

The wolf's claws cut deep grooves in the wood. Its teeth snapped inches from one of Hodge's boots, but he managed to scrabble skyward. But climbing higher was useless if the wolf brought the tree down.

Fury set Halston's blood aflame. *Not Hodge.* He'd tear the beast apart with his bare hands. He'd—

Hodge fired. Halston's ears rang.

Halston looked down to see that the shot hadn't struck the wolf at all. Instead, it sent the monster into a frenzy. A note of sheer fury pierced its cry, and it tossed its head wildly from side to side as it trampled around the tree.

Pandemonium. Hodge shot at the wolf again as it bucked and writhed in a desperate dance across the earth. Dread began to staunch Halston's breathing. The air grew thick with the smell of gunsmoke.

But Hodge's next bullet hit the wolf's paw.

The monster's wail pierced the night. It pranced around in a circle, yelping, and Halston swore he saw it limping. The wolf cried out again, then bolted off into the trees. Blood stained the ground where it ran away, its prey forgotten.

Halston was breathing heavily. "Are you alright?"

Hodge didn't answer him. His entire body shook with each heavy breath, and he faced the direction in which the wolf had fled, a look of pure fire in his eyes.

Hodge clambered down the branches. Halston followed. Before Halston was even close to catching up, Hodge's feet touched the ground. Without warning, he sprinted after the wolf.

"Hodge!" Halston descended swiftly as he could, though each step down made his stomach pitch. If he fell, he could break a bone, and then there was no running after his brother. Twigs scratched his cheeks, one so deeply that he felt the sting of a cut forming there, but he pushed himself to ignore it.

At last, he reached the bottom of the tree, then broke into a run, following Hodge's fleeing form.

There was no point in yelling at him to come back. They had to find the wolf, now. If they didn't, one of the others would pay the price. Who would they strike down first?

Halston tried not to think about Jae.

No.

Halston stopped running. What was he doing? He was unarmed, perhaps worse than useless.

But whatever end Delgon had planned for them, he couldn't let Hodge face it alone.

So he kept on running.

Chapter 17

There was a wet spot on Hodge's shirt. He glanced at his stomach, fearing the worst. No—it was only sweat. He hurried onward.

It had taken everything in him not to curse his rotten luck when the wolf had bolted out of his range, but he couldn't afford to curse his luck right now. He needed every bit he had.

He began to run faster, and his legs strained at the slight incline up which he charged. Still, he raced along, willing his pounding heart to keep him going. On and on. He could do this. He *had* to.

Hodge couldn't resist smirking at the path before him. They hadn't killed the wolf, but they'd weakened it—from the trail of blood it left, that much was certain.

Still, he couldn't let his guard down. He kept running, fighting to keep his breathing from turning shallow.

Everything in these mountains was larger than life.

Now, he needed the bravery to match it.

Dazed with feverish determination, he focused on every rock

and root in his way, trying not to trip. Every few paces, he glanced at his hand to make sure he still held his gun. Four rounds left. No extras.

He didn't dare dream of what the wolf would look like dead, how it might feel to show Delgon its stiff body, to get the others out of that damned pit. There was only *now*. Turning, running, turning again. Nothing else was real.

He was ready for the wolf to leap from the shadows, to feel its breath, hot and steamy, on his face. To face the jaws nipping just an inch from his skin. As long as he could still shoot, he didn't care how close it came.

He wouldn't lose. He wouldn't, he wouldn't.

"Hodge!" From a distance, his brother's voice cut through the damp air.

Tempted as he was, Hodge wouldn't let him catch up. Halston had no weapon, and in his heart of hearts, Hodge knew that now, this was his battle alone. He sensed the wolf's presence nearby—it was waiting for him. It wasn't going to go down without a fight, and neither would he.

"Hodge!" Halston called again.

Like *hell* would he let Halston get close to that thing. "I've got it!" Hodge cried back, willing it to be true.

He followed the blood spatters to a nearby hill and bolted up the slanting ground. Then, he glimpsed a paw print twice the size of his head in the moist earth. Any man with half a mind would have turned around at the sight. Good thing Hodge was feeling as out of his mind as he ever had. The trail of blood climbed the hill. Somewhere, over this mound, his opponent was waiting for him.

Hodge broke into a sprint. The slope threatened to slow him down. His legs trembled with every step. Hodge kept moving purposefully, urging his motions to keep him from falling. One stumble would cost him precious time, or worse.

He had fired this gun so many times without fail. On jobs for Sterling, in Coy's shooting pit . . . He could do it once more. Yes, once more.

He gritted his teeth.

A half-hundred images flew around in his mind, fluttering like leaves caught in a powerful gale. Returning to the pit, marching through the caverns, opening the portal, seeing his mother and Lia once more . . .

Every moment in that half-there future that he'd ever dared to imagine was with him, dangling above his head like bait. Gleaming while he gasped, hunger clawing at his belly, lips parted for the hook.

All of it.

All of it came after this shot.

Hodge reached the summit of the hill. There was no sign of the wolf at the top. Downhill, the trail of blood continued to a stand of trees screening a stretch of small cliffs, and in the center . . .

The mouth of a cave.

Hodge took off downhill, bound for the cave. Yes, this was where it had to be. The entrance was enormous, but behind it, there was nothing but blackness. Could the wolf smell him?

Hell, he hoped it could. *Get out here.*

His lungs heaved. Though he gasped for air, it tasted rank in his throat. He forced himself to steady the shaking in his limbs—any stray move here could be a death sentence.

He peered around at the surrounding trees. *Wood.*

Hodge touched his pocket. The lump of flint was still there, and he could have sung for joy. They might have taken everything else . . . but there'd been no need to snatch away his flint when Delgon's prison was all stone!

He'd make sure to thank Delgon when he got back.

The sound of breathing came from within the cave. Not hungered breaths, but angry ones—breaths that seemed to say the beast thirsted for his blood, for the snap of his bones.

Time, time, time.

Hodge turned, reached out and gathered up a fistful of pine needles, then placed them at the mouth of the cave. There was no time to gauge how dry they were, to guess whether or not it would actually catch.

He hurried back to the mouth of the cave, then took the flintstone from his pocket and began to strike it against his gun. *Snap, snap.* He'd lit Sterling's stable on fire all those months ago. That same madness overcame him now. *Snap, snap, snap.* The stubborn needles wouldn't catch, wouldn't light. They seemed determined not to burn.

He wanted to shout at them, curse, like that could make it work. *Light, dammit.*

The breathing turned to a snarl.

Stay put. Just a little longer.

And at last, the sparks caught. The little fire sprang to life. Hodge wanted to worship that flame. Before it could wink out, Hodge jogged a few yards back into the trees, grabbed a fistful of the driest twigs he saw and wedged them into the flame. He ran back. Grabbed a few more. Into the flames they went. Quickly as he could, he piled wood into the fire.

And the flame began to lick at the wood, and smoke—smoke more precious than anything he'd ever held in his hands—bloomed from it.

The smoke filled his nostrils. Hodge coughed. Being quiet didn't matter anymore. The wolf knew he was here, and it knew what he wanted.

It was the wolf's life, or his. One of them would not walk again after this night.

First, Hodge saw the glint in its tawny eyes. It came close enough to the cave's mouth for Hodge to make out the shape of its snout.

Then, Hodge was flying over the earth.

He hadn't even seen the wolf's paw lash out at him. The force of a runaway train barreled into him, knocking out his breath. His body skidded over the ground. Pine needles cut into his cheeks, and dirt filled his mouth, melding with the ripe taste of blood.

He pushed himself up. Fresh cuts stung his face. Behind him, the wolf was barking so loud his ears stung. Hodge thought back to the hungry cattle dogs on Gus Emberhill's ranch.

His gun lay a couple yards ahead of him. The feeling of his naked shooting hand was worse than the pain in his newly throbbing chest.

The growls got closer, deeper, and a shadow fell over him.

Hodge rolled over and came face-to-face with the beast. It was close enough for Hodge to make out the ashy flecks in its black fur, its dark pupils, its twitching ears. The wolf's jaws opened up. The stench of its breath overwhelmed him.

A drop of its saliva rained down on his head. Hodge was staring straight down its throat, past the rows of spear-like teeth. There was nowhere to move.

At least it was going for his head. It'd be over quicker, this way.

Would they still find the dagger's other half without him? The thought of Halston never making it home frightened him more than his own death.

The wolf tensed, bracing itself for the death bite.

Then, a shout came from behind them. "Hodge!"

The wolf's ears pricked up, and its eyes flicked in the direction of Halston's voice.

His brother had bought him a moment of priceless time.

Hodge rolled over, clawed his way up from under the wolf, and leapt to his feet. The wolf let out an aggravated roar. Hodge didn't turn back. He raced for his gun, swept it off the ground, then spun back around.

Hodge didn't think about it a second longer than he had to. He raised his gun and fired a bullet straight into the wolf's eye.

The beast let out a long, ragged cry, spine curling as its muscles began to twitch. Blood streamed from the ruined socket, and Hodge scrambled out of its way.

For a moment, the creature faltered, wavering like a candle's flame touched by a draft. It strained to let out a thin, faint whine. Then it crumpled to the ground. It let out one huff, then two, and then at last, it died.

In death, Hodge expected it to look smaller, but it somehow looked far larger—much too large to be anything he had brought down with a bullet. It was still shuddering . . . Nerve endings, Hodge imagined.

His stomach turned over as he knelt, and the ripe tang of blood filled his nostrils. He didn't want to think about how this creature had strode over the earth and howled just a few moments before. All that strength, gone in an instant.

A silhouette appeared in the corner of his eye.

Halston had caught up to him.

Hodge was breathing like he'd just been saved from drowning— it was the sweetest air he'd ever tasted. Halston was frozen in his spot, standing a few yards away and shuddering slightly. For a minute, he just looked stunned.

And then, the brothers began to laugh. The relief was just too much to keep down. They laughed until it hurt—Hodge's chest burned so much that he nearly forgot all of his scratches. Tears pricked the corners of Hodge's eyes.

"Hodge," Halston whispered between laughs.

Hodge stood. "Hal."

"Gods above."

"We did it." Hodge wiped his eyes. "We did it."

He threw his arms around his brother, and they held each other for a long time, until they finally managed to stop laughing.

Hodge couldn't quite believe it. The now-motionless body didn't look quite dead yet, despite the blood streaming from the wound. He still tensed up when he met its remaining yellow eye, blank and vacant.

"What are we doing?" Hodge snapped himself out of it, thinking back to the others, who were probably beside themselves in that pit. "We've got to get back."

Halston placed a steady hand on Hodge's shoulder. "Hodge?"

"Yeah?"

"I'm proud of you."

Hodge just blinked, because he could scarcely believe his own ears.

He'd never heard that from Halston. Other good things, sure, from time to time, but never the word *proud*. "You are?"

"Of course I am."

Hodge wasn't sure why he started laughing at that, but the laughter came over him anyway. Maybe it was because it was sheer nonsense. They had fresh blood on their clothes and the body of a monstrous wolf at their feet. Their friends were fearfully awaiting their return. Yet they were shooting the breeze and talking about . . . pride?

"Don't be proud of me just yet," Hodge said, turning back in the direction of the caves. "One day there might be a pinch that I don't get us out of."

"Well, in that case, it'll be my turn."

Well . . . that was true. They'd been taking turns for years now. And Hodge couldn't help but smile at the notion.

They put out the scanty fire. Hodge wished the mountain men hadn't taken his knife so they could bring Delgon the wolf's pelt, but he hoped that the bloodstains on his shirt would be enough proof for the Nefilium lord . . . at least enough to convince him to follow them back to the body. So they left the wolf and let it lie. Perhaps, after they showed it to Delgon, it would be food for some lucky creature passing by. They hustled back to the caves as quickly as they could. There was no more time to waste. They had friends to retrieve, a cavern to cross, and a world to go home to.

Chapter 18

The Drifter woke to the sound of scratching outside.

His eyes flew open. Half-caught in a stupor, he floundered, trying to steady himself and stand. He looked over the dim room, across the wooden floorboards and the old man's now-empty chair. The room was warmer than when he'd fallen asleep, and he noticed a small fire now blazing in the hearth.

The scratching came again.

"Dammit!"

The old man came striding out from the shadows with a shotgun in hand. The Drifter's heart twisted—he'd give anything to carry a real weapon here. He wondered why the old man had been allowed to have one.

"Damned vipers," the old man muttered. "I've been killing the same creature for years now. Always comes back."

"It . . . comes back?"

The old man ignored the question. "I'll be back. Stay put." He cocked his gun, then fled the house.

The Drifter didn't look out the window. He heard shouting, screeching not unlike that which had come from the creature he'd slaughtered in the desert before he'd come here. His pulse refused to calm.

He should go outside, help his companion slay whatever wailing creature had traipsed onto his land. Trying to keep his breathing even, he searched frantically for something he could use to defend himself. He settled on the fire poker.

The Drifter worked to free the poker from its holder, but as he got a firm grip on the sooty metal rod, the shrieking stopped.

The Drifter hesitated. He didn't trust the quiet, certainly. Slowly, poker in hand, he slunk to the window and peered outside. The flimsy wooden cross still marked the grave of the old man's companion. Streaks and dips marred the sand—perhaps they were footprints, though it was hard to say for sure. Outside, everything was perfectly lifeless.

The flames in the hearth turned to faint embers. He waited for a voice, a flicker of motion, a sign that the old man would come back. He never showed up.

The Drifter's bandage had grown so worn that it refused to stay tied around his hand. But the cut still had not scabbed over. He sighed, mopping up some of the blood with a clean spot of his sleeve.

For a while, he sat there, staring idly around the room. A sense of white-hot fear rippled through him every few minutes, where he felt certain that all of his surroundings would collapse, or a tract of dark emptiness would open up beneath his feet and swallow him whole. Even so, the world around him stayed frozen. Stagnant. Waiting, as he was, to change.

He stood a while longer, braced with his poker. Maybe the old man wasn't really a man at all and was in fact a monster, waiting for him to survey the sandy plain outside. No. He'd stay here. Perhaps he should go upstairs and get a better look at the ground below.

The Drifter took a few tentative steps toward the stairway. A few more. One foot on the first step, then on the second. Gradually, cautiously, he scaled the stairs.

There was a hallway at the top of the stairway, empty save for a door at the end. Half-alert, the Drifter ventured toward it. He lifted his arm. His hand found the knob. And there, he let it rest. Behind the door, he sensed something comforting, enticing as berry wine.

"It's alright," a soft voice said from the other side. "You can come in."

The Drifter opened the door, then stepped into the room. The floor was bare, but tapestries covered every inch of the walls and ceiling, their textures desecrated by dust and wear. A sad-looking girl sat by the window. Before her was a loom. Her dark hair was very long, long enough to drag on the floor behind her if she were to start walking. Gauzy robes hung from her delicate arms, and she turned around to gaze at him with wide, pale eyes.

For a second, she looked almost ready to cry, but instead, she offered him a small smile. "I heard you talking to him last night."

The Drifter nodded. "He was . . . helpful." That was a lie, but he couldn't think of anything else to say.

The girl toyed with the shuttle in her hands. "He has always been kind to me."

"Is he your father?"

She shrugged. "Who can say?"

Well, at least the old man wasn't a monster. The Drifter wished there was something he could offer the girl. Food, maybe . . . He had none, of course, but she was so frail. "What are you making?"

"A tapestry. I do nothing but weave." She pointed to the half-finished tapestry on her loom. "It helps me to chronicle the years. I may include you in this one, if that would be alright with you."

"Alright."

She turned back to finish the row. Her nimble fingers worked eagerly at the loom. The Drifter tried to take a closer look at her handiwork on the walls, but he could see nothing decipherable in them. Colors, shapes without meaning. Perhaps they only made sense to her.

"He went to go kill a monster," the Drifter said, though she probably already knew. "He says he has to kill it every few months."

"Oh, yes."

"Is it true?"

"Sure it is. I haven't seen the monster, though."

"He hasn't come back. Should we go out and look for him?"

The girl shook her head. "No. He comes back every time."

"He could be dead."

"I doubt he'd mind that."

In their brief exchange, she'd already woven several more rows on the loom. The Drifter wasn't sure how it was possible. Then again, it seemed absurd to fret over impossible things in a realm with no sun, where starvation and thirst didn't exist.

"Do you remember what you came here for?" she asked, turning back to the loom.

The Drifter said nothing, and for a moment, he just looked around at the tapestries covering the walls. Still, he couldn't make out anything meaningful in the web of woven threads. "For the ones I love."

"I see. How are you going to get out?"

"I have to speak my name at the gates."

"Hm." The girl tapped a finger against her delicate chin. "Do you know how far you have to go?"

The Drifter shook his head. He didn't want to think about how far away the gates might be, how long it might take for him to reach them.

"Well. In that case, I have something for you." She spoke as if she'd known him all her life. "Hold out your hands."

The Drifter hesitated, but he discerned no deception in her eyes. The deepest part of him knew that like him, she was a prisoner here. She just seemed less hungry to escape.

The weaver passed him a small bundle. He unraveled it to find it was a long length of cloth, slightly frayed at the edges, and the color of newborn grass. He ran it over his fingers, and as he did, his skin felt new. He gasped. When the cloth slipped from his palms, he found that the bleeding cut had turned into smooth, soft flesh. The scratch he'd received from the monster was gone. It hadn't even left a scar.

"It took me ages to figure out how to craft that cloth," she said with a proud grin. "But it will protect you. From whatever lurks out there."

"Thank you." He blinked at the cloth, half-afraid that it would disappear. "Thank you."

"You could stay here." It sounded less like a suggestion and more like a plea. "You'd be good company, I'm sure."

Her clear eyes were full of enough longing to destroy her.

Then, *her* face surfaced inside his mind.

Before he'd come here, he'd spent his nights grieving for her. She'd been torn from him. Taken from his grasp without warning. He wasn't even sure if she was alive, and if she was, if he would ever find her again. But he planned to die trying.

He didn't want to entertain the thought of staying here for a moment, but he couldn't let her generosity go unappreciated. "Why are you giving this to me?"

"It's been ages since I've met someone who remembers why they're here. Someone might as well use it." She turned back to her loom. "You'd better get back out there. If you want to find the gates."

"Thank you." And there was no other way to thank her—all he had were his words. But that would have to be enough.

He wouldn't turn to bones. His mind wouldn't crumble into dust, like everything else here did. He would go on.

And now he had to flee.

"You could come with me," he offered as he wound the cloth around his waist, then tied it off with a snug knot.

"No," the girl said without looking back at him, once more absorbed in her weaving. "There is nothing for me out there. All my life is here."

As he stepped out of the room, all he could do was hope keenly that he would remember her.

The Drifter ventured downstairs, then to the threshold of the house. He paused. He listened for the sound of the man battling the beast that wouldn't stay dead. There was only a silence, beckoning to him, challenging him to join it.

The Drifter checked that the cloth still bound his waist. Yes, it was there. So, with that, he started back out into the world.

Chapter 19

When they'd returned to Delgon's abode, bruised, battered, and bloody, a haughty look came over the face of the mountain lord. He'd seemed loath to believe Halston when he said the deed was done. They'd come to him, speaking through heavy breaths, and the bloodstains on Hodge's clothes were still fresh.

Halston hadn't been able to get a good look at the others. Delgon's band of soldiers blocked his view of the pit. Delgon told them that he would not let them speak to the others until he saw the wolf's body.

Now, they stood looking over the dead animal with Delgon—gore now matted all across its fur. The lord of the mountain men was quiet, almost infuriatingly so. Halston bit down on his tongue. If he'd had a shred more courage, he might have demanded that Delgon say something.

Despite the long stretch of silence, Delgon eventually murmured, "You killed it." He made no attempt to mask his disbelief.

Hodge frowned. "Yeah, we did. So can we go through your pass now?"

Halston's throat went tight. If Delgon changed his mind, forced them back into the pit or worse, he wasn't sure he'd have it in him to restrain himself. For once, he'd lose the battle to keep his composure.

"Of course," Delgon replied with unexpected sincerity. "I gave you my word." Whether he'd believed they could kill the wolf or not, a vow was a vow. A part of Halston almost admired him, but that part was overpowered by a tidal wave of relief.

They were going through the Nefilium Pass.

They were going to reach the Outlands.

Delgon said something to his soldiers in their own language. The scouts' shoulders slumped with relief. They bent over the fallen beast, then set to skinning it. Did they plan to use the pelt, or would they take it as a trophy? Either way, it was probably better not to ask.

The odd party trailed back to the caverns with Delgon and two of the scouts. They passed the pine where the wolf had cornered them, the bloodstains on the rocky ground, and the enormous Genia Tree with its stone altar. The ropes still lay in a pile at the trunk, and Halston couldn't fight the grin that came over him.

They'd done it. They'd won.

On the way back to the caverns, they said nothing, and when they finally returned to the pit, Halston wanted to jump and shout for victory. But it wasn't a look of triumph that crossed the others' faces. They all seemed to slacken with disbelief.

Something bright was swimming in Jae's eyes. Whatever it was, Halston couldn't quite name it, but he wanted to stare at it for longer than time allowed.

The soldiers tossed a rope ladder into the pit, and the others scaled it eagerly. Nobody dared speak yet. There was an unspoken understanding that saying the wrong thing might just land them back in that stark prison.

To their surprise, the soldiers gave them back their supplies. They followed Delgon back up the stairs and to the caverns' entrance. He motioned for them to approach the gates, and as they neared the opening, Halston could almost feel the overwhelming darkness turn its head to stare at them. When they came closer to the great doors, Halston could make out rows and rows of inscriptions etched into the dull, stone-like metal. He wondered who had scrawled them there, and what they meant.

"Magic lights the way," Delgon explained. "The *bluecaps*. Don't venture from the light of their flames. Even a few strides off the path could lead you to a swath of pure darkness."

With that, he placed one enormous hand on the gate's center. For a moment, there was total stillness. Then, a groan emanated from the cave around them, shaking the stone beneath their feet. Halston almost lost his balance and fell to the ground. Slowly, the gates lurched, then parted to allow them entry into Nestor's Caverns.

"Be cautious. It's a day's trek to the other end." Delgon motioned to one of his scouts, who came hurrying over with a torch in hand. "The bluecaps will come to greet you a ways down. In the meantime, this light should suffice." He passed Hodge the torch.

For a few moments, they stood and faced the darkness. Gryff's nostrils were flaring, and he seemed to be eyeing Delgon with an air of suspicion. Tsashin was hanging her head, and Lorelin had one hand on her shoulder. And Jae . . . Jae was looking at the path ahead as if she were about to charge down it with a knife in each hand.

She ventured into the shadows first. Then Gryff, Lorelin, Tsashin. Before Halston and Hodge could trail behind them, Delgon stopped them both. "Wait."

To Halston's surprise, the mountain man was smiling.

"Thank you both," Delgon said. "For what you did for my people."

Delgon's grin reminded Halston of his father, in those rare moments when his brusqueness slipped away.

"Pleased to be of service," Hodge said. "Hope that wolf lad stops giving you trouble."

"Wolf lord," Delgon replied.

"Oh, yeah." Hodge tipped his hat at Delgon, then swaggered off down the path.

And for the second time that day, Halston followed his brother without an ounce of doubt to slow him down.

Bathed in torchlight, they started on their path, sparing a glance back at the gates as they rumbled again and drew together once more. Halston watched Delgon's massive shadow retreat from the gates and disappear.

Halston looked away from the entrance, only to find Lorelin just inches from his face.

"The two of you are downright *crazy!*" Lorelin exclaimed, throwing an arm around each of the brothers. "And don't you *ever* get better."

"*Watch it,*" Hodge wheezed through Lorelin's bone-crushing hug, trying to keep the torch away from everybody's hair. "I'm holding a flame."

Gryff took the torch away from him as Jae joined their huddle, then Tsashin. Lost in a sea of arms and warmth, they stayed that way a while, and their chatter of relief and reunion echoed off the cavern's walls.

Gryff stood back from their cluster, but when they spread out at last, he chuckled, clapping Hodge on the shoulder. "Look at you. Done it again, kid."

Halston met Jae's eyes. Her mouth stretched out into a wicked grin, and she threw herself at him. She nearly knocked him down, but he didn't mind in the slightest. And besides, he caught her.

"I made it," he said to her.

"You made it," she replied, sounding breathless.

When he kissed her, he felt as though he'd never die.

"Ha-hem," Hodge cleared his throat emphatically. "Hate to say it, but we didn't just kill a *wolf monster* so the two of you could suck on each other's faces all night. Now let's get going."

It turned out that the mountain men's return of their packs had been a hollow victory.

The mountain men had given them back their knives, except for Halston's boot knife, and their guns, but they quickly found that the soldiers had taken all their ammunition, save for what Hodge still had in his gun. Three bullets. They divided them amongst Halston, Hodge, and Jae, though Hodge put up a fuss over having to share.

Now, they were nearly lost in the darkness. Jae squinted at the stony passage unfolding in front of them. The flame on Hodge's torch had faded until it was pitifully small. Apart from the rough texture of the walls, there wasn't much they could make of their surroundings.

"How much further?" Hodge asked for at least the fourth time in five minutes.

"It can't be much more," Lorelin said hopefully.

Jae frowned. Their waterskins were still full enough, and their packs still held roots, nuts, and a bit of dried meat for them all. They had enough to get by, if they were careful. Still, Hodge's torch was on its last legs, and without light, there was no point in going any further.

"We should turn back," Gryff said.

"Not now," Lorelin argued. "We still have light."

"Not for much longer," said Gryff.

"I say we go back if the bluecaps don't show up for another minute," said Jae. Even if it meant facing the mountain men again, it was better than stumbling blindly through a cave. There could be a deathly steep drop somewhere up ahead, or worse.

"What if Delgon isn't there anymore? Then what?" asked Lorelin.

"This is ridiculous! We're wasting time!" Hodge unslung his pack, then passed Jae the torch and began to rummage through his bag. "There ain't much of the oil rag left on the torch head . . . maybe some kindling will keep it going long enough."

"Delgon told us that the bluecaps would light our way," said Tsashin. "All we have to do is wait for them."

"I ain't waiting longer. It'll be pitch dark in a minute." He stopped fishing through his pack, then turned to Halston. "Where's that piece of wood you were staring at the other night? Didn't you put it back in your pocket?"

". . . No."

"Yes, you did," said Hodge. "I saw you holding it yesterday. It's shaped like a pear."

"It's a *bird,*" Jae said before she could stop herself. Not that it mattered.

"Who *cares?*" Hodge blurted. "Where is it? We can burn that until—"

"No." Halston stepped back.

"Just give me the wood, Hal!"

"It's not for—"

"*Stop,*" said Jae.

They all fell silent. Above Hodge's head, a blue flame winked into being.

The flame was small, no larger than a man's fist. It floated in a delicate sort of way, like a set of gauzy curtains wavering by an open window. It was blue as the heart of candleflame—the most beautiful blue Jae had ever seen.

Another flame joined it. They hovered together for a moment, flitting close to one another, as if whispering their thoughts. Then their light disappeared, leaving the party in total darkness.

And then, they returned with hundreds more.

Jae's breath escaped her. More bluecaps than she could count lit up along a path twisting through the chasm and into the darkness ahead, and what a *wonder* it was.

The ceiling was so high her breath hitched at the merest glimpse of it. Stalactites hung down from the canopy like teeth sprouting from a monster's jaw. There were dozens of shapes within the rock—towers and dips and basins and spheres. The stone was a muted, silver-yellow, like the moon when it was low in the sky. She had been in caves before, but nothing like this. Jae had never seen a place so vast—like a home built for gods. A certain energy seemed to flow from it—something that felt exactly like the last few moments of a dream.

Around them, the bluecaps danced. "They're here." Jae was almost laughing with relief.

One of the bluecaps—perhaps the first one that had shown itself—drifted closer and closer to Hodge's face. He shrank away from it, and if he was trying to hide his discomfort, he was not succeeding. "What's it doing?"

Tsashin giggled. "I think he wants to say hello."

". . . Hello," Hodge said. His throat trembled a little.

Jae couldn't help laughing. "You just finished slaying a gigantic *wolf*. You can't tell me you're scared of these guys."

"I ain't *scared* of them," Hodge said, but he took two big steps away from the bluecap.

Lorelin put her hands on her hips, looking upon the glowing bluecaps with a satisfied grin. "Well, we aren't getting any younger."

Together, they drifted down the path, though their focus did not stray from the bluecaps' display. As they moved, the bluecaps darted ahead of them to continue lighting their way. Eventually, they came to a pool at the side of the path. It was shallow, and beneath the bluecaps' light, the water was the exact color of Lorelin's eyes. They reckoned it was finally time to rest. Uncomfortable as it would be in a cave, they wouldn't get much further without some sleep tonight, and nobody had shut an eye since their capture. They refilled the canteens and waterskins, and Hodge finally had a chance to rinse the blood from his shirt. Jae made a somewhat comfortable spot for herself with her jacket and bedroll and sat for a while sipping water. It was marvelously cold.

Before long, Halston joined her, but his focus belonged to the wonders surrounding them, his gaze darting across the ceiling over and over again.

Jae nudged him in the shoulder. "Looks like someone put you in a trance."

"It's incredible," he said, almost under his breath. "It reminds me of the epic of Kamal."

"Who's that?"

"He was a Suryan prince. In the story, he goes to the underworld to get his lost love back. I always pictured the underworld looking something like this."

Jae blinked. "Would you do that?"

"Do what?"

"Go to the underworld to . . . Never mind."

He said nothing more about it, thank the gods. Jae hoped that he'd have forgotten the question by morning. "Why don't you go ahead and rest? I'll take the first watch."

"No you ain't. You and Hodge ought to sleep first."

"I'll be awake anyway. I don't think I'll be able to sleep for a while."

Jae knew the feeling. She'd never been able to drift off the night after hauling a man in for a bounty, especially after he'd put up a fight. It always caused a war in her mind, one that refused to settle when she tried to let her body rest.

"Alright. Well, don't stay up for too long." There was no real reason for her to move, but she gathered up her things and shuffled over to where Lorelin was lying, watching Jae with an unmoving smirk.

Jae tried to set out her bedroll again, but she could feel Lorelin's eyes boring into her, and it was mighty distracting. Jae was already bracing herself for the earful. When she finally sat down, Lorelin jabbed her elbow playfully against Jae's arm. "I heard that whole thing, you know."

"Oh, could you? I couldn't tell."

Lorelin raised her eyebrows. "You were so close! Why'd you stop there?"

Jae shrugged. "I don't know. It was a stupid thing to ask."

"No, it wasn't."

"It *was.*"

"He'd do it, you know." Lorelin beamed with a wicked grin.

"Do what?" Jae realized that she'd been inching away from her friend.

"Cross into the underworld for you."

Jae waved a hand. "I don't wanna talk about this, okay?" They had *real* things to worry about.

Lorelin huffed and rolled her eyes, scooching back to rest her head on her pack. "I swear. I'm gonna lock you two in a closet or something. Then you'd have no choice."

"Good thing there ain't any closets in this cave," Jae said, spreading out her arms.

"Jae." Lorelin glanced back at Halston. Hodge had joined him, and the brothers were chuckling about something, now. "Enough games. Listen. Some days, all I can think about is Martina. All the things I never said to her."

"What's that got to do with anything?" Jae felt herself tense up for a moment, and then, she admitted to Lorelin what she hadn't yet dared to tell herself. "It can't last forever, Lorelin."

"Who's to say that?"

"I am. My life's here. His is . . . somewhere else."

"That's down the road."

"Not far down it."

"Still." Lorelin took Jae's hand in both of hers. It caught Jae off guard, but the gesture was so comforting Jae couldn't bring herself to pull her hand away.

"It doesn't matter if you have to part later," Lorelin whispered. "You love him *now*. Why don't you tell him so?"

A gunfight erupted in Jae's mind. Every part of it was sounding off, and the gunsmoke clouded her head. Inside, she was screaming. She wanted to disappear. Shrivel up and blow away.

"I've decided we're done talking about this," Jae said, and with that, put her head down to sleep.

Lorelin laughed softly, then Jae felt her hand brush a few stray hairs off her forehead. She pretended not to hear what Lorelin said next, but she knew she'd be thinking of it for days to come.

Lorelin sighed. "Dear Jae. I'm just trying to save you from regret. The stuff stings like nothing else."

Chapter 20

$\mathcal{H}$alston was about ten yards away from the others, sitting beside a knobby arch of rock and running a hand along the foundation. Above him, the bluecaps shone like stars. He had been staring at them for so long that his eyes were beginning to strain. They were mesmerizing, the way they rippled and wavered.

There was something almost childlike about the way they fluttered about, and Halston felt the ghost of a smile tugging at his mouth. What *were* these strange little spirits? Had they been human, once?

Halston rolled back his shoulders and closed his eyes for longer than a blink. He supposed there wasn't a real need for someone to keep a watch down here, but between habit and restlessness, he'd stayed awake. Still, the fatigue was finally beginning to weigh on him.

All at once, the bluecaps shifted.

"Huh?"

A few of the bluecaps remained floating to mark the path, but a dozen or more of them began swirling in the air like a cyclone. Two of them flitted close to Halston's face, bobbing up and down as if they were afraid.

There was a rattling noise from somewhere nearby.

Every muscle in his neck went tense. Halston glanced backward. The path was empty, and everyone else was sleeping. Everything was quiet as it had been for the whole night thus far.

Then the noise came again.

It sounded like pebbles pattering on the ground. Then, the unmistakable sound of a footfall followed it. It was soft. If he'd been a yard further away, Halston might have missed it.

There were certain feelings Halston had grown remarkably familiar with these past few years: being chased, being feared, and being watched. And then there was being hunted, which was what he felt now.

His stomach jerked into a knot, and a knifelike pain pierced his chest, but he stood up slowly, slung his pack over his shoulder, then carefully drew his gun. He couldn't make too much noise, and he only had one bullet. He'd have to be careful.

Halston jogged about twenty yards down the path, braced to shout to wake the others if anything emerged.

He was only able to take one step.

Something beneath him shifted—Halston lost footing, and his body slammed into the ground, knocking the wind out of him. The sudden fall threw him into sheer disarray.

Halston got to his feet, half-drunk with confusion. He was thrown off his balance again—the ground disappeared from under his feet. A cry tore out of his throat. He was falling.

He tumbled downward, the blackness around him spinning, turning darker, growing more complete. The rock battered his muscles. Somewhere during the fall, he dropped his gun. When he finally came to a stop, he lay still, throbbing and helpless.

Halston's blood roared through him, the pain searing in his skull and limbs. He forced himself to sit up, but as he came to his senses, there was only darkness staring back at him.

There was nowhere to run. He was as good as blind down here.

"Hodge! Jae!" he shouted. His body was screaming in agony, but he urged himself to keep moving. His hands fumbled across the cave floor, searching for his gun but finding only grit and stone. Now, he was trying with all his might not to choke on his own terror. "Gryff!"

A few painful seconds ticked by. Then, a glow emerged and he could see where he was . . . a wide stretch of rock. Three bluecaps came fluttering from over the slope he'd tumbled down—a slope that had come out of nowhere.

Was he mad? He couldn't have imagined it. The ramp of stone— rising gradually to a point about fifteen feet above him—hadn't been there before he'd fallen.

Several more bluecaps joined the first few. Halston almost wanted to sing praise to them. At last, he had light! The bluecaps were moving frantically again. Halston braced himself to start scaling the slope. The angle was gentle enough that he could climb it swiftly.

Then, at the top of the slope, a silhouette emerged. At once, Halston's breath stopped.

Halston couldn't make out much—a shapeless cloak draped over invisible limbs, a hood drawn over the figure's head. A band of cloth concealed the lower half of his face, but the whites of his eyes glinted in the bluecaps' glow.

Then, Halston spied his gun gleaming in the same blue light— it had landed several feet away. Before the man above him could move, Halston leapt for his weapon and snatched it up.

"Stay where you are, and don't make a sound," the figure

commanded, raising his arm in a steady, crisp motion. It was a man with a thin, almost grainy voice. There was no malice in his tone, and he spoke matter-of-factly. It was then Halston glimpsed the faint outline of a knife in the man's hand.

Unbridled desperation seized every part of him.

Halston took aim. He braced himself to send his only bullet hurtling into his enemy's skull. He pulled the trigger, and he fired.

The noise rattled his senses. He was certain he'd aimed well, but a moment later, the man came bounding down the slope, right toward Halston. He'd missed!

The next second lasted an eternity.

Halston glanced backward, but he couldn't make out what was behind him. He wasn't sure if there was anywhere to run, if this plateau of stone led to another path, a dead-end, or a deep chasm. Instinct curled his free hand into a fist, and he braced himself to deliver the first blow.

His enemy rushed to meet him. Halston swung at the man's torso, but his fist struck his shoulder. His opponent dodged back for a moment, giving Halston enough time to remember his pack. In it, there was a hunting knife, along with his broken conduit. If he could just grab one or the other in time, he would at least have a weapon.

If he could grab it in time, he'd start slashing like a man possessed.

Above them, the bluecaps were whirling. Before Halston could reach over his shoulder to try and fish for his knife, the man's foot slammed into Halston's stomach. Halston lost his breath, but managed to deliver another hit to the man's chest. He shuffled to the side, then stumbled over his enemy's outstretched foot and crashed into the ground again. The sharp tang of blood flooded his mouth.

Fingers closed around his shirt collar and yanked him skyward. There was no time to catch his breath, to plan his next move, to even entertain a second of panic. Cold metal stung his throat. He gripped his useless gun tighter, waiting for the blade's bite, but it didn't come.

"*Don't move,*" the voice hissed.

Immediately, he froze. Even a quiver could earn him a slashed throat. Halston didn't even dare to breathe as his captor's head shifted. In his periphery, Halston saw a pair of oddly wistful looking eyes.

He'd seen these eyes before.

He couldn't place them, but there was no doubt in his mind that he'd once met this man's gaze. Here he was, teetering on the edge of his own death, and all he could do was wonder where he'd first seen those eyes.

As he was silently seeking the answer, Halston watched the regret clouding in the man's eyes.

The blade was colder than anything Halston had ever felt. A lone thought surfaced from the panicked chaos inside him: *Who are you?*

A new cascade of yellow light—certainly not from the bluecaps—fell over them. It was then a second figure revealed itself at the top of the slanted stone—this one brandishing a torch. This figure was slow-moving, emaciated, robed in threadbare clothes and a hat peppered with holes. Human in shape. The face . . . utterly blank. No, not a face. A mask. Fashioned from dull iron or stone, featureless except for the bolts that held it together and two slits for the eyes.

But where the eyes should have gleamed, there was nothing.

Nothing at all.

"Hold still," the new man said. His voice was impossibly cold— pure ice. "Hold still and come with—"

Halston felt his captor's focus shift to his scrawny companion. He seized the moment, and with a burst of almost stupid desperation, slammed his heel between his captor's legs. He howled, releasing his grip, and Halston whirled around.

The masked stranger raised one thin arm. Halston fell, and the ground beneath him crumbled into a small pit. The stone was moving as if it had turned molten, lurching and melding into new formations while the masked man stood above, unmoving.

Halston *wasn't* mad. The masked man was the one shifting the stone around. This was magic, plain as day.

As Halston tried to regain a steady stance, he spied the gaunt figure up above twisting and writhing his fingers, his hollow gaze steadfast on the stretch of rock beneath him.

He'd trapped Halston in his newly fashioned pit, which was about two yards across. When the ground solidified again, he fumbled desperately at the rim of the cavity. This new-made hole was shallow—he could hoist himself out of here, if he got his hands free for a moment. He shoved his gun back into his holster, ready to leap.

One of the men screamed.

Halston finally got hold of the edge. The bluecaps were swarming around his two attackers like an army of vengeful bees. There were so many circling round the masked man that Halston could no longer see him. The man in the hood batted desperately at the bluecaps, but his efforts were in vain.

Three of the bluecaps darted out of the swarm and raced to meet Halston, then spun in several circles over his head before zipping in a new direction. *This way!* they seemed to cry.

That was good enough for him.

With all his strength, Halston pushed himself out of the hole, then raced after the bluecaps, swifter than wildfire. The bluecaps didn't lead him up the slope and back to the path, but he put his faith in the little flames.

He cursed under his breath. They were well outside the path now, and the cave here was a far cry from flat. Whirling around stone towers and stalagmites, he hoped with all he had that the obstacles wouldn't slow him down too much. A few precious seconds could spell his doom. He had no choice but to believe the bluecaps would guide him to safety. They were still fluttering several paces before him, and he wouldn't dare let them out of his sight.

Behind him, his enemies were shouting. They were still close.

He didn't know where he was going, or how far he was from the others. Had the commotion roused them? Were they somewhere nearby?

A new sort of fear began to lay waste to his senses. A sharp, prolonged terror, like a metal spike twisting in his stomach and plunging deeper and deeper. The sting of familiarity made it sharper, and all the more inhibiting.

He kept running. His enemies weren't shouting anymore . . . Had he outrun them? A stitch formed in his side, and his lungs felt paper-thin, but he kept hurrying around spikes and dips of uneven stone.

At last, the floor evened out into a relatively flat stretch. The ceiling was lower here. Was he nearing some passageway?

Halston sped up. He was running like a wild beast. There was nothing in his veins but raging, maddening fire.

Behind him, something rumbled. The stranger, stirring the ground with his magic? Creating a string of craters for Halston to stumble into headfirst? If he fell again and the rock struck his head, he might lose consciousness. He'd be entirely powerless. *Or* he'd die in an instant.

He couldn't shout for the others again. If he did, he'd alert his attackers, and he was certain the bluecaps were trying to get him as far from them as possible. But gods above, where were they? He had to warn them! If these two assailants were hell-bent on taking him, were they after the others as well?

He had to find his way back to them. Darkness be damned— he'd never forgive himself if he didn't find them in time. But the bluecaps seemed to be leading him somewhere else entirely.

After what felt like eons of tearing through darkness, something stung his eyes. Up ahead, an opening in the cave, and through it, a square of daylight. *Daylight!* The bluecaps came to a wavering halt, and before Halston took off for the exit, he whispered, "Thank you!"

Though no amount of gratitude would ever repay the bluecaps, they still seemed to acknowledge him by flying in a sweeping formation, like the arm of an old friend waving goodbye.

Time and distance had turned to a blur. If he'd crossed a mile in two minutes, or half a mile in ten, he didn't know. He didn't even remember stooping under the exit. The soft sunlight of dawn swallowed him.

Before he exited the caverns, he was half-dazed with pain and exertion. But when he tore through the shrubs and lost footing on the steep incline before him, everything turned crystal clear.

He fell and fell and fell again. The ground pummeled his chest, his limbs, his head, each blow sending a new jolt of pain through his body.

Halston was already half-gone when he stopped rolling. He was faintly aware of the wetness covering him when he finally blacked out.

———————

"There he is!"

"Halston!" Halston hadn't heard Hodge cry out like that since they were small. "Hal! *Hal!*"

The voices stirred together, growing more frantic the closer they got. Halston forced his eyes open, then closed them tight again—the sun burned like an iron brand. Every part of him ached. He knew he should rise to his feet, stagger toward them on shaky limbs if he had to, but he couldn't budge.

He became aware of his soaking wet legs, and the sound of gently trickling water. He opened his eyes again to find that he lay on the banks of the river. They'd made it to the Glenn River.

They were in the Outlands.

"Hal!" Jae cried. She was near enough that he could hear her hurried breathing.

Trying not to groan, Halston rolled onto his side. Mud sucked at his hands as he tried to push his body upright. A sour stench flooded his nose. His shirt was damp. Gods. He'd vomited before losing consciousness.

Then the memories seized him.

The strangers!

"Stand back!" he shouted. Halston jumped to his feet, ignoring the throbbing in his limbs so he could fill their pursuers with bullets.

The others leapt back as Halston cocked his gun and aimed at the caverns' exit above. The strangers couldn't be far behind. When his attackers emerged from the caverns, he would fire. They'd fall. It would all be over soon.

He waited. He didn't dare release his grasp on the gun, despite the ten bewildered eyes staring at him. The burning in his battered muscles was growing worse with every breath he took, but he couldn't pay it any heed. Not when he needed to focus.

Halston stood unwavering, panting, hardly even daring to blink. Breath escaped his lungs in thin, papery huffs. His cheek stung; perhaps he'd nicked himself.

Then, he remembered that his gun was empty. Halston let out a defeated sigh.

He wasn't sure how long he'd been unconscious, and he realized the sun had fully risen by now. The rest of them all stood there, trapped in their own confusion, but nothing changed. Part of him wondered if they were just humoring him. The surrounding forest was silent, and the river kept on singing.

Had he escaped? He wouldn't let his guard down. Not yet.

"Wait," he breathed. What had he just *seen?* He touched his throat, trying to recall the feeling of his attacker's arm against it. Would the skin bruise? Leave a trace of proof that he wasn't losing his mind?

"Hal." Hodge touched Halston's arm. "What happened?"

Halston ignored the question. "How did you get out?"

"The bluecaps woke us," said Tsashin.

"Scared us half to death," added Gryff, making a circular motion with one clawed hand. "They were swarmin' like hornets, and when we came to our senses we found that you were gone. Just about sprinted out of there, we did. Right down the path the bluecaps showed us. What happened, kid?"

Halston couldn't bring himself to look away from the exit when he told them what had happened. His finger didn't move from the trigger. His rapidly pounding heart betrayed his tongue, but he spoke clearly enough to get the gist of what he'd seen across to them.

Hodge drew in a breath. "Let's get out of here. I ain't taking any chances with a warlock."

"Wait! Halston's hurt," Lorelin said as she reached for Halston. "Let me see."

Halston flinched from her. "No. We have to move." There was no point in tending to his injuries until they were *all* out of harm's way. He looked at Jae. She knew this country well. Maybe she could share her knowledge and tell him exactly what kind of spirit, magic anomaly, or monster he had just encountered. But all she offered him was a blank, bewildered stare.

"You're *hurt*," Lorelin almost snapped. "Now hold still."

"We're not staying here! We've got to move!"

It took a few moments of quarreling before they compromised. Nobody seemed to doubt Halston's story, and they couldn't stay here, but Lorelin wasn't going to ignore his injuries. She forced him to drape either of his arms around her and Hodge so they could half-drag him back onto the path.

The trail ran next to the sweeping river, but Jae led them sideways to a point where the earth wasn't so damp that they'd be leaving plain-as-day tracks on the way. Here, they could still travel upstream without walking directly on the trail. After two or three miles, they found a copse of short trees and thick, leafy shrubs. There were plenty of shadows and branches to conceal them, and Halston figured they couldn't gamble on finding a better hiding spot for the time being.

When they entered the copse, he vomited again.

Lorelin made him sit down, then slowly drink an entire canteen of water. Halston felt as though a blacksmith had split his skull with a hammer and chisel. Gradually, the pain began to lessen, but as it faded, an overwhelming certainty filled him in its place.

Beyond a shadow of a doubt, he knew that unless they got far away from here, the warlock and the cloaked man would come back for him.

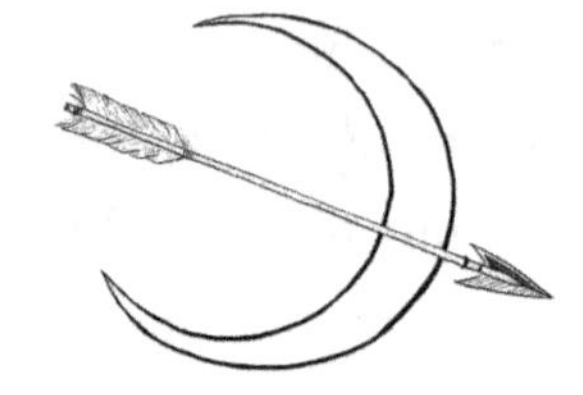

Chapter 21

Two days of loosely following the river passed, and there was still no sign of a masked warlock. Even though they were still only in the shallows of the Outlands—Pa had always told Jae that the most wondrous things were further north—they'd already wandered past no shortage of oddities.

Their first night in the Outlands, they passed a small grove of trees with curved stumps and leafy tops that shone blue and violet under the moon. Close to the river, they came across a trail of footprints, and though they were human in shape, each print was no bigger than Jae's fingertip. They passed trees and stones on which Rangers had scrawled runes, though nothing said anything more interesting than *berries in area* and *hot spring near*. And later, they stumbled across a Wydrian memory of a young, smiling girl beaming shyly at the ground, planted there by someone long forgotten.

Jae wondered why somebody had planted that memory there. The memory of the girl didn't speak, didn't share any directions or warnings. Then again, maybe such spells didn't need to be so practical. Maybe someone had loved her and felt the need to capture some of her loveliness. The thought brought a smile to Jae's face.

Three nights after their exit from the caverns, the trail began winding along a ridge, and the Glenn River cut through the earth around sixty feet below. Even from this high, Jae could feel the river's mist on her face. Below, it gleamed like a silver ribbon.

They circled up to camp in an aspen grove a ways off the trail. Jem greeted them shortly thereafter, looking cheerful, despite the circumstances. "I've got good news. We're just twenty miles from the Shroud. Still no sign of anybody following us."

That was good to hear. It hadn't been easy for the gang to let their guards down since they'd found Halston lying by the river. They'd been careful to cover their tracks best they could, and everyone had kept a vigilant eye on the surrounding forest and shadows.

As soon as Jem had rejoined them after the caverns, Halston asked him about any warlocks Sterling may have worked with who could move the ground itself. Jem hadn't the faintest idea, but he'd immediately taken to the woods to scout the area for anyone following them. So far, no signs of pursuit.

Jem let out something between a sigh and a whistle. "Can't imagine what a warlock would want with y'all. 'Specially if he ain't someone Sterling knew. Anyone else you might've . . . I don't know, riled up?"

Hodge snorted. He took his hat off and spun it on one finger while he spoke. "Bunch of ranchers in Arrowwood that Elias pissed off. Folks we robbed, of course. But nobody with *magic*."

Halston said nothing. He was sitting with his back against the narrow trunk of an aspen, knees drawn up to his chest, speaking to the soft bed of grass at his boots instead of the others. For days now, he'd been quiet and twitchy as a startled rabbit.

Jae took out her compass and flipped it open. "Still north along the trail?"

"Yes. We should be getting close around sundown tomorrow. I'll meet y'all then." The white bark of the aspens behind Jem's bluish form were the exact color of the early morning sky. With that, he winked out of their sight.

Twenty miles from the Shroud.

Jae lay back on her bedroll, tucking one hand behind her head, wondering what, exactly, had cursed and killed all the folks in the Shroud. Settlements in the Outlands were few and far between. There were a few scattered native tribes—the Konohe people included—and before the Banderra Rangers had cracked down and imposed the passage laws a couple decades ago, a handful of settlers had come to try their luck north of the Cannocs, despite the Nefilium and monsters . . . The land was dirt cheap. A few villages remained here and there, and from what Jae understood, the Rangers let the folks there be . . . as long as they didn't stir up trouble. They were hearty people. They had to be.

Did the Rangers know about the Shroud? It was the sort of case Pa would have been assigned to in his Rangering days.

Jae snorted at the thought of the Rangers. If she hadn't been in the saloon that night Hodge had gotten into a brawl, she'd still be on her way to joining them. All for passage into the Outlands. On another night, she might've laughed at that. Here she was, no badge required.

Of course, now they had the Rangers to worry about, in addition to the nonhuman things that roamed the Outlands. Jae had pushed the idea out of her mind. Gods above, what would she even do if they ran into a unit of Rangers? Because she couldn't leave her gang behind and flee. She couldn't get herself thrown into a cell, either. All she knew was that she wasn't leaving Halston.

Not yet.

But when?

Ever?

Dammit, Gryff was right when he'd told her to be careful . . . but she'd rather fling herself off a ledge into frigid waters than say it out loud. That was the thing about honesty. It was just and it was right and it still hurt like a barrage of stones. She was beginning to understand why so many folks surrounded themselves with liars.

These woods reminded Jae of the forest that had sheltered Tsashin's makeshift tomb: watchful and quiet, but *alive*. It was late enough that Jae's eyes were starting to burn with each blink. Halston was awake, too, and Jae was certain he hadn't slept a wink since they'd left the mines, despite all of Lorelin's fussing. Hell, she'd hardly even seen him *blink*.

Jae looked at Halston, but he didn't glance back at her. He was too busy staring into the shadows and thumbing the broken adamite knife, like that masked warlock would jump out of the treeline at any moment. Jae swallowed. Only having two bullets between all six of them was almost laughably unlucky. If they didn't find somewhere to get more ammo soon, what would happen? They still had their knives, and Gryff had an axe, but could *anything* protect them from a warlock who could move the ground itself? Having Jem to scout the area was hardly a comfort.

Then, a new thought bored its way into her mind: one of Halston lying dead in the spot where he was sitting now, drenched in blood, a man in a mask bending over him. It forced his name out of her lips. "Hal?"

"Hmm?"

I ain't gonna let him get you. I'd kill him with my own hands before I let him get to you. "You should get some sleep. I'm worried . . ." *I'm worried sick about you.* "You'll start seeing things or something."

Then, Halston started looking as if he might collapse.

It was the same as that night in Sterling's cellar—when he'd ripped open the air itself and threatened to heave Halston back into Median. The panic seemed to be controlling his entire body like a puppet. His breath hitched. One hand reached clumsily for his chest, and Jae didn't need to touch it too to know that his heart was hammering like thunder underneath. Before her mind could even register the motion, she'd linked her arm through his.

"Breathe," she whispered, knowing there was nothing to do but wait it out with him.

They stayed that way for a couple of minutes before Halston's breathing slowed.

"Better?" she asked.

Halston nodded, not quite meeting her eyes. "I've been meaning to ask. Did your father ever see anything like the man in the mask?"

She should've told him no, that there was no point in talking about this now, that he needed to rest and think about something else. But there was no moving on until she gave him an answer. "Yeah."

"Like what?"

"He saw a beautiful Nefili woman who could open her mouth and swallow men whole. He watched her kill somebody that way. There were trees that moved their branches like arms and tried to break his bones. And once there was a gaunt, boney creature that came out of a well and tried to drag him down."

Halston said nothing. He didn't look surprised. Jae reminded herself that he'd seen strange things, too.

"I mean . . . he lived, didn't he?" said Jae. He'd kept winning. Until the ghosts came.

Halston let out a long, shaky breath. "He looked so familiar. I just can't place it. I'm worried it's . . ." He didn't finish.

"It's what?"

For a long time, Halston was quiet. Finally, in a hushed voice, he said, "The warlock . . . I don't even know if I can call him that. He didn't look *human*. It doesn't make sense, but . . . there was something about his presence that was just . . . lacking. There was no *warmth* coming from him. And I'm wondering if he could be . . ." Halston's fingers started drumming on the ground. "Bear with me. This could take a while."

"I ain't got anywhere to be."

Halston hesitated, and Jae sensed the thoughts spinning in his mind, struggling to form themselves into words. "Alright. When the voyagers came through the portals, they settled on different islands and elected lords to govern them."

Jae recalled what Halston had told her about the settlers who'd come from this world—travelers from Alfir, Quierra, Surya, and the Marchant expedition in Hespyria—and how they'd all entered Halston's world through portals.

"There were centuries of unrest when they came, but after several resource wars, they united and formed the Order of the Second Realm. My father. He . . . he was the lord of our isle. Each lord was an admiral, of sorts. They commanded the ships that explored our world.

"He wasn't especially liked by everyone. Some of the other lords said that he was unfit to find the Source, and—"

"The Source?"

He answered so quietly, Jae almost didn't catch it. "The Source of the monsters."

It took Jae a moment to reply. "What monsters?"

"Just . . ." He made a vague gesture. "The *monsters*. It's strange. My father told us that when he was a boy, all he'd ever known was peace.

"Then the monsters started coming. Out of *nowhere*. People have lived in our world for centuries now, but nothing like it had happened before. Sometimes, months would pass without an incident. Then a few ships would set sail and never come back. There'd be a week of peace, and then terrible news. Sometimes, they'd find headless corpses on the shoreline. My sister's friend was torn apart. She wasn't even ten years old."

Jae shut her eyes, trying not to imagine what it must have been like, the fear that must have shackled them all.

"It was a horrible year, just before we came here." Halston's hands were trembling slightly. "Got to a point where my mother wouldn't let us go outside. I'd just sit in my room and wait. There were days I felt like I was going to live my entire life under that roof."

Though she felt she might regret the question, Jae asked, "Did anybody ever . . . see one?"

"Once. They attacked a ship on an expedition, and only one of the men survived. He wouldn't speak for days when he returned. But when they finally got him to talk, all he'd say was . . . 'Darkness. Darkness with a mouth.'"

A shiver ran through Jae's whole body.

"They talked about escaping," Halston went on. "Through the portal on our land. But that portal . . . we didn't understand it. It wasn't like the portals that the settlers could create with conduits and silver. It was . . . leftover. From forever ago. We knew it led to the First Realm, but we didn't know what waited in-between. Nobody had ever gone through it before. We weren't even sure we'd survive passing through it. And some of us were getting desperate enough to try, but most of the lords didn't want to take the risk. They felt there had to be another way.

"My father's duty, and his father's before that, was to explore. To come to know the new world as their ancestors had known this one. It changed. They figured that if the monsters were running rampant, there had to be a Source.

"He left for a voyage one day . . . and when he came back, he was . . ."

He said nothing more, but Jae knew what he meant. She'd met men who'd seen things that they couldn't—*wouldn't*—speak of.

"He didn't tell us what he'd found. I don't know if it was the Source itself, or some . . . something that came out of it. Whatever it was, something came for my family after he returned."

Jae didn't ask it out loud. *What was it?*

"At first, I thought it was a storm. A mass of black clouds. But when the darkness began to swallow our home . . . he just told us we had to run. So we ran to the one-way portal while the darkness covered everything. And the last time I saw it, it was reaching out for my mother. And Lia.

"I don't know if they're alive. I watched my father jump to his death. Maybe they joined him. I don't know.

"If we make it back, if we open up a portal here . . . I don't know what I'll find. Maybe it'll still be the home I remember. Maybe I'll find a wasteland. If so . . . we'll come back to this world, I guess.

"But I can't leave them there. If my family, my *people,* are suffering. I have to carry on what my father started. If there's anyone left to save . . . then I have to go back for them."

How do you know *that there's anything left?*

As soon as the question entered her mind, a wave of shame washed over her. She'd never ask such a thing out loud, never hurt him like that. Anyway, she knew what he would say. She was quite familiar with that answer herself. Because it was love, it was *madness* that pushed him to find the truth. She knew it all too well.

"You think the warlock is somebody from your world?"

"I don't know. It could be." He pressed three fingers to his temple. "And that man in the *cloak* . . ."

Jae wished she could tell him what it was that had come after him, or at least give him some comfort. Perhaps she could start by holding his hand, so that was exactly what she did.

"Jae," Halston said softly, "will you promise me something?"

"What is it?"

"Whoever—whatever—I saw in the caverns . . . if they come back to kill me, then—"

Jae squeezed his hand, perhaps a touch too tightly. "It ain't gonna kill you." *Because if it comes to that, I'll kill it first.*

He ignored that. "I know you need to find your father. But if they come back for me before that, and I don't make it out this time . . . I want you to stay with Hodge. Protect him for as long as you can. He acts strong, but . . . he's reckless, Jae. And I worry that he'll do something stupid and get himself killed if I'm not around to talk him out of it. Will—will you do that for me?"

"You ain't gonna di—"

His hand found her cheek. "*Jae.* Can you promise me that?"

She ran out of breath. "I promise."

And it killed her to think about it, but if she couldn't at least promise him that, then she was worse than useless.

He thanked her with a kiss.

Jae thought back to their evening by the pond. It was the closest thing she'd ever had to a perfect summer night—the kind of night folks wrote songs about, with words that didn't make sense till you lived something like it yourself. Until Gryff had ruined it, at least.

With his mouth on hers, her body folded in his arms . . . she felt like the greediest creature that ever did breathe. All she could think about was how much she wanted. She wanted more time with him.

She wanted a different life with him, one where the years would draw them to the same spot. She wanted him. She wanted *all* of him.

And she could never *have* all of him.

So she would find a way to make peace with their borrowed time, learn to grieve its passing without falling to her knees. She would watch the grains of sand slipping through her fingers and piling up. She'd stare at that pile of lost time long after it had passed. And the whole time, she would curse the earth and the sky, because there was nobody else to blame. Not even the Wandering God could re-arrange this for her.

When she pulled herself from him at last, he finally told her he was ready to sleep. She told him she was glad; he needed rest, after all.

She hoped to the gods that he hadn't seen the tears in her eyes.

Chapter 22

There were hunters in these woods.

The Drifter was getting good at hiding from them. He'd been spending most of his time in these woods running and listening for them. The path cut through the trees, and though he didn't dare walk on it when the hunters came, he never strayed so far that he could not see it.

He'd only caught glimpses of the hunters: thin limbs, yellow-gray flesh, moving swiftly as the wind. They were fast, but fortunately for him, they were also *loud*. He could hear their hawk-like yelps and pattering feet. Each time he heard the hunters coming, their predatory laughter filling the night, he'd take to a tree. There he'd stay. Then they would run off, and he'd be back on his way.

Some time ago, he'd stopped by the path to rest and woken to find that the world had changed while he was asleep. When slumber found him, he'd been among the rolling dunes, and now he was in a forest of thick, leafy trees.

The cloth was still bound around his waist. He'd made a habit of looking at it often, tightening the knot whenever it seemed to loosen. Each time, he thought about the weaver, safe in her dim, tapestry-clad room. He was beginning to envy her. He'd trade feeling like startled prey for another night in that quiet room.

But he had to find the gates.

He'd come to a spot in the forest where the trees grew sparsely. Every couple yards, he'd find a sturdier one, with branches thick enough for him to scale. He'd also passed a tree with a trunk made of moonlight, and another which sprouted fruits resembling chunks of sulphur. The bark smelled of brimstone. He'd steered clear of both trees.

The ground here was soft and spongy. Parts of it smelled sweet as molasses, and there were patches of grass that looked softer than featherbeds. But tempting as it was to lie down in them, he ignored them.

The Drifter had been crossing this wood for what felt like months. Sometimes, he found himself talking to the stars. They had yet to answer him, but he didn't really mind. He liked pretending that they could hear him.

He was beginning to wonder if he would become a part of this place, like the old man and the weaver. Whenever the fear crossed his mind, he repeated the names of those waiting for him. He imagined their faces, always smiling, always laughing, always glad to see him. And then, he was not afraid.

But he was afraid now.

He heard the hunters coming, dozens of feet scrabbling on the earth, and at once, he broke into a sprint. The pack called out to one another somewhere behind him. Their calls reminded him of crows . . . hungry, beckoning. *Were* there crows here?

Running, running.

Would the hunters strip the cloth from his waist? Without it, he was vulnerable. The thought spurred him to run faster.

He finally found a tree to climb, one with maroon bark and hefty limbs. He flung himself at the tree, and almost recoiled in shock. He'd expected rough bark, but the tree had the texture of firm, gamey flesh with strong bone underneath. But the tree wasn't moving, nor was its skin pulsing, and it would have to do.

He began to scale the branches. He climbed until at last he found a fork where he could roost.

He didn't look down. Still, when they came, their cries grated on his bones. In the corner of his eye, he glimpsed a swarm of pale figures scurrying beneath, cawing, cackling, sounding hungrier than anything he'd heard before. Hungry for more than just meat. A mouthful of flesh would not be enough to sate them. They were starving for bone, for screams.

"No!" a voice cried. The scream was close.

The Drifter almost winced. He pressed his body closer to the trunk.

"No!"

The voice chilled him to the core. He hadn't seen anybody else here, but it was the voice of a man. It held an enduring, unbearable pain.

"No! Please!"

The hunters were laughing, and their chortles were dripping with relish. The Drifter listened to them cackling at their victim, who was still pleading with them. Their fiendish laughter began to drown out the sound of his cries.

Fight them, the Drifter thought. *Fight with everything you have.* Maybe the man *couldn't* fight. Perhaps begging was all he had left.

"Please!" the man cried. His voice was paper thin, now. Soon, he would have no voice left— death or pain would take it away.

Footsteps pounded on the ground. The Drifter could feel the earth reverberating, the vibrations traveling underneath the surface and up through the roots of his fleshy tree.

He closed his eyes. He leaned his head against the tree, listening for motion, for the grating laughter of the hunters passing by . . . but now, there was only stillness.

He released a breath. With that, the Drifter scurried back down the branches and hopped to the ground. Nearby, the path was waiting for him. Onward he'd go.

Soon after he broke back into a brisk walk, a voice up ahead said, "Please."

His heart sank.

Just several strides away, bound to another tree with rope, arms trapped at his sides, was the victim.

He wasn't a man, like the Drifter had imagined. Actually, he wasn't sure *what* this creature was. He was shaped like a human, but scraggly gray fur covered every inch of his body. Two nubby horns sprouted from his head, and dark circles surrounded his eyes. The creature was naked, but dark spots splattered his fur. The Drifter got closer, and realized that the spots were blood.

The creature stared down at him with large yellow eyes. "Please."

Why had the hunters left him here? Why hadn't they finished him off?

The creature's fingers trembled. Each one ended in a short, dull claw. "Please," he begged, sounding weaker now.

The hunters couldn't be far. Any moment now, they could return. When they came back, surely they'd finish this creature off, and likely the Drifter with him.

But the Drifter couldn't bring himself to ignore the pain brimming in the creature's eyes. A pain so deeply human.

The Drifter treaded closer to the creature. Without meeting his eyes, he reached out for the ropes. His fingers touched dampness. He tried not to wince at the feel of the creature's blood.

The knots were taut and numerous. The Drifter tried not to curse. Frustration would only slow him down. He got to work, plucking, pulling, unwinding, plucking again.

In the distance, the hunters' cries resounded. The Drifter yanked tirelessly at the knots. Snap, snap. Little by little, the ropes gave way.

Run. The thought ran down every alley of his mind. *Get out of here.* Though his instincts implored him to flee, his hand refused to obey them. He worked at the ropes, even when the screams came closer.

If he left now, the vision of the creature, bound and bleeding, would haunt him all the rest of his days.

At last, he unwound the final knot, and the ropes fell away. For a moment, the creature was still. His belly swelled as he took in a labored breath and gazed down at his bloodstained fur. He took a step, another. The Drifter hoped that was a good sign—perhaps the wounds would not kill him.

The creature looked at the Drifter with an expression of gratitude so strong he almost shrank away. For a moment, he could almost picture the creature's entire life, as if he'd lived it all himself. He imagined him venturing back to a green countryside, where a clan of creatures like himself waited for him, and there, his life would go on.

A life not unlike his own.

"Thank you," the creature breathed.

The Drifter glanced down at the creature's bloody fur. "Where are you hurt?"

The creature waved a hand. "I can care for myself now. Thank you, stranger."

The Drifter found himself unable to speak, but he did give the creature a small smile before taking off down the path, racing with renewed strength.

He would find the gate soon. He had to.

Chapter 23

Several days after leaving the caverns, they came to a post manned by a Konohe family. They had their wares laid out in the center of a wide glade with goldenrods, harebells and emerald grass, rimmed by lofty fir trees. There was a man, perhaps forty, sitting beside a wooden cart piled high with furs, saddles, and woven blankets. Nearby, a round-faced woman sat cradling a baby while two little girls laughed and chased grasshoppers through the flowers, their black braids flapping over their shoulders.

Jae gave them a polite tip of her hat, then whispered to Halston, "Want to see if they have bullets?"

Hodge answered for his brother. "*Please.*"

Jae, Halston, and Lorelin stepped up to the Konohe man.

"Good afternoon," Lorelin bid him with a courteous smile.

The man furrowed his brow. "Rangers?"

Jae shook her head.

His eyes gleamed with understanding, then. "Took the caverns?"

Was it that obvious? None of them denied it, but the trader just raised a hand. "No concern of mine."

Lorelin held out the brooch from Argus' pocket. "Do you have any bullets?"

The trader blinked in surprise, glancing from the jewelry to Lorelin's beaming grin. Jae sensed the confusion lurking behind his brown eyes. He already knew they weren't in the Outlands legally, and he was probably certain that they were thieves with not-inconsiderable bounties on their names. Still, who could say no to a deal like this?

They bought every bit of ammunition the trader had, along with dried venison, several rations of bread, salt, and even a bag of sugared apricots. How *marvelous* it was to have a loaded gun once more. Though in truth, Jae was the most excited about the apricots.

———————

The longer they spent in the Outlands, the more Jae was starting to sound an awful lot like Pa used to, relentlessly throwing out warnings.

'If you see a tree growing in the center of the path, don't touch it. Walk 'round it.'

'If you hear a nearby scream, ignore it. If you hear a far-off scream, light a torch.'

'If it starts seeming like we're going in circles, we stop. We arm up and face out.'

It was all advice Pa had just about smothered her with ever since she'd learned to talk, and he'd forced her to repeat it back till she was tired of her own voice. Through it all, he'd made one thing very clear: one could never be too cautious in the Outlands.

Nobody questioned her advice, and they hadn't run into trouble yet—at least, nothing more troublesome than their own twitchiness. Jae hoped to the high heavens that it would stay that way. And she was praying to the Wandering God, Hemaera, and all the others that the masked man would not reappear.

Pa used to tell her about places where the air itself felt weary and callous. Until now, she hadn't understood what he'd meant. She felt like a stranger to the earth itself, and now it was growing suspicious of her.

The trail was still marked, but it had become thinner and far less straight. There were points on the path where the trees grew so close together they might as well have been brick walls rising up on either side of them. At one point, the pines cleared to make way for a stretch of mud covered in hoofprints the size of wagon wheels. Once, Jae and Hodge swore they heard somebody singing, but as soon as they looked into the forest, it stopped.

They'd been weaving a plan for confronting Flint when they found him. Jem swore that he didn't know anything about him other than that he was young, a treasure hunter, and relatively quiet.

When it came to it, they figured they'd have no choice but to find a way to get him to a secluded location. The plan was to send Lorelin to go and sweet-talk him, and she'd give them a signal if Flint gave them no choice but to do things the ugly way. If she couldn't charm an answer out of him, they'd force one out of him.

Maybe it wouldn't come to that. Maybe Flint would spare himself a quarrel and give it up. Any man with half-good sense would yield if he were outnumbered by a handful of gunslingers and an Azmarian the size of a boulder.

I can't afford to think like this. I can't afford to worry. Jae was used to taking risks. She'd learned to tune out the thoughts of failing, of dying . . . fears like that could only slow her down, and she hated slowing down.

It was early in the night, now, and Jem had led them down a narrow trail a mile or so from the river. The woods here weren't terribly thick, but they were awfully quiet, without the sounds of hooting owls or crickets to break it. Jae wondered if perhaps the Shroud's curse had caused the surrounding lands to go mute.

Tsashin had helped fill the silence with her stories. Jae's favorite was the story of how the Cannocs had formed; a few thousand years ago, the bison lord had lost a bet to the hawk lord, and his herd was transformed into the mountain range.

Jem was having a much easier time staying with them now, and he'd taken a turn telling his own stories. How his pa drank too much and his ma died when he was twelve years old, and he'd lied and said that he was sixteen so he could go work in the mines. He'd been tall for his age, so he'd gotten away with it.

"I never did like working at the mines. I once saw a fella bleed to death—got into a fight with someone else over a gold nugget. Both of them said they'd found it first, but only one of 'em had a knife. Then a few years later some miner came with news of an adamite deposit up north and convinced a bunch of folks to go find it with him. They never did come back. I think it was the greed that killed 'em.

"I should have quit mining. Found other work. Guess I was scared of a change. I was saving up to go off and make a life for myself when it all came to an end. It's just like that, ain't it? You make up your mind about something, then it slips away from you all at once."

Before long, the trees became thinner, more scattered. They walked along the snaking trail for a while and soon came across a dead tree rising like a knobby post beside the trail. The trunk was so crooked that it was a wonder it stood up on its own. Across the bone-dry bark was a message.

VISTRA WAS HERE

Dangling from one branch was a gnarled bit of rope that ended in a noose. Ancient looking. That rope could have hanged the first man who'd set foot in this wood.

Nobody had suggested they stop, but they came to a halt anyway. For a time they lingered there, eyes drifting across the strange writing on the tree.

A heavy knot tied itself in Jae's chest. She started feeling like she had to move away from the tree, as if its branches would sprout big hands that would reach out and crush her ribs.

"Don't like the look of *that*," Hodge said with a snort.

"I reckon that's been there forever. Might not mean a thing," Jem said.

Jae knew better. She was sure they all did. It had certainly meant something to the person who'd bothered to scrawl that message on the trunk.

After a couple moments, they pulled themselves away from the site. Nobody spoke of it, but Jae couldn't keep herself from wondering who Vistra was.

Not long after passing the tree, the trail began to rise. They passed another dead tree with *TURN AROUND* scrawled into the bark. Jem caught Jae eyeballing it.

"Don't worry. I reckon they just put that there to keep living folks away," he said gently.

A small bit of fear budded in Jae's chest, but she reminded herself of all she'd learned of ghosts, and of Jem. Besides, they had Zeph's potion.

The path carried them to the summit of a large hill. Below, the woods cleared, making way for an expanse of overgrown flatland that must have once been used for farming. The land was framed by a length of stony cliffs on one side and more woods on the others.

To the south rose the Cannocs, casting their shadow over the town which could only be the Shroud.

There were two lines of flat-topped structures that formed a main street, with scattered houses and log cabins dotting the rest of the area. Jae guessed that it could host around a hundred residents. It brought to mind places she'd passed through as a child, towns that were full of people who smiled readily and welcomed strangers. Nobody passing by would ever guess that it was full of the dead.

There was one structure that Jae kept squinting at to get a better look. It sat around a half mile from the rest of the town, and judging by the spikey, branchlike arms jutting from the top, it might have been a tree. But the trunk looked too thick and square for something natural.

"Got the potions?" asked Hodge.

"Not so fast," Gryff said. "Jem. You go down there first. Can you ask around for us? About Flint? They'll trust you. We ought to use a *real ghost* before we disguise ourselves."

"On it," Jem said brightly, then floated downhill into the town.

The moon rose higher in the sky, and Jae's eyes began to itch with the urge to sleep. The others were getting restless, too, and before long they were all sitting with their backs against the trees. Jae began drawing circles in the dirt with her thumb. She guessed that Jem had been gone for around two hours.

"What's taking him so long?" Hodge muttered. "This town ain't that big. Only so many folks he could talk to."

"Maybe he's being personable," said Lorelin.

"He's *dead*. What good is being chatty gonna do?"

Lorelin shot him a glare. "You could learn a thing or two from him."

When Jem finally reappeared, they were all just about jumping to hear from him.

"They told me that we ought to go to Mr. Elm's Place," Jem explained. "That's where Flint lives. Told me how to get there and everything."

Mr. Elm's Place. The name itself sounded like any other old town roadhouse or inn. Nothing special, but Jem had spoken in a slight hush, like he'd just whispered the name of some legendary king's palace.

"In that case," Gryff said slowly, retrieving the potions from his pack, "it's time."

Jae had never thought much about what drinking a potion would be like. It was cool as springwater, but with the metallic tang of copper. It finished with something like a spark of lightning burning inside her stomach.

The rest of them took turns sipping from the vials. Jae waited and examined her own features as she did. The effects came on slowly. She didn't feel too different. Just as on-edge as she had been for nearly three years, now. But her veins were gone, her freckles vanished, and her skin was the same shining, half-transparent blue as Jem's.

She faced the others. They made a rather lively looking pack of ghosts, shining there under the moonlight. Their disguises brought an involuntary grin to her face.

Not dead, but they'd pass for it.

———

Jae had imagined that a town full of ghosts would be quiet as the grave, but the Shroud was anything but silent.

A mother walked-hand-hand with her little son, and off to their right, a group of young men were joking about something that must have been very funny indeed, judging by how loudly they were laughing. An older couple swayed in each other's arms on a nearby porch, though to what music no one could tell. Perhaps touching things of this world was a challenge for ghosts, but touching one another was no more difficult than a live man reaching for another's hand.

And Jae could do nothing but look at them with surprise, because they didn't frighten her. Not in the slightest. They were just . . . people. Barely there, but people all the same.

The buildings weren't in a horrible state of disrepair, like Jae might have guessed. They looked worn and shoddy from years of going unused, but nowhere close to collapsing. The windows were grimy, the wooden boards splintery, the shingles loose. Still, they stood strong.

Jae had had a hunch that 'Mr. Elm's Place' was the strange, tree-like structure she'd spied up on the hill. As Jem led them down the main street, past a few cabins, and onto a more secluded part of the cleared land, Jae found that she was right.

The structure looked as if someone had taken the lower half of a church and the top half of a tree and smacked them together to make whatever *this* was. Bark and gnarled branches surrounded a few windows, and a row of wide steps led to a rectangular entrance. The branches on the roof grew vertically, circling in spires that reached for the wide-open sky. The house-tree looked lonely. A stop along the road beneath a million stars, with only the silent, empty space to keep it company. It was offset from the rest of the town. Hardly a part of it at all.

It didn't belong here, that much was for sure. The hand of a god might have uprooted it from another world and planted it here instead.

As they entered, they found that it was dim but not dark. The walls were wooden, but the grain was smooth, like it had been carved out and polished into a room from the inside. There were two rows of wooden pews lining either side of a wide aisle, and to the side of one row was a narrow stairway.

In every Church of the Wandering God Jae had ever stepped into, the aisle between the pews led to an altar, but this one led to a bar with a stone fountain sitting next to it. There was a man standing behind the counter, in the middle of a conversation with two spirits shimmering in front of him. He was not a ghost. His face was ageless, his skin was dark as the night, and his eyes were apple-green.

If this was Mr. Elm, the name certainly suited him.

As they moved down the aisle toward the bar, Jae noticed that the spirits standing across from the man were a boy and girl, neither one older than eight. Jae swallowed, trying and failing to keep her heart from sinking.

The ghost girl leaned forward and spoke, voice moving swiftly as a hummingbird. "I saw a weatherbird last night, Mr. Elm."

Mr. Elm had a kind smile. It was the kind that Pa had given Jae all the time when she was a child. The sort of smile that hid the sadness of an understanding that the little one almost certainly lacked. "Did you? Will you describe it to me?"

"He had wings of gold, and eyes bright and blue. Just like you told us."

The boy wrinkled his nose. "I think it was just a regular bird, Lottie."

Jae couldn't help but grin at how much he sounded like Halston. *That tone must come hand-in-hand with being an older brother.*

Tsashin was the first of the group to step forward. "I think you might have seen a sunbird."

Lottie's eyes widened. "Really?"

"Yes," Tsashin said. "There are stormbirds, too, and rainstorms follow wherever they fly. You said he was gold, and the golden birds bring the sunshine. I imagine tomorrow will be sunny."

Lottie smiled wide and nodded. Then, her smile slipped away. "I wish we could still see the sun."

For a moment or two, Mr. Elm studied the group more closely, and a flicker of wariness flashed across his face, though he didn't follow it with wary words. "Lottie, Ray, why don't you go outside? I haven't had a chance to greet our new *visitors*."

Ray glanced the gang of unfamiliar ghosts up and down. "How did you die?" he blurted at last.

"*Ray*, that's *rude*!" Lottie snapped.

"River accident," murmured Hodge.

"Neat," said Ray. "But our story is better. A monster ate us."

Lottie rolled her eyes. "Dying's not a *contest*."

"Hey, off with you now," said Mr. Elm with a flourish of his hand. The little ones floated away and passed right through the wall.

Mr. Elm stepped out from behind the counter. His clothes were strange—a wide-brimmed hat and a gauzy poncho swaddling his torso. Beneath, he wore bright green pants. On his feet were flimsy-looking leather shoes that seemed like they'd be hardly better than no shoes at all. He wore a tarnished brooch on his lapel, too worn to tell if it had ever once had a shape.

He spoke in an assured sort of way—Jae knew at once that he was the sort of man who never stammered. "Using spirium? Clever. No need to look so stunned. I never turn a soul away, dead or not, but mind you—the spirits here may not be so forgiving. They're rather protective of this town. Now then. Are you lost?"

Already, he had seen right through them. Would the townsfolk do the same?

They began swapping befuddled looks with one another, and it took them all a moment of gaping like dunces before somebody spoke up. "No," Halston finally replied. "We're looking for a man named Flint."

A sigh escaped Mr. Elm's mouth. "Did he steal something from you?"

Halston shook his head. "Not . . . exactly."

"Well, I imagine he'll be home before long. You won't have any trouble *finding* him. Getting him to *cooperate* with you is another matter entirely." Mr. Elm reached for a short glass of shimmering violet liquid, raised it to his lips, and sipped. "Might I ask what business you have with him?"

"He has something of ours," Halston said. "He didn't *steal* it from us, necessarily, but . . . do you think he'd accept a trade?"

"I wouldn't know. Flint is . . . a closed book. He's my sister's son, and I still don't know him half as well as I should."

The group exchanged sullen glances. *What now?*

"I imagine he'll return soon enough. If you need a place to stay the night, I don't mind putting you up," said Mr. Elm. He motioned in the direction of the stairwell. "It's been a long time since I've had a guest. I never turn away travelers, but you'll have to pay upfront."

"How much?" asked Hodge.

"One memory for the night."

For a moment, they glanced back and forth at one another. They waited for Mr. Elm to chuckle, then reveal what his true price was. Instead, he merely gave them a knowing smile. "Come. This way."

They followed him to the fountain at the side of the bar. When they came closer to the liquid pooling at the bottom, they found that it didn't ripple and shine like clear water. It was cloudy and motionless, as if it had frozen over.

Tsashin craned her neck over the fountain. "What's this?"

"The pool of memories," said Mr. Elm. "I keep it here for the spirits. If they ever need a change of scenery. There's not much in the way of entertainment in this town."

Jae peered at the hazy water, wondering what sort of memories lurked underneath. What would it be like for these waters to cover her head? "Like Wydrian?"

"Exactly," said Mr. Elm. "You'll still have the memory yourself. You're simply . . . transferring its essence to the waters. For others to enjoy as they please."

"Can't we just give you three crowns and call it a night?" asked Hodge.

Mr. Elm chuckled. "Crowns aren't much good in a place like this."

"Oh, for gods' sake," Jae muttered. "I'll do it."

Mr. Elm grinned and gave her a nod. "Excellent. It won't be painful—just touch the water when you're ready. Let the memory play out. Don't force it."

Jae sucked in a breath, then knelt before the fountain. She shut her eyes, then reached out and placed one hand in the water.

In images shaped of blue and white threads, she watched the memories unfold.

First, she glimpsed a wedding during the first breaths of spring, with a laughing bride and groom and a whole town of folks cheering in the pews. She saw men driving livestock over the pasture, wagon wheels turning, bringing up clouds of grit. The dust flew up and settled down, and on that same ground, there were children running and hollering. She saw a family sitting at a table, passing around steaming plates of potatoes and cornbread and sharing stories from the day. She saw a dance hall full of people spinning, a stage with musicians singing and plucking at fiddles. Somehow, both on their own and altogether, the memories flowed through her like water lapping at a shoreline, moving, going still, coming back.

There was laughter.

So much laughter.

And Jae thought of a summer day she'd spent with Pa on a lake-shore in Banderra. It was early, but she wasn't tired in the slightest. That was the day he'd taught her to skip stones. He spoke gently as he helped her find a flat one, then stood behind her and helped her position her arm and hand correctly. Sunlight, casting rings on the water. The freshwater smell, making the whole world feel clean and new. She'd felt as though she were the queen of everything when she finally got the first stone to hop along the water, and her ribs ached from how she'd laughed.

Mr. Elm didn't tell her when to come back. Somehow, she just knew when it was time.

Jae opened her eyes, then drew her arm out of the water. It was still dry.

Already, she longed to go back.

"Thank you." Mr. Elm pointed to the stairway once more. "You may choose any room upstairs but the one with the white door. That's Nova's room . . . You may hear her, but I assure you she's no threat. She just prefers to be alone. That said, be careful not to re-veal yourselves. If the townsfolk decide they don't want you here, I won't be able to stop them from chasing you off."

Hodge leaned over to Halston and whispered, "Ain't sure how I feel about staying here."

It wasn't quiet enough. "You'll fare better under my roof than out in the streets," said Mr. Elm. "I'd imagine you don't want any of the spirits to catch you sleeping."

Sheepishly, Hodge looked down at the floor.

"Much obliged, sir," Halston said quickly.

They all took turns thanking him, then ventured upstairs. Jae's heart fluttered when they stepped into the hallway with eight doors. As per Mr. Elm's instructions, they ignored the one with the white door and entered the first room on their left.

The room was surprisingly large, with six small beds set up in neat rows. The covers were so dusty that Jae wasn't even sure what color they were, but after weeks of sleeping on the ground, a bed still seemed a luxury. There was a wide window in the center of the wall, letting moonlight stream onto the wooden floor.

They shut the door and got settled for the night, though everyone was too tired to do much more than wipe some of the dust off the beds and drape their bedrolls over them. It was strange to see everybody lying on the beds when they all still resembled ghosts— save Jem, who quietly floated around the room for a few moments before disappearing off into the night. Down the hall, somebody was weeping.

Jae kept willing herself to drift off, but the crying was keeping her awake. It was the most hollow sound she'd ever heard. *Nova.* It had to be the spirit Mr. Elm had mentioned, and Jae figured that the poor ghost must have swallowed every bit of suffering she'd felt in life and stored it away. Now, it was bursting out of her like water from a shattered dam.

Before long, Jae gave up and opened her eyes. Halston was still awake, sitting with his legs draped over the side of his bed, facing the big window. Jae rose from her spot, shuffled over and sat down beside him. The springs of the bed creaked.

Halston exhaled. Without speaking, he reached into his pack and pulled out his half of the adamite knife. Jae's breathing turned shallow.

Halston set the knife down.

And up above, there was another world.

There wasn't much Jae could see, but past Median's stretch of scattered rock and gray sky, there was a rolling pasture of emerald-green. Beyond that, a faint ribbon of sea.

"There's hardly any Median here," Halston said in a hushed voice, then pointed to the circle. "That's . . . that's it. Right there. That's my realm."

He kept on staring through the void separating him from his home . . . but Jae kept on staring at *him*. There was something in his gaze Jae had never seen before. It was like he couldn't believe his own eyes.

That was it, then.

They were nearing the end.

Jae threw her arms around him, unable to tell if she felt like she was rising out of deep water or spinning uncontrollably in a current. Still, she needed to cling to him, to keep herself from sinking.

"Hal," she whispered, willing her voice not to break. "You did it."

"Shh," he said. "I don't want to wake anyone now. We can't get our hopes up just yet. We still need the other half."

After that, Jae imagined they'd settle all those questions they'd been too afraid to discuss. *What now? Who's going with you? Who's staying behind?*

What comes next? Gods, oh gods, what comes next?

"*After* we get the knife," Halston continued, "we'll need to get to the Yunah nation. Find somebody to take care of Tsashin."

And uttering her reply may very well have been the hardest thing Jae had ever done.

"I'll take her, Hal," she said. "When I go looking for my Pa again."

Halston's face fell. "You will?"

"I will. I'll protect her. I'll find somebody who can help her figure out who she is."

In the darkness, he knotted his fingers through hers, and like that they stayed.

What was there to say, anyway? That she was grateful for their borrowed time? That she'd treasure it always? Could one even treasure something after it was gone? There was nothing to marvel at, then. All she would have was grief.

Somehow, tiredness overcame her, and she parted from him without another word. She took two steps back to her bed and quietly flopped onto it. Before long, she began drifting off to the glowing memories she'd relived in the fountain downstairs. She understood how they could bring a dead man some comfort. She was a live girl, and they'd given her more warmth than she'd known in years.

And she needed it now more than ever.

Chapter 24

The next day passed by painfully slowly. Jem had vanished sometime during the night. They had to stay in Mr. Elm's place until sundown, where they passed the time with Lorelin's deck of cards, playing just about every game they knew.

"These poor ghosts." Hodge took a peek out the window and frowned at the still-bright sky. "No food, disappearing every day at dawn . . . They can't even leave this place. I'd lose my mind."

They'd just finished their fourth game of faro, and Lorelin gathered up the cards to shuffle once more. The edges were ragged, 'well-loved,' she kept saying. "Perhaps they make the most of it. I think I could make do as a ghost here as long as I was surrounded by the right people."

Tsashin laughed behind her hand. "I'd be happy to stick out a curse with you, Lorelin."

"I wouldn't wait out a curse with *any* of you," said Hodge.

Jae swatted at his arm. "What, you don't want to while away eternity with us?"

"I mean no disrespect," Hodge said slowly, "but if I have to spend another day losing at cards with y'all, I'll have more than a few choice words for Flint Barrow. If we do find him."

"We will," said Lorelin.

"What if he doesn't show?" Hodge asked. "Then what?"

The first round of spirium had worn off this morning, but there was no reason to dip into their still-plentiful supply before nightfall.

Lorelin said, "Maybe we ought to look for other leads. Talk to the other ghosts around here. See where Flint's been. It can't hurt."

At dusk, they decided that Lorelin's idea was as good a plan as any. The others volunteered to head outside and speak to the spirits around town, and Jae would see if she could glean anything else from Mr. Elm. Jae would have been fine striking up a conversation with one of the Shroud's ghosts, but since their meeting last night, she'd been itching to speak to Mr. Elm again. They all took extra sips of spirium and watched their skin turn ghostly once again.

After the others disappeared, their newly wispy forms fleeting out the doorway, Tsashin stayed behind. She sat in the corner, knees up to her chest, eyes open but somehow still looking half-asleep.

"You alright?" asked Jae.

"Not especially," she said. She wrapped her arms around her legs, drawing further back into herself. "I hate this. The uncertainty of it all. It's driving me mad."

"I know." Jae sat beside Tsashin, placing a hand on her delicate shoulder. Although her barely clear hand looked as though it would pass right through Tsashin, she could still touch her friend, and as cold as real ghosts were, both of them were still warm. "My secret is to just . . . not think about it too much. To just keep going."

"How do you *stand* that?"

'*I don't,*' Jae wanted to say. '*And I'm a liar. I feel like I'm clutching onto a thread for dear life. It'll snap any day now.*'

"You don't have to worry," was all Jae said.

Tsashin hesitated, then said, "I heard what you said to Halston last night."

Jae only blinked. "And?"

"I'm glad you want to protect me. But Jae, I'm . . . I'm not *weak*, am I?" she asked, sounding more hurt than angry.

"Of course you ain't weak!" And that was true. *But you're too kind for the likes of us.*

Tsashin thoughtfully scratched her temple. "I'm just not sure what the point of it would be—going home when I can't even re-member it. And . . ." Her throat bobbed with a hard swallow, and she whispered, "I'm not ready to say goodbye to them, Jae."

Jae squeezed Tsashin's shoulder. "I know. I'm not ready either."

A year ago, she never would have uttered such a thing out loud. To do so would have been to admit a weakness . . . but maybe, she realized now, there was more strength in honesty, in making peace with the truth.

They sat in the corner for a while, Tsashin perfectly quiet, Jae thinking of something she could say to make it all a trifle better . . . but talking hardly ever seemed to make things better. At least not in the way that getting up and *acting* did. Still, she was just glad to know she wasn't alone, and she hoped it was a comfort to Tsashin, too.

Before long, Tsashin rose to her feet. "I'll be alright. Thanks, Jae. Ready to head out?"

"Sure." Jae smiled slightly. Tsashin would have a whole trove of tales for her family, when she got home. Jae just prayed that— by some miracle or wish come true—Tsashin's memory of them would return first.

Jae was glad they were headed out now. As soon as they had both risen, the ghost down the hallway started wailing again.

They traveled downstairs and parted ways, Tsashin heading

down the aisle and out into the night, and Jae drifting over to Mr. Elm, who was still standing behind his counter. Since the last time she'd seen him, he hadn't budged a bit.

"Good evening," he said, without looking away from the small glass bottle in his hands. He was polishing its surface with an old, threadbare rag. He had a gentleness about his movements, wiping the surface in steady, circular motions, as if that little bottle was worth a great deal of gold.

"Hi." Jae headed over to the counter. "Is . . ." She wasn't quite sure how to put it. "Is that weeping ghost alright? The one upstairs?"

She ought to ask more about Flint, but she wasn't sure how to lead into the subject just yet. Besides, she'd never heard crying like *that* before. It was so fraught with pain that she already knew she'd remember it years down the road.

"No," Mr. Elm replied. "It brings Nova some comfort to stay here, though. Some spirits take longer than others to make peace with their own deaths."

"Does she remember who she is?"

"Yes. I believe she's still grieving the life she's lost."

Jae nodded, not quite meeting Mr. Elm's eye. If she died on this very night, she was certain that she'd feel the same. She'd mourn for her unlived life, for all she'd left undone, but she might become a ghost that cursed and shouted for all time instead of weeping.

Jae stretched out her arms. Fatigue had made her bones heavy. Though she'd tried, she hadn't slept well.

"You should watch your movements," Mr. Elm warned. "Ghosts have no muscles. They tend not to stretch."

Jae corrected herself. He was right. She'd have to be more careful.

The room was quiet. Mr. Elm placed the glass bottle back with the others lining his shelves. They came in every color and size.

"What's in those?"

"Water from the fountain. Sometimes, I can isolate the memories. These are the . . . most powerful of them. Most of the spirits find them too overwhelming." His shoulders went slack. "But some of them *ask* for the most powerful ones."

"Why?"

"I'm not sure. Perhaps they find the stronger memories the most sincere."

Jae said nothing to that. Instead, she took in their surroundings, the wooden pews, the smooth countertop, the rainbow of bottles. "Did this place used to be a church?"

"Yes," said Mr. Elm. "A sanctuary of Argun, in fact. Before I turned it into an inn."

The faith of the Wandering God said that he appointed lower gods to watch over the worlds he created, before he continued his travels across the stars, worlds growing wherever he moved. Most churches weren't devoted to any singular god, and one could pray to whomever they pleased. But in the old days especially, folks built them in spots to honor specific gods—deserts for Cressien, mountains for Petreos, watersides for Nerea . . . forests for Argun.

"Ain't that . . ." Jae trailed off. There was no way to ask it politely.

But Mr. Elm finished for her. "Sacrilegious?" He chuckled, picking up another bottle to wipe down. "No. Argun told me he doesn't mind."

Jae's mouth parted. Was Mr. Elm a deeply religious man, or a crazy one? Jae believed in the gods, and every so often she'd pray to them for good fortune, but she was fairly certain they didn't speak to mortals. At least, not in a way that let earthly men know whether they could turn their churches into roadhouses.

Jae studied his face carefully. This man wasn't just a live one. Perhaps he was a warlock, but something about him made her reckon that he was less than half human. He had some of the same quality that she'd seen in Zeph and Delgon, one that ordinary folks lacked. He might have even been one of the Nefilium . . . but even if he was, what would a Nefili man want with a town full of lingering mortal souls?

Maybe he would tell her. "Why are you here, Mr. Elm? You ain't a ghost."

Mr. Elm arched a thick brow, then cleared his throat. "Duty. I survived the attack on the town while so many did not. The least I can do is . . . help the spirits."

"They seem happy enough from what I've seen," said Jae. "I mean, apart from the one upstairs."

Mr. Elm shook his head. "Some of them are, but it took a while for them to become so. Many of them have managed to find a sort of joy in this state. I do what I can to keep them that way. Others aren't so content. They stay inside their homes, haunting their own hallways. Sometimes, you can hear them wailing from the outside. They're desperate to move on, and they can't. Still, I'm hopeful that I can ease their suffering. While the Shroud is still here."

"What do you mean?"

"Until the curse is lifted." He hung his head. "Other spirits can move on to what comes next, if they choose, or wander the earth itself, though that has its own difficulties. But the curse keeps the spirits here rooted to this place. They can't leave the borders of our town, and not even god-ore can set their souls free."

Jae shuddered. "Then . . . what's gonna break the curse?"

Mr. Elm set one of the bottles down. "That's the problem. Nobody knows. My wife left several years ago in search of a solution. I haven't seen her since."

The poor man. "I'm so sorry."

"It's alright," said Mr. Elm, and he hardly sounded sad. "She's the boldest soul I've ever known. She always finds her way back eventually. But I do miss her."

Behind them, the front entrance creaked. Footsteps padded across the floor, and Mr. Elm leaned to look over Jae's shoulder.

"Good to see you, *Flint*," Mr. Elm said, placing a great deal of weight on his name.

Jae whirled around.

She bit down on her cheeks. It was all she could do to keep from gasping out loud.

This was Flint?

She'd been expecting a rugged-looking man around Sterling's age, muscular, covered in scars. But this man—boy, really—was probably as old as Halston, and certainly no older than twenty-one. A loose duster jacket swallowed his body, but Jae could tell that underneath it he was slim but sturdy. A battered hat crowned a head of coiled black curls, and his skin was smooth and deep brown. His movements were self-assured. Despite the strange, wistful gloom that hung over the place, and a long, scabbed-over slash on his cheek, he was grinning.

He had a friendly face. Certainly not the face Jae would have expected from a confidant of Sterling Byrd. He gave Jae a pleasant smile and a tip of his hat before he bustled up to the counter as if he didn't have a care in the world.

"You should have seen it, Elm. The caravan was *glorious*."

Mr. Elm just frowned, eyeballing the scab on Flint's cheek. "No trouble this time, I hope?"

Flint's face morphed into a sheepish grimace. "Well . . ."

Mr. Elm heaved out an aggravated breath. "*Flint.*"

"I'm as careful as I can be," he said. "You know that."

"I worry about you."

"You don't have to."

"Clearly I do, since one of every three of your excursions seems to end with you nearly dying."

"Oh, come on, it's closer to one in four."

Mr. Elm didn't laugh.

Flint's grin slipped away. "I appreciate you looking out for me, but there's no need. Anyway, I brought you a Midsummer present." He took a cloth pouch from his pocket, then slid it across the counter.

Midsummer. Already? Jae tried not to snort. Time really did seem to be slipping through her fingers.

Mr. Elm opened the pouch and removed a blue bottle with a trumpet-like spout and pale, shimmering flecks in the glass. Jae thought back to a magnificent sculpture she'd once seen a Quierran trader selling in a square. *Blown glass,* he'd called it.

Mr. Elm gave Flint a suspicious glare.

"I *bought* it. Cross my heart." He tapped four fingers against either side of his chest.

"I certainly hope so." He added the pretty little bottle to his collection. "But thank you."

Flint took a few steps back toward the front door. He pursed his lips, retreating a bit more, hands in his pockets. "You aren't gonna . . . ?"

"No. If you've gotten yourself into another mess, you can work it out yourself. Besides, I have a guest right now."

Flint took another step away from the counter, then tipped his hat at Jae once again. "Evening, miss." Before Jae could even think about speaking to him, he was out the door.

She turned to Mr. Elm, who just waved a hand. "You wanted to speak to him, didn't you? Go after him."

Good thing Mr. Elm had given up on meddling in Flint's problems. If he hadn't, he might've stopped Jae from following him out that door.

But follow him, she did.

———

Jae followed Flint out of Mr. Elm's place, across the tract of barren earth, and into the heart of the Shroud.

He wasn't that much further ahead of her. Flint walked with purpose, moving swiftly and pointedly, but the spirits didn't seem concerned by his presence.

Jae noticed that there were wildflowers spread around either side of the street. Perhaps the ghosts had put every bit of concentration they could into gathering and scattering them.

Midsummer. Jae hadn't celebrated the feast day since Pa's disappearance, but she had fond memories of the holiday from her childhood. Pa would often take her to one of the nearby towns where folks would dance to the fiddle in the street and feast on skewers of meat and hand pies from roadside vendors. And everywhere, on every surface, were flowers of every color.

At once, Jae's heart was warmer. Perhaps the ghosts couldn't play fiddles or eat food, but at the very least, they could have flowers.

The streets were crowded. Dozens of ghosts stood gathered together, talking and laughing. Through the haze of laughter and conversation, she made out one specific tiding.

"To a bountiful harvest!" somebody hooted, and the ghosts around him laughed.

Jae quickly scanned the area for one of the others, but she couldn't make any of them out in the sea of glassy spirits. Unlike last night, where only a few souls had been out, it seemed that the entire town had wandered out into the main street. She stopped trying to find the others and Flint, who was traipsing on the edge of the buildings about ten yards ahead of her, well-removed from the spirits. Soon, he veered in between two of the structures and disappeared.

Jae didn't waste another moment trying to find the others. She wasn't about to lose Flint.

She picked up after him, moving swiftly, but not quickly enough to call attention to herself. Jae turned and glided down the same alleyway into which Flint had disappeared. At the end of it, she stopped and looked around the corner.

Flint was walking briskly toward a house which sat about a hundred yards off from the rest of the town. It was a large house, two stories high, with plenty of windows and peeling white paint. He edged around the side of the house, then Jae lost track of him.

Jae made her way across the empty, overgrown field leading to the house. There was nobody out here, and that was a good sign. As she came closer to the house, her stomach got heavy, as if dense stones were rolling into it. Layers of muck and dust covered most of the windows, but a few were broken. There might have been an awful smell coming from inside, but maybe she was imagining it.

Jae forced herself to take a few more steps toward the house. She was close enough to touch it, now, though she was in no hurry to do so. The walls were so cracked and full of holes that she wondered how they hadn't collapsed yet.

As she was pacing along the east side of the house, she heard someone crying, followed by the sound of Flint's muffled voice.

Jae crept to the source of the sound, then crouched down and peered through one of the holes in the wall.

Oh.

She blinked a few times. It was all she could do to make sense of the sight before her.

The room was almost empty, save for a tarnished bed frame without a mattress and a threadbare rug covering half of the battered wooden floor. Flint knelt beside the back wall. Moonglow from a small, circular window shed a light on him . . . and a ghost.

The spirit was a young woman about Flint's age. Faint as her form was, Jae could make out a head of curly hair, a baggy dress, and round, sad eyes with delicate lashes. She looked at Flint with a fond softness. The look was gentle, barely there: a whisper, the hint of a breeze, the first drop of a short-lived sunshower.

The ghost spoke. "She hurt you again."

"What, *this?*" Flint pointed to the slash on his cheek. "This is nothing. I've had worse, you know that."

"It *could* be worse next time." The ghost girl caved into herself like a tulip at nightfall. "I haven't forgotten what you told me last time—of the man who lost his mind after he displeased her."

"That won't be me, Daisy. I've never let her down."

"You can't do this." Daisy lifted one slender hand. "You—you can't keep putting yourself in danger for me."

"She'll release me soon. A few more talismans, that's it, and then she'll grant me my wish. You'll have your body back in no time."

"A body will do me no good if you're just a shell of yourself. A body will do me no good if you're *dead.*"

"I'd come back for you. As a spirit. We could be like this, forever." Flint motioned to the dusty world surrounding them.

Daisy glared at the floor. "That's not funny."

"Who said I was kidding?"

"It's no *good* like this, Flint. It's no good." She was crying now—weeping without any tears to shed.

"Hey, hey. It's alright. I'll be alright." He reached for her, but there was nothing to embrace. His face came close to hers. The longing there, growing heavy between them, cut sharp as a knife.

Daisy spoke so softly, then, that Jae scarcely heard it at all. "I hate this. I hate it here. I want to be somewhere else."

"Do you want to come outside? It's Midsummer. We can go and have some fun."

Daisy only shook her head.

So . . .

This was Flint Barrow.

A man who had fallen in love with a ghost.

A thousand feelings were swimming inside of Jae, and she couldn't name most of them. She had to find the rest of the gang, but the thought was impossibly quiet beneath the roar in her mind. *Flint loves a ghost.* She couldn't keep her mind from steeping in the strangeness of it all.

She was still lost in the revelation when a freezing hand closed around her ankle.

Jae's captor yanked, bringing her to the ground. The impact knocked her breath out. Hot fear flooded Jae's body. For a moment, she couldn't even scream. Whoever had taken hold of her was now dragging her across the gravelly ground.

"Halston!" she cried. "Gryff!"

Jae was on her stomach, and though she was struggling with all her might, she couldn't roll around and see who had grabbed her. Grit and tiny rocks cut her skin. To hell with blending in. She clawed at the ground, wildly kicking her free leg, but her captor held fast. They hauled her over a stretch of earth, then through an opening in the side of the house. Jae kept writhing as they dragged her over grimy floorboards and into a large, empty room.

Finally, the hand released her leg. Jae placed her palms on the floor, ready to push herself upright and fly out of here, but it was no use. She was surrounded.

All around her—leering at her like flames in the darkness—were ghosts. The room was impossibly cold, cold as the woods when Pa had been taken away. Beneath this throng of ghosts, Jae felt as small as she'd ever been.

The spirits' gazes were somehow empty and angry at the same time. There were six in all—a woman with an eternal bruise around one ghostly eye, a few girls around twelve to eighteen, with gray splotches on their skin, thin lips and hollow cheeks, and a middle-aged man.

The man was glaring sharply at her. The spirit was tall and muscular, and Jae could make out scars and pockmarks on his face. In his eyes was a fury so deep and powerful it dug all the way to Jae's bones.

The man's face was cold and cruel, but all of the women appeared to be frozen in terror—eyes like the full moon, mouths agape.

Why were they afraid? They had no reason to be scared.

Without looking away from Jae, the male ghost said, "She's alive."

And though Jae should have been the one to cry out, all of the women began to scream.

Jae should have tried to run, but she threw her hands over her ears. Their shrieks were louder than a train barreling off its tracks, and the sound burned like boiling lead. She waited for them to stop, but they just kept screaming. And screaming. And screaming.

And then, they came at her.

White-hot panic tore through Jae's body. She began thrashing beneath them. The cold swallowed her, a thousand times worse than it had been when she'd hidden from the raiders who took Pa. So cold she could hardly keep moving.

The ghosts kept grabbing for her, reaching, desperate to take hold of her clothes or limbs. Every couple seconds, she felt the grip of a solid hand, but mostly, the ghosts kept passing through her . . . and it bought Jae a few seconds of clear, beautiful relief.

Concentration. Ghosts had to try very hard to grab something. So far, they were failing. And she could keep it that way.

So she started making a ruckus.

She started screaming nonsense, wailing. She bashed the floor with her fists and kicked like a pillbug on its back. *Distract them.*

A hand grasped at her throat.

Jae reached for her neck. The ghost of the furious-looking man had a hold on her. He didn't stop staring down at her. Jae tried to grab his forearm, pry his deathly grip from her throat, but already the dizziness was laying waste to her mind. A fire swallowed her chest, spreading, growing. She couldn't breathe. His focus must have been unshakable. She was—

"Pa! Let her go!" somebody screamed.

Something flew through the air and crashed into the wall. The ghost released Jae's throat, and she scrambled backward on her hands and feet. A flimsy old chair lay on the floor, newly split in two, and the ghosts had all turned to look at it.

It bought her just a moment, but that was all she needed.

Flint hurried into the room, looking urgent but not frightened, followed by Daisy, who began screaming at her Pa, asking what he was doing. Jae barely had time to regain her breath when Flint bent over her and lifted her off the ground like she weighed nothing.

And Jae had no choice but to trust him fully.

Flint sped with her across the room, then into a hallway, into a second room, and out the lopsided, doorless frame Jae had first been dragged through. The night air's kiss was the greatest mercy she'd ever known. Together, they escaped the house.

But when they were far enough away from it, Flint didn't set Jae down gently. He didn't exactly drop her, but when he spilled her on the ground, it took her a moment to gather herself back up.

She was gasping, breathing harder than she reckoned she ever had before. Tears pricked at her eyes. Would the ghost's chokehold leave a bruise on her throat that showed through the spirium?

Flint narrowed his eyes on her.

What was he going to do? Should she thank him? Run from him? Both?

Flint thrust his pointer finger at the house. "Listen. You stay away from the Audley house. You hear me? Don't you *ever* snoop around there again."

Jae said nothing. The most she could manage was a terse nod.

Flint blew a puff of air from his lips. "And I'm sorry to be so frank, but you're doing a terrible job at passing for a ghost. I don't care what your business is—I suggest you leave this place as soon as you can. Some of the ghosts here," he said, pointing to the house once again, "ain't as nice as I am." Without another word, he turned from her and headed back to the town.

Jae wanted to run after him, but her body wouldn't obey. The ordeal had sapped the last of her strength, and she collapsed on the ground. For a moment, she faced the stars and gulped down the night air like it was clear, cool water.

What had she just seen?

Gods above, what had she just lived through?

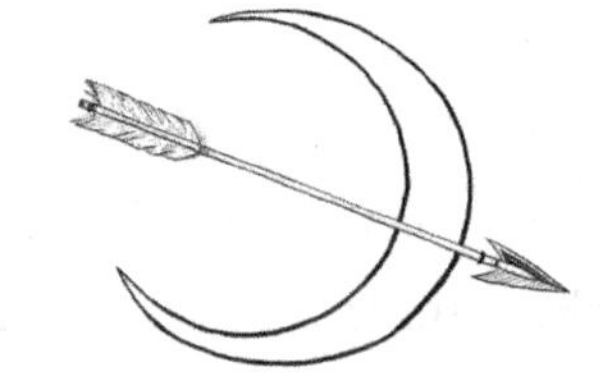

Chapter 25

*H*alston had to pace himself once they left Mr. Elm's place. He spared a quick glance at his hands. Still translucent. Ghostly.

Where did they even begin?

They'd split up. Jae was to stay behind and talk to Mr. Elm, Tsashin and Lorelin would go north, and Gryff would go west. Halston and Hodge traipsed down the east side of town in silence.

"Well," Hodge said at last, "who do we speak to?"

Halston shrugged. "Might as well start with anybody."

They made their way toward the center of the town. Ghosts filled the streets, bustling with merriment. There were far more of them now than there had been on the night they'd arrived. Halston hadn't seen a crowd like this in ages.

There were so many of them. How were they supposed to find the others?

Halston began drifting toward the crowd, paying mind to his motions and trying to move with that wispy softness that the others ghosts had. Still, he was struggling to concentrate on his actions. How could he when all of this surrounded him?

Beneath the turning stars, the ghosts continued gathering. A group of them started cheering.

"To the summer!" somebody hooted, and the others whooped in response.

That's right. It was June.

Midsummer. It had been years since Halston had celebrated it. But every once in a while, he and the gang had come across towns where folks still had time for such things. They'd build bonfires, dance, and drink freely, celebrating how June made the whole world swell with life.

There was no fire here, but there *was* music. In the center of the crowd, there was a quartet of young men singing without any instruments to accompany their tune. All the same, it was a lovely song. They layered their voices in just the right way, and Halston couldn't help but wonder how much time and patience it had taken them to master their harmonies.

The cheering grew into a joyous uproar, then the ghosts broke into a dance. It had been ages since Halston had heard so much laughter. And in spite of himself, a thousand warm winds stirred inside him.

The songs sounded old. Mosaic pieces of a time long before Halston's life. As he perused the dancing crowd, he caught snippets of each story the songs told—wolves running, free and wild, loves that stood like pillars of stone against the storms of time, lost ships and wagons going west and rivers that wrapped around the entire world. Stories made deathless in each song.

They stood in place for a while, listening to the music and watching the ghosts spin and leap through the street. Halston didn't notice it at first, but he'd been tapping his foot in time to the tunes.

A female ghost with a cheeky grin stepped out of the crowd. She curtsied at Halston. "Care to dance?"

"*What?*" he blurted without thinking.

The ghost blinked in surprise—perhaps she wasn't used to that sort of response. "C'mon. It'll be fun." She was pretty. Once upon a time, she must have had that sort of girlish, rose-tinged beauty that made the poets and painters leap.

Halston thought of Jae's beauty. Wild. Storm-like. Unkempt.

Halston almost froze in place. He saw other ghosts dancing close to one another, hands clasped together. Maybe it was a struggle for ghosts to touch earthly things, but touching one another was just fine.

Still, even after they'd swallowed the potion, they'd found that their bodies still felt warm. They didn't radiate bitter cold, the way that ghosts did.

"No, thank you." Halston tried to keep his voice from trembling. "You see, dancing . . . it reminds me of my wife. *She's* still alive, and . . ." He tried to feign a catch in his throat.

The ghost girl gave Halston a wide-eyed look. For a moment, Halston was worried that she wasn't buying his disguise, but then she just gave him a sympathetic smile. "I'm sorry to hear that. You're newly dead, then?"

Newly dead. "Yeah."

"You must have died awfully close by," she said, though she didn't quite sound suspicious yet.

"We did. I'd . . . I'd rather not talk about it."

"I'm sorry about that." The girl tipped her chin up at the crowd. "I'm sure you'll be pulled back to haunting your deathplace soon, but I'm glad you found your way here. You picked a good night to drift by."

The other ghosts were dancing with zeal, caught up in the music and laughter. Some were dancing on the rooftops or floating above the buildings and hooting like drunk men in a saloon. Others stood amongst the flowers scattered about the streets, watching the dancers with wistful smiles.

"I don't get it," Halston said. "What's . . . what's there to celebrate?"

The girl laughed. "No reason not to. Hell, I'd say we have all the more reason to celebrate. It ain't like we'll be stuck here forever, right? Might as well make it bearable till somebody breaks the curse."

So this was death, then. It seemed it didn't make vengeful ghosts out of everybody. Like Jem, the dead could be patient and cheerful and kind.

And this flood of dancing, hollering, laughing ghosts were proof death itself wasn't strong enough to take hope away. The thought of that filled Halston with something brighter than the burning stars.

"Do you know Flint Barrow?" he finally asked. He figured there was no point in being subtle about it.

"Sure I do. Nice fella." She tilted her head. "Are you here to haunt him?"

"*What?*"

She chuckled. "I guess not, huh? I was just curious. It's happened before. Some fella came back here after death, complaining that Flint stole something from him."

"Stole what?" *Treasure hunter.* Did Flint Barrow raid tombs, the living, or both?

"Not sure. Could've been anything. Mr. Elm says that Flint steals all sorts of stuff. I don't know him too well . . . spends all his time in the Audley house whenever he's here," she said, then lowered her voice. "Stay away from that place, by the way. Those folks *always* gave me the creeps."

It was then Halston spied a shadowy figure with twin braids, watching him from the frontside of a ramshackle building. Jae. He almost called out to her, but then, he got a better look at her face.

The look in her eyes was utterly hollow, like her mind and soul were elsewhere . . . somewhere far, far away from here. She was petrified. Over the past couple of months, he'd seen Jae when she was frightened, but not like this. This was the sort of fear that didn't spur one to run or fight, but to go still.

Whether she needed him now or not, Halston had to go to her. "I've got to go," he said, stepping away from the ghost girl.

She started to protest, but he was already on his way. He passed around the crowd of ghosts, careful not to pass directly through any of them, though it was difficult to dodge them. The celebration went on, and none of the ghosts seemed likely to slow down or go quiet just yet.

"Jae!"

She tipped her head up only slightly. Halston reached her, and Hodge followed.

"What happened?"

"I found Flint."

Although she'd stated it mildly, as if she'd just found something as simple as a cairn of rocks by a riverside, the harrowed look in her eyes kept Halston from speaking right away.

"Where'd he go?" Hodge blurted.

"I don't know." Her voice was dull, like somebody talking in their sleep. "But . . . something happened."

"What?" he asked desperately.

Something heavy seemed to hold Jae's tongue for a moment, then she finally told them what had happened without meeting their eyes: how she'd followed Flint to the strange house sitting apart from the rest of town. When she spoke of the spirit who had dragged her through his halls by the ankle, chills fell over him, but when she told him how he'd wrapped his hand around her throat, roaring heat took their place.

"Where'd he go?" asked Hodge.

Jae gestured vaguely to the north. "That way, but I lost track of him. He wasn't real pleased with me for going into the house. And he figured me out. He knows I ain't really . . ." She waved a hand over her chest. *Dead.*

Their plan would still work as long as the phantom townsfolk didn't know they were ghosts. They just had to keep from being chased out long enough to confront Flint . . . But now, they'd have to be careful that they didn't give him a reason to blow their cover.

"Listen," said Hodge. "Jae, I'm real sorry that happened, but we can't waste any more time. We've gotta find him."

Hodge started off in the direction Jae had pointed out, and they followed after him quickly. Along the way, all Jae could talk about was Flint and the ghost girl. *Daisy,* he called her. She told them every detail about what she'd seen, right down to the way Daisy had begged Flint not to return to *her.* Whoever that was.

"What's this ghost girl got to do with anything?" asked Hodge.

"Hodge, he ain't . . ." She hesitated for a few long moments, glancing up at the moon. "I don't think Flint is *dangerous.* We may be able to reason with him."

"He's in love with a ghost. That doesn't mean he can't be dangerous."

"He saved me. I . . . I don't know. I don't feel right about threatening him."

"Noble, huh?" Hodge said with a frown. "Well then. Maybe you're right. Maybe we *can* reason with him. Either way, I ain't leavin' this town without our knife, or without having some idea about where it is. Now let's go find him!"

They found Gryff easily. He was lingering by an old cabin, staring at the ground and looking lost in thought. It took them longer to find Tsashin and Lorelin, but they did at last. Lorelin was caught up in a conversation with two ghosts around her age, laughing and joking, while Tsashin sat idly by, gaze running across the bounty of flowers littering the street.

Jae described Flint to them all as best she could, and with that, they set out to find where he'd gone. They spent so long walking through the crowd that the faces and figures seemed to start blending together.

But after several rounds of walking along the edges of the street, Jae pointed. "That's him."

In spite of his height, Flint carried himself discreetly. A speck, a shadow. He was standing a good distance off from the main street, leaning against the porch of a log cabin.

Halston's feet started moving before his mind could catch up to them. He reminded himself to be slow, like a coyote stalking through the grass.

Flint was watching the bobbing spirits with keen eyes. In his hand was a knife with a short blade. He was fidgeting with it, moving it in quick, round motions like he was trying to cut a circle from the sky.

Halston squinted. No, this wasn't their knife. This one definitely had a handle, and it lacked the unmarred, pearly sheen of adamite.

Flint stood in sight of the ghosts, but behind him, the cabin sitting next to the one where he leaned formed a narrow alleyway. If Lorelin got in front of him, and the others stood behind, they'd have him cornered.

"We'll have to be quiet," Halston whispered. The ghosts were still dancing, hopelessly lost in their merriment, and he figured it would take a real ruckus to take them from their revels. But Halston's gang had a knack for creating a ruckus.

Lorelin flashed the rest of them an impish grin. "Who wants to bet me I can get it out of him in five minutes?"

They'd come too far to start making a game out of this, but Hodge still joined in. "Ain't your record fifteen?"

"Ten, actually." She tilted her head. "I'll bet he's shy. He looks like the stuttering type."

He definitely *didn't* look like the stuttering type, but Halston didn't say so.

"I don't know, Lorelin," Gryff said. "Somethin' tells me a living man won't exactly fumble over a dead woman."

Jae and the Harney brothers exchanged a quick look.

Lorelin lifted her chin with an air of self-assurance. "I'm an extra special dead woman."

"Eh," Hodge said with a shrug.

Lorelin shot him a glare. "If we hadn't worked our fingers to the bone for these potions, I'd stomp on you. Now then. If I move my hair from my right shoulder to my left, then I'll need you to back me up. I'll coax him into the shadows over there. Get into the alley, alright?"

They exchanged terse words of agreement, then Lorelin traipsed in Flint's direction, slinking toward him like a fox.

They took a long way around the buildings, circling around the two cabins, careful not to draw Flint's attention, or the townsfolk's. The space between the cabins was wide but short, so Halston merely poked his head around the corner to watch while the others waited behind them.

Flint had his back turned to the alleyway. Lorelin was giggling, moving fluidly, accenting every word with a wave of her hands, but Flint seemed to be getting stiffer by the second.

Lorelin talked. And talked, and talked.

It was becoming painful. Never, even once, had Halston seen Lorelin look *frustrated* when trying to sweet-talk a foe or potential ally.

Flint said something to Lorelin at last, and as he spoke, Lorelin draped her wispy hair over her left shoulder.

Halston's heart sank. He should have been ready for this. More than once, they'd had to resort to force, but still . . . he'd dared to hope that it would stay in their past.

But now, there was nothing to do but proceed.

Carefully, the gang shuffled into the alley. It didn't take long for Flint to turn around and spot the gang approaching him, and a befuddled look came over his face. Halston's insides twisted when the confused look turned into one of exasperation, then he realized it was aimed at Jae.

"Miss," he said to Jae, his tone courteous but firm, "I promise you, I wasn't trying to be uncouth when I told you to get out of here. It's for your own good."

Jae merely stood there, stiff as a lamppost. Hodge tensed. Bracing himself to leap, no doubt. The potions had made their guns look no more formidable than puffs of smoke, but they could still shoot.

But Halston raised a hand—just enough to signal to Hodge to wait. Something told him that there was no need for threats, or intimidation yet.

"We need to speak to you," Halston said with as much tact as he could muster.

Flint folded his arms. *"All* of you are alive, aren't you?" he said, a little too loudly for comfort. "Did somebody send you? If it's Radcliffe, *please* tell him that he's out of luck and his pearl is long gone—"

"Nobody sent us. We've got our own reasons to talk to you," said Halston.

Flint smirked. "Heard about me through the grapevine, eh? I'll spare you your time, then. I'm not the son of a god. I'm not an exiled prince from across the sea. And I'm definitely not an heir to a lost city of gold." His words sounded rehearsed to the point of perfection. "If I was, then my debt would be gone."

"Was it to Sterling Byrd?" asked Lorelin. "If so, you don't have to worry about that. He died more than a month ago."

"I know," said Flint.

Lorelin blinked. "Then . . . who are you in debt to?"

Flint waved a hand. "It's not important. Listen—who sent you? Don't beat around the bush, please. You folks look like you've got somewhere to be. I'd hate to waste your time."

It was tough to say if the sentiment was sincere. Still, Halston gave him a fair answer. "Did Sterling give you an adamite blade?" He left it at that. No point in naming a price, no reason to talk it over . . . like gentlemen did—especially if they wound up having to take it or get an answer by force.

Recognition flashed in Flint's dark eyes. "The snapped blade? With the runes on the flat of it?"

Halston did his best not to start celebrating within just yet. "Yes."

A painfully long moment of silence unfolded. "Sure did. He had me hold onto it for a while."

"*Where is it?*" Lorelin, Gryff, and Hodge all blurted at once.

For the first time that night, Flint looked something close to frightened. He tried shrinking closer to the cabin. "I don't have it anymore."

"Then where is it?" asked Hodge, gliding closer.

"When I heard that Sterling died . . . there was no reason for me to hold onto it. I . . . I gave it to Rogue." His gaze swept over them all, and then he began speaking a mile-a-minute. "It helped pay off some of my debt to her, and—"

"*You what?!*" Hodge cried.

It happened far too quickly.

Hodge had leapt in Flint's direction, his shooting hand braced to grab Flint's lapel. Reflexively, Flint had lashed out with the knife.

Hodge let out a roar of pain. In return, Flint yelped in alarm, then darted between Jae and Lorelin and into the crowd of ghosts.

"Hodge!" Halston cried. He jumped for his brother, half-expecting Hodge's hand to fly to his stomach, staunching blood from a fresh wound.

But when Halston got closer, he nearly keeled over with sheer relief. They'd been lucky. The blade hadn't slashed anything vital.

But even though his skin was still pale and sheer from the spirium, the blood pooling from his cut was easy to see—the bright, burning red of a living man.

And now, the eyes of several dozen startled ghosts were fixed on them all.

Chapter 26

"*Living!*" somebody shouted.

It took a moment for the song and scattered laughter to cease completely. A few angry shouts took their place, but mostly there were startled cries. The ghosts pinned their gazes on the gang, then plunged in their direction as a horde, moving swiftly as a raging river.

Gryff's reptilian eyes went wide "*Run!*" he yelled.

And they ran. Like scared rabbits, like startled bats, like the gods-damned thieves they were, they ran.

They were close to the edge of the woods. Up ahead, there was the start of a trail leading from the town to the woods, disappearing into the dark safety of the trees. Without wasting another second, they tore down the path.

They weren't even thinking about blending in. As soon as a hundred ghostly eyes had leapt to Hodge's bleeding hand, it was over. There was no remaining in the Shroud.

"They can't leave," Jae hissed between brisk, labored breaths. "They can't leave the town."

They just had to make it to the woods, then. A little further. Just a little further.

Halston risked a backward glance. Flint was long gone, fleeing town in a different direction or lost in the ghostly mob. Halston met the stares of a hundred scorned ghosts, and what he saw sent a pang of surprise through him.

They weren't the faces of angry men, but desperate ones. He could see it in their eyes. The spirits—people—wanted to protect themselves, their loved ones, from living outsiders who would violate their peace, gaggle and gawk at the cursed souls, their haunted town, their inability to move on.

And Halston couldn't blame them. All they wanted was to preserve their solitude. It was all they had left.

But it didn't matter whether or not they knew that Halston understood, because the ghosts were coming at them fast.

A trio of spirits popped up in their path, reaching out for them, or perhaps motioning for them to stop. Their hands began swatting at the gang before they could all veer away from them. An icy hand seized Halston's arm. He hollered, and the ghost lost focus. His hand sank into Halston's shoulder, and the cold nearly sent him doubling over. It was like a knife of pure ice biting into him. The ghost met Halston's eyes, and there was a horror-stricken look on his face, and Halston thought the ghost might have been scared he'd hurt him.

But Halston didn't look at the ghost again. They kept running. The rickety structures and log cabins whizzed past them, and the cries of the townsfolk got fainter and fainter. When they reached the treeline, Halston peered back at the Shroud once more.

The ghosts were no longer chasing them. They merely stood there in dismal clusters, helplessly watching the fleeting forms of Halston and his gang. For a second, Halston imagined himself in their place, watching his own ghostly figure sprinting into the woods. He didn't know what to make of their faces. Every one of them looked ready to curse or cry or both.

There was no time to dwell on it, but Halston would remember that sea of wistful eyes for all his days.

They escaped into the cover of branches and thick shadows. Still, they didn't slow down. They charged over the twisting trail until their chests felt ready to burst and the air tasted stale and thin in their mouths.

Halston was the first to come to a standstill. "Stop," he gasped out between quick, heavy breaths. When they finally stopped in the middle of the woods, he wasn't sure why they'd bothered running this far, but part of him was glad they had.

The trail was straighter here, but the forest was denser. The trees grew so closely that there was hardly any space between them at all. At least here, it would be tough to stray from the path.

Only then did it really sink in.

They'd failed. They'd been run out of town with empty hands.

The other half of the blade was somewhere else, and there was nothing they could do.

Halston raised his eyes to the canopy of branches, to the barely visible sky above. The trees seemed to shake their arms in contempt. *Failure.*

They stood and caught their breath in the dead-quiet woods. Should they even move on? Why continue to face these woods and everything lurking in them when the blade was beyond their reach now?

Where on earth were they supposed to go?

"Dammit!" Hodge lifted his hand. The bleeding had stopped, but clammy blood caked his knuckles and wrist. The red was prominent on his translucent skin. He began pacing across the trail. "This ain't good. This *ain't* good."

"Settle down, will you? We made it out okay," said Gryff.

Hodge spun on his heels. "I ain't settling down! Our knife is *gone!*"

Gryff flexed a hand, claws glinting in the scanty starlight. "It ain't *gone,* it's just not where we thought it'd be. Gripin' won't do you a bit of good, so how's about we put a plan together instead of workin' ourselves up?"

Hodge waved an arm in the direction of the Shroud. "What *plan*, Gryff? In case you haven't noticed, we're just about out of options here."

"We *aren't,* and if you don't get a grip *right now,* I'll box your ears, so I suggest you *listen* to me. We've got a name," Gryff said. "*Rogue.* That don't count for nothin'."

"Do you know who *Rogue* is?" Hodge asked.

"No," Gryff said confidently.

"Then it sure as hell counts for nothin', thanks."

"Hodge, stop it." Lorelin took a step toward him. "Gryff's right. Complaining and *quarreling* won't help."

The footsteps crunching behind them should have alarmed Halston more than they did.

He whirled around, and staring back at him with a grim, puzzled look . . . was Flint.

Halston froze. Where on earth had he come from? Halston had looked back several times, and he hadn't caught so much as a glimpse of Flint running after them.

The others went tense. Gryff's hand drifted closer to his rifle strap. Hodge fingered the knife in his belt.

"Why did you follow us?" Halston knew that his frustration was leaking into his tone—but he hoped that his budding fear wasn't apparent. He couldn't blame Flint for trying to defend himself, but still, if Flint had been an inch closer, or moved his knife with an ounce more force, he could have hurt Hodge terribly . . . or worse. "What are you doing here?"

Hodge was fine, but now, all their travels had been for nothing. Flint Barrow had given away the key back to Halston's world.

Lia. His mother.

With the knife, his chance of finding them was miniscule. Without it, it was nonexistent.

"I mean you no harm. The spirits didn't send me," Flint said coolly, then motioned to Hodge's still-bloody hand. "Are you hurt?"

"I'm fine," Hodge muttered, so softly Halston knew Flint could barely hear it.

"I'm sorry," Flint said with unmistakable sincerity. "I was on edge, and when you came at me . . . I should have been more careful, but . . . I wasn't sure what else to do."

Hodge ignored his apology.

Flint cleared his throat, then faced Halston again. "I want to make you an offer."

Was this a trick? "Go on."

"You killed Sterling, didn't you?" Flint said, with a note of surprising hopefulness, though something in his eyes told Halston that he already knew the answer.

"Yeah," said Jae. She must have figured there was no use lying about it.

"In that case, you did me a favor." He paused. "Did you kill Argus, too?"

Jae raised a hand, and Halston understood that she was gesturing for them to be silent. If Argus had promised Flint a resurrection for his lover, then that meant the outlaw's death had ruined Flint's hope.

"Because if you did, then I owe you even more," Flint said. "Sterling had me robbing graves for him for a couple of years. The first time I was late on an assignment, he told me that if it happened again, he'd have Argus bring Daisy back to life—so he could kill her himself and make me watch."

Stoney silence held his tongue for a while, then he continued. "I promised it would never happen again, but that was a vow I couldn't keep. On my last assignment, I *was* late. I thought up a plan to talk myself out of it, but I was certain Argus would do what he promised. But when I showed up to meet him for my last job, two days past what we'd agreed upon . . . he never came." His throat bobbed with a hard swallow.

It was Jae's turn to jump in. "Think he was bluffing?"

"I don't know, but I was doing everything I could not to find out," said Flint.

In Flint's eyes, there was an understanding almost strong enough to startle Halston. Another man haunted by the distant spirit of Sterling Byrd. Flint's duster jacket concealed most of his skin, but beneath his clothing, Halston wondered if there were scars from Sterling's whip.

"Argus and Sterling ain't what you owe us for." Hodge held up his hand, drawing everybody's attention to his still-fresh cut. "You already gave up what we needed."

"*Hodge,*" Halston whispered.

"Why did Sterling give you our blade, anyway?" asked Hodge.

"He . . . thought it would be safe with me," Flint said slowly. "And he told me that he'd kill Daisy if I ever lost it. I'm sorry it's gone, but I've come to make you an offer."

He spoke with such calm that Halston was struggling to keep up his anger. Flint hadn't known all that knife had meant to them. Until tonight, he hadn't known they existed. Any reasonable soul would have tried to find a buyer for half an adamite knife.

"Alright," Hodge said at last. "What's your offer, then?"

"Like I said: I sold half the knife to Rogue. That blade alone subtracted half my debt to her. But she may be willing to give it back to you."

"Who is Rogue?" asked Gryff.

"A witch," said Flint. "She issues challenges in exchange for . . . well, anything one desires, I imagine. She lives in an underground palace at the bottom of a caldera. *Telin,* she calls it."

"Telin?" Jae said, narrowing her eyes in what could only be disbelief. "*Telin* is *real?*"

Flint's lips drew upward into a joyless grin. "It sure is." He went on before Halston could ask for an explanation. "She'll give you a challenge in exchange for your knife, but listen here . . . I don't encourage you to go after her. If you can get by another way, I think you should do it. I'll turn back now and never bother you again. But if you really do need that knife—"

"We need it," said Halston. There was no question about it.

"How badly?" asked Flint.

Halston didn't speak again, but something in his eyes must have given it away.

Flint said, "Hmm. I'm sorry I asked. Something tells me that nothing short of death will stop you."

That was the truth. As sure as the sun rose, as certain as the wind blew, it was the truth.

"What sort of *challenge* would she give us?" asked Halston.

Flint just shrugged. "It depends. Everything she's given me has involved stealing."

Halston snorted. He'd stolen enough for one lifetime, but for his key home, he could do it again. Once more.

Besides, after years of service under Sterling's watch, a challenge from a witch seemed almost merciful.

It was then Halston saw Jae taking out her map. "Telin," she whispered. The map went blank, then the road to Telin began to unfold.

Flint's amazed eyes stayed glued to the paper as he spoke. "*That's* a treasure, right there."

Jae shot him a frown, then pointedly put her map away.

Flint chuckled. "No worries. I don't steal anything that Rogue hasn't told me to steal. But if I were you, I wouldn't go into Telin on your own."

"Why not?" Lorelin asked.

Flint crossed his arms and tapped his fingers on one elbow, perhaps searching for the right words. "Rogue enjoys . . . disorder," he said at last. "When travelers come to her palace for the first time, she . . . likes to manipulate the palace walls. She has complete dominion over her halls, and when people first seek her, she likes to create . . . obstacles for them."

"Obstacles?" Tsashin piped in, her voice even smaller than usual. "Like what?"

"Well, for me I had to cross a whirlpool, and then get past a monster that was . . ." Flint scratched his head. "The best way I can describe it is if a goat, a lizard, and a god of fire found a way to meld themselves together."

An image of the monster knit together in Halston's mind, and he pushed it away at once. "So we'd have to battle that ourselves?"

"No," Flint replied. "Not if you were with me. I've passed her initial test, and if I led us there, we could enter freely."

Halston tried to steady his mind. The possibilities were roiling through him, visions of the near-future, of everything Telin could possibly be. How could they reason with a witch who sowed discord and strife? Would Rogue conjure up beasts and perils for them anyway, even if they went with Flint? What sort of challenge would she give them? Was the conduit further from their reach than ever before?

But if this was the only chance they had . . .

As Halston was considering it all, Flint spoke again. "Well, I'm headed to Telin one way or another. You can follow me if you like, or not. Again . . . I wouldn't get involved with Rogue, but if there's no other way . . ."

"There's no other way," Halston said firmly. When he met his brother's eyes, he knew that they didn't have to say it out loud.

For them, there was no other choice.

"Alright, then," Flint said. "Telin it is."

———

It took them a while to find a spot where the trees grew far enough apart that they'd have space for their bedrolls. Everyone was too tired to bother with a fire. Jae insisted on taking the first watch that night. Flint made his own camp about a dozen yards away from the others, and he seemed to fall asleep faster than anyone Halston had ever met. Somehow, he looked alert even in unconsciousness, lying stiff as a board with his arms at his side, as though the slightest rustle would rouse him at once.

Halston certainly didn't trust him fully, but he wasn't worried he was plotting against them. They had no choice but to follow him, and Flint seemed too absorbed in his own affairs to pay those of the gang too much mind.

Besides, Halston couldn't forget that Flint had saved Jae's life.

Sleep came to him easily that night, but later on, Halston woke to somebody shaking him by the shoulder.

He came to his senses and found Jae leaning over him with a wild glint in her eyes. Halston shot upright. "What is it?"

"*Telin*," said Jae. "Listen here. I ain't heard of this Rogue witch before, but I *have* heard about Telin, and . . . Hal. I ain't sure about this."

Halston frowned. "Why not?"

Jae began nervously fidgeting with the hem of her shirt. "Well . . . I've heard a few stories about Telin, and it's different in all of 'em. Sometimes it's a maze, sometimes it's a castle or something, but there's usually some witch or warlock or monster who lives there and gives challenges to travelers, just like Flint said. But it's stuff like stealing a star out of the sky or finding a seed in a whole sea of clovers. Always something ridiculous or impossible. And if somebody wins the challenge, they're granted a wish."

"That's—"

"You didn't let me finish," Jae said with an urgent flick of her hand. "In some of the stories, the folks *don't* win. And then . . . horrible things happen. They go home and find that their entire families have forgotten them. Or they see monsters and demons following them everywhere, and they lose their minds waiting for them to attack. Stuff like that."

This *was* the Outlands. Halston supposed he shouldn't have been surprised. "Did you . . . Were they true?"

"I didn't think so. They were always silly to me. Sounded like stories kids would tell to scare each other."

Halston was relieved to hear that . . . but even in the most absurd sounding stories, there were often grains of truth.

"Silly or not, I've got a bad feeling about it," Jae added quickly.

"Flint says the witch has him steal for her," said Halston. "If it's no worse than that, then I'll take it. As for the monsters in the palace . . . well, we've faced worse. Besides, we won't have to face them if Flint is with us."

Jae said nothing to that. Surely, Jae knew that nothing was going to stop him now. They'd come too far.

"Hate to say it, Hal," Jae murmured, "but you've gotten yourself into a real mess here."

Halston couldn't help but laugh. "It's been a mess this whole time, Jae. I can't imagine this witch will make it much worse."

"You don't know that," Jae said without meeting his gaze.

Halston placed a hand on Jae's wrist. It was then he told her: "We've come far. It's been years. And I don't have forever, Jae. I have to get the blade back. They're waiting for me."

Slowly, Jae glanced up at him. *What if they aren't?* her eyes seemed to whisper.

Even if it meant he'd starve, bleed, and burn, he had to try. For Lia. For his mother. For his ravaged world, waiting for him on the other side of Median.

Jae flexed her fingers and said, "If that witch sends a demon to come and haunt you, I'll toss her to the wolves."

Halston grinned. "I don't think it'll come to that."

Jae squeezed his hand. "There's no talking you out of this, is there?"

He traced his thumb along the side of her wrist. "I'm afraid not."

"I kind of figured. Just thought it was worth a try."

And so they let the night pass them by, waiting for the dawn, and all that came after it.

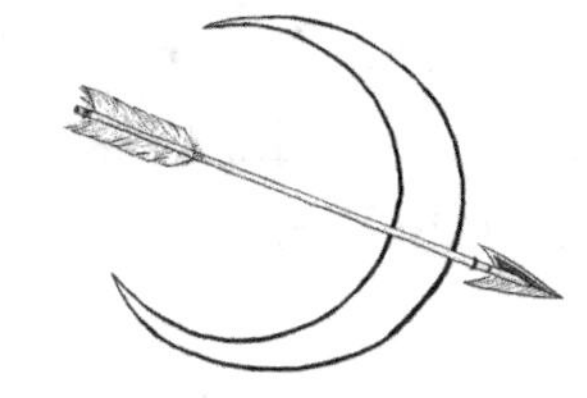

Chapter 27

That morning, Jae woke up with a start. The sun stung her eyes. Gods, she'd dozed off on her watch! Trying not to curse, she rubbed the tender spot on her cheek where her fingers had been cradling her chin. Already, her back was hurting from sleeping slouched over.

Jae had dozed off in the shadow of a broad-trunked fir, just a yard from where Halston still slept soundly. Moss carpeted the bittersweet-smelling bark. The morning was bright, not a cloud in the sky, and from the gentle slope on which they'd camped, she could make out the faint outline of the dirt road beyond the trees.

She should have woken somebody else sooner, but she'd been certain that sleep wouldn't find her, anyway. Visions of those vengeful ghosts had haunted her some of the night, but they'd been overcome by thoughts of Telin and the witch who lived there. She wouldn't grant herself more time to dwell on that haunted house. Because the second she had a chance, she was going to wring every drop of information about Telin out of Flint.

She'd be polite as pie, of course. After last night, she owed him that much.

Maybe it really wasn't half as bad as the children's fables she'd heard all those years ago, but if there was any chance they would leave that place accursed, then she had to find out right away.

Sometime during the night, the spirium had worn off. Gryff's scaly green skin returned, and the others regained their healthy glow, their color, their visible veins. Jae was relieved to look like herself again.

Now, it was time to wake Flint and speak to him. She stood, then surveyed the sleeping figures of her companions . . . only to find that Flint was not among them. There was no sign of him, his supplies, or his bedroll.

Where *was* he?

Jae wandered over to where he'd slept that night. He'd stationed himself a ways off from the group, but he'd still been in their sight. All that remained was a patch of bare earth where he'd swept aside the pine needles and twigs to sleep.

Jae *did* curse then.

She took off her pack and painstakingly rummaged through all her belongings. Yes, everything was still there. Gryff was a light sleeper, so she prayed they still had all the silver.

Footfalls seized her attention. Jae turned to where they were coming from. She narrowed her eyes. The steps were rustling the undergrowth to her right, and by the sound of them, whoever they belonged to had to be just a few yards away.

But there was nobody there. Just the empty air.

Until, directly *from* that empty air, Flint appeared carrying two dead rabbits by the ears.

Jae's scream woke everybody up.

The others all started shouting at once, leaping to their feet, drawing their guns. Embarrassment didn't strike her until they were all up and alert and staring at nothing but a frazzled girl and a young man holding a pair of dead animals.

"What's going on?" Halston gasped out.

". . . I didn't mean to startle you," Flint said. He faced the others, then announced, "Alright, just so there are no more surprises, let's get this out of the way. Everyone take a look at what I can do."

He was there for a moment, and then he wasn't. Flint's body, clothes, and even the rabbits he was holding vanished with him. A few seconds later, he reappeared a couple paces away, looking just as self-assured as before.

"Warlock?" asked Gryff, sounding almost amused.

Flint answered with a nod that was closer to a bow. "Really, it makes robbing a little *too* easy."

Of course—*this* was why Sterling had trusted him with the blade. If anyone tried to snatch it from him, all Flint had to do was disappear.

Flint passed Halston the rabbits, and everyone thanked him for catching them breakfast. Lorelin and Tsashin got a fire going, and Flint offered to head down to the Glenn River to refill the canteens and waterskins. Jae insisted on going with him.

She followed Flint into the woods and downhill. Before long, the hefty rush of the river greeted them. The silvery waters cut through a valley beneath, plentiful with summer runoff.

Flint bent over the river and dunked his canteen in the water. "You still look startled."

He spoke so agreeably that it was hard to feel upset with him for scaring her half to death. "I ain't startled," she lied. "And . . . thank you, by the way. For saving me last night."

"Don't mention it," Flint said, glancing down at his feet for a second.

Jae was trying to figure out the best way to bring up Telin, then decided that there was no point in trying to dress up her curiosities. "What *is* Telin? I've heard a million different things about it, and if you've seen it for real, then . . . I want to know what it is you're leading us into. Before we get ourselves killed."

That last word came out far harsher than she'd meant, but Flint didn't look taken aback. He just nodded in understanding.

Conduit or not, she couldn't let Halston wander into a place that might claim his life. Jae remembered how frightened Daisy had been talking to Flint about his debt to Rogue. Who knew what this young man had gotten himself into? If they weren't careful, he might drag them all headfirst into the same fate.

"Well," Flint said slowly. "If it helps, you won't *die*. Rogue . . . she doesn't *kill* anyone. I think she'd find that boring."

"I know about the challenges," said Jae. "In the stories about Telin, there's always a monster or warlock who gives them to travelers. But if they fail, awful things happen to them. Is that true?"

"Well, *I* haven't failed her yet. But . . . yes. Hearsay is that the price of failure is a curse."

"Then what are we going to do?"

Flint shrugged. "Don't fail, I guess."

"You ain't helping."

"Sorry. I thought you wanted the truth."

He was right. She didn't have a single right to get angry with him, and there was no talking Halston and Hodge out of going. She wasn't sure *anything* could scare them out of it, if it meant finding their way home.

"Alright," Jae said slowly, her voice soft under the rush of the river. She shifted back and forth on her feet, feeling the mud sink slightly under her boots. "So, Rogue is a witch who lives in Telin. What else?"

He tapped his fingers against his canteen. "Telin isn't her home, exactly. It's more of a prison. Somebody shackled her there, and she can't leave the grounds, but she can do as she pleases with her magic. She has some . . . connections to other worlds. She's sent me to several of them to get treasures for her."

"Other worlds?"

"Yes. They exist."

Jae knew that already, but now she was wondering if this witch might have a power similar to Sterling's . . . in addition to conjuring monsters and shaping the palace grounds to toy with new coming travelers, apparently. "She doesn't sound like a witch," said Jae. "She sounds more like a god."

Flint only shrugged. "She damn well could be."

If Flint had survived every challenge that Rogue had tasked him with, then maybe they would be up to the task as well. Maybe Jae wouldn't have to talk the Harney boys out of this after all.

Deeply, Jae breathed in the smell of the world around them. Mist on stone, pinewood, damp earth. "Why you, then?"

"Huh?"

"You told us we shouldn't get involved with Rogue, but you wouldn't stop us if it was what we really wanted. So why are *you* working for her if she's so terrible?"

Flint's shoulders sagged. "She told me that if I stole enough treasures for her, she could grant me a wish."

Jae made no reply. Flint was gazing thoughtfully at the river, as though he were considering wading into it. Lost in his own thoughts of Daisy, surely. Jae recalled Daisy's delicate face, her sad eyes, and wondered what she might look like if she regained her skin and bones.

Then, Jae shuddered at the thought of that icy grip on her ankle, how helpless she'd felt in Flint's arms when he'd hustled her out of that house. "Those ghosts that got ahold of me," she said. "Are they Daisy's folks?"

"Yes." Flint took a hurried sip of water from his canteen. "Her pa was a bastard in life and is still a bastard in death. I'm just trying to get her away from him, once and for all. He beat Daisy senseless while she was alive. Same for her mother and sisters."

Jae flinched. How could any man raise a fist against his own wife, his own daughters?

"I tried to kill him once," said Flint.

"*Kill* him?"

"I tried to send his spirit away. And I used that adamite blade of yours." Flint released a short breath. "I went right up to the open window and threw the blade at his spirit.

"It didn't work. It just passed right through him. He looked at it for a second, and then he forgot about it. Just left the room. So I picked it off the floor and got the hell out of there."

Jae thought back to what Mr. Elm had said, about how even *god-ore* couldn't set the ghosts free. She wondered why he hadn't passed that information on to his nephew.

"It's awfully brave of you," said Jae. "To visit Daisy while he's still there." She couldn't imagine summoning the courage to set foot in the Audley house a second time.

"I've gotten good at sneaking in. I just keep a window open. Climb out if he catches me. His fists can't hurt Daisy anymore, but his words can. The others . . . they've all forgotten who they were in life. Daisy says that all they do is roam the halls, now. She says that they don't even speak. Her pa remembers, though. Daisy's gotten good at hiding from him, but he's even warier of outsiders than the other ghosts." Flint motioned to Jae's neck. "He always enjoyed causing others fear. Dying didn't change that."

Jae pictured Daisy coming back to life, her skin turning rosy once more, eyes brightening, the grief draining from her heart. Maybe they'd ride off to somewhere peaceful together. Somewhere they wouldn't have to think of the Shroud or Daisy's pa ever again.

And she couldn't help but want that for them.

"Reckon it's none of my business but . . . how'd you meet her? I mean, you and Daisy . . . it's something out of a fireside tale. Ain't something you see every day."

Flint smiled shyly. "Well. I grew up. Went out into the world to find my fortune. My mother told me where my uncle lived, if I ever needed help. And I . . . I did wind up needing help. Took me ages to admit it, though.

"The Shroud had been cursed for several years when I finally came to it. It took me ages to warm up to it. It was just too strange, being around the dead all the time. But Daisy . . . I saw her floating on her porch one night, staring up at the sky like she was waiting for the moon itself to speak to her. And somehow, I *knew*. I went up to her, we spoke, and . . . and it was like I'd known her my whole life."

For a while, they sat and listened to the river. The air in the Outlands always seemed to have a chill laced through it, but today was unusually warm. Jae enjoyed the gentle kiss of the sun on her neck.

Eventually, Jae gave Flint a small smile. "You're kind. Doing all this so she can get her life back."

Flint chuckled. "My uncle says I'm mad. He doesn't have to remind me. I already know." He was grinning at the ground now. "I don't mind, though. Being mad for Daisy."

Jae nodded. Hmm. Maybe Flint was growing on her.

"What about you?" asked Flint, eyes flicking back in the direction of their campsite. "Have you ever loved anybody like that?"

Jae hesitated. "I don't know." Already, her cheeks were flaming hot.

"Well, if you're not sure, then I reckon the answer is no. If you find it one day, there won't be a shred of doubt in your mind."

Do you think we ever . . . make that doubt? For ourselves?

For gods' sake, why was she talking about all this with a stranger? They had better things to do. Working out a plan on where they were headed next, for one.

Still, there was something about this stranger that made him tough to ignore. He could speak of himself and his travels for hours, and Jae was sure she'd listen the whole way through.

"I don't get it," she said. "Sterling aside . . . why help us? Seems like you've got your own knots to untangle."

"That's true. But even if you hadn't a clue who I was a month ago, as far as I'm concerned, you still saved Daisy—which means you saved *me*." Then, his voice took on a teasing lilt. "Besides, I know a pack of stubborn pigheads when I see them. Something tells me we'll all get along just fine."

Chapter 28

Flint took them further north into the Outlands, to a steeper part of the trail running past the Glenn River. Here, the river was so swift and clear that the waters shone bright turquoise, and the air was so cool and fresh it tasted of spring water. They walked through the near-endless sea of pines, listening to the river's song.

"Let me get this straight," Hodge said, half-breathless from their current uphill trek. "You robbed the grave of a *king?*"

"Well . . . king is the closest word for it in our tongue. Most of the Nefilium have their own titles for their rulers." Flint was leading the group, stepping steadily across the path, as if he'd hiked this very trail a hundred times before. "And breaking into his tomb for his circlet was the easy part. It took me weeks to work out a way to steal the armor I needed to pose as one of his guards."

All day, Flint had been dazzling them with tales of his journeys and heists. He'd stolen plenty of treasures from men who were still alive, but it sounded like raiding tombs and digging up long-forgotten fortunes made up the bulk of his job. Jae wasn't sure how she felt about taking from the dead, especially since she was still convinced that was a surefire way to earn yourself a curse or a haunting. Just being in the Outlands likely doubled the risk of that. But even if a ghost or two had shown up at the Shroud to gripe about what Flint had taken, vengeful spirits still seemed the least of his worries.

"What did he rule, exactly?" asked Lorelin.

"The Inahi canyon," he said. "It's a fascinating place. The Nefilium hewed a thousand tunnels and halls out of the earth there. It used to be full of amethyst, I heard. Before they mined it dry."

"It sounds like Nestor's Caverns," Tsashin said. "Have you been there?"

Flint nodded. "A few times. The mountain men are . . . gruff, for certain. Is that how you crossed under the Cannocs?"

"Yeah, they almost killed us. It was fantastic," said Hodge, rolling his eyes.

When the sun went down, they ventured a ways off the path to camp for the night and settled in a small clearing among the trees. The pine needles smelled sweeter here, somehow, and in the shadows cast by the pines there were still a few patches of hardened snow from the winter. Jae smoothed out her bedroll in the shade of an especially big fir tree, breathing in the fresh smell of its bark.

They dug a pit for a small fire, and as they clung to the warmth of its flame, Flint told them the best story of the day: how Rogue had sent him to another world to find a warrior's buried sword. All Jae could think about was how much Pa would love to hear it . . .

. . . but right when Flint got to the part where he'd found an entrance behind an enormous waterfall, Jem popped into the air, the smoke from the campfire floating directly through his form.

They hadn't seen him since before fleeing the Shroud, and now, Jem was looking positively frazzled.

"I've been trying to catch up to you," he said, somehow sounding almost breathless. He looked down at Flint, then arched one faint eyebrow. "Who's this?"

Flint offered Jem a polite wave. "Pleased to meet you. Flint Barrow."

They took a moment to explain how Jem had joined them, and when he told Flint about his pact with Argus, Flint's eyes sparked with understanding. Jem described how Argus had given him a body as leverage for working alongside him, and how on the night of Dolorosa's raid, he chose his ghostly state over a knavish life with the Byrds' gang . . . the only life Argus could offer him.

"Well, if it's any consolation . . ." Flint started, "it didn't work out for me, either. Not with Argus, at least."

They swapped stories—Jem of his yearning to live once more, Flint of a shared life with his beloved. And when Flint mentioned the offer Rogue had made him, Jem glowed like a thousand burning stars.

"Would she . . . could she do that for me?" he asked, gliding higher into the air.

"Worth a try," said Flint. "I'm taking your friends to Telin. You're welcome to follow us."

Jem flew upward with so much excitement that he disappeared.

"Well," Flint said after a stretch of silence. "There's that."

"So the sword," Tsashin broke in, leaning forward. Jae had never seen her looking so eager. It was like she'd burst if Flint didn't finish the tale.

"Oh, yes!" Flint cleared his throat. "There was a chamber there, and the sword was lying in the center. It was the muggiest place I've ever been in. I thought I'd drown in the air itself. Not suffocate, *drown*. But I picked up the sword. There were spots of rust and mold all over it. It shouldn't have been beautiful, still, but . . .

somehow, it was. I've never seen craftsmanship like that. Not in this world, at least.

"I stepped out of the chamber, and before I passed back around the falls . . . I saw a face in the waterfall."

Tsashin's eyes went wide. "A face?"

"Just barely there, at first. If it hadn't started speaking to me, I might have walked right through it. But I could make out every one of its features . . . I almost fainted." Softly, he laughed at himself. "It was the warrior."

"What was his name?" asked Tsashin.

"Hardreth," said Flint. "He wasn't angry with me. He told me I could take it, as long as I promised to use it well." His gaze fell to the campfire, and a grave look came over him. "I'm not sure I *kept* that promise."

Like everything else, that sword had gone straight to Rogue.

Jae didn't make him say so out loud, but . . . perhaps using it to pay for Daisy's life was noble enough. Of course, that depended on the sort of fella this warrior was. She wanted to ask, but they wouldn't make it any further to Telin tomorrow if they stayed up listening to stories instead of getting some rest tonight.

Hodge took the first watch, and though she hadn't rested well for several days now, Jae couldn't sleep. Her mind had been refusing to quiet down. She tossed and turned for an hour or two as the moon crossed the sky and the campfire withered down. Perhaps her mind was playing tricks on her, but it was beginning to feel as though she'd been awake for days instead of hours.

Jae swallowed. Her tongue slid around her dry mouth. She sat up, tucking her knees to her chest, and peered into the forest beyond.

The trees stretched on for miles around them. It would be so easy to disappear into these woods. They weren't unlike the ones where she'd lost Pa. All the forests through which she'd traveled south had blurred together in her memory.

It was lonely out here.

How had she done it for so long? Spent her days all alone? She should've gone mad years ago.

Why are you still here?

They were in the Outlands. The Harney boys had a plan to get their knife back. She didn't have to go to Telin, or meet Rogue . . . Right now, she could get up and start her search for Pa again. She had no reason to be here.

That's not true, she told herself. *I've got a thousand reasons to be here.*

The most glaring one was that she didn't have the strength to walk away.

As she had that thought, far away, there was a scream.

Jae leapt to her feet. It had been faint. If she'd been closer to sleep, she would have missed it.

Jae took a step toward the treeline. Her hand reached for her gun. The forest was too still, too silent.

She glanced over her shoulder. Hodge was standing a couple paces behind her, eyes fierce and wide despite his sleep-rumpled clothes.

"You heard that, too?" she whispered. Hodge nodded.

Then, it hit her like an icy wind: there were eyes watching them. She couldn't see them, and she didn't know where they were. But she felt their gaze.

For a moment, clarity left her. Jae found her will again, her focus, and when she faced the dark woods again, the fear left her body.

She couldn't speak.

It was like a day hadn't gone by. Standing just a few yards away, he looked exactly as he had the day he'd been taken away from her. His brown eyes, smiling, warm as honey. He waved at her, and now . . .

He was *there.*

Pa.

She was paralyzed with joy.

No more wandering.

No more bounties, no more spreading herself so thin. No more nightmares. No more ghosts. No more sleepless nights, awake and asking *why, why, why.*

He was here.

Safe. Alive.

"Jae," he said. "Is it really you? By gods, you'll be tall as I am, soon."

Jae didn't speak, and her heart caved in on itself.

Something about his voice wasn't right. It was Pa's voice—but it didn't belong to him. She couldn't name it, but something was missing—some crucial part of his soul.

Jae gasped. She'd been caught in some trance, and a split second had made her lucid. Her blood froze.

If you hear a faraway scream—

Then, there were footsteps next to her. Hodge came closer. He was staring at Pa, too.

He took a few steps in Pa's direction. "Lia?" His voice was so thin, so unlike *Hodge.*

The deep boom of a rifle cracked. Pa stumbled, one hand reaching for the blood bursting from his hip. Raw, hungry pain tore at Jae's chest, but she was too stunned to make a sound. Once more, she forgot what she'd known just seconds earlier. All she could see there was Pa bleeding out.

Pa's skin rippled for a split second, revealing bone-colored flesh stretched over a gaunt frame—it was *then* she screamed.

Gryff stepped out of the shadows, edging close to the treeline, rifle aimed at Pa.

Part of her mind tried scolding her. *It ain't Pa! It's something else! Help Gryff. Shoot it back to hell.* But that part of her was silenced by fear and confusion so powerful that they burned away every other trace of herself.

Then, Hodge started striding in Pa's direction—had he seen the flash of yellowish skin? Without a second thought, Jae leapt for him, locking her arms around his chest to hold him back.

"Let me go!" Hodge spat, struggling against her.

"It's not Lia!" Jae snapped, and she squeezed her eyes shut for a moment. *Not Lia. Not Pa, either.*

The second shot found Pa's shoulder. He cried out again, but this time, there was something animal in that cry. His face rearranged itself into long nostrils, black eyes and pointed teeth. Just for a moment. Then it was Pa again, just Pa.

"Holy hell," Hodge breathed, and Jae released him, thanking the Wandering God that he understood what it was, now.

"Jae! Make him stop!" Pa wailed.

She wanted to black out. Make it all go away forever. She shut her eyes. *Make it stop.*

"Jae, Jae! Please!"

Hurried feet and cries of confusion drowned out Pa's begging. Halston called out Jae's name. Something had turned her feet to roots and tethered her to the ground.

But another force was tugging at her. She could stop it. Stop *this.* A draw, a shot, and she could *end* whatever was attacking them.

If it weren't for the sound of Pa's pleading.

A firm grip yanked at her arm. Jae opened her eyes. Halston stood beside her. Pa was staggering on trembling legs, trying to trudge closer to them.

Something was wrong.

Lorelin's face shone with fresh tears. She had her gun in hand, but she wasn't shooting. Halston and Hodge were doing the same. Tsashin's face was a blank slate, but she held fast.

The only one moving was Gryff, and Jae saw a trail of pine needles stirring under what were surely Flint's invisible feet. She couldn't even see his gun.

The pine needles stopped stirring around five yards from the monster. A shot rang out, and the bullet struck Pa's calf.

Pa was gone, replaced by a shrieking tangle of flailing limbs and unnaturally stretching skin.

There wasn't a moment to curse herself for lost time, for her own damn foolishness. The monster's maw was huge.

"Fire!" Flint shouted, revealing himself at once.

Hodge squeezed his eyes shut, then pointed his gun at the beast writhing on the ground.

"NO!" Flint shouted as Hodge's bullet plowed into the creature's gut, making it gurgle. "*Flame!* Burn it!"

Flame.

Jae made it to the fire pit in two strides. Behind her, Pa—no, the monster—was screaming out Pa's groans of agony. She began reaching for the smoldering wood, searching for a piece she could grab without singing her palm, but every passing moment drained her. She was growing heavy—those cries, her name, repeated with growing desperation each time—were turning her blood into lead.

A small shadow fell over the fire. Tsashin.

Tsashin had wetted one of her sleeves with water, then tugged the fabric over her hand. She bent down and pulled a branch from the wood. The wet cloth hissed on one end of the stick, but the flame continued to flicker on the other. Her quick feet carried her to Flint, who had one hand outstretched, ready to grab the burning branch.

At the same time, the monster lunged for Lorelin.

But Lorelin didn't throw up her arms, made no attempt to shield herself. The creature became a blur—but Jae swore it morphed back into Pa when it threw itself at Lorelin.

Gryff leapt forward, swinging his rifle in one fluid sweep. It slammed against the creature's neck. It fell and cried out Jae's name again.

And gods, thank gods, by the time Flint was on top of it with his brand, it wasn't Pa anymore. Human shaped, with wiry limbs, black eyes, and visible veins running along its legs and up its gut, pulsing, bulging.

The thing's flesh caught like tinder.

It let out a scream straight from hell. The sight of the flames burned Jae's eyes. Long, crooked fingers reached toward the sky and grasped at nothing before curling into a lifeless fist and falling.

It just burned and burned and burned.

It was quick, but it smoked like a chimney. The skin fell away in fragile black flakes, giving way to narrow bones. Bones that, if one didn't know better, would have looked ever-so *human*.

Only Flint and Gryff seemed relieved. Everyone else stood stone-still and dead silent. Tears shone on Tsashin's cheeks. Lorelin vomited.

"Are you hurt?" Flint asked as he rushed to her side.

She moaned. "Martina." She dug her hands into her hair, then raised a fist to her mouth, biting down on her own skin.

Martina.

"It wasn't Martina," said Flint, though the name sounded foreign on his tongue. "These things . . . shifters . . . they get into your head. Morph into what—who—whoever you want most. It wasn't Martina."

Panting, Hodge turned to Halston. "Did you see Lia, too?"

Eyes wider than saucers, Halston nodded.

When the body had been more or less reduced to ash and bone, they heaped soil over the dying flames. And just because she could, Jae spat on the dirt. A funeral fit for a beast. Dead and gone and done with.

For ages, they just stood there by the creature's remains, trying to get themselves to start breathing a little easier. The skeleton poked through the earth . . . They hadn't done a great job of burying it, but nobody was in the right frame of mind to give this monster its last rites. Still, despite its narrower frame, the skeleton looked eerily human.

She'd known about shifters. Pa himself had warned her about them every year before they traveled south to Mesca. They'd never run into one, thank the gods.

She'd thought it would be different when she saw one. *If* she saw one. That somehow, she'd be an exception to what they could do, the way that they tempted you, lured you in and devoured you. Foolishly, she'd assumed that she wouldn't fall for its ruse.

Jae accidentally inhaled some of the leftover smoke. She coughed. Tears welled up in her eyes. Her chest felt thin and dry.

"Will there be more?" asked Tsashin. The poor girl's voice was thin as thread.

"They don't usually hunt in packs," said Jae, forcing her tone to stay level. "I reckon we'll be fine."

"We should get going, anyway," said Flint. "Get away from here. Packs of shifters or not, I don't feel good about staying here."

Nobody was in a rush to disagree with him, but how on earth could he be so cool about it? Jae couldn't bring herself to start moving yet. The others kept staring down at the charred bones, looking just as lost as Jae felt.

Flint frowned at them all. "We're wasting time. I hate to

be so callous, but whatever you saw—it wasn't real. We have to move."

Lorelin started, "Who did you—"

Flint waved a hand. "It morphed into Daisy's ghost."

Jae wanted to tell him that of *course* this had been easy for him. Even if Daisy's ghost had appeared, it wasn't like Flint could kill *her*.

Before they started down the trail again, Jae looked at the misshapen lump of dirt and ash. She hadn't had the will to fight it. If it hadn't been for Flint and Gryff, they all would have been at the mercy of its magic.

Perhaps she wasn't as strong as she thought.

Tsashin was moving more slowly than the rest of them. She was shivering slightly.

"Are you alright?" Jae whispered to her.

"I saw a man," she said. "Perhaps forty. His clothes were like mine . . . his *face* was like mine. He was . . . smiling, with his arms outstretched, like he wanted to welcome me."

Jae swallowed hard. "Your father?"

"Maybe?"

Jae slung an arm over Tsashin's shoulders and gave her a slight squeeze. "It's alright. We're alright."

Maybe these woods were full of horrors they had yet to see, but . . . they had one another. And for now, that had to be enough.

Chapter 29

No one was itching to speak after the shifter attack. They'd continued on the winding trail diligently, braced for anything else that might leap out of the woods. Halston just wished he could blot the vision of Lia bleeding out from his mind.

Hodge had seen it, too.

They'd taken the ordinary wolves, cougars, and lawless men from the south for granted. Here, there were monsters who could delve into their minds and draw up their worst fears before their very eyes.

"Should we stop?" Lorelin said after what felt like an eternity of silence.

Halston wasn't sure what the point was. Nobody was going to sleep after what they'd just seen.

He was about to say so when thunderous hoofbeats conquered the silent woods, overpowering the sound of the river nearby.

They froze. Halston listened. By the time he realized they were coming from behind, not up ahead, he had turned to see the riders already veering around a bend in the road and heading straight for them. He could only see two from where he stood, but judging by the hoofbeats, he guessed there were at least six of them.

A voice as hard and heavy as steel sounded from the group. "Banderra Rangers. Halt and drop your weapons."

There was no urge to move that found Halston's feet, no desperate burst of courage in his veins. The Rangers rode toward them, and by the time Halston could make out the individual faces of each man, there was no chance for escape.

Run. Hide. Fight.

Fight?

"Hold still," Jae hissed through gritted teeth. "They'll gun us down if we try anything."

Her father had been a Ranger, and Halston had every reason to believe her. He froze.

Around them, the abysmal forest stretched for what might as well have been eternity. There was nothing to run into but the darkness, and whatever lurked inside it.

An austere-looking man with sharp features led the group of Rangers—eight in all, Halston saw now, surrounded them. All of them wore identical riding boots, crisp breeches and button-down jackets, with badges glinting at their breasts. He couldn't get a good look at their faces, as their wide-brimmed hats shaded them, but he could see that each one was armed with a rifle, two revolvers, and bandoliers full of cartridges.

The man fronting them hadn't drawn his weapon, yet, but the hand on his holster suggested that he would as soon as the situation demanded it. His thin lips pursed under his ashy blond goatee, and his cold eyes found Halston. Their icy clarity reminded him of Sterling.

Perhaps he was imagining it . . . at least, he hoped he was

imagining it, but Halston thought he caught a flash of recognition in the Ranger's eye.

Halston tore his gaze from him for a moment to look at Jae. Though she faced the Rangers with her head high, he could sense that she was afraid, like he could feel her heart pounding from where he stood.

"We were tracking the *shifter*," the man started, "and passed a smoldering pile of ash on the trail. It appears you took care of it for us?"

"Yes, sir," Halston said, hoping he sounded unassuming enough.

The Ranger's brow creased. He let the silence simmer until it was almost unbearable.

"Seeing travelers in these woods is . . . unusual," the Ranger mused. "We'll need to see your permits. I assume the outpost in Analisa issued them to you?" The pitch of his voice ascended with disdain. He already had them pinned down by the wrists, and he knew it.

Jae leapt to their rescue. "A band of Nefilium bandits stole them from us."

The Ranger's mouth stretched into a hardened line. "Yet it seems that all of you still have your packs."

Jae motioned to Tsashin, who was still looking sullen and drained after the shifter's attack. "*She* had our permits on hand. She went into the woods to hunt, and—"

"I've heard enough. If you don't have the permits with you, then you'll have to come with us and settle this at Fort Marksdale."

Halston's head started spinning. He'd already seen a monster morph into his sister, scream bloody murder, and die tonight. It had mimicked the exact cadence of Lia's voice—a voice surprisingly high and bouncy for Lia's temper—a fire she'd always shared with Hodge.

They'd been had.

Caught, forced to negotiate, when nobody's mind was braced for it.

Now, it was either run into a forest of certain death, draw, or surrender.

When the Rangers dismounted, took their weapons, and bound their wrists, no one was brave enough to object. They went for Jae last. Halston saw her lip quivering, eyes darting all over the place, conflicting emotions flashing across her face. What was she going to try?

"You listen here!" Jae yelled as one of the Rangers grabbed her shoulders. "I'm *Ven Oldridge's* daughter!"

And for some reason, that was enough to get them to pause. None of the Rangers stopped their business, but for a moment, they went still.

"Ven Oldridge's daughter, eh?" asked the leader.

"Yes, and if you don't let me finish, I'm going to—"

Jae wasn't cut off by words, but with loud, dismissive laughter.

"Even if it's true, that wouldn't do you a bit of good, miss." The Ranger motioned to one of the deputies with his thumb. "We are all equal under the law. Now, I suggest you hold your tongue until your trial."

Jae didn't say another word, but the glare she gave the lot of them could have punctured pure steel.

The wheels of Halston's mind began churning as they bound his wrists, then hoisted him onto one of the horses. He felt helpless as snared prey sitting pressed against his own captor. Beside him, Jae and Tsashin were being hauled up onto another saddle, and Halston could almost feel the fire roaring inside of Jae right now.

No. They hadn't failed. Not yet. He refused to believe it.

We'll find a way out of this. He caught her eye and passed the message on to her silently, and the slight nod she gave him let him know she understood.

———

The ride was short. They rode about a half mile away from the Glenn River to a stretch of rocky land running parallel to an enormous ravine that wound far into the distance. Jae couldn't see the bottom of it, nor could she guess how far it stretched—its end was well beyond her sight. In the distance, sitting amongst the boulders and a handful of skinny pines, was Fort Marksdale.

Jae had never been to a fort in the Outlands. Like all the forts in Banderra and northern Monvallea, Fort Marksdale was an elongated log structure surrounded by a palisade of sharp wooden stakes. There was a smaller cabin beside the central building, perhaps a bunkhouse. Two flags fluttered on top of its roof. One was the Hespyrian flag—a golden star at the corner of a sea of blue— and another displayed the mark of Hemaera, the arrow crossed with the crescent moon.

The mark of Hemaera. A half-goddess, a *woman,* who had charted the Outlands herself centuries ago and given the map and the gift of Wyrdrian to the first Rangers. Rangers who had apparently forgotten the origins of their order, seeing how they'd taken Jae's chance to speak and slung her over a damn saddle. Like she was nothing more than a feedsack, a carcass with no mind of her own. She was shaking, now—half from shame and half from anger.

One of the Rangers picked her up like she weighed nothing, then set her down. He was gentle about it, and that made it easier for Jae not to call him a colorful word or two.

"Alright, Miss *Oldridge,*" said the leader, a captain, she now realized, observing the heavy gold star on his chest. "You're up for questioning first."

The Rangers prodded them into the fort like cattle. Lamplight nearly blinded Jae when they stepped over the threshold. At once, her eyes craved the darkness. They passed through a dusty-smelling common-space, with a round wooden table, several chairs, and a wood-burning stove. The room was large, with several hallways branching off into other wings of the fort. Several men stood by the stove and eyed the gang with suspicion before they were led through a door and down a short, rickety stairway. The bottom floor was surprisingly long and held a wide stretch of iron-barred cells, all of them empty.

Jae swapped a look with Flint. He was probably regretting not disappearing the first chance he'd had. Now, he was bound, and his face was just as dismayed as the rest of them. Maybe he knew a lost cause when he was in one.

No, this *couldn't* be a lost cause. Jae would talk her way out of this. Hell, if it came to it, she'd *fight* her way out of it.

The deputies corralled their party into three different cells. Flint, Halston, and Hodge to one. Tsashin and Lorelin to another. Gryff had his own. Jae was bracing herself to be nudged in with the other girls when the captain yanked her away and clasped a pair of metal cuffs over her wrists. Her skin ached at the cold, merciless grip of the steel.

Her lips were free, but she knew that she could only speak to Halston with her eyes. If she said too much too soon, she might just add fuel to the already roaring fire beneath the pot they were in. *It's alright. I'll figure a way out of this.*

She was Ven Oldridge's daughter, for the gods' sake. This was no damn time for modesty.

The captain led her back upstairs, then down a side hall to a small, dimly lit office. He motioned her to sit in a chair across from his desk.

Sitting and facing a lawman. She'd done this many times before—but not for a long while, and certainly not while under arrest. Jae read the shining nameplate on his desk. *Carlisle Crane.*

The captain sat across from her, every one of his motions smooth and calculated. Every part of this man was sharp. Pointed nose, angular chin, and long fingers steepled, his elbows on his desk. Since their arrest, she hadn't even seen him blink. How long had it taken him to perfect his unmoving stare?

Gods . . . she was an *outlaw* now.

Despite its truth, she didn't *feel* like an outlaw, like the wretched scum the captain seemed to think she was, based on the way he was leering at her now. Lawless or not, she didn't feel that she'd crossed some line into wickedness. Everything she'd done had been for her gang.

Had the men Jae had hauled in for bounties felt the same way?

As much as it startled her, she couldn't bring herself to dwell on it for longer than a second. Right now, all that mattered was finding a way out of this.

Jae struggled to sit comfortably. Surely she was imagining it, but the cuffs seemed to tighten around her wrists every few moments.

"Is there a way we can get new permits?" she asked, keeping her eyes level with the captain's. Liars' eyes wandered like lost, scared souls. Honest folk stared dead ahead. Now, she needed to masquerade as an honest woman.

Captain Crane's stare did not dither. "No. Not that you had any permits to begin with."

"We *did.*"

"Alright, then. You're making things difficult for yourself. So, I'll give you another chance to tell me the truth, and if it doesn't add up with what the others tell me, this could lead to a much lengthier trial."

Jae bit down on her cheeks. Time, she needed *time*—a precious extra moment to think up a lie. But what good would lying do? She could weasel her way out of a pinch with a scoundrel. A lawman was another story.

"We *did* have permits. We got them at Fort Crawley." She recalled Pa being friends with a Ranger there . . . Damn it, what was his name?

"Interesting," Captain Crane replied, leaning in her direction "Though something tells me if I send word to Captain Hall at Fort Crawley, he won't have any recollection of giving permits to the *Harney gang*."

Jae's stomach shrank. She fought to keep her expression blank, though right now she wished she could turn into a pile of dust.

They were in deep, deep shit.

"Sir," she started. "My name is Jae Oldridge. I'm—"

"Whether or not you are Ven Oldridge's daughter is irrelevant." His tone was biting, razor-sharp.

"I wasn't *finished talking*." She didn't think before speaking. Maybe being fresh with him would only tighten her noose here, but if he wasn't going to budge anyway, she didn't see why she should bother acting courteous. "You want proof? I'll tell you the stories. I know his life forward and back."

"Including his discharge from the Banderra Rangers?"

It struck her like a falling axe.

Dis—what?

Was this some sort of sick new ploy? A way to make her shrink back and give it up? If it was, it wouldn't work. This captain couldn't fool her. "I don't know what you're talking about."

"I can show you the court records if you'd prefer," the captain said flatly.

"That's ridiculous. Pa couldn't have been—he would've—" *He would have told me about it. He would've . . .*

He . . .

"No, surely you'd know," Captain Crane went on, though by now she felt like a dead moth under his heel. He'd already crushed all the life out of her, and anything else he said would just be grinding her into a pulp. "Twenty years ago, Ven Oldridge and his unit were sent to capture a band of robbers led by a warlock . . . Amon was his name, I believe. At Lake Arania, they were ambushed. Oldridge *fled*. He abandoned his men to their deaths. I've heard the stories. Amon died in the shootout, but his bandits slaughtered Ven's unit. None of them survived."

Her mind turned to fog.

"Many of those men were young. They had wives. Children. Entire lives ahead of them."

Jae couldn't bring herself to look directly at the captain, but in the corner of her eye, she could see its expression shift from a blank, stony stare to one of anger.

"If you are indeed Ven Oldridge's child, then you are the daughter of a coward."

"Shut the hell up," she muttered under her breath, though by now, she didn't care much whether or not he heard.

"I beg your pardon?"

She forced herself to raise her head. "He wasn't a coward."

Captain Crane gave her a dismissive snort. "If you have nothing useful to say, then I believe our questioning is over." He stood and pulled Jae up by the handcuffs, and it took every little bit of resolve left in her not to slam her head into his throat.

What had the years turned her into?

She'd be a stranger to that girl clutching the magic map—that girl who feared ghosts and distrusted thieves. That girl was gone. Jae had shaped her into something else entirely, somebody who'd turned into stone and made herself a woman of the law for Pa—Pa.

Pa, who hadn't told her the truth.

Jae was in a daze as they shuffled back through the office space, then down the flimsy wooden stairs into the cell block. Captain Crane removed her cuffs after he'd unlocked her cell. Jae wished that it could have been a relief, but now, she hardly noticed. The reek of rotting wood flooded her nostrils. The captain shoved her back, and she retreated into the cell. Tsashin and Lorelin greeted her with sad, hopeful eyes.

Jae sank to her knees. She overheard Crane leading Flint away for questioning, but her trembling shoulders made it impossible for her to pay them too much heed. Lorelin might have also said her name.

Jae slinked over to the wall, pacing around a few crooked straw pallets. She ran a hand over the cheap whitewash . . . yes, it was hard. She tossed her hat to the side, then slammed her temple against the wall and relished the jolt of pain. Again and again, she let the wall strike her head. She wanted to drive it all out—every last thought of tonight.

Soft arms gathered around her waist. "Stop! Jae, stop it!" Lorelin yanked her away from the wall.

Jae didn't try to break away from Lorelin. She was too busy fighting the tears that came, but it was no use. Though she tried holding them back, they began raining down her cheeks. She gave up and rested her head beneath Lorelin's collarbone. Somehow, she still smelled beautiful and sweet. Gently, her hand stroked Jae's hair, and Jae felt small but not hopeless as she had a moment ago.

On another night, she might have felt ashamed, but tonight, she didn't care about looking helpless. She wanted to get out of here. Tear this place down plank by plank and *run*.

She let herself cry a minute longer. "He lied to me. My Pa lied to me."

Chapter 30

Jae woke up to Halston whispering at her from his cell. "Jae?"

Jae scooted up to the iron bars on her knees. Halston sat in the cell across from her, his fingers curled loosely around one of the bars. His face was dark, grim, but not quite fearful.

Somehow, Jae had managed to sleep. There were three straw pallets in each cell, and though the hay poked out of the fabric, they were still far better than sleeping directly on the hard-packed dirt floor. Jae had only stirred once all day, when a baby-faced deputy came to bring them all water and gruel. She'd eaten her ration in four bites and lay back down to sleep again.

Now, Lorelin and Tsashin were asleep on their pallets. She saw the still shapes of Hodge and Gryff lying in Halston's cell, and Flint slept in the cell to their right.

"What time is it?" she asked.

"Around nine, I think," Halston replied. "They said they'd bring us more rations around dusk, but . . . well, that must've been a lie."

Of course. Jae was surprised she'd managed to sleep the whole day, but she was glad she had. Her mind felt clearer, now, as though the day of rest had washed the worst of her pain away like rain clearing the grime from a windowpane.

Jae leaned her forehead against the metal of the cell door. It was slightly tarnished, and the rust made her skin itch. Her head had stopped throbbing by now. Mostly. Gods. It'd been stupid to hurt herself like that.

For the first time since coming here, she got a decent look at the cell block. There were four cells on either side of a wide aisle, which trailed to the narrow stairway leading to the Rangers' office space. At the other end of the cell block was a door, but there was no hope of opening it, as an enormous padlock and a length of chain banded it shut.

"Did they question you too?" asked Jae. Fatigue had seized her shortly after she'd come down from her own discussion with the captain, so she wasn't sure who else they'd brought up.

Halston nodded. "I didn't say much. I told them I wanted to wait for our trial and held my tongue. Told the others to do the same. Sterling always said that the best thing to do if we ever got caught would be to keep our mouths shut till the trial, then find a way to run off *before* the trial." He sighed, running a hand through his dark hair. "I always hoped it was advice I'd never need."

Halston caught Jae looking at Flint, then.

"I told him to tell them that he wasn't involved with us. They didn't believe him."

Of course they hadn't. Jae just hoped that they wouldn't somehow sniff out Flint's line of work. The Rangers certainly wouldn't let someone off easy for looting graves and stealing treasures.

"We'll get out of here," said Jae, though even now, she wasn't sure she quite believed it. "I'll think of a way we can get out of this. I mean, my first idea didn't work, but . . ." She breathed in, gripping the bar more tightly. "I kept trying to tell him that I was Ven Oldridge's daughter. I mean, *everybody* knew my pa when he was young. He was a high-ranking Ranger, and . . . I thought that had to count for something, so I kept trying to get him to believe me."

"Did he?"

"No. I mean, I don't know. But it doesn't matter. It didn't help one way or the other." She took in a long, heavy breath. "Turns out my a pa was discharged from the Rangers. He left his men to die, and he'd been keeping it from me all my life."

Jae couldn't read Halston's expression. Either way, it wasn't like she could make him understand. Hal loved his own pa—she knew that much. Still . . . Hal had other loved ones, too. He'd grown up with a handful of heroes. He'd had his ma, his brothers, his little sister. Pa had been the only non-stranger in Jae's world. Until her gang.

But even Pa hadn't told her the truth.

He hadn't left the Rangers of his own accord. He'd fled. He'd been a . . .

Liar.

Coward.

Traitor.

Jae wanted to cover her ears. She couldn't make herself believe that Pa was a coward. She wanted to erase everything that Captain Crane had told her. Hell, she wanted to call *him* a liar, but what reason would he have for lying about something like that? It'd do him no good, as much as she'd hoped it had just been a ploy.

"Pa told me *everything,* Hal. He told me all his stories from his Rangering days. And I . . ." She swallowed, suddenly feeling less angry and more numb. "I don't know if it was the only lie. There could have been more."

"Maybe there's more to the story," Halston said hopefully, but she reckoned he was just grasping at straws to make her feel better.

"Maybe." Jae just shook her head. "But if he abandoned them, then—"

At once, she stopped talking.

The ghosts—

Their pure, untamed fury . . . They had been searching for Pa for *years* . . .

Her heart just about stopped.

The men Pa had abandoned.

It was *them*!

Though she'd spent so much time trying to blot that memory out of her mind, now, she unearthed it as clearly as she could. They'd been riding horses, wearing uniforms . . . Rangers. They'd been *Rangers!*

Jae's hand jumped into her pocket. The map—thank the gods it wasn't in her pack—she still had it!

She unfolded the map with trembling hands. Blank, but not for long. She was shaking so much, she thought she might accidentally tear the paper, but she fought against her shivering and managed to hold it steady enough. Then, she whispered, *"Lake Arania."*

The magic got to work, and the pathway began to spread slowly, like a bloodstain on cloth, reaching from Fort Marksdale to Lake Arania. A restless sea began crashing inside Jae's chest.

Because the lake wasn't far at all. It could fit on the map from where they were now . . . forty miles away, give or take a few.

"It's here," she breathed. "I see it."

"What's here?"

Jae stood up and began pacing beside the cell door. She tried to make her footfalls soft to keep from waking Lorelin and Tsashin, but she couldn't hold still at a time like this. She explained the story of the unit Pa had abandoned, and how Captain Crane—*bless him*—had dropped the name of their deathplace. Lake Arania.

"I can't imagine who else those ghosts would be," Jae said, holding the map just in front of her face. "Jem says ghosts are bound to the place they died. And if I find Lake Arania . . ."

I find the ghosts, and then I find Pa.

Liar or not . . . Pa couldn't be far. And even if he wasn't with the ghosts, they had to know where he was, at least. Unless he was dead.

No, he wasn't dead. Some part of her, all this time, had just known that he was alive. Maybe it was foolish, but she'd never trusted anything more in her life.

And Halston said, "I'm coming with you."

Jae blinked. "What?"

"We're going to find him together. Zeph says that adamite can destroy ghosts, right? We've got half an adamite knife—" He reached over his shoulder for his pack, then his mouth fell into a frown. "—somewhere upstairs."

"Hal, you can't . . ." *You have to get home.*

"Yes, I can. And I'm going to."

"What about Telin? What about Rogue?" She stopped pacing. "Hell, what about getting out of here?"

"We're going to get out of here. Besides, the lake is on the way to Telin, isn't it?" He tapped his fingers against the bars of his cell. "But even if it wasn't . . ."

"No. You can't go out of your way for me."

"I will if it means helping you find your father."

"But why? Why do you want to come with me?"

"Because it's *you and me.*"

Jae's mouth fell open. For a few moments, she couldn't do anything but stare. She didn't want to turn away from him.

How did he do it?

How could Halston take a night straight from hell and . . . still somehow give her a moment that she wanted to hold onto till her last days?

Jae raised an arm to the ceiling, then motioned at the dingy cells around them. "You're right. We'll get out of here," she said, and the smile that came to her mouth wasn't forced in the slightest.

Halston smiled right back. "I know we will."

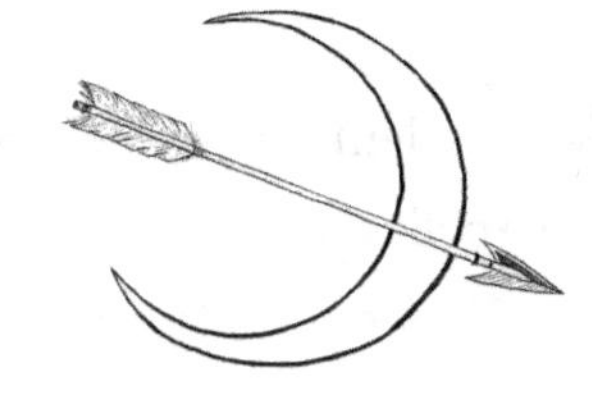

Chapter 31

Some time after she and Halston had talked, Jae managed to get some more rest. She was lost in a blissful, deep sleep when she woke to a scream.

She sat bolt upright, then crawled over Lorelin and Tsashin to shake them both by the shoulders. They stirred, murmuring in confusion. Upstairs, something cracked. There were men shouting, hurried feet scrambling on the floor above them. Then came a screeching noise, gunshots, something crashing down to the floor.

"What's going on?" Tsashin got to her feet and hurried to the bars of their cell, her black hair flying behind her. "I don't see anything."

Jae fought the urge to let out a stream of curses. Whatever it was, they had nowhere to run, no way to escape, and no weapons to defend themselves.

The door at the top of the stairway flew open, and the narrow shape of a man came hurrying down the steps and into the cell block. A small, brass deputy badge glinted on his chest, and keys jangled in one of his hands. Swinging from his other hand was a lantern, and the glow lit his face—showing his terror clearly, and how young he really was. He was at least a year younger than Jae. Just a kid, really.

The boy only began explaining himself after he'd jammed the key into the lock of Jae's cell.

"*Warlock,*" he breathed, twisting the key. "Run. Get out of here."

A sickening pit formed in Jae's stomach.

Right away, she knew who had come for them. Judging by just how wide Halston's eyes had grown, she knew that he was thinking the same thing.

Jae helped push the door open, and she, Tsashin, and Lorelin filed out into the aisle between the cell blocks. The deputy dashed to Halston's cell and began unlocking it as well.

Hodge flew out of his cell as soon as the deputy had pulled the door open. "Where are our guns?"

"Upstairs," said the deputy, already hurrying toward the back exit at the other end of the cell block.

"Where?" Hodge fired back.

"Captain Crane's offi—"

Hodge bolted for the stairs.

"Hodge!" Halston yelled, and he ran after his brother. Gryff hurried after them, too, swearing up a storm.

Jae's gaze leapt from Halston to the young deputy, who had just finished turning the lock to Flint's cell. He reached for the handle and yanked, tugged, yanked some more . . .

"It's stuck," he said, voice thin as thread.

Hodge, Gryff, and Halston stopped dead on the stairs to look down at the cell. Flint's face fell into a look of horror. For a few moments, they all just stood there, gaping at the door. Halston had paused halfway up the stairs to look down.

"I'm sorry," the deputy said at last, then took off toward the back door.

Lorelin, Tsashin, and Jae ran for Flint's cell.

"Get it open!" Halston shouted at them before bolting up the rest of the stairs. "We'll go get our gear!"

Flint lingered by the door, saying nothing, but pushing against the iron bars with one shoulder. Lorelin gripped the handle, and Jae and Tsashin each took one of the door's iron bars. Together, they worked at the door with all their strength.

It creaked one inch, two, grinding against the floor. Jae's muscles strained with each motion, and their breaths grew labored. The smell of smoke flooded into the cell block from upstairs, and Jae tried not to choke—or let the thought of the boys caught in the fire keep her from moving.

More, more. They kept pulling, pushing, tugging . . .

"One big pull!" Lorelin shouted. "On the count of three! One, two—"

They yanked with all their strength a second early. They managed to pull the door further open, adding just another whisper of space, but that was all Flint needed to squeeze through at last.

Jae gazed at the open door for a moment, then spun on her heels to face the back exit. While they'd been trying to free Flint, the deputy had removed the lock and chains and left it open. Jae wondered how far into the woods he'd made it by now. But there it was: their way out.

Instead, Jae raced to the foot of the stairs. "Halston!" she cried. "Gryff! Hodge!"

Halston tore after Gryff and Hodge, gun at the ready, braced to fire on the warlock the first chance he got.

They ran into the common space only to immediately begin coughing on the smoke that filled it. They were the only living souls in the room. The warlock was nowhere in sight. In the corner, a table lay on its side, flaming. The chairs lay scattered about the room, along with a mess of empty bullet casings. Halston's insides twisted when he saw the bodies of two Rangers lying in the opposite corner, fresh blood pooling beneath them.

His stomach lurched when he looked upon the face of the dead Captain Crane.

Hodge grabbed Halston's wrist, rousing him from his temporary stupor.

"Where is he?" Halston spat the question out. It was an effort not to swallow more of the smoke. These men had only been dead for moments. Where had the warlock gone?

"Come on," Hodge urged him, dragging Halston in the direction of the office.

Halston let his brother pull him back into a run, but he spared a glance over his shoulder, surveying the smoke for that stony figure in the mask.

Together, Gryff trailing them, they fought their way through the smoke and down the hallway leading to the captain's office. The door had been left open, the captain's belongings strewn over his desk. They found their packs and weapons in an armoire in the corner, and Halston thanked the gods that it hadn't been locked.

Halston slung his own pack, Jae's, and Lorelin's over his shoulders, staggering under the weight, then drew his gun before they slipped out the door. His eyes watered and burned as they dashed back into the common space. The fire had spread, licking at the floorboards, but it had not yet reached the doorway to the cell block. Halston drew his shirt up over his mouth and nose and strode over the debris, careful not to step too close to the flames.

Halston heard Jae call their names from downstairs. He stopped by the doorway, letting Hodge and Gryff lumber into the cell block first. Before he joined them, Halston turned and took one last look at the burning room . . .

And despite the fire's heat, his blood ran cold.

A footstep creaked against the floorboards. Through the smoke, a dark figure loomed, with a mask of dull metal and an unwavering gaze.

He'd found Halston.

And his steady, unyielding stare told Halston that this wouldn't be over anytime soon.

Halston turned his back to the masked warlock and hurtled down the stairs. "He's back!" he cried, feeling only fleeting relief when he saw that the others had freed Flint from his cell. He tossed Jae her pack, then returned Lorelin's.

They all threw him stricken, understanding stares, but there was no time to waste. They bounded out the back door into the night— to some unforeseen end.

They ran downhill, away from the fort, then Halston threw a hand out, motioning to the west. "The river!"

Lorelin's head whirled around. "What about it?"

"We'll have to jump in," Halston forced out between hurried breaths. "The river will carry us away from here. Fast."

Halston guessed it was about a half mile from the fort. From what he recalled from their ride over, the road ran parallel to the ravine most of the way, then crooked into a turn leading to the river. Besides, if the warlock started stirring the ground up again, then the sooner they all got off the dirt road, the better. His gang could do it. They could make it.

But Halston wouldn't be following them for much longer.

Onward they ran, bolting past the ravine, boots flying over the muddy road. Hodge led the group, one hand reaching toward Tsashin, who flew next to him, light and swift on her feet. Close behind them was Lorelin. Gryff, Jae, and Flint ran on the flanks, with Halston running at the tail end.

He began to stagger his pace. A little, at first, then more. None of the others had chanced a look back yet. *Good.*

When he'd allowed several yards of distance to accumulate between himself and the gang, Halston twisted around and raced back in the direction of the fort.

This was *his* battle. Halston would not let the others be dragged into it.

Halston fought against the pain that struck inside him after turning back, knowing that if he'd taken even a second to say goodbye, they'd have followed him at once. Still, he summoned every bit of courage he could, desperate to smother the rising panic in his chest.

Don't turn back, he commanded himself. *Don't turn back.*

The road was empty. Behind them, the fort still stood, but now, smoke billowed from its foundations. Halston guessed that the surviving Rangers had all fled into the night. He kept running, though there was no sign of the warlock.

The hammer of a gun clicked behind him. Halston looked back over his shoulder and shouted at the figure standing there.

"*Jae!*" he wanted it to be a command, but his heart made it sound like a plea. "Get out of here! *Now!*"

He should've known he wouldn't get away with it. Jae was ready to aim and fire. Her gaze was as hard as ancient stone. She ignored his plea. "Where'd the bastard go?"

"I don't know! Get out of here! Run!"

"I ain't running." She slid her thumb up the grip of her pistol.

Halston was about to try yelling at her one more time when the ground disappeared from under his feet. His body slammed against the earth, then he felt himself rolling down another gods-damned slope. Beside him, Jae was cursing and screaming, clawing at the slanting ground.

The ground ceased moving, and Halston and Jae stopped tumbling. Halston got to his knees, loose dirt falling from his pants, then held an arm out to help Jae rise, who was picking up her pistol with a trembling hand.

They stood, hurriedly trying to catch their breath and take in their surroundings. They were stuck at the bottom of a new-made basin—around three yards high and perhaps ten yards across. Two skinny pine trees had fallen in as the ground had caved in. One lay crookedly in the center of the pit, and the other sprouted outward from one of the curved walls like an arm outstretched from a damp, earthy shoulder.

Halston remained standing, letting his gaze run around the rim of the basin, waiting for the masked warlock to appear. Surely, *he* was here. When he showed himself, Halston would be ready for him.

He just hoped he'd be able to shoot quickly, before the warlock could even think about getting Jae out of the way.

After a few moments of painful silence, two figures *did* come into view at the top of the crater, but the warlock was not among them. Shafts of moonlight caught on their badges, and Halston was relieved.

At first.

They were standing utterly motionless on the ledge, as still as stakes firmly planted in the ground. One of the men was short and muscular, with a dark beard and big hands. And the other one was Captain Crane.

Halston blinked. Were his eyes tricking him? He had seen the bodies of both these men inside the fort—and their shirts were still soaked with blood.

There wasn't a trace of consciousness in their eyes. They stared at Jae and Halston with stony, vacant stares.

Then, with the speed and grace of cougars, the men leapt into the basin and landed steadily. Without the slightest stagger or briefest hesitation, they bolted for Halston.

Before Halston could stop her, Jae let out a raw scream and dashed straight for the men. She shot once, twice as she ran. The first bullet struck Captain Crane's shoulder, and the second found the other man's temple.

Despite the glaring hole in his forehead, the Ranger kept moving. No blood streamed from his wound.

"*Revenants!*" Jae screamed.

Revenants—Sterling had told Halston about them before. Dead men, reanimated through a warlock's magic . . .

Warlock.

The masked man had to be near, but right now, they had to get the hell out of this basin and away from the revenants.

The undead men were blocking Halston's path to Jae, still making a beeline for *him*. Halston rushed to the other side of the basin, heading for the pine tree jutting from one of the earthen walls. It was their best shot at climbing out of here.

He reached the tree, grabbed one of the branches and hoisted himself onto the horizontal trunk. When he turned around, he came face-to-face with the two revenants scrabbling to grab his legs, their bloody hands clawing at his pant legs.

Halston kicked Captain Crane squarely in the nose. The revenant lurched back, but its stone-still expression did not falter.

"Halston!" Jae cried. "Your knife!"

"What?"

"Adamite!" He watched her bend down to snatch a stone off the ground.

"Will that *work*?" Halston cried back, slamming his heel on top of the short man's skull.

"*Yes!*" As she cried it, she threw the rock, which struck Captain Crane on the head, though the revenant's focus did not waver.

Halston reached over his shoulder, desperately trying to unhook the clasp of his knapsack. As he finally managed to reach through the outer flap, the revenants came closer, their hands swatting at the barrier of pine branches. One impossibly cold hand locked around his ankle and pulled. Halston used his free hand to hold tight to the branch, but each tug from the revenant jostled him. Pine needles scratched his face and prodded him through his clothes.

Where was it? Halston's hand scrambled over his blankets, a pack of jerky, a length of twine . . .

The branches rustled at his side. Jae had made it to the tree, and now, she was crawling her way to him.

When he at last touched the cold surface of the knife's hilt, Halston almost screamed for joy.

In one swift motion, Halston drew the knife from his pack, leaned forward, and swiped it across the short man's forehead. Halston's eyes went wide at what he saw.

Immediately, the Ranger's body turned to black dust. In less time than a finger snap, his remains crumbled and rained on the earth, indistinguishable from the dark, loamy soil of the basin.

But there was no time for Halston to slash at Captain Crane.

Without warning, the earth rumbled around them. Halston and Jae lost hold of the branches, fell, and collided with the ground. Halston's vision clouded over as he felt the hard soil rearranging itself around them. When he came to his senses and the earth was once more at a standstill, he rose to find that the basin had shrunk in on itself. Now, it was far smaller, horribly cramped. He and Jae were trapped between the tree and a newly formed wall of earth that had cut the hollow in half.

The wall arched around them, barricading them from the rest of the basin. They had to move higher. It was their only chance.

"Climb!" shouted Jae.

Through the branches, thrashing on the other side of the tree, Captain Crane's revenant was still trying to grab them. Halston's heart sank when he heard the branches cracking, then falling to the ground. If the revenant climbed over the tree to them, then there was no escape.

Halston struggled to lift his arms, finally managed to get them up, then put the knife between his teeth and fumbled for the branches, searching for places to put his hands and feet. Twigs and needles jabbed at his cheeks, his neck, his stomach. Sap clung to his palms, and his shaking hands made it near impossible to grasp anything. A stream of blood trickled down his cheek and between his lips, and its coppery taste filled his mouth. Then, the earth shook again, and Halston fell to the bottom of the pit once more.

Halston took the knife out from his mouth, and as he sat upright, the bittersweet smell of pine overcame him. Halston looked up above. Overhead, standing at the ledge on the other side of the basin, was the masked warlock.

But he wasn't moving, and neither were the trees or the earth. He'd trapped Jae and Halston in this little prison, and now, he was still.

Halston almost froze. Why wasn't he trying to stir the soil anymore?

Then, he recalled how Sterling had once said that he'd often have to stop and rest for hours or days after using his powers to open a portal. Magic could be draining.

And thank the gods it was.

Jae raised her gun and fired at him. The bullet missed their captor, but it startled him backward, and he darted somewhere out of their sight.

Then a dark, hulking shape leapt into the pit with a furious roar. Gryff.

Halston heard Gryff lumbering across the basin's floor. He couldn't tell how much space there was on the other side of the tree, but it sounded like Gryff had plenty of room to move. He could still see Captain Crane through the branches. The crack of Gryff's rifle clubbing the revenant over the head came from the other side of the tree, and the living corpse fell to the ground.

As Gryff continued bludgeoning the revenant, Hodge appeared at the edge above Halston and reached out.

He came back for me.

"Climb!" Hodge yelled.

Jae was closer to Hodge than Halston was. She passed Halston a look of reluctance, but Halston said, "Do it. Go first."

She hesitated, then seized two branches and heaved herself upward, crying out as she lifted all her bodyweight from the crevice between the wall and tree. Her right arm shot up as if she'd just punched a hole in her own casket, and Hodge took hold of her wrist. Grunting, he pulled her from the basin.

Once she was at the edge, Jae turned and fired at something Halston could not see. Was the warlock still here?

Halston wheezed. His body was broader than Jae's, and he was straining to pull himself from the trap. His face was caked in blood and dirt, and the branches restricted his movements. He kept trying to take Hodge's hand, like a fish trying to swallow bait, but it was just out of Halston's reach.

"Die, dammit!" Gryff shouted. Halston heard him strike the revenant once more.

"It's a *revenant*, Gryff!" Jae called back from the ledge.

"A what?"

"Oh for the love of—just keep hitting it!"

Halston bit down on his blade again, then continued trying to raise himself higher, desperate to push the branches away. He tried moving his feet, searching for spots he could position himself without falling. He drew in a deep, long breath, then grabbed a sturdy branch, braced his foot against another, and pushed himself skyward. Slowly, he came closer to Hodge. A little more. He stretched out his free hand.

At last, Hodge took it with a whoop of triumph. Huffing, pulling, squeezing, he pulled Halston from the prison at last. The warlock was nowhere to be seen. Halston watched Gryff give the revenant one last blow to the chest, and it staggered backward. Gryff sprinted across the basin, then smacked both clawed hands on top of the ledge and pulled himself out.

"The river!" Hodge cried when Gryff had freed himself, then motioned to the west. "Come on!"

The warlock had formed the basin just a stone's throw from the ravine. They sprinted alongside it, leaving the chasm of scattered earth and uprooted trees behind them.

Together, they dashed down the edge of the ravine. There was a short breadth of clear ground between the ravine and the trees, just wide enough for them to hustle side-by-side. Halston tried not to look at the sprawling ditch to his left. He couldn't tell how deep it ran, or how steep the sides were, but he was in no rush to find out if losing his balance might leave him splattered at the bottom.

Still, slowing down could mean an end just as grisly.

They kept on racing, bound for the river, not daring to look back. The ground before them remained unmoved. In the near distance, the sound of the rushing current thrummed.

"We're almost there," Hodge said breathlessly. "The turn is coming up, we—"

An enormous burst of earth shot up like a geyser from their path.

Halston fell, and his body slammed into the ground, knocking the wind out of him. Jae screamed, and he wanted to cry out her name, but he had no breath for it. The entire world had become a blur. Everything was spinning, and he realized that he was rolling down a hill.

A tree finally broke his fall. Halston crashed into the trunk. The impact rattled his senses. Still, he forced himself to push through the immediate throbbing in his body, to rise and face what lay ahead.

To his left rose an enormous mountain of soil, tall enough that he couldn't see over it, though he knew the ravine was on the other side. To his right, there was nothing but forest. He didn't see the warlock, but surely, he was close by.

There was no sign of Gryff or Jae.

"Jae!" Halston screamed, and after her name left his mouth, his throat felt as though someone had rammed a dull blade down it. He took two strides toward the freshly formed hill. It was too steep to climb, but damn it, he might try. "Gryff!"

Far on the other side of the magic hill, Jae's brittle voice cried back, "Hal!"

And then the earth shifted again. Halston and Hodge jumped backward, away from the land as it rapidly ascended before them, gathering, accumulating into the warlock's hill, that wretched barrier dividing them from Gryff and Jae.

Hodge seized Halston's wrist. Before Halston could fully process what was happening, they were sprinting into the trees. The sound of the river grew louder. They ran in its direction, weaving in and out of the scattered pines, not daring to look back and see if the earth was caving in or rising up behind them.

Halston's thoughts finally overcame his instinct. What were they doing? Gryff and Jae were trapped! "We can't leave them!" Halston shouted.

The words had barely left his lips when a dark shape sprang out of the trees, cutting off their path.

Halston and Hodge leapt backward just in time to dodge a swipe from a familiar long-bladed knife. Its wielder spun on his heels, making his enormous cloak billow around his limbs.

"You!" Halston snapped without thinking.

The man said nothing, but looked at Halston with wide, round eyes. There was no malice in his gaze, just determination . . . and maybe Halston imagined it, but he also thought he saw a faint tinge of regret. Folds of cloth still concealed the lower half of the man's face, and Halston still couldn't place him.

"Stop moving," he commanded. "And no harm will—"

Hodge fired at the man's arm. He yowled, and the knife tumbled from his grasp before Hodge seized Halston's wrist again and took off.

"Stop!" Halston cried out, though he wasn't sure if he was speaking to Hodge or to the cloaked man. They'd barely made it ten yards before Halston looked back. Already, the cloaked man pursued them. He'd transferred his knife to his left hand, but thick rivulets of blood already dribbled down his right forearm.

Despite his injury, he was quick.

"I'll go with you!" Halston shouted, yanking against Hodge's hold, hoping to free himself from his brother's iron-grip. "Just st—"

"Like hell you are!" Hodge spat, picking up the pace.

Halston watched the cloaked man speed up with them, ignoring the fresh wound from Hodge's bullet. The man said something else, but the roar of the river had grown too powerful for Halston to make out his words.

Halston looked forward again just in time to see the silver streak of water below, cutting beneath the stony ledge they were about to cross.

"Jump!" Hodge cried.

As the ground left their feet and their bodies plunged into the water, Hodge did not let Halston go.

Chapter 32

Around halfway through her fall, Jae became aware of her own screaming.

She was tumbling down a muddy slope, her body spiraling out of control. Damp grit filled her mouth, making her choke. Down, down, down.

The ground finally leveled out, and Jae slowly rolled to a stop. Her body groaned everywhere as she lay still. Her clothes were damp. Had she landed in a puddle? She forced her eyes open and faced a sky of spinning stars.

Far above, softened by distance, Halston cried her name, then Gryff's.

There was blood and dirt in her mouth. Still, she managed to ignore her shaking limbs and throbbing head to summon the energy to shout, "*Hal!*"

But there was no answer. There was more shouting—far, muffled. She placed her palms on the springy earth and pushed herself upright. At least her body, or skull, hadn't struck stone.

Jae's fall had taken her to the bottom of the ravine. She hopelessly scanned the walls. They weren't quite vertical. She supposed that was a good thing. It was the slope that had likely spared her life. The long fall down had been merciful, but there was no hope of climbing out of here. Not without someone to throw down a rope to the top. Jae peered back and forth, hoping to find an end in sight. In either direction, the ravine snaked on to somewhere unseen.

A low groan came from a few yards away, startling her. Jae looked in the direction of the noise and saw Gryff's massive shape rising, his clawed fingers rubbing at his temple.

"Gryff!" She hurried up to him, then half-knelt, half-collapsed beside him. "Gryff! Are you hurt?"

"Reckon not," he grumbled, though she could barely make out what he'd said through his grunting. His fingers prodded his head again, and he let out a strangled groan as he sat upright, then got to his feet.

Jae raised her head to scope out the ledge above. The fresh hill the warlock had summoned still sat at the top of the ridge. It was large enough to hide their view of anything overhead, a dark mass beneath a web of summer stars.

"The warlock," she said, still trying to steady her breathing. "Where is he?"

"Runnin' after Halston, I'd wager," Gryff snarled. He looked hopelessly up at the ravine's rim.

A chill that could have frozen a June desert ran through Jae. If the warlock knew they were down here and hadn't bothered with a chase . . . maybe Halston was right. The warlock was only here for *him*.

Jae hurried to the wall of the ravine. The angle was too steep, too much. It wasn't rocky here, and the earth was damp from its nearness to the river. Hell, parts of it were almost *slick*. There was nothing to cling to, nothing to climb.

"We've gotta get out of here." Surely, panic was creeping into her tone, but right now, she hardly cared about sounding like a mess in front of Gryff.

"Kid, settle—"

"They're gonna get Hal!" She pressed her hands to the ravine's wall and dug her fingers into the damp earth, so hard and deep it hurt the skin beneath her nails. Her limbs were trembling. Each one of her muscles was screaming with agony from her fall, but she *had* to climb out of here. Pain be damned, gods be damned, everything but *getting out of here* be damned . . .

"Gryff?" she felt childish, suddenly, a small thing lost in the wilderness. Helplessly, she stared up at the far-off lip of the ravine. "What do we do?"

She hadn't expected a hopeful answer from him, but his reply still stung.

Gently, Gryff raised his hands. "Wait."

———————

The river's cold reached all the way down to Halston's bones.

When he plunged into the waters, the rush of the chill drowned out all his senses. He held his breath, and began to paddle with all his strength. Halston couldn't remember the last time he'd swam.

The current finally forced Hodge to let Halston go.

Halston sank under the surface for a moment, then broke above the water once more. "Hodge!"

"I'm right here!" his brother called back. He was close.

"Keep going!" Halston answered, though it seemed futile to tell Hodge to keep swimming.

Elias' bloated face flashed in Halston's memory. Halston kept treading water, trying to drive the thought out of his mind.

As the current carried them downriver, Halston fought to keep his head above the water. He kicked and thrashed like a man possessed. It shouldn't have been so hard. When they were children, he and his brothers would swim like minnows. His earliest memories were of the water. Water, cradling him as a child. Water, smelling of salt and fish. Water, all he could see for miles—nothing more than a comfort, an old, familiar friend.

The *sea* was a friend.

The river was a murderous stranger.

Halston kept thrashing against the current. The water's cold dulled his senses, but his eyes kept darting to the rocky bluffs above, waiting for Gryff and Jae to emerge.

No. There was no sandy shore here, just high rocks on either side of the river. Until they reached a flat bank, there would be no climbing out of the water, no tearing back into the woods to find them.

Gods above.

How on earth could he have left them behind?

Before long, the current dipped around a bend, and Halston didn't have to tread the water so violently. He floated closer to Hodge, close enough that they could almost touch. Up ahead, they heard shouting. Faint starlight softened three silhouettes. Lorelin, Flint, and Tsashin waited on a narrow stretch of shore, waving frantically.

"We're here!" Halston shouted. His own voice burned his throat.

"Hurry! Grab the branch!" Lorelin's shadow ordered.

The current brought Halston and Hodge closer to the bank. Halston could make out their features, now—moonglow glinting on Lorelin's golden hair, the long scab on Flint's brown cheek, Tsashin's half-relieved, half-horrified expression. Lorelin and Flint had grabbed a thick, knobby branch and lowered it into the river. They were coming up fast. Halston braced himself.

His hands closed around the wood. Pain bit at his left palm and rushed up his arm. He hadn't realized that he'd cut himself. He felt Hodge's weight clinging to another part of the branch, then gritted his teeth and fought against the tug of the current.

The brothers kicked toward the banks as Flint and Lorelin pulled. Fatigue was tempting Halston, but he pushed himself to cling tighter to the branch.

Flint and Lorelin gave it a mighty yank, and Halston had never been so relieved to feel dry air on his skin.

When his body finally flopped onto the shore, he didn't move. Halston lay there, perfectly still, eyes half-closed. Nearby, insects sang in the water plants. Gravelly mud stuck to his cheek.

"Hal, come on," Lorelin said. The gravel crunched as she knelt over him. "Hal?"

Halston rose up on his knees. To his surprise, Tsashin's slender arms gathered around him, and she put her chin on his shoulder.

"We thought we'd lost you both," she said, her voice wavering with relief. She turned to Hodge and pressed her face into his shoulder. "I'm so sorry. We got too far ahead and jumped like we planned. We . . . we didn't realize that the rest of you had turned back."

Lorelin touched Halston's shoulder. "Hal. *Did* you turn back?"

"I wanted to fight him," he replied, trying not to sputter. "It was my battle. I . . . I couldn't let any of you put yourself in harm's way for me."

"Why? Why on *earth* would you martyr yourself like that?" Hodge said in turn, though he sounded a far cry from angry.

Halston wondered what had been running through Hodge's mind when he'd realized Halston hadn't followed the group. He wasn't sure why he'd been so certain that he'd get away with turning back on his own. Nothing short of an iron barricade could have kept his brother from following him.

But Halston didn't bother with an answer. "Gryff. Jae." Each name tightened his chest with pain. "We lost them."

Lorelin's eyes darkened. "They didn't come after you?"

A futile question.

"The warlock," Halston coughed, then forced the explanation out. "He threw up a big heap of earth and separated us. I think Jae and Gryff fell into the ravine. Then the cloaked man chased us to the river."

"You mean they're trapped?" asked Tsashin, her voice thick with fear.

Halston faced the restless waters, hoping that by some stroke of luck he'd glimpse a pair of flailing arms, Jae's chestnut hair or Gryff's mossy green scales. He shoved a hand against his chest, feeling as though his beating heart might leap right out of it. He looked at his brother, and the distant, forlorn gleam in Hodge's eyes told him that Hodge was feeling just as regretful as he was.

Halston tried to keep his breathing steady. Lorelin remained at his side. All the color had drained from her cheeks.

"We've got to find them," he said at last. "That ravine looked like it ran for miles, it . . . it can't be hard to find." The rocky cliffs continued on the riverside across from him, but where they stood, the shoreline was flat and ample.

"Gryff! Jae!" he shouted at the river, like that would somehow summon them. Then, he raised his voice to the cliffs looming above the waters and cried their names vagain. This time, the shout left his throat raw, but all he had to answer him was the river's clamor.

Halston reached for his pocket and felt the comforting shape of his weapon. Yes, he hadn't lost the knife. Somewhere along the run, he'd saved it, though unconsciously.

"We've gotta move," Flint said finally.

Halston shook his head. "We're going back. We can't go on without them."

If the warlock and his henchmen had killed them, Halston would never forgive himself. They could be dead—already cold—right now.

No. Halston couldn't think like that yet. Sharp, splintering pain roared inside him, but he couldn't give in to it now. If Gryff and Jae were waiting to be rescued, they couldn't waste a second fretting over their misfortune.

Flint said, "They're not here."

Halston ignored him, then started moving downstream. He drifted to the very edge of the riverbank, just before the water met the earth. "Let's go. We've got to find them."

Flint started, "Hal—"

Halston whirled back around. "I'm not going on without them. Follow me or don't. *I'm* going back to look for them."

He took a few more strides downriver. When he looked back over his shoulder, he saw that everyone had followed him.

They made their way down the bank, looking from the narrow strip of land they walked on, to the river itself, to the short but un-scalable cliffs rising on the other side of the water. There was no hope of getting to the other side. Halston kept hoping he would glimpse Gryff's hulking shape, or Jae's slim one, running along the bluffs, but all he saw were still and silent trees.

The thought of the warlock confronting Gryff and Jae burst up in his mind. Halston's stomach clenched. Would he capture them? Kill them outright? Pass them right by in hopes of getting to Halston again?

They were here for me, Halston thought. He wished he could place a message in the care of the wind itself, carrying it to the man in the dull gray mask. *Spare the others. Come and get me.*

"This warlock," Flint said slowly, a note of suspicion leaching into his tone. "What does he want with you?"

"I don't know," Halston said. He figured he might as well tell Flint about the caverns, to buy them more time to wait if nothing else.

For a while, after Halston finished his recollection, Flint said nothing, but there was a look of faint regret in his eyes. Halston knew that Flint was wondering what the hell he'd gotten himself into.

But they kept on. They walked until the shore ended and the flat, sandy land became a stretch of short cliffs once more. They would have to turn back. There was nowhere else to go.

Instead, Halston just stared down at the restless current lapping at the sand. He was close enough that if he fell face-first, the river would swallow him whole.

They waited there on that riverbank until the sky began to pale with the first whispers of sunlight.

Finally, Flint said, "We should go back."

"No," Halston said. He squinted at the cliffs on the other side of the river.

"We can't cross here," Lorelin said, though the grief in her voice was heavy as lead. "We should go upstream. We can . . . we can look for them in the daylight."

It was a pointless, fruitless suggestion, and Lorelin must have known it. But Halston had never known her to voice pessimism out loud, however bleak things seemed. He wished he could do the same.

But they couldn't just give up.

"We need to move," Flint said. "It'll be best for us all if we put some distance between ourselves and the revenants. I'll take us to see my friend Levi. He's . . . familiar with these sorts of things, perhaps he can—"

Halston cut him off. "Not yet." He hardly cared about being impolite right now.

Flint stared at him for a moment. "I don't know what sort of mess you're in. But your gang," he said, nodding at Tsashin and Lorelin, "saved my life at the fort, and I won't forget it. Besides, I promised to help you, and I've never been a man to go back on his word. I'm taking us to see Levi. He can give us food, more ammo. We'll rest there, and then we're going to Telin."

"We can't *give up on them,*" Halston replied, unable to bring himself to look away from the river.

Though Halston didn't dare say so out loud, he knew Flint was right. There was nothing anyone could say to change this. No amount of time spent waiting at the water's edge would get Jae and Gryff to reappear. The river was utterly impassable for miles.

But Halston still couldn't tear his gaze from the water. Had his pursuers killed Jae? Gryff? Were they lying dead in that ravine? Maybe the warlock had tossed them into the river, and the current would carry their bodies downstream until they were unrecognizable.

Just like Elias. Gods above, Elias first, and now . . .

No. This wasn't real. Surely, the two of them would appear. Soon enough. They'd all be together again. Halston's breathing still hadn't slowed.

"Hal, you're crazy if you think we're leaving you behind." Hodge touched Halston's shoulder, but it wasn't enough to rouse him from his stillness. "What if the warlock catches up to us?"

That was it, then. If even Hodge could bring himself to keep moving . . .

Hodge whispered, "We'll find them. They're strong, Hal. They can take care of themselves, and we'll find a spot where we can cross the river and head back. I'm sure of it. But we ain't gonna find them by standing here and staring."

He was right. They had to keep moving. Waiting here would accomplish nothing.

Halston finally managed to pry himself from the water's edge. Without another word, he rejoined the pack, and they trekked onward into the night.

But two burning thoughts plagued him every step of the way.

The man in the mask wanted *him,* and if he'd managed to track Halston down twice before, it was only a matter of time before he did it again.

The second was that if Gryff and Jae were lost, captured, or worse because of him . . .

Then he hadn't a single right to still be walking down this road.

Chapter 33

The skin on Jae's hands was raw and pink.

The moon was not yet setting, and the sky had not taken the first gasps of dawn, so they had at least a few hours of darkness left. After walking for what Jae guessed was around two miles, she and Gryff had finally found a decently rocky part of the ravine. Still steep, but at least there might be some decent handholds here.

Jae had spent the last fifteen minutes leaping up for the ledge, desperately trying to find a dent in the rock. Maybe she could get a grip and lift herself up, find some footing, and climb out of here. It wasn't *too* steep. She could do it.

"Will you cut that out?" Gryff finally said. "You're wasting your energy."

Gryff had been sitting a few paces away, slouching on a short, slanted rock, rifle on his lap.

Here she was, working her fingers to the bone trying to find a way out of here, and he was just . . . sitting there. Jae bit down on her cheeks and glared. It was all she could do to snuff out the sparks of her anger. "I know what I'm doing."

"No, you don't. Listen. It's dark. We'd better rest for the night. When the sun comes up, I'll help you."

She turned her back to him. "I don't want your help."

She remembered that night by the pond. Gryff, sticking his scaly nose in business that wasn't his. If he wasn't going to find a way out of this with her *now*, then that suited her just fine. He could climb out of here tomorrow. Halston and the others needed her *tonight*.

Her aching limbs and frustration were nearly bringing tears to her eyes, but she wasn't giving up yet.

"For the gods' sake, just listen to me for one—"

"Why?" She bit down on her cheeks, trying to keep tears of anger from welling in her eyes. "So we can get stuck in a *different* mess?"

"Gods above, you're actin' like . . ." Something made him stop speaking. A second thought? Guilt? Patience? Jae didn't know, but she was still too mad to care.

She finally looked over her shoulder at him. Tough as it could be to read the emotions on his snake-like face . . . there was no mistaking the sadness there. There was a distant look in his yellow eyes.

Jae swallowed, then turned from him again. Had she somehow managed to hurt *Gryff's* feelings, of all people? Gods. If that was the case, she was wretched.

Gryff had been right about one thing: she'd been wasting her energy. Suddenly, the top of the ledge looked farther away. She swallowed at the thought of thousands of unseen terrors lurking in the darkness up there. Would the warlock and Captain Crane's revenant return?

A new fear seized her. The thought of never seeing any of them again— the girls, Hodge . . . Pa . . . Hal. The idea had been too wholly impossible to cross her mind. Now, she wasn't just aching.

A wave of sickness seized her, like she might lose what little food was in her stomach.

She should have been ready for this. She was going to leave them one way or another. They'd all have had to part ways eventually, and likely . . . soon after this.

But not like this.

Never like this.

Jae dragged herself over to a flat rock and sat down. She kept her back turned to Gyrff, taking a few moments to breathe deeply and let her churning stomach level out. She wasn't feeling hot headed anymore, but her attempt to climb out of here had left her feeling sore, her already-sore muscles tingling like she'd just scaled a mountain. Alright, she'd take a break. Just a short one, then it was back to climbing.

As usual, Gryff was quiet, but he didn't look so forlorn anymore. She sensed anger simmering inside him—then again, there *always* seemed to be anger simmering inside him. She just didn't like knowing that this time, she'd caused it.

Who *was* she? What had she been thinking, snipping at him like a child?

"I shouldn't have snapped at you," she murmured, though she didn't dare raise her voice much louder than a whisper.

"It don't matter," Gryff said, though his voice didn't depart from its usual tone. "Get some sleep, will ya?"

Jae tapped her fingers against the rock. "I don't want to rest till we're out of here."

"Alright, do what you want. I ain't arguin' with you no more." He leaned back against his own rock and shut his eyes.

Jae undid one of her braids, then the other one. She ran her fingers through the tangles, then braided her hair once more while she waited for the moon to disappear. It had not budged much.

"I'm sorry," she said, though it was tough to force it. It was a phrase she wasn't used to . . . and perhaps that was a bigger problem than she'd realized. "I get real angry when I'm scared."

"I've noticed," Gryff grumbled. "Does it *help* you to do that?"

"Do what?"

"When you start yellin' like thunder when somethin' frightens you. Does it help?"

For a second, she thought he might be trying to ruffle her feathers, but she heard a strong dash of patience in his bluntness. "Sometimes." She swallowed. "But . . . I'm usually better off when I keep a cool head."

Without opening his eyes, Gryff said, "Then I reckon you ought to try keepin' a cool head *now*."

A cool head . . . Gods, it shouldn't have been this hard. Jae wished they'd made it to the river so she could dunk herself in the water. She settled for breathing in deep, facing the stars for a few moments, on focusing on their beauty, on what a gift it was that they showed up, night after night, unchanging, and what a real gift that was.

Jae tapped her fingers against her knee. Gryff might have been asleep now, but she couldn't stop herself from speaking her one burning thought. "Who was I acting like?"

Gryff's eyes opened slowly. "Huh?"

"You were about to say that I was acting like someone."

Gryff was quiet for so long, Jae figured she might as well just drop it. But then, he said at last, "Her name was Lexa. Don't matter, though. She ain't here anymore."

"Who was she?"

Another lengthy stretch of silence. Then: "My daughter."

A *daughter!* "You never told me—"

"I don't tell *anybody* about her." His voice was straining like the last gasps of a dust storm. "Don't tell anyone about Kalea or Idrex either."

Jae didn't repeat the names aloud, but her lips began trembling, trying to take on the shape of their names. Strange names, but beautiful, like thick frost on wildflowers.

Then, Gryff began to chuckle a little. There wasn't a hint of mirth in the sound, though. "Like I said. They ain't here anymore, but . . . they've gotta be out there somewhere, don't they? 'Specially Lexa. Takes more than a falling roof to snuff out a spitfire like her. Nothin' in this world can kill a spirit like that."

"Falling roof?"

Gryff cleared his throat. "Listen here. I reckon that you ain't gonna rest, however many times I tell you to. But if you really reckon we can get out of here tonight, I'm all for it. So . . . are we gonna spend all night talkin', or are we gonna think of a way out of here?"

Jae swallowed hard. "Yeah. Yeah, let's get out of here."

"Good. Will you listen to me then?"

Jae nodded.

Gryff let out a long, thin breath and began to fidget with something on his back. His hand came forth holding his lasso.

It took less than a second for Jae's anger to come rushing back. "You had that the whole time and didn't tell me?"

"I've my reasons," Gryff said with surprising coolness.

"But we could have used it sooner!" Jae wanted to blow up again, but she made herself pull a new puff of air into her chest. She began breathing from her gut instead of her chest, reminding herself to keep a cool head, even if it felt almost as tricky as getting out of this place.

Gryff pointed to the ledge. "Walk along south and see if there are any tree stumps or boulders we can catch this on. I'll go north. Let's meet back here in a quarter hour."

Jae parted from Gryff and paced south as quickly as her feet would carry her across the rugged ground. She looked every which-way, surveying the jagged tops of the gorge. The land was mocking her. She walked for half an eternity and there wasn't a single anchor to toss a rope around.

In defeat, she trudged back to the spot where she and Gryff had camped in the first place. He was standing firmly planted on the ground, running a thumb over the length of gold rope, staring up at the ledge as if eyeing it down would somehow make a stump sprout up right before them.

"No luck," Jae muttered.

Gryff sighed. "In that case, we should rest. We'll try again in the morning."

"I told you, I'm not resting."

"We'll have better luck in the daylight, kid. At least one of us should have a rested mind."

"You go first."

"No. Now go lie down before I eat the last of your rations."

Jae was too tired to pick another argument. At least the night was warm enough. She bundled her jacket into a makeshift pillow and lay down. She didn't bother covering herself up with a blanket from her pack; she didn't plan on sleeping long.

She relaxed her muscles and faced the eternal sky. Usually, the stars were one of her greatest comforts, but now she felt very small and weak—like she was swimming through open water with no shore in sight.

A thought came over her, and she acted on it before she'd even had the chance to dwell on it. "Gryff."

"Hm?"

"I don't know how they died," she said, and she wasn't sure why. And just before sleep took her, she finished, "But it wasn't your fault."

Chapter 34

Jae woke to an ear-piercing screech.

Before she'd even come to her senses, her limbs were already flailing wildly. In her first second of wakefulness, she meant to stand, but a muscular arm hooked around her waist before she could. She nearly screeched in terror before she realized it was Gryff. He flung her over his shoulder like a sack, and Jae almost cursed at him. What was he *doing?*

But before she could demand he put her down, he hissed *"Quiet,"* through his teeth.

Jae caught a glimpse of gray sky, and by the scanty light, she figured it was barely daybreak. Gryff hurried across the ravine's floor, leaping over rocks and darting around boulders. Jae was getting tossed around like beans bouncing in a jar, and she couldn't see a thing, save for a vast shadow circling on the ground—a shadow that did not belong to Gryff.

The shadow disappeared when Gryff dipped beneath a large, flat slab of rock leaning against the gorge's wall. There was a space for them to shelter in, just wide enough for them to crouch in and peer out.

Jae dusted herself off after Gryff released her, not sure if it was even safe to ask him what the hell was going on.

A deep rumble echoed somewhere overhead. Jae squinted at the swath of darkness that began climbing over the ravine, bathing everything in shadow. Then, it began to rain.

But this wasn't a regular rainstorm. It came on all at once. A moment earlier, this place had been bone-dry. Now, the raindrops came swift and heavy, with no buildup to signal its incoming.

The screech came again. Through a gap in their shelter, Jae could see the gigantic shape swooping overhead. A bird with a wingspan as wide as three wagons pushed together, and feathers dark as pitch.

Jae swore under her breath. "A *stormbird.*"

Jae had never seen one before, and she'd thanked her lucky stars for it. South of the Outlands, they were rare, but the birds' appetites were as large as their bodies. Always hollow were their bellies, and all they wanted was *flesh.* The more, the better.

And Gryff and Jae had plenty of it.

Jae recalled Tsashin speaking to that little ghost girl about the *sun*birds, who brought the sunshine. When she spoke of them, they'd sounded about as scary as a house cat with a limp. Damn it, why couldn't one of *those* come instead?

All around them, the storm raged on as the bird swooped in wide circles overhead. The rainfall kept coming, and the thunderous wings kept beating. The downpour muddied the ravine, throwing up splatters, gathering in pools. Jae stayed close to Gryff while she tried to steady her mind long enough to think up a plan. If the bird kept flying over them, the sky would keep raining. If it kept raining, how long would they have before the ravine filled up and the water swept them both away?

The bird cried out again. With its cry, another rumble of thunder rattled their surroundings. The ground itself shuddered. Jae planted her feet, determined to remain standing.

Maybe the monster would feast on them, maybe they'd drown, or maybe the ravine's walls would melt into a landslide.

"It's circlin' us," Gryff muttered. "It won't leave till we come out. It knows we have nowhere to run."

Jae didn't dare think of what it would feel like to have the beak of a house-sized bird plunge through her chest. To be torn apart, limb by limb. Her fingers began to tremble, but she couldn't let the fear break her down. "Let's shoot it."

"We don't have enough ammo to fell somethin' this big. Comin' out of here to aim is *suicide*. I reckon it'll just dive for us straight away."

"We can't just wait it out."

Gryff's yellow eyes were still bright in the shadows. Jae took a good look at his slitted pupils, his rugged scales. There were moments when she found him almost frightening, but not now. Still . . . she wished that he was intimidating enough to scare off a stormbird.

The rain drumming on the rock shielding them was about to drive her mad. Already, she felt the water seeping in through her boots, and her hair was sticking to her damp forehead.

She realized that the raindrops were getting heavier. Gryff shouted something. Jae didn't hear it. The boom cut him off.

The flash blinded her, and the blast threw her backwards.

Jae crashed into the ground. The impact knocked out her breath. She opened her mouth trying to gulp down air, but the rain filled it, making her sputter and choke. She forced her eyes open, and the whole world looked hazy. Her eyes still burned from the lightning strike, and she was already soaked to the skin.

Jae pushed herself upward just in time to see that the lightning strike had thrown them clear out of their hiding spot. Gryff lay about two yards away, still splayed out on his back. The lightning hadn't hit either of them directly, but the relief was short-lived.

The stormbird dove from the sky, and when its talons struck the earth just in front of Gryff, the impact of its landing shot through the ground. Already, its beak was wide open, prepared to bite. It fanned out its wings, throwing back its head to let out a harsh, hungry cry.

Jae forgot herself. All the feeling in her body disappeared. She was all mind, all spirit. It was as if she were watching the whole thing from the top of a raindrop, slowing time for a moment in midair.

Because the stormbird was *beautiful.* It had the sort of beauty that drove men mad, that only gods were supposed to behold.

Its feathers shone like dark glass. Tufts of cloudlike vapor plumed from its body, following each of the bird's movements. In its eyes sparked veins of lightning, so bright they burned.

In all the men she'd tracked and killed, in all the beasts she'd stumbled across, even in the eyes of the Nefilium . . . she had never seen such blind fury.

When its head plunged toward Gryff, there was no time. No time for Jae to do *anything* but scream his name.

The damned rain blurred it all, but when she watched its beak meet Gryff's neck, a ragged scream tore at her throat.

Not Gryff!

She waited for the bird to pull away from him, Gryff's head in its beak, the rest of him left sprawled out on the ground. But that didn't happen.

Gryff was still moving—yes, he was still moving! The bird was writhing, and though it didn't have Gryff in its mouth, it was holding on fast to something. Then Jae made out the outline of a straight rod propped in its beak, Gryff gripping with both hands and pushing back with all his might.

His rifle!

It would buy him time, but not much.

Jae staggered two steps back and drew her pistol. Godlike monster or not, she'd never heard any learned traveler say that an old-fashioned bullet wouldn't still do the trick on a stormbird. And so she shot.

She didn't see where the bullet struck it, but Jae was certain she'd hit the bird, because the thing bucked up at once, rifle falling from its beak, and let out a scream twice as loud and piercing as all its others.

The bird recovered itself, then fixed its furious gaze on Jae and leapt over a hefty rock that lay between them. The rugged terrain in the ravine might slow the bird down, but it would limit Gryff and Jae's movements as well. Jae watched Gryff jump back up to his feet, and as fast as she could, she shifted backward, trying to get her arm steady enough to shoot again. The stormbird veered sharply to Jae's right, then lashed forth, beak snapping.

Jae dodged, the bite missing her by just a hair. The rain beat down on her head, and already, she was starting to feel the haze of dizziness. The bird's head snaked away, then it leapt for her and snapped again. She shuffled back, then to the left, nearly losing her balance on the slick mud before ducking behind another rock. Another clipped screech escaped the stormbird's beak.

Gryff was on his feet again. Swiftly but steadily, he took up his rifle and aimed at the monster. The low crack of the gun split the air. The stormbird shrieked and lifted one of its feet. Perhaps it was only rain, but Jae swore she saw a few drops of blood stream from its talons.

Gryff had bought her just enough time to take three big strides backwards. At last, she could shoot again. She aimed for the bird's head.

Just as she fired, another blast of lightning shook the whole world and threw her off her feet.

This time, Jae's head broke her fall.

She blacked out a second. Her senses came back quick enough— rain, rain like she'd never felt, pounding on her skull and flesh so hard it ached. She opened her eyes. The first thing she saw was the bird, tossing its head wildly from side to side, deep red blood gushing from one of its eyes. Though she was still caught in a daze, some small part of her was grateful she'd hit it in the eye.

Gryff was standing next to her. He wasn't looking at her, but then his rough hand nudged something into her own. "Grab it."

Jae's fingers closed around a thick length of rope. She sat up, and her vision trailed down the line of Gryff's golden lasso. The other end sat just by the stormbird's feet. It didn't notice the rope. It was still thrashing and wailing over its ruined eye. Sitting just before it was the rest of the rope, ending in a wide loop, lying slack on the ground.

Gryff tossed a stone in the bird's direction, startling it a few hops forward. One foot landed just inside the loop.

Then, Gryff shouted, *"Hold on!"* And like a madman with a death wish, he pulled the rope.

"Gryff!" Jae screamed, but somehow, her hands knew what to do. They clutched the rope so tightly they ached.

No—

Was he—

When Gryff yanked the rope, the loop closed around the bird's ankle, then he tossed another rock at the stormbird's chest. Once more, it shrieked, then it took off, and the gust of wind from its wings hit Jae like an iron board slamming against her entire body.

Jae was too frightened to even scream as the rope pulled tight and lifted them off the ground.

She gripped the rope with all her strength, praying to the gods that her wet hands wouldn't lose hold of it, and managed to squeeze the lower part of it with her legs. The lasso was rough against her cheek. Up, up, up they soared. The bird brought the storm with them, leaving the ravine behind, forgotten. Each beat of its wings sent a new wave of thunder rolling over the earth. They were *flying*.

Jae's heart dove into her stomach, but she held fast to the rope so tightly her hands burned. It was shaking madly with Gryff's weight up above.

The stormbird's screeches were like knives in her ears, but the sound was an afterthought. Above, Gryff was *scaling* the rope, and Jae could make out the outline of his knife between his lips. Each one of his movements threatened her grip on the lasso, but she clung with all her strength.

Jae looked down and only half-regretted it. They weren't too far off the ground. Their weight was keeping the stormbird from taking all the way to the skies. If they fell . . .

It would hurt.

They might crack their ribs, or legs, or leave with a few scars.

They might not live.

But if they did . . .

Gryff took one hand off the rope to grab the knife from his teeth. He was just a whisper of space from the bird's feet, where he'd looped the rope. Then he shouted, "Get ready to fall!"

And he began to saw.

The bird kept squawking, and with each pulse of Gryff's blade shooting through the rope, it warbled. Jae glimpsed sparks of gold flying from the rope as he severed it—she'd forgotten that the rope was magical.

They were both shaking. The stormbird swooped lower to the ground, and the tips of Jae's boots skimmed the piney treetops. Her breath caught. If they fell here, the branches could spear straight through them. Then the bird rose again, higher this time.

Gryff kept on sawing. The bird wavered and rose, shuddered and sank. Each frenzied motion threatened to send them both plummeting.

Then, the final snap came.

Their weight was held by the air alone.

And as they fell to the earth, only one thought entered Jae's mind.

This was gonna be one hell of a story.

Down, down, down, and then they hit the ground. She didn't register whether she landed on her feet or knees. Impact shot up her legs and threw her to the side. She broke into a roll and let the sodden earth pass beneath her body. The sky and ground became a hazy blur. She rolled until a thick tree stump put an end to her progress. The rush was gone. Pain took its place.

Jae bit down on her tongue. The taste of blood pooled in her mouth. But she was breathing—breathing deeply, greedily.

For a while, she lay there, eyes shut, savoring the feeling of breath traveling down her throat and into her chest. Her head and limbs still ached, but the initial pain of the impact slowly trickled into a duller one. She was alive. By the gods, she was *alive*.

She knelt, then stood. She could stand without roaring pain in her legs, so at the very least she knew those bones weren't broken. Shade from a pine thicket shielded her from the sky. Somewhere, a ways off, the bird's screeches still reached them, but its shadow wasn't on the ground, and its shape wasn't in the sky.

It wasn't raining anymore. The storm had passed. Spots of gray clouds dotted the sky, and Jae wasn't sure whether the stormbird had created them, but there was just enough daylight to get a good look at her surroundings: tall firs and scattered bushes.

Her hands stung. Jae raised them to inspect the damage and winced at the sight: pink flesh, blood gathering in shallow scratches running like latticework across her palms.

A hearty voice groaned and said her name. "Jae."

"Gryff!" She took off in the direction of his voice. "Where are you?" Near. So very near. First, she saw the golden rope, and she followed it like a trail leading to a place of refuge.

She found him lying limp in a heap of bushes. He had crushed them upon landing. His rifle lay beside him, and ten feet away his hat lay forgotten, looking as crumpled and defeated as he did.

"You hurt?" Jae finally breathed out, fearing her heart might stop. She wasn't Lorelin, or Martina. She could patch a wound well enough, but she lacked that magic touch that could keep someone from stepping too close to death's door.

To her relief, Gryff shook his head. "Patted myself down. Nothin' broken. These here broke my fall," he said, wincing as he motioned to the bushes.

Jae felt her mouth twist into a tight, burning smile. An urge to shout worked its way up her throat. It turned into a laugh. And she laughed harder when Gryff's eyes widened at her reaction. She had to shove a fist under her rib cage to keep herself from snorting and howling. With their luck, the bird would find them here again if she couldn't shut herself up.

"Kid?" The bushes rustled as Gryff pushed himself up.

"You're *crazy*!" Jae could barely push the words out through her laughter.

Gryff just snorted. "Had no other choice."

Gryff let her laugh herself into a state of calm, but it took a while. She understood it, now, why some folks laughed at times when doing so would've seemed batty to anyone else. There was just too *much* stirring inside her. She had to get it out, send it all somewhere else.

Jae helped him get to his feet. For good measure, they patted themselves down once again. Cuts here. Gashes there. They patched themselves up the best they could. Jae had some spare cloth they used to wind around the open wounds.

When they were done tending to themselves, Jae asked, "Should we keep going?"

"Hell no," said Gryff. "We're *restin'*. And then we're findin' somethin' to eat."

Jae nodded. They'd fallen in a nicer part of the woods—here, the trees were sparse, and the air smelled nice. Fresh, almost sweet. Like unripe strawberries.

"Gryff?" Jae said after a beat of silence.

"What?"

"I just gotta say. I'm . . . I'm glad I got stuck with you."

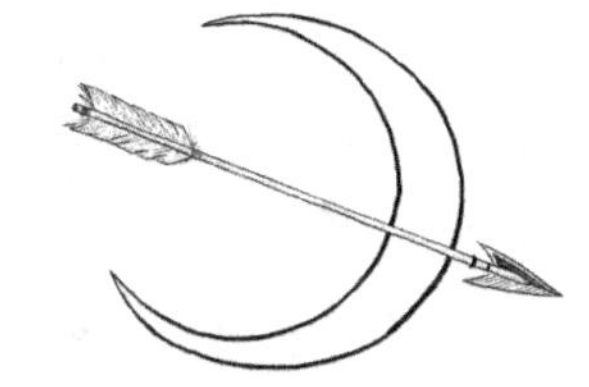

Chapter 35

The stars weren't bad company. For years, they'd been the only beings Jae could count on seeing every day without fail.

Gryff wasn't bad company, either.

They sat beneath the stars, nibbling on the raw roots and greens they'd gathered earlier. Gryff had muttered something about needing real meat, but after the shifter and the stormbird, neither one was keen on announcing their presence with any more gunshots. No need to rouse the attention of any other monsters in these woods.

There was no need for a fire tonight, but the ground still felt cold through Jae's jacket. Everything here was damp—soil dark and thick with moisture, dew glimmering on the leaves and stones, dripping from the twigs.

"Why's the lasso gold?" Jae asked, twisting a dandelion leaf between her fingers.

"I don't know."

"Sure you do."

Gryff shrugged. "Zeph just made it that way, I guess."

Jae swallowed a bite of the greens. She'd kill for a cut of real venison, right about now. Or a turkey leg. "What's it for? You never told us."

No response. Gryff began inspecting one of the cuts on his forearm.

Jae was tempted to pry . . . but perhaps he had his reasons for keeping quiet about it. She did her best to ignore the curiosity gnawing at her, finished off her paltry meal, then stretched out her arms and smiled at the stars. For the first time in weeks, she didn't feel as if she were teetering off a ledge. She was still on the ledge, wherever it was, but she no longer felt that she was about to fall.

Gryff said he'd take the first watch. Jae knew she should try to sleep. Each time she shut her eyes, a few bleak moments would pass, and she would feel the ground lurch from under her and shoot bolt upright. But everything was just the same as when she'd lain down.

She gave up, then spent a good while counting the stars, losing her place, and starting over. It wasn't working. Finally, she said, "Do you think we'll find them?"

"Sure, we will," Gryff said, though he sounded more wary than assured. "If we head to Telin, I reckon we'll find them somewhere on the way. You've got that map of yours, right?"

Jae hadn't bothered checking her map yet, but she figured she might as well do it now. She took it from her pack, unfolded it, and whispered the name. At once, the path to it appeared. A three-days' journey, perhaps two if they hurried.

"We might be too late," she said. "They might not be there anymore. They might—"

"We ain't gonna just lose 'em, Jae. We'll find 'em if they don't find us."

Us. "Are you . . ." She swallowed. ". . . going with them? Once they open the portal?"

"Sure," said Gryff. "There ain't nothin' left for me in this world. Might as well try the next one. But to tell you the truth, I've never thought that far ahead. All I've thought about for years is runnin' from the law and keepin' us alive. I always reckoned I'd go with 'em if they ever did get the whole knife back, but . . . it ain't often I thought about anythin' past tomorrow."

He sounded almost scared. Jae thought back to being small and looking forward to growing older, because she'd assumed that fear was something that only children felt. Surely it would go away when she grew up. That was why Pa wasn't scared of anything. She missed that. Believing that she could someday be courageous without a second thought.

She put her map away, then lay back down and rolled onto her side. Gryff was staring up at the stars as well. She'd once heard somewhere that the Azmarians were skilled sailors, that they figured out how to use the stars to navigate the seas long before humans could. Watching Gryff sitting there, she thought of the courage it would take for one to leave his homeland and journey to a new one, to the other side of the world.

"Why'd you come here, Gryff?"

"Come where?"

"Ain't many Azmarians here in Hespyria," she said. "I've always wondered that about you. What brought you to our side of the world?"

Jae wasn't sure why she'd asked him. She'd fully expected silence. Some rebuff if not.

But . . . he answered her.

"Well, I wasn't born in Azmaria. Never even been there. But my folks came from there," Gryff said with an air of fondness.

"There's a reason there ain't many humans in our country. Work ain't easy to come by there. Bunch of rocky islands, little farmland. So they packed up and left. Sailed here to Hespyria.

"They came with six other families, but had no luck in the east." He grunted with a touch of disdain. "This was before all the factories sprang up . . . too little land, not enough work. So they spent everything they had on wagons to come out here. Built cabins in Banderra and raised livestock. Had families.

"That's where I was born. Had our own little village, just our kind . . . It was a good life. Simple. Wasn't excitin' enough for me when I was young." He pointed at her. "You keep that in mind, kid. Excitement is the last thing you'll want when you're older.

"My pa died in . . . gods, I don't even remember if he was huntin' or fishin' . . . maybe he fell? Some sort of accident. My ma lasted a few more years. I think she got sick. I wandered downstairs one day and found her lyin' cold. Just never woke up.

"When we got older, my brother went east to work in the factories. He told me to come with him. We could do the work of three men and make good lives for ourselves. There were more Azmarian girls east, anyway, but I . . . ." He paused for a long time, and Jae started to wonder if he'd forgotten what he planned to say next in the middle of his sentence. "I didn't want to leave her."

Jae didn't need to ask who she was. Gryff told her right away.

"Kalea was her name. You ever heard anythin' so beautiful? And she was smarter than anyone else I've ever met."

"Even Halston?"

Gryff nodded solemnly. "Even Halston."

"Damn."

"No kiddin'." He might've even chuckled at that. "She was so hard to please. But that just made me wanna try harder. Only agreed to marry me after I'd built a house and reared a few oxen for the two of us. I got the job done.

"We had a bad frost one spring. My crops made it, but her folks' fields all died. They figured they could either eat paper-thin roots all year or move south. So they left. But Kalea stayed with me.

"It was just us in that house for a little while. That valley was our world. Belonged to no one else." He spoke with a warmth Jae had never heard in his voice before.

She pictured a tiny cabin bordered by towering cliffs and swathes of rolling green. Two Azmarians in the northern country, building a life for themselves. "Just the two of you?"

"For a while. Lexa came two years after," said Gryff. "Then Idrex. Quiet one, my son was. Didn't say a damn word till he turned four. When he fell on the floor and spat out his first curse word, I knew for sure he was my blood." Gryff let out a broken laugh. "He liked to sit on the back fence and watch the sky change. Bored me half to death at the time, but now . . . I wish I'd done it more—just sat and watched the blue turn gold with him. I think he had a knack for *appreciatin'* things. Wish I'd been able to learn that from him.

"And Lexa was the wild one. Never could stay put. Played by her own rules. She used to wander for miles into the woods, searching for ghouls and the Nefilium. She'd leave offerings for them. Bundles of flowers and buttons. Once she took my wife's jam jars, and I'd never seen her so angry."

A dark look fell over his face. "I should've asked Lexa to be honest about where she'd been. No, *told* her to be honest. Then maybe . . ." He just shook his head.

Despite the sinking feeling in her chest, Jae asked, "Maybe what?"

Gryff did not face her when his answer came. "Then maybe that monster wouldn't have found us." His voice was the lowest she'd ever heard it, thrumming with a growl.

A chill ran through Jae's blood. "What monster?"

"It was . . . like a man, made of dust, ridin' on a whirlwind. I don't know why it spared me. For a long time, I wished that it hadn't. But after it was finished with what it'd came to do . . . it just rode off on its spiral of wind, swarmed over the hills, and disappeared." Gryff's voice began straining, and Jae knew that he was fighting the pain, the scars his memory had prodded at. "I don't know why it came for us, why it brought the house down on them. I don't know what Lexa did to anger it. But when I came home from town that night, to our house lyin' in shambles, it was waitin' for me, lookin' over the wreckage. I swear I heard it laugh at me before it whisked itself away."

Jae shut her eyes, doing everything in her power not to imagine the scene. Gryff's house, collapsed . . . him sifting through the rubble, finding his wife . . . his son . . . his daughter . . .

Now, Gryff was holding the lasso, running his hands over the golden fibers. "I spent years hoppin' from town to town, traipsin' through the wilds . . . I looked everywhere for that demon. I stole, I fought . . . whatever I had to do to keep goin'. I just wanted to figure out a way I could find it, and destroy it once and for all.

"When I met Zeph . . . when I won the bet with him . . ." he lifted the lasso, holding it just in front of his face, "I thought it was pure luck, even if Zeph was furious about givin' it up."

Jae thought of how the lasso sparked when Gryff had sawed at it. "What does it do?"

"It can harness the wind," Gryff said, and Jae could hardly believe that he'd finally told her the truth of it. "I knew that if I caught the demon with this, it would never break away from me. I didn't even know how I'd *kill* it, but I knew this would be a start."

Jae could hardly believe it. Gryff had never found the demon, but why hadn't he used the lasso? Surely, harnessing the wind would have gotten them out of a pinch or two. "Why—"

"—haven't I used it?" Gryff asked.

"Yeah."

"Don't know how. This is a Nefilium tool, crafted by a Nefili man, to be used by Nefilium." Gryff sighed. "Zeph gave it to me, but refused to teach me how to use its power. Still, like he said . . . it's bound to me, and I can't surrender it.

"I spent a few years searchin' for someone who could show me how it worked. But then I joined up with the Harney brothers, and . . . I just stopped."

Jae blinked in surprise. "You stopped?"

Gryff's shoulders slackened. "I stopped."

"Why?"

"I don't know." Gryff pensively ran a claw down the length of the rope. "Had other matters to occupy my time. The days went by, and I thought about the demon less and less. Sometimes, I'd look at this thing, and wonder why I'd worked so hard to find it. Just didn't seem worth it anymore. Maybe I realized that even if I *did* find a teacher, and learned to harness the wind, and got my vengeance . . ." He sighed. "They'd still be gone. I won't say I gave up. If that demon poked its head out of the woods right now, I reckon I'd take my chances with it. But . . . what's done is done. Took me a real long time to realize that."

Maybe that was true. But Jae knew that if she was offered the power to change the past, mold it however she wanted, she'd take it. Sometimes, dwelling on it was all she could do. Doing anything else felt impossible.

Gryff said nothing more. But those names were precious, more valuable than the purest gold. Kalea. Idrex. Lexa. He said them so delicately. Like they were secret treasures a thief might come and steal.

Jae knew better than to press further. Pain was a stubborn thing. It softened but never healed, shrank small enough to be ignored, but it was never forgotten entirely. And she couldn't have Gryff draw it out further. Not after all he'd done for her. They were outcasts in these dark, forsaken woods . . . and though she'd acted like a wretched beast to him, he'd kept her alive.

What's done is done.

Perhaps he hadn't found all of it . . . but Jae hoped that someday, Gryff would find all the peace he deserved.

Jae stood up, then made her way to where Gryff sat. He didn't glance at her until she placed a hand on his shoulder, then turned and faced her with a look of pure surprise.

"Thank you," she said. "For keeping us alive."

He laughed softly. "Least I can do."

Speaking of pain, the day had left her sore. Maybe a night of rest would make it all go away. Jae ventured back to her resting spot, and at last, she drifted off.

Chapter 36

They'd searched far-and-wide for Gryff and Jae, and there was still no sign of them.

Several hours after they'd fled Fort Marksdale, when the day was young and the sunlight was faint, they'd finally found a spot in the river that was shallow and tame enough to cross. They headed back in the direction they'd come, though they didn't dare stray out of sight from the road along the riverbank. Flint reminded them at least once every half hour that losing themselves in these woods could very well be a death sentence.

But eventually, they made it back to the bend in the river where they'd jumped and followed the current to the road they'd sprinted down the night before.

They braced themselves to encounter the warlock, for the land to cave in, for the cloaked man or the cold-eyed revenants to leap from the trees. The thought was terrible, but the thought of going on without Gryff and Jae, they all agreed, was far worse.

As they searched, Halston didn't let go of his gun even once.

When they reached the road down which they'd first fled, the warlock was not there, nor were the revenants. It was midmorning, now, and the earth was far damper than it had been the night before. Halston squinted at the ground. There hadn't been a cloud in the sky that night.

They moved down the ravine, and soon spotted the fresh mound of earth the revenant had summoned, still rising like an upraised fist from the ravine's ledge. In the distance lay the smoldering remains of Fort Marksdale. Now, it wasn't much more than a pile of blackened logs.

Halston gazed down hopelessly into the ravine. The walls were certainly too steep to scale. He squinted at the bottom of the gorge, trying to make out footprints.

"Jae!" Lorelin called out, her hearty voice echoing through the trench. "Gryff!"

No answer.

So they marched along the edge, boots treading over the muddy road. The ravine was like a long, ragged gash in the forest's skin. In silence, they went in the opposite direction of the fort and followed the ravine for miles, walking as morning turned to noon. The endless pines cast their shadows over the forest floor, bathing them all in tangles of darkness. Along the way, nobody spoke.

Late in the afternoon, the ravine came to an end, halting in a solitary, rocky wall beneath a scraggly hemlock grove.

Halston closed his eyes.

Along the way, all they'd seen below was a continuous stretch of loamy earth and rocks at the bottom. There had been no sign of Gryff or Jae.

For good measure, he called their names out one last time. All that came in turn was muted birdsong.

Halston kept his eyes shut, wordlessly praying for a miracle.

"They must have gotten out," Tsashin said, and he felt her small hand tenderly touch his arm. "Right?"

"They must have," Flint agreed, with a note of cautious optimism.

"Then they'll probably be headed for Telin," Lorelin said.

Telin. Yes, that was right. Jae still had her magic map. She could find the way.

If they were headed anywhere, then certainly, it was Telin.

Halston just couldn't push away the vision clouding his mind— the warlock appearing at the ravine's edge and burying Gryff and Jae with a landslide.

"We should get going," Flint said gently, then turned back in the direction they'd come. Slowly, with a hint of reluctance, Lorelin followed him, then Tsashin. Halston remained by the ledge, his boots just inches from the open air.

Hodge strode up to his side. Together, they studied the rocky pit of the ravine together, watching a blue jay swoop over the stones and back toward the treetops.

"We won't find them if we stop moving," Hodge reminded Halston, placing a hand on his shoulder.

He was right. Nothing good could come from standing here.

But when at last they turned away, Halston couldn't keep from cursing his own name.

Two days passed. Then three, four. Flint said that they were getting close to Levi's village, and soon after, they'd reach Telin.

The entire time, Hodge had scarcely left his brother's side. Halston was even quieter than usual. Jumpier, too. Like at any second, the ground would fall out from under their feet and the man in the mask would come to entomb them all.

It was morning, and Halston and Hodge had found a spot where they could watch the sun rise. They'd settled on a hill for the night, and from the crest, they had a decent view of the dawn.

Hodge had never been one for mornings, but he liked watching the sun reappear. Maybe it was just the certainty. The sun could keep rising. They could survive another day. Dawn would arrive. They would wake up again. And again, and again.

When was the last time they'd done something like this? Not for ages, that was for sure. It just hadn't crossed their minds that they could sit in the quiet and enjoy something, just for the sake of it.

They watched as the sun scaled the sky, turning it from black to blue, then gold streaked with pink.

After a time, Hodge said, "I think they'll find us."

"You do?"

"Yeah. Jae's got her magic map."

"It doesn't work on people. Only places."

Hodge scratched at his throat. "I'll bet they killed that bastard in the mask. I'll bet Gryff beat the other one senseless."

"Hodge."

"I mean it! He's gonna find us and tell us all about it. Who knows? If Gryff and Jae took care of them for us, maybe you've been getting worked up about nothing."

For the first time in ages, Halston began to laugh. "When did *you* get so optimistic?"

Hodge shrugged. "I don't know." *Maybe I don't have a choice anymore. Maybe it's all I've got to keep us going.* But he couldn't keep it up for long. "We can't go home without the silver."

They all knew it, but no one had mentioned it. Gryff had been the one carrying it. And Gryff was . . .

Not here. Hodge still hadn't found it in himself to entertain the thought of any other possibility.

Hodge wasn't sure if he believed in gods, but if they were real, maybe they were playing tricks on them. If any power beyond their reach had a hand in this, it certainly didn't want them going home.

The rose-colored clouds were beginning to fade. Dawn to day.

"Do you ever think we would've been better off just . . . accepting it?" asked Halston.

"Accepting what?"

"Everything. This world. We could have walked away from Sterling the second he offered us that knife. Maybe we didn't have to choose this life."

Hodge tried not to roll his eyes. "Of *course* I think about that, Hal. Maybe we could've had an easier life. Or we could've found ourselves in some other mess. Point is, there's no good thinking about it now. Listen: I've had a feeling inside me that they're still out there. Our world is . . . it's there. It's waiting for us. It's still our home. And I don't care if I spend another eighty years here trying to crawl my way back to it. We'll find more silver. We'll get our blade back together. We'll open that portal, and we'll *run*."

Halston was nodding along to everything Hodge said, but Hodge couldn't tell if he was just trying to be agreeable. Halston pinched the bridge of his nose. *Gods, he looks tired.* "They might not find us."

"No. We're gonna see Gryff again. And Jae. And Lia. And Mother."

The older they got, the harder Halston was to read. Sterling had whipped the openness out of him, likely. His face was a blank canvas, even in places like this, when there was only *peace*. But Hodge had seen Halston slip out of it a few times since Sterling's death. Maybe someday, he'd forget it entirely. Maybe laughing could come easily to him, again. Maybe soon, he'd really, truly feel free.

Maybe they'd *all* feel that way.

"You believe me, don't you?" said Hodge.

"Yes," said Halston. "I do."

Perhaps it was a lie. But it certainly didn't sound like one.

"Hodge?"

"Hmm?"

Halston placed a hand on Hodge's shoulder. "I never thanked you. For coming back for me. For . . . for saving us that night."

Hodge recalled looking over his shoulder, then swearing up a storm when he'd realized that Halston had run back into the fight. He hadn't been thinking quite straight . . . All he'd known was that he couldn't leave Halston behind.

Hodge clapped Halston back on the shoulder. "You know I had no other choice."

———

Flint had led them somewhere far off the trail. There were a few times when Halston was almost certain they were lost, but Flint insisted that he knew what he was doing. Levi had had to build his village far away from the roads, Flint explained. If he hadn't, the Rangers would have found him long ago and sent him packing back across the Cannocs.

They arrived at Levi's village late in the afternoon. It was hardly even a village, really, and certainly too small for a name or a pinpoint on a map. Eight cabins were scattered around a firepit in the center, where a grimy cookpot swiveled from a stand. Most of the surrounding trees had been cleared, and the buildings sat on a long stretch of loose earth, the soil rich with decades of rotted foliage.

Lorelin leaned forward and looked around, blonde curls bouncing over her shoulders. "It's awfully quiet."

"Just how everybody here likes it," said Flint.

"Why here? Why deal with the . . ." Lorelin gestured vaguely,

"Well, why deal with the woods? There are better places to build a settlement, if you ask me."

Flint pursed his lips. "It's better than prison. Levi and his wife used to be part of a gang. They're wanted in the provinces, territories, and Quierra."

"Damn," Hodge whistled. "What'd they do?"

"Stole from Kalstira's governor."

Hodge snorted, sounding almost impressed. "*There* it is."

"When they wanted to settle down . . . they figured they would pick somewhere out of the way," Flint continued. "Took a Nefilium Pass up north, built a village, and never looked back." He waved a hand at the forest beyond. "They have some sort of pact with the Nefilium who live nearby. The Nefilium protect them from the Rangers, and in exchange the village helps keep the woods free of monsters."

Flint led them up a pathway to one of the cabins. From the looks of it, it was quaint and well-kept. There were no holes in the rooftop, no cracks in the walls. A garden bloomed outside, framed by a modest fence, swarming with honeybees. Yellow curtains covered the two windows at the front.

Flint stepped up to the door and knocked thrice.

"Come in, Flint," came a dull, raspy voice from the other side.

"I brought some friends, if that's alright."

Footsteps pounded on the floor inside. A tall man with brassy hair and a stubbled chin opened the door. Halston guessed he was around forty. A sizeable collection of tiny scars marred his face, neck, and forearms—markings from years on the road, no doubt. Halston wasn't sure they'd given him a reason to be glaring at them. Then again, maybe he was the sort of man who didn't need a reason.

"What happened?" asked Levi. "Been a while since you brought somebody here. Last time was . . ."

Flint smirked. "Never?"

Levi arched a brow. "Yeah, never. What's going on?"

Flint motioned to the group. "We . . . well, I'm helping them out. I owe 'em one. They need to settle something with Rogue. I figured they'll fare a lot better if I—"

Levi threw up a hand in exasperation, then turned on his heels and retreated inside. "Your soft heart is gonna get you killed one day. Don't I always say that? Not that you'd know. You never listen to me."

Flint drew in a breath, then pinched the bridge of his nose. "For goodness' sake, Levi, learning a little understanding would do you good!"

"It's all wonderful, I'm sure, till they take all your things and leave you on the roadside in the middle of the night," Levi hollered back from inside.

"I *trust* them, Levi!"

Halston heard Levi rummaging through what sounded like a box of clay and iron. "Fine. You trust 'em. They can stay the night if they fix the fence out back."

They stood out in the garden for a while, staring into the open door until Levi finally called, "Well, you coming in or not?"

Flint leaned over to Halston. "You get used to him fast," he whispered before leading the others through the doorway.

Inside, it was warm. A fire blazed in the hearth, wide flames lapping at a hefty log. Something was simmering over the fire, and the smell made Halston's mouth water. An enviable stack of firewood climbed the wall. There was a bearskin hanging on the parallel wall, and beneath it, a brass bed covered in a raggedy quilt.

A flaxen-haired, tired-looking woman lay demurely across the mattress with an open book in her hands. She glanced up at the strangers who had just entered her home, then her eyes returned to the book without a second thought.

Levi wandered over to the front door and kicked it shut. "How's Daisy?"

"Fine. Dead," said Flint.

"Nothing new, then." Levi made his way to the pot on the fire and gave it a stir.

Halston glanced out the window. There was nothing to see but dense woods. He noticed two long, suspicious stains on the windowsill, and his stomach lurched.

Levi caught him staring at the stains "From a lycan that tried to get in here last winter. Haven't seen one since. Last thing that gave us trouble was a shifter a month ago."

"I wonder if it was the same one we ran into," Flint muttered.

After they'd set their belongings down, Halston and Hodge volunteered to go out back and fix Levi's fence. He showed them the damage, and Halston was pleased to find that it wasn't bad. Just a couple displaced posts that needed to be pounded back into place. He'd seen to worse as a cowhand. Levi gave them nails and a pair of hammers, and the boys got to work.

"Been a while since we've done this," said Hodge, struggling to get the first post back into its spot.

"No kidding." And the truth was, it was a good feeling. It reminded Halston of when things had been simpler.

They set to work, and before long, the job was nearly done. But after a while, Hodge wasn't looking at the fence anymore. Halston followed his gaze to . . . of course. Flint and Tsashin were out back, and she was laughing at whatever he was saying.

"Hodge," Halston said. "Let it go."

"Let what go?"

"They're just talking."

Hodge furrowed his brow. "He's a natural," he muttered.

Halston just ignored him. There was no point in arguing about this. Halston got back to the fence and started tapping at a nail again. Flint came over to join them, then. "How's it coming along?" he asked.

"Fine. What were you talking about back there?" Hodge asked, and his attempt to sound unconcerned was downright painful.

"She was asking me about Hardreth again."

"Oh, *Hardreth*," Hodge mused. He started fiddling with his hammer, spinning the handle in his hand.

Flint's brow creased, then a look of understanding crossed his face. "Oh, I see. Pardon me if I crossed a line there. Tsashin was just . . . curious."

Halston could see every step of Hodge's thought process passing over him. Doubt, then consideration, then sheepish acceptance.

"How did you do it?" Hodge asked. "I can never seem to make her laugh like that."

Flint shrugged. "I don't know. Have you tried doing anything interesting?"

Hodge stopped moving the hammer at once. "What do you mean, *interesting*?"

"Forgive me. Didn't mean to sound so blunt. It's just . . . she seems to enjoy hearing about adventures."

Hodge began trying to jam one of the fence posts back into place. "She's been on lots of adventures with us. Maybe the stories ain't as good when you've lived through them."

Flint let out an exasperated sigh. "I can't believe I have to say this, Hodge, but you have absolutely nothing to worry about. I've all but sold my soul to a *witch* for the sake of the girl I love. If that doesn't convince you . . . well, I'm not sure what will. Good luck!" And he sauntered back toward the house.

Hodge didn't seem to notice when Halston finished setting the last post. "I was a jackass to him, wasn't I?"

"Well . . ."

"You can say it."

Halston didn't say 'yes'. If Hodge already knew it, then that was enough. Tsashin had gone off somewhere, and Halston couldn't help but recognize the eagerness to go and seek her in warring with hesitation his brother's eyes.

"Hodge." Halston let out a staggered breath. "You should talk to her."

"Why? She ain't gonna . . . I mean . . ."

"You should *still* talk to her." It didn't matter how Hodge's statement was meant to end. It didn't matter where he was going, where Tsashin was going, how near or far it was. "I don't want you to run out of time."

Hodge's lips parted. "Hal?"

Halston swallowed hard.

A moment later, Hodge continued with a lighthearted snort. "You didn't run out of time. We're gonna find them again, remember?"

Tough as it was, Halston made himself smile and nod. "Right. Right."

"What would you say to her, if she were here now?" Hodge asked.

Halston could hardly bring himself to tell his brother the truth, but somehow, he managed. Really, there were a *thousand* things he wanted to say to her, but if he had the chance, he'd start with the most important.

"That I loved her."

"You do?"

"Yes," said Halston. "I do."

And now that it was too late, there wasn't a shred of doubt in his mind about it.

"It's just like that, isn't it?" Hodge said with a touch of dryness. "So hard to say these things, till you run out of time to say 'em. Then it's the easiest thing in the world."

Chapter 37

For the first time since coming here, the Drifter saw sunlight. He'd been walking through the woods—never straying far from the path—and he'd grown accustomed to the sight of nothing but dark sky and scraggly pines. Things had been almost pleasantly quiet since he'd cut the horned creature's bonds. A rank smell had started to permeate the air—something rotten and vaguely metallic, but he hadn't stumbled across the source of it yet.

As he was walking, he came to a glade. The clearing basked in a shaft of sunlight with no apparent source—it seemed to be streaming from the treetops themselves, though there was no sun at all in the sky. In the center of the glade was a mound of earth coated in especially soft-looking grass, shaded by a leafy tree with vines of ivy circling its trunk.

Sunlight.

How long had it been since he had felt *sunlight* on his skin?

The Drifter took a step toward the tree. He felt tired.

The sunlight was just warm enough. The whole world smelled

sweet. He lay back onto the grass and stared off into the branches. It was faint enough that he might have imagined it, but he thought he heard birds singing nearby.

Rest. He could finally rest.

So for a long while, he lay still.

Half-alert dreams overflowed inside him. He was a child again, young enough to believe that death wasn't real—or at least did not come for everyone. Around him, the world was made of muted color and sound. He dreamed that he'd stepped into a hall filled with candlelight. Summer rain was drumming on the roof.

Nothing could touch him. Nothing at all.

A voice whispered over him, and though it was beautifully familiar, he couldn't place it. "You're going to come back, right?"

"Hmm."

"I said, you're going to come back, right? Please answer me."

He was too tired to lift his tongue, to open his mouth. Sleep. He wanted to sleep.

This was a good place to rest, after all.

He woke to something scraping against his arm, then encircling it. Something thick and rope-like had a hold of him, and it tightened, tightened.

Someone was screaming. It might have been him.

The Drifter's eyes flew open. The vines around the tree had reached out and begun wrapping around his wrist. Beneath them, his veins were standing out. They sank further into his flesh, threatening to cut it open.

The sweet smell succumbed to the stench of rot and decay. Around him, the world was breaking away. Gloom snatched the sunlight from the sky, and with it, the blue. Gone was the grass, the tree.

The vines thickened, then turned hard. Green to gray, frigid iron. The shards of his vision whirled around him, light and colors chasing one another in a restless whirlwind, reforming into something new. The Drifter felt himself slipping into another time, another place.

At last, the scene around him ceased changing, but he wasn't back in the fog-veiled forest. Instead, he stood on a path of stone, not unlike the one he'd been following as long as he'd been here. This one was rod-straight, leading toward a knobby, cave-like building. Lumps of hewn rock formed spires and domes over its foundations, and in the middle was a massive, arched entryway.

The smell of death overpowered the air.

On either side of him, as far as he could see, there were statues. They weren't uniform— some had swathes of space all to themselves, others lay stacked on top of each other, or stood so close they brushed elbows and knees. Some embraced one another. Some were alone. He spied faces of every age among the horde, men, women, children . . .

Had they brought him here to join them?

A sharp force prodded the back of his shin. He glanced over his shoulder, but there was nothing there. Whatever it was, it poked him again, this time on the small of his back.

He moved forward. Though the chains bound his arms, he could still walk quickly enough. The Drifter staggered forth until he passed under the stone arch.

He entered a great hall. A shaft of light streamed in from a wide window on the other side of the hall, revealing that the room was barren. In spite of that, it was vast. Once, it may have been fit for kings, but time had worn at the walls and floor, and the smell of death was even thicker here than it had been outside.

The force hit him again, this time, sharper than ever, like a dull blade twisting through the back of his knee and shooting out the other side. The Drifter gritted his teeth and kept walking until he halted just in front of the enormous window. The glass of the pane was foggy, and sitting on the stone sill, just in front of him, was a lit candle, wax dripping down its sides.

Rooted to his spot, arms still constrained by the chains, the Drifter looked out the window.

Outside, there was an enormous pyre. It must have taken the wood of a hundred trees to construct.

Five figures were tied to the pyre, shoulder-to-shoulder, eyes closed. Though their heads hung limply, chins pressed to their shoulders, he could still see their chests rising and falling with breath.

The Drifter mouthed their names, then cried out to them, and though he tried to shout as loudly as he could, his voice came out as a hoarse whisper. He slammed his head against the windowpane. The glass rattled, and pain shot through his temple. He had to break the glass. He had to get to them. He'd tear this place down from the inside out if he had to.

As he was trying to shatter the glass, a presence manifested next to him. Was it what had led him here? The Drifter found the courage to turn to it.

Beside him stood a being a head taller than him. There was a longbow in its gloved hand, and a quiver of arrows on its back. A thick robe wrapped its body, and an enormous hood shielded its face with shadow.

"Can they see me?" the Drifter asked.

"No. But they're waiting for you." Its voice was sexless, ageless, without cadence or emotion.

The chains binding the Drifter tumbled to the floor with a piercing clatter. The being next to him unslung an arrow from the quiver on its back, then motioned to the candle on the windowsill. "Lift it."

The Drifter reached for the candle and wrapped his fingers

around the stick, trying in vain to steady his shaking hand. His gaze fell to the delicately wavering flame. In his periphery, he watched the being nock the arrow.

"Light my arrow," said the being without feeling. "And I will shoot it into the pyre."

The windowpane disappeared. Now, there was no barrier between the pyre and the arrow. A cold breeze kissed his face. The Drifter wanted to scream at them to wake up, but what good would that do? He couldn't free them, could do nothing but stare.

"Help me set fire to the wood," the being said again, "and then you may leave."

He pictured the fire swallowing them. Would it wake them, or would they remain unconscious as the flames overcame them? "Will they die?" A stupid, worthless question.

"Of course."

The Drifter said, "I won't do it."

"You may leave," the being said, its tone a warning this time. "When the arrow has been fired."

The Drifter snuffed out the candle's flame between his fingers. "I said no."

"Very well, then."

Everything faded all at once, and then, it was as if none of it had been there in the first place. But the chains remained tight around his chest and arms. Now, they were spiraling down toward his legs. Thickening, tugging, threatening to squeeze the breath from his body.

And around him, wheezing out breaths and faint laughs of disdain, were the hunters.

Naked. No eyes. Skin, tight over their skulls and limbs but bagging around their torsos. Their bellies were large, guts swelling— with what, he dared not guess. Wide red mouths, prominent against their pale flesh as rubies in the snow. Rows of jagged teeth, flashing as they whooped and roared.

"Help!" he cried out.

The hunters only laughed. They had crafted their bait just for him, and now, they were devouring their prey. His terror. His helplessness.

He ground his teeth together as the chains tightened. Were they going to crush his chest? Hang him from the nearest branch?

"We would have left you alone," one of them said. The cadence of its voice grated on the Drifter like a nail scraping on granite. "If you'd let them burn."

It wasn't real.

Those bodies on the pyre, a mere illusion. The people who would have burned . . .

They weren't here. He should have known that. They were waiting for him worlds away.

They stepped aside to reveal a casket sitting beside a deep, freshly dug grave. Constructed of flimsy wood, it waited for him, the lid unhinged. Empty. Ready to seal him inside. Before the Drifter could even scream, they yanked him toward the casket, shoved him downward, and a dozen fingernails clawed at his face and clothing, bundling him inside. Before the darkness covered him, his attackers looked upon him one last time.

"*Remember,*" they spat. One last taunt before the lid of the casket slammed shut.

The casket hit the bottom of the grave with a thud, but the fall had seemed to last half a lifetime. A thread of hope—hardly any at all—spurred him to try to move. But they'd bound his limbs well.

He wished that they'd untied the cloth from his stomach, and he wished that he could reach it now.

As long as he had it, no harm could come to him.

Even down here.

Remember.

And the Drifter remembered.

For a little while.

But there was darkness, and there was darkness, and there was darkness.

And he didn't remember anymore.

Chapter 38

"Lake Arania," Jae whispered to the map.

Jae almost could have leapt for . . . not joy, but something close to it.

She imagined this was what it was like to spot land from the bow of a ship. Weeks, months, years at sea had brought her to this.

And it was better than she could have hoped for. The snaking trail on her map showed that it was four miles away. If she was quick, and the land was flat, it would be just over an hour's hike. She almost hugged the paper to her chest like a long-lost friend.

Good thing the night was still young.

Sure enough, Gryff was still sleeping. She'd have to take extra care not to rouse him.

Jae reached into her pack for a pencil and dug around for one of her old bounty receipts. She almost laughed when she picked it up. It seemed like she'd earned this one a lifetime ago. When she grabbed them, she started moving more slowly and spared a moment to look back at Gryff. He was motionless as she'd ever seen him, and by the looks of it, sleeping very soundly. Still, she wanted no surprises. She couldn't wake him. If she did, he'd come right after her.

Guilt was already plucking at her heart. Gryff had to understand, though.

She'd bled for this. Fought for this. She'd lived through what felt like another lifetime, just to hear that name: Lake Arania.

But . . . Gryff would be furious with her if she left.

No.

That didn't matter. She'd come all this way, and she was far too close to the end to turn back now.

And so she wrote Gryff the letter.

Gryff,

I'm going to Lake Arania to find my Pa. It's four miles from here.

-Jae

P.S. I'll be back.

She thought about adding another post-script, one where she asked Gryff if he would give the others all her love if she did not return. She tried to add it, to start the sentence, but she couldn't get the pencil to budge again. A blind, mad certainty stilled it—that she would return, and that Pa would be with her.

And after that, they'd get to Telin, and they'd find the gang.

It was that same certainty that drove her feet to start moving in a new direction. And so, with a flimsy knapsack, a gun, and not much else, Jae Oldridge set out to find her father.

———

This place was strangely familiar.

Jae wandered through the forest, pushing her way past shrubs and weeds, basking in the shadows of the pines. Closer. She was getting closer.

This wasn't where she'd lost Pa, of course. They'd been south of the Cannocs when they'd taken him away, close to Banderra's border. Still, somehow, the woods brought that place to the forefront of her memory. The air was heavy with mist, with a strange and otherworldly coldness about it. The surrounding trees were tall, with thick trunks and a godly fierceness. It was summer, still, but she was freezing. She wished she could have set out in the daylight, but then she'd have had to think up a way to get Gryff off her back.

She kept on listening for hoofbeats, for thin, wispy voices, or even, by some slim chance, Pa's voice.

She felt like a stranger, a trespasser. She was hiding in the pines like before, while the spirits rode off with Pa in their clutches. At once, she was fifteen again, that girl who'd dreamed of the world and the sea. Back then, her only worries had been for things she now realized hardly mattered. Once more, she was a child who had never spilled blood herself.

She'd been braver, back then. She was sure of it. Right now, she needed some of that girl's spirit.

Jae trembled with her next step. The cold, earthy smell around her was almost overpowering. She passed through towering pines, around moss-covered boulders and bushes swarming with brambles. The forest was dead-quiet.

On the night they'd stolen Pa from her, she had torn apart woods like these ones, searching until her fear made her feel half-crazy. *Don't you know?* The trees seemed to say. *Don't you know it's in vain? You tried before. Why on earth are you still trying?*

But there was nothing short of death that could have stopped Jae from marching onward. Her legs began to burn from the hike. Breathing deeply soon started to feel near impossible, and evil visions of failure threatened to smother her mind. Still, she marched on.

Jae alternated between hiking and checking her map. She was getting closer. She kept moving, forcing her feet to fly as quickly as they could without stumbling. The lake was two miles away. Then one.

She stopped to take a drink from her waterskin. Fogginess was beginning to ravage her head, and her hammering heart refused to settle down. The water slid down her throat, and she made herself take several long, drawn-out breaths. She felt better.

She just wished that, after all this time, she'd have found a way to summon all the courage she needed for this day. Maybe she'd never truly expected that she'd make it here. Still . . . here she was.

And whether or not she was ready, Pa needed her.

In spite of the lies he may have told her, she couldn't imagine herself willingly leaving this place without him.

At the very least, she had to try.

The path on Jae's map was hardly wider than a grain on the paper. She glanced up. The pines were thick here, but as she moved downhill, a dank, fishy smell filled her nostrils. The air was damp. She hurried forward several more yards, then glimpsed the rippling sheen of water through the treeline, moonlight shining on the surface.

There it was.

But before Jae could make her final stride for Lake Arania, a biting voice boomed from behind.

"*Kid.*"

Oh. No.

Jae couldn't look at him. *Run.* She had to get away—get herself to the lake before Gryff made her leave. He'd scoop her off the ground and haul her back kicking and screaming if he had to. She knew that much.

And yet, she couldn't get her feet to budge.

"I've been followin' your trail. The hell are you doin' out here?"

She kept her back turned to Gryff. She didn't have it in her to face him, yet, though she was already bracing herself to run. "Didn't you find my note?"

"Yeah, I sure did. And if you pull a stunt like that again, I'm gonna *carry* you the rest of the way to Telin."

Jae took a giant step away from him. "I've gotta find Pa."

Gryff answered with a sigh. "Jae, listen. I wasted years of my life huntin' down the monster that took my family. And I never found it, but even if I *had,* it wouldn't have done me a lick of good. They were already long gone. Nothing would've changed that."

Jae spun around, expecting to see an angry-looking Azmarian, but instead, she found Gryff looking the same way Pa had when she'd snuck out for a late-night swim and been gone for hours. *Don't you ever do that to me again. Do you have any idea how worried I was?*

"This is different!" shouted Jae. "He's alive!"

"How do you know?"

"I just *know!*"

Gryff raised a hand, as if motioning for her to stand back. "You're makin' this harder than it needs to be. I'm givin' you one more chance before I *drag* you back with me."

"You can't."

"I swear, if your ramblin' don't kill me first, I'm gonna—"

Gryff didn't need to finish. Jae would never learn what he'd meant to say.

Ever since that long night, she'd been trying to drown out the memory of those hoofbeats. In vain, she'd struggled to bury the sound under days of riding and hunting, and nights trying to stay warm. But if Jae Oldridge saw a hundred years, she'd still have recognized the barrage of ghostly hoofbeats in an instant.

They were here.

"*Run!*" she cried.

Jae waited for Gryff to sprint off. But his iron gaze—that suddenly reminded her so much of herself—let her know that he wasn't going anywhere. Like a pillar of pure iron, he remained where he stood.

And even when the ghosts came—looking just as she'd remembered them—Gryff stayed right with her.

All around them, like a sudden, raging storm, the ghosts swarmed. Jae found herself in the eye of their storm, trying not to freeze in the icy miasma they brought with them. But this time, she was not hiding. She could see their faces, plain as day.

The spirits of the men leered down at her. In death, they still wore their Rangers' uniforms, and on the chests of a few, she could make out their badges. Captain Crane had been right. Though the sight of their faces was fleeting as they rode in circles around her, she did not glimpse a single old man amongst the horde.

I know why you're here, she wanted to say to them. *I know why you're angry.*

Their gazes tore straight through her. A haggard, thin voice struck her then and there . . . *"Oldridge."*

That was all she knew before a cold grasp seized her ankle from behind. She screamed as she fell, and a rock struck her on the head.

Then all she knew was darkness.

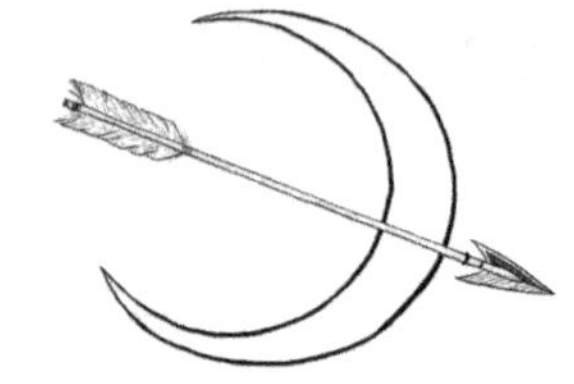

Chapter 39

Jae's eyes fluttered open. She lay on her side, damp gravel prodding her cheek, and instantly, she became aware of the rough touch of rope binding her wrists. The ground was hard beneath her, and the back of her head throbbed relentlessly. She moaned, then swore under her breath.

Quickly, she scanned her surroundings. It was still dark, and the moon was still high in the sky, so she mustn't have been out for long. The rope bound her to the trunk of a spindly fir tree just beside the shore of Lake Arania. There was a thick fog hanging over the lake, and she couldn't see much beyond the thin, muddy shoreline and the rippling shallows. Gryff was also tied to the tree behind her, snarling as he tried to free his thick wrists from the bindings. Their weapons and knapsacks lay in an unreachable pile against a heap of stones several yards away.

The ghosts were nowhere in sight.

"Gryff?"

Gryff didn't meet her eyes. "They're waitin' for you to wake up. Said they had a few questions."

Her head was aching. Impatience heightened her pain.

She was tired of silence, tired of watching, waiting, watching some more. Wander here, search there, haul some crook to the county jail, scream every now and again. She was *tired.*

It ended *now.*

"Come out, damn it!" she shouted. Her hollering made Gryff jump. "I ain't chasing you no more! Come talk to me! I know you're here!"

"Jae," Gryff said gently, sounding very, very tired.

"Gryff ain't who you want," Jae went on. "He did nothing wrong. Let him go. It's me you want, ain't it? Here I am. Come and get me. But let—" Was he here? Was Pa watching her, hidden where she couldn't see? Or was he held captive somewhere deeper in the woods, or across the lake? "Let my Pa go, too."

She'd stand before him again, but not as the child he'd left behind. She was different. Now, her feet had trodden over hundreds of miles of earth, and her hands had drawn blood. There were stains all over her once-golden heart.

Jae was not his wide-eyed wanderer anymore. Just a hunter, a drifter, a thief. But she was still her Pa's girl.

They came slowly, emerging from the fog, drifting over the lake's murky waters like the shadows of storm clouds crawling over the earth below. The souls of men who'd died too soon came from the mist to look upon her, broken remnants of the men they were in life.

So many faces. A crowd of souls, their translucent forms shimmering under the faint moonlight. There was a whole cavalry of them. For the first time, she noticed the dark splotches staining their spectral clothes and faces, and realized now that it was blood.

Some had bullet holes in their chests, their heads, and others had faces so mangled they scarcely resembled men in death.

She'd imagined that they'd stare her down with anger, when she finally arrived. And many of them did. But like so many of the ghosts in the Shroud . . . some of them only looked sad, heavy with grief for their unlived years.

Jae wouldn't make peace with them, nor would she forgive them. She'd do whatever it took, now, to get them to take her to Pa . . . but after so many years, she finally understood them.

Here were the spirits.

Here were the ghosts that had taken Pa from her, robbed him of his freedom, and stolen the life of wind and walking that she had prayed for as a child. She had spent a great deal of time wondering what Pa ever could have done to make them hate him so. And now, she knew. Tonight, she would put an end to it all, or she would die.

The throng of spirits stopped just paces from her and Gryff, lining up on the shore as though they were ready to charge. They were utterly, disturbingly silent. Were they waiting for her to speak first?

"I know who you are," she said, pushing back her shoulders. Even if she had no more power than a prisoner, she could at least keep from shivering, from showing them a trace of her fear.

There was one ghost, sitting on the spirit of a glossy-maned pinto, heading the troop. He tipped his chin down at Jae, furrowing his brow. He was older than the others, perhaps fifty, with hair that brushed his shoulders. She recognized him. This was the ghost who had told Pa that they'd been searching far and wide for him. "*Do* you?"

"You were in my Pa's unit," she said. "You were on a mission to stop Amon and his gang, and my Pa left you behind."

The ghost hesitated, then nodded grimly. She expected the whole unit to start shouting, to curse Pa's name and drag it through the mud, but none of them spoke, save for the ghost at their head.

"We were his companions," he said slowly. "And some of us were his friends. We came here, hoping to arrest Amon and his gang. They ambushed us, and to our surprise, we were outnumbered. Ven fled the moment he knew we were lost. He ran faster than I'd ever seen him run before. Left us to the mercy of the bandits. We still remember the pain."

Jae shut her eyes. She squeezed them till it hurt. She'd throw her face in the sand before she let these spirits see her shedding tears.

Still, she wouldn't waste her time being penitent. "Tell me what you want."

"Rest," he said, and his tone made Jae think of Halston whenever he spoke of going home. That unbreakable longing for something so far out of reach. If this ghost hadn't taken Pa away, she might have pitied him.

"Great," she said. "So how do I give that to you? Cut you down with adamite or something?"

"It will not work," the leader said dismally. "The curse has bound us to the world."

"Curse?" Jae thought of the Shroud, of Mr. Elm, and how the spirits there didn't even know how to break their own curse. "What sort of curse?"

"There is a Nefilium lord," their leader said, "who inhabits the lake. Amon's father. Ebdiel is his name. Ven killed his son as he fled the fight."

Jae heard another one of the ghosts mutter, "Was the only useful thing he *did* in that fight."

A moment of wretched silence passed. Then, "Ebdiel has cursed our souls to wander this earth until Oldridge's blood pays for the life of his son."

No. This couldn't be . . . "My Pa is dead?"

"No."

Jae ground her teeth, then grasped for every trace of courage within her before she spoke again. "What do you mean his *blood*? If you'd killed him, you'd be at rest. You're telling me he's *alive*?"

"He's marked."

"The hell you mean, he's 'marked'?"

"He made some sort of pact with a Nefili. The Nefilium can't kill him, nor can the undead. Only a mortal can take your father's life." He exchanged a sullen look with his comrades. Jae wondered if they were all remembering an attempt to take her father's life, and the thought of it made her blood boil. "A ghost cannot kill your father. We've tried, and each time, the magic has protected him. But we need his blood to rest. To leave this world."

His blood.

Oldridge blood.

Jae raised her chin a little higher. "So you brought me here to take his place."

The head ghost lowered his head. "We did," he admitted. "*Would* you take his place?"

"Jae," Gryff broke in. He began struggling wildly at his rope tethers. "We're gettin' out of here."

Jae didn't even look at him. If she did, she might break down entirely, and that couldn't happen.

Whatever Pa had done, whatever lies he'd told . . . he'd raised her on his own, and despite it all, he had built a good life for the two of them. He may have hidden a truth from her, but none of that could change the past, nor could it change that when these ghosts had come, he had saved her.

He'd thrown himself in harm's way for her. If the ghosts had taken them both, she'd have died years ago. Pa had given her that time. And in that time, her gang had come to her.

Halston had come to her.

Pa had given Jae her life, and he'd made it gold. Not even a lie could tarnish that. Now, it was time for her to do the same for him.

"Yes," she said. "But . . . will you let me see him?"

The ghosts said nothing, but two of them emerged from the crowd and bent over her. Goosebumps prickled on her arms, and their freezing auras sent chills down her spine. As they released her from her bindings, it took everything in her not to break down.

Gryff kept on protesting. "Jae, stop this! We're leavin'. We're turnin' back." He let out a low stream of curses, then looked at the ghosts and shouted, "Let her *go*! You there! Listen to me!"

The ghosts ignored him.

"Will you let Gryff go?" asked Jae.

"When the debt is paid," the ghost said with a grim bow of his head.

Jae smiled at Gryff, who was pulling at his ropes so hard she thought he might pull the tree down with him. "It's alright. Gryff . . . thank you. Thank you for saving me. Thank you for *everything*."

"I swear, kid, if you go with them—"

"*Gryff*," she said, struggling to keep her voice level. "When you find them . . . tell Lorelin that I hope she finds joy. Tell Tsashin that I want her to remember her old life and tell stories till she can't speak. Tell Hodge that I hope he gets home. And tell them all that I'll miss them wildly."

"Get *back here*."

"And when you meet my pa and he asks what happened . . . tell him that I love him with everything I have. Tell him I forgive him for everything he kept from me. And that I'm sorry I couldn't see him again. And tell him thank you, for me. For everything he gave me." She was crying, now, but she no longer cared if the ghosts saw it. "And Gryff . . . will you tell Halston that it was all real? Will you . . . will you tell him that I loved him for me?"

She'd been so foolish. She'd wasted all their time, and now, she was out of it. Still, he had to know, somehow. She'd come back as a ghost and haunt him if that was what it took for him to hear it. Maybe they could even be like Flint and Daisy.

That thought brought her some comfort.

Gryff didn't give her a 'yes.' He just kept rambling. "Get back here now! You ain't throwin' yourself into this." The ghosts led her away, but tirelessly, he kept on shouting. "Let go of her! Jae, get back here!"

He'll tell them, Jae thought as the ghosts led her across the shore. *He'll tell them what I asked.*

They made their way along the shoreline. The lake was the exact color of thunderclouds, so murky Jae couldn't even see the stones lurking at the bottom of the shallows. Water lapped gently at the sand. It was so foggy that she couldn't see five feet in front of her. Still, she trudged on with the ghosts.

My own little funeral procession. She snorted at the thought. Perhaps she ought to feel important.

"Where is he?" she asked at last. "Show him to me."

"We're almost there," the leader assured her.

And he was right. Just a minute or two later, they came to a rockier part of the shore. Jae's boots made the stones and pebbles crackle. As they moved forth, a knobby stone tower came into their view, about as high as a man was tall, rising from the sand like a great railroad spike. It lay about three strides from the waterline. A length of rope wound around the pillar, snaking down to . . .

To . . .

Jae sank to her knees.

"Pa?"

It was him, but not like she thought she'd find him.

Pa lay in the sand, and though his chest rose and fell with his breathing, he didn't look *alive*. He was thinner than Jae had ever seen him, and he was nearly as pale as the ghosts themselves. The blue veins on his forearms stood out like ink on snow. Eyes closed, arms slack, ropes circling his legs and torso like a fish caught in a net. There were lines on his face that hadn't been there before.

"What happened to him?" She glanced down to find that she'd unwittingly curled her hand into a fist.

"Ebdiel can't kill him," said the ghost. "So he cursed him instead. Ven will sleep until the debt is paid."

"No less than he deserves," another cavalryman murmured.

"So he'll be like this forever?" she asked, unable to raise her voice above a murmur.

"Until the debt is paid," the lead ghost repeated.

This was no way to live.

How on earth could she ever go on knowing that Pa was still lost in an unnatural sleep, wasting away, never to open his eyes and face the daylight once more?

But she could save him. She could set him free.

She trudged over the gravelly shore to where Pa lay, then knelt down. Dampness seeped into her pant legs. She smoothed a hand over Pa's forehead. His skin was cold as ice. She drew in a breath, letting the misty air travel down her throat, hoping to ease the storm in her chest, if only a little.

I hate this.

It wasn't supposed to be like this.

Had Pa ever thought about her dying? She'd certainly never thought about *Pa* dying, at least, not until she'd lost him. It had always seemed as impossible to her as the sky falling down. She thought of their years on the road together, how he'd shown her how the world's green glory lurked everywhere, if one knew where to search. He'd shared the beautiful parts of it with her and done all he could to shield her from the ugly ones.

What would it be like for him to wake up and learn that she was gone?

There was nothing she could do but trust that Gryff would remember what to tell him. And she *did* trust that. For now, that had to be enough.

"I love you, Pa. Goodbye." She pressed a kiss to his temple, then stood, and turned. "I'm ready."

Half the ghosts disbanded from the pack. They floated out onto the lake itself, then disappeared into the fog.

"Where are they going?" asked Jae.

"To summon Ebdiel," the leader said steadily. There was a note of muted anticipation in his voice. "To let him know you've arrived."

Time crept by like molten iron slinking down a wall, slowing every second, hardening, becoming entirely still. Jae didn't bother asking what this *Ebdiel* was going to do to her. In a while, it wouldn't matter. She just hoped it would be quick.

Just as she was starting to wonder whether anything would happen at all, the water began sinking back. Then, just before her, the water churned, then parted to form a path, holding itself on either side of a strip of moist sand, pebbles, and water plants . . . a little aisle for her, formed from the lakebed itself.

Sweet Wandering God.

Jae stood, frozen in place, staring down at the path before her, the walls of water supported by magic alone.

The ghosts said, "*Go.*"

She wouldn't waste a minute longer here. If she did, the fear would only spiral, grow to something she couldn't control.

And that was enough to make her take the first step. Then another. Slowly, she began to tread down the strip of the lakebed.

Jae felt she ought to pray. She and Pa never went to church much when she was younger, but Pa had always told her that there was a world across the stars for those who prayed to Argun, the guardian-god of this world's woods, where the forests were lush and green and endless. She thought what it might be like to wake up there, in a patch of velvety grass, the warm sun kissing her skin.

She wasn't sure how much time there was for penance, but in her mind, she whispered, *I'm sorry for all I did wrong. Hope I'm not too far-gone for that forest.*

She wasn't really expecting a reply from Argun or the Wandering God, but still . . . it might have eased her mind to hear them speak.

The walls of water came higher and higher. For a second, her fear slipped away and turned to awe. The water, though held in place, still rippled and gleamed in midair. For some reason she couldn't name, it took her breath away.

Then the magic released its hold.

And the water came crashing over her head.

Chapter 40

Halston stood looking out Levi's window, watching the sky turn from dusky gold to deep blue above the sea of trees. There were a few lone, early stars out, barely visible. Over and over again, he pictured it: Jae and Gryff, stepping out of those thick shadows, whole and sound and smiling.

One night here, and then they had to move on. And a dust-sized, hopeful part of Halston prayed that Gryff and Jae would be with him soon.

There were times when he forgot that he hadn't known Gryff all his life. All throughout the day, he'd kept turning, half-expecting to see Gryff's enormous shadow beside him. But Gryff was somewhere far away.

And Jae . . .

He'd lived several thousand days without her, but now, he felt as though he were trying to fumble his way through the world without his sight or hearing. One of his senses was gone.

Telin was so close.

Lorelin was out on the front porch, chatting with Levi's wife. Halston couldn't help but chuckle slightly at the sight. It took almost nothing for most people to warm up to Lorelin. Hodge and Flint were warming themselves by the fireplace, and Tsashin was sitting on the fur rug next to Halston, legs-crossed, gaze running over the ceiling boards as though she were trying to read them.

Halston thought back to Jae's promise to take Tsashin back to the Yunah nation. His heart sank an inch, then he knelt down beside Tsashin.

"I'm going to speak to Levi tomorrow. I'll see if you can stay with him for a while. I doubt he'll mind. Then maybe somebody could take you to the Yunah nation. I'm sure he has connections . . . it seems like he's been all over. I'll pay him, if we need to."

Tsashin sat up straighter. Her inky eyes were wide. "What?"

Halston's heart felt cold. He should have spoken to her sooner. "Someone has to get you home. Jae said she would, but that was before—"

"Halston." She raised a hand to quiet him, and then, her voice was stone-firm. "I said it to Hodge, and now I'll say it to you. In the time I can remember . . . you're the only home I've known. You're my *friends*. All of you. I can't leave."

"We want you somewhere safe."

She smiled faintly. "I'll be safe. Have you forgotten that I'm clever? Who knows, perhaps you'll need *me* to face the Witch of Telin."

So much warmth seemed to radiate from her. Halston swallowed. "Are you sure?"

"I'm sure." Her shoulders rose with a heavy inhale, then, "I hope we see them there."

Halston sighed. "I know. So do I."

He pictured Gryff and Jae walking through the woods, bound for Telin, checking Jae's map every step of the way.

Tsashin joined him in watching the faltering flames. They didn't fall down her cheeks, but there were tears glimmering in her eyes. "I'm worried about them."

"I know. So am I."

"Do you think they'll find us?"

"I do," said Halston, even though he didn't quite believe himself.

Something in Tsashin's eyes told him that she understood he wasn't quite sure. "I don't like this. The thought of . . . not knowing." She drew in a sharp breath. "I can't stand it."

"Neither can I," Halston said softly.

Tsashin wiped one eye with the back of her hand. "Can you carry it with me?"

"Of course I will."

Maybe they wouldn't manage. But they could certainly try.

Something nudged him on the shoulder. Levi was standing behind Halston, holding a wooden bucket by its rope handle. He passed Halston the pail and said, "We'll need three buckets. Flint will take you to the well."

Flint and Hodge stood in the center of the room, each holding an identical wooden pail. Hodge arched a dark eyebrow. "You sure it's safe?"

"Sure is." Levi gestured to the fading light outside. "Nothing ever comes out of the woods at dusk. It ain't till late night that you really gotta start to worry."

Halston followed Flint and Hodge out the door and through the garden, into the cool, twilit woods. Around them, the shadows danced, and the crickets were beginning to sing. Flint led them down a narrow dirt path, starting at the garden and reaching into the pines. Halston took a few unsure steps down the path, thinking of the shifter that had taken Lia's shape, but Flint was moving without hesitation. He'd been here before. Halston needed to trust his judgment.

The well was around a half-mile from the village, Halston wagered. It sat in the center of a small clearing, ringed by tall, lush grass and delicate white flowers. Moss carpeted the stones forming its wellhead, and its steepled roof was slightly off-center.

Jae would like it here.

"Halston?" Flint's voice cut through the air.

"Hmm?"

Flint regarded him with a look of concern. "Are you alright?"

Halston said nothing. He just made his way to the well, slipped his bucket over the hook, and began turning the crank. He tucked his head beneath the eaves of the well's small roof, taking in the coolness beneath.

"Jae's still got her map," Hodge reminded him. "I'll bet they'll be waiting for us at Telin."

Halston began bringing up the bucket, listening to the creaking crank. "I hope they aren't. Without Flint . . ."

Halston recalled what Flint had told them about the tests that Rogue liked to put newcomers through, the monsters and visions she conjured for those who stumbled unwittingly upon her abode.

He lifted the now-full bucket from the hook, then glanced at Flint. "What's she like? Rogue?"

"Frightening," Flint said bluntly. "But reasonable enough for a crater-dwelling witch. As long as you do what she asks."

Halston snorted. "Well, I've always been good at doing that."

Flint chuckled humorlessly. "I'm sure Sterling played a part in that."

Halston placed the bucket on the ground, then sat down with his back against the well. "Yeah. He sure did."

Flint cleared his throat. "Forgive me for being so forward. It's just . . . he was the same with me. I never could rest on the nights I was supposed to meet with him."

Halston wondered what their heists would have been like if Flint had been a part of their little wayward gang. Some part of Halston had always known that if it weren't for Hodge, Gryff, and Lorelin, he wouldn't have been able to keep going. Without them, Sterling would have ended him. Crushed out every bit of Halston's spirit, if not his life. He couldn't imagine what it would have been like to do the same work on his own, to face Sterling without anyone by his side.

Halston's gaze passed over the surrounding woods. The air was fragrant with the smell of pine, and his eyes were half-burning from fatigue.

"I'm sorry," Flint said. "That we lost them. I was . . . callous to you, by the river. I shouldn't have been."

Halston shook his head. "It wasn't your fault. I don't blame you."

And for Gryff, for Jae . . . he'd remain hopeful. It was all there was left to do.

"If it helps, I've been looking for them, too," came another voice.

Halston looked at the treetops. There, rising just above the well as though he were claiming it as his territory, was Jem.

Halston couldn't fight the smile that came to his face. "Any luck?"

"None, I'm afraid." Jem gave Hodge and Flint a polite wave, then looked back down at Halston. "What happened?"

Halston let Hodge explain things to Jem. He wasn't ready to recount it just yet.

"Gryff and Jae are a pair of strong spirits, Hal," Jem said brightly. "I reckon they're both just fine."

Halston drew in a breath. "It's my fault."

Flint and Hodge swapped a sullen glance. Jem just came down from the top of the well. "Oh, come on now. What makes you say that?"

"I should have turned back for them before we jumped." Halston closed his eyes, recalling how he'd shouted for the two of them when he'd finished tumbling down the earth and how faint Jae's reply had been. Surely, she'd been hurt.

"We would've *died,* Hal," said Hodge. He sat next to Halston, then, slinking down against the well's mossy exterior. "That fella in the cloak almost had us."

Perhaps that was true, but Halston still felt that he should have gone with the cloaked man . . . even though he knew that Hodge wouldn't have let him.

"Perhaps it don't mean much coming from me," Jem started, circling around the well, "but you can't live your whole life with one foot in yesterday's troubles. I reckon you did all you could to find them, right?"

Halston didn't answer, mostly because part of him felt he could have done more, but Hodge said, "Yeah. We did."

"Then there's no use blaming yourself," Jem went on. He moved closer to Halston, close enough that Halston could feel the ghost's cold aura on his skin.

Halston took a good look at the strange spirit next to him. Jem really wasn't that much older than him. Just looking at him, Halston guessed he couldn't have been any older than twenty-five when he'd passed.

There was no guarantee that he would ever experience life again, at least not in the form he longed for. But he'd stayed by them this long and helped them where he could.

"Jem?" said Halston.

"Yeah?"

"Thank you," he said. "This whole time, I don't think anybody has bothered to say that to you. And I'm sorry for it."

Jem just waved a hand. "It's what we're all here for, ain't it?"

"For what?" asked Hodge, tilting his head.

Jem looked at Hodge with an odd, almost wistful expression. "I hope you never have to learn this, Hodge, but nothing makes a man more aware of wasted time than a life cut short. When I get my body back, I'll make better use of my time on earth. I plan to actually help a soul or two, from time to time. But I realized I might as well start—"

Before he could finish, he winked out of their sight. Back to the mines, Halston supposed. His death place. Halston couldn't imagine what it would be like to wake in the spot he'd died, night after night, year after year.

Halston reached into his pocket, hand closing around the wooden bird Jae had carved for him. He took it out and rolled it between his thumb and forefinger, feeling the rough planes of its head and chest, the knobby point she'd whittled for his beak.

She'd made it to remind him of the hydrells back home, of the only time he'd really felt invincible.

He certainly didn't feel invincible now, but for Jae, and for Gryff . . . perhaps he could try.

In a companionable silence, they made their way back toward Levi's house. More stars had come out, and there was a thin breeze in the air. For the first time in days, Halston found that he was eager to sleep, to finally get some rest.

About halfway down the trail, a distant scream echoed through the night.

Halston froze in his tracks.

The lone scream turned to a cacophony of frazzled shouts, all coming from Levi's village.

Halston didn't realize that he'd broken into a run until he heard Hodge calling after him. His pant legs were damp, and he glanced down. He hadn't noticed when he dropped the bucket, either.

But now, he was sprinting down the trail, Flint and Hodge tailing after him.

Halston tore past the trees, and as the shouts grew louder, dread flooded his chest like water overflowing from a ditch. As they ran, the shadows seemed to thicken, knitting together like a vast barricade over their path. But Halston had to ignore them and be swift as possible.

Before . . . before . . .

When the village finally came into their sight, a knife of bitter fear seemed to cleave Halston through the center.

Men were shouting, braced with their shotguns and pistols, leaning over windowsills or peering around the corners of their cabins. In the center of the little village, standing squarely beside the fire pit, was Captain Crane's pale-faced revenant, a man swaddled in a cloak, still hiding his mouth and nose, and in between them, the warlock in the slate-colored mask.

The warlock was holding a young, copper-haired woman to his chest, one arm around her stomach. Halston didn't recognize her, but he figured she could only be one of the villagers. In his hand was an elegant knife, its blade touching the woman's bare throat. Though he was still a stone's throw away from the village, Halston could see that she had her eyes squeezed shut, fingers hooked helplessly over the warlock's forearm. Halston had never seen a person shake so violently.

Surrounding them, all freshly bloodied, were bodies. All men, all villagers, all strewn before the warlock like soldiers in the aftermath of a battle. There were six in all.

"Please, remain still and no one else shall have to fall," the warlock announced. Even from where Halston stood, his voice was still clear. Worse—it was entirely *indifferent.* He spoke in the same tone that Halston had heard merchants using to discuss prices with one another. "When our demands are met, I will release her. We know that the Harney brothers are here. If you surrender just *one* of them, no harm will come to anyone else. Or to *her,*" he said as he jostled the woman in his arms, making her wail.

Halston looked at Hodge.

Hodge looked at him.

All this time, they hadn't needed *Halston.* They'd just wanted one of *them.*

Two things happened at once.

Halston started racing toward the village, and Hodge tackled him to the ground.

"Hodge!" Halston shouted, struggling to throw Hodge off his back. Hodge had taken hold of his shoulders and was pushing Halston toward the ground as if trying to force-feed him the dirt.

"You ain't going!" Hodge's voice was rife with terror.

"Stop!" Flint yelled, though Halston hardly heard it.

It killed him to do it, but Halston threw back his head, striking Hodge in the nose. Hodge cried out, his grip loosening, and Halston threw himself to the side. He took Hodge with him.

They rolled and grappled, grappled and rolled, all while Flint stood by, shouting at them to let each other go. In the village, the people were still screaming. There were three gunshots. Hodge smacked Halston in the temple, making him fall to the side, then pinned him down by the shoulders. Halston turned his head to find that another man lay dead at the warlock's feet.

"I'm here!" Halston shouted, but the villagers' screams drowned out his voice, and the distance didn't help. Before he could shout it again, Hodge clapped a hand over Halston's mouth.

"It's me!" Hodge yelled. "Take me in—"

Halston wriggled one arm free and delivered a blow to Hodge's stomach. Hodge yelped and doubled over, then Halston got back on top of him and clamped one hand firmly over his brother's mouth.

He hated this. They'd never fought like this before, but if Halston had to give his brother a few bruises to save his gods-damned *life,* then he'd—

The screaming got louder.

Halston looked back at the village, and his mind went blank.

The bodies were gone—no, not gone. They'd simply stood back up.

With the same dreary, far-off emptiness in their stares, they'd lined up before the warlock like blank-faced guardians. Eight in all, including Captain Crane.

"I can make a soldier out of anyone who uselessly forfeits his life tonight," the warlock said dully, his voice passing like a gust of wind over the revenants' heads. "I will have them search your cabins, if you do not surrender one of the Harney brothers to me first."

Halston's mind went blank. In the corner of his eye, floating above them, was a faint, bluish mass. Halston looked up. Jem was back.

Jem regarded them with a tender but determined glance, then flickered out of the air. He reappeared just over the warlock's head, and the screaming recommenced.

Jem paid the screams no mind. He dove for the warlock, perhaps hoping to distract him, but the warlock waved an arm, batting at the ghost like a housefly. Jem lost his focus and vanished.

"I'm here!" Halston cried, just as Hodge shot up straight and clocked him in the throat with his head. Halston choked, slumping for a moment, voice gone.

It was then a shot cracked from a few yards away, and one

revenant—what remained of one of the villagers—burst into a cloud of ash and disappeared.

The warlock staggered backward, still holding the keening woman, and though his mask hid his entire face, Halston knew that if he could yank it off, he'd look startled. Though Halston couldn't see where Levi stood, he heard his voice shout:

"*Adamite!*"

Halston tried to get to his feet, but Hodge grabbed his wrist and yanked him to the ground.

Just after he struck the earth, Halston pushed himself back up and tried to shout again. Before he could open his mouth, Halston glimpsed several men reloading, and then, the shots began, drowning out anything he might have said. Around the warlock, clouds of ash exploded like dirt clods hitting a stone wall. Halston didn't see how many more revenants they took down in those few seconds. The cracking of guns and the dusty clouds came too quickly.

Halston *did* see Jem reappear, manifesting just before the gang of revenants. He had just enough time to open his mouth, but Halston would never know what Jem's last words were.

Because he had appeared right in the path of an adamite bullet.

Surely, it couldn't have hurt. Jem had died before. Ghosts couldn't feel pain. Could they?

There wasn't much time to wonder. For a moment, Jem was there, and as soon as the bullet passed through him, he was gone.

It wasn't like all the other times he'd disappeared, when the unyielding pull of his deathplace kept taking him away. This was different. Each time before had been like the last second of the setting sun, the wink of time between dusk and night. A break, with a promise to return—eventually if not immediately. This was like a spark going out. Final. Eternal.

Jem—the spirit who had selflessly saved Jae, who had led them to the Shroud, with no real guarantee of a new life, a life he'd wanted more than anything else . . . was gone.

"I've got five more adamite bullets in this gun here," Levi finally shouted at the warlock. His voice was dripping with venom, raw and potent. "I'll use every last one of 'em if I have to. And every man surrounding you has just as many."

Halston opened his mouth to shout again, and Hodge tossed him to the side once more, clamping a forearm over his chest and a hand over his mouth.

Though Halston lay pinned beneath Hodge's weight, he could turn his head to see six remaining revenants. Beyond a doubt, their pursuers were outnumbered, and the warlock heeded Levi's warning. He thumbed the talisman dangling from his neck, then raised a thin hand to the sky. Behind him, the air rippled, then knit into a hazy circle. Halston knew what came next. He'd seen Sterling do it a hundred times over.

And the warlock and his revenants disappeared into the portal amid the rippling air.

Halston couldn't bring himself to look away from the empty air, where the portal had been just moments earlier.

For a few moments, they just lay there. Pain from his brawl with Hodge finally began to tug at his body, but Halston hardly noticed it. Flint paced up to them, then froze in his tracks.

When Hodge finally released his hold on Halston, Halston meant to say, *'You should have let me go.'*

But he didn't have it in himself to speak just yet.

Hodge got off of him. They stared at one another, their breathing labored, neither daring to say anything out loud, to try and make sense of everything that had just happened.

Without looking back at Hodge and Flint, Halston ran into the village.

None of the villagers had moved from their posts. They stood firm, most of them still aiming their weapons, and as Halston entered the space between the cabins, he felt their stares piercing him. The red-haired woman sat on her knees, face buried in her hands, letting out sobs that shook her whole body. Halston had only heard tears like this once before: when he'd come home to find his sister mourning her best friend, who'd been found torn apart by monsters earlier that morning.

Halston could live to be older than the forest itself, and he would never forget those sobs.

Halston paced over the ground, boots stirring the bloody pine needles. He stared at the spot where the warlock, cloaked man, and revenants had disappeared, and couldn't bring himself to move. Perhaps the masked man had cast some lingering spell on him, to keep him rooted to that spot, dumb, motionless.

Tonight, several men were dead on his account, made into weapons that would surely follow him to the ends of the earth if he didn't find a way to stop this soon.

"Halston!"

Lorelin's voice shattered his trance. She came running toward him, sea-green eyes watery with tears. Tsashin hurried behind her, and when she came to a stop behind Lorelin, her whole body shook like a stone rattled by the hoofbeats of a stampede.

A third shape came trudging behind them.

Levi.

In one hand, he still held the gun he'd used to kill that first revenant. He surveyed the bloody ground for a few seconds, then he fixed Halston with a look of pure ire. There was no grief in his eyes. Only fury.

Halston raised one hand. He was shaking. There was no bringing back those dead men, they would never see Jem again . . . and now, there wasn't a shred of doubt in his mind that the warlock would return for him.

He had to apologize. He had to vow to pay for those men's lives, somehow. But when he opened his mouth, his mind refused to work, to summon any words that could possibly bring any of the villagers some comfort.

Footsteps crunched behind Halston. Hodge came to his side, then Flint, though neither of them said a word.

Levi thrust a finger in Flint's direction. "Get them. The hell. Out of here."

"Levi—" Flint started.

He was not allowed to finish. "I don't care where you go. I don't care if you ever come back. Just get them *out* of here." He looked at Halston, and each of the rest of them, with a stone-cold scowl. "And I don't give a damn what sweet hell you've gotten yourselves into. Nobody in my town dies to save your sorry skin. *Nobody.* You have one minute to run and *never* come back."

No.

This had to end.

Halston was still half inside a daze when they fled down the road. He wasn't focusing when they left Levi's village behind, left that circle of cabins and all those people, mourning for their fallen.

The next thing Halston knew, they were deep in the woods again, at the mercy of whatever might come out of the dark forest. He could almost feel the pines watching them, their spirits glaring, angered by the blood that had watered the earth that night.

Halston couldn't shake the notion that all of it was on his hands.

"Stop," Flint ordered after a time, and they all staggered to a halt.

Halston knew what was coming, but nothing could have prepared for it. "Flint—"

"Don't." Flint lifted a hand. "*Don't.*"

And Halston listened.

"Did you . . . know them?" Hodge asked in a hushed voice.

"Not well, but that doesn't matter," Flint said. He began pacing back and forth. His breaths were shaky. "This wasn't their fight."

"I know it wasn't," said Hodge. He gave Halston a look of desperation. "They—"

Flint just cut him off. "Listen. I'll keep my word. We're a day's journey from Telin, and I'll honor my promise to you and take you there. You saved me back at Fort Marksdale, but once I've repaid that, I'm *done*. Whatever mess you've gotten yourselves into isn't mine. Not if folks are paying for it with their lives."

"I understand," Halston forced out.

They'd been so close, he thought, to being friends.

Flint reached into the large pocket of his duster jacket, then pulled out a small cloth pouch and motioned to Halston. "Here. Hold out your hand."

Reluctantly, Halston did so. Flint poured six bullets into Halston's cupped hand. At first, he thought they were ordinary, then he noticed the tiny, pearly-white flecks glinting in the metal. "Are these—"

"Adamite infused," Flint said. He gave another handful to Hodge, then to Lorelin. "I picked them up at Levi's place, and I hope to the *gods* we won't have to use them. I don't have many left. If they come again, we'll have to aim carefully."

Halston looked into the expanse of trees ahead. If he knew beyond a shadow of a doubt that he could run into these woods— without awakening some monstrosity—and confront the warlock once and for all, he'd do it. The parts of him Hodge had hit during their quarrel still hurt, and he knew they would bruise.

He wouldn't fight his brother again, but he knew that if he tried to flee, Hodge would not let him. There was no breaking away from the others, at least not while they were all alert.

Flint broke back into a stride, moving down the road once more. Without speaking, they all followed after him. Halston was glad to put distance between themselves and the village.

"What is it?" Flint asked, throwing up his arms. "What do they *want* with you?"

"I don't know!" Halston wished there was something he could say to make Flint believe him, to make him know that he was just as lost as the rest of them. "I've been trying to figure it out for weeks!"

"Flint," Lorelin said slowly. Tears glistened faintly on her cheeks. "Could it be someone Sterling sent?"

"Maybe? I don't know." Once again, Flint stopped moving. They stood there for a while, and the only sound around them was the night breeze faintly rustling through the branches above. A calculating look fell over his face as he studied the rest of them intensely. "You really haven't a clue, do you?"

"We don't," Hodge replied. If he was making any effort at all to keep from sounding exasperated, he was failing. "That's what we're trying to tell you."

Halston closed his eyes and endured the next few moments of silence. He couldn't keep them shut for long. The memory of those bodies lying on the ground taunted him, somehow more potent than when he'd seen them in real time.

"Let's go," Flint said at last, and started down the trail without looking at them again. Nobody had it in them to protest.

And so they bounded down the trail. Unharmed. Alive. And as they began their final trek toward Telin, Halston made a silent promise.

When the warlock returned, no one else would die in his place.

Not his gang. Not Flint, not Tsashin, not Lorelin.

And certainly not his brother.

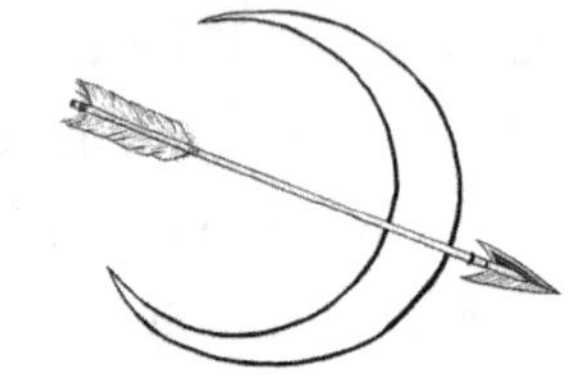

Chapter 41

Jae wasn't drowning yet, but the water's cold burned like nothing she'd ever felt.

She kicked and flailed. Already, her chest was hot. White bubbles swarmed around her in frenzied clouds. They rose to the surface with ease. To the air she'd never know again.

It was then something firm and slimy looped around her leg, then it tightened and tugged. It began to drag her down, down, down. She glanced at her ankle. Though she could hardly see a thing down here, she glimpsed the outline of some sort of rope.

It had her.

Then a thought hit her, and it burned worse than her chest did right now.

She wasn't brave.

What came after this? When the pain ceased—and her life with it—what followed?

I don't want to know. I don't want to find out.

Panic made her stupid. Instinct overcame her, and she tried to swim to the surface.

Jae thrashed and squirmed against the binding. The light at the surface got further and further away. Slipping from her reach. Her salvation.

But she couldn't fight the force pulling her down. The faint sphere of the moon glinted far overhead, and though she reached for it, she felt herself drifting further and further down, until at last, her body hit the bottom.

The darkness was incomplete, but that was no comfort. She'd have preferred to drown in pitch blackness. But her writhing body sent bursts of mud flying upward, and tangles of water plants wavered at her side. A pair of fish darted past overhead. They almost seemed to gawk at her. The drowning girl had disturbed their peace.

When her chest felt like little more than a paper husk, she couldn't fight it any longer. Her lips surrendered. Water filled her mouth and charged down her throat.

Just like Elias.

At least Elias had hit his head first.

Selfish girl.

That would have been her last thought, too—if a shadow hadn't risen before her like the sun over the bed of plants.

Somewhere inside her mind, there came a pinprick of curiosity, though it hardly stood out through her terror. The water made her heavy. Darkness took her.

Then, she could breathe.

She rose, fast as an animal freed from a trap. The rope which had bound her lay in severed tangles at her feet . . . a rope made of water plants, she now realized. Her fingers sank into thin, waterlogged mud. It was still dark. She was soaking wet. Drenched. Dizzy. But *breathing.*

She lifted a muddied hand. Above her, the waters of the lake still rippled. Some sort of air pocket had sheltered her.

And someone had taken the water out of her chest.

What was this? Was she imagining things? Had her mind painted this picture, made it seem real as possible to comfort her in her last moments?

She touched the ceiling of the air pocket. Her fingertips slipped into the water. The dome was just large enough for her to sit up comfortably.

When she saw him looming over her, she almost jumped right out of the bubble.

The stranger's skin was almost invisible against the lakewater. It was smooth as glass, and muddy gray, like stones burnished by years of a current's push. His eyes were large, but dull, and his long, silvery hair wavered like steady ripples. In his hand was a blade, some sort of long knife or short spear. His other hand was empty, and when he flexed his fingers, Jae noticed thin webs between each one, like the feet of a duck.

He was big—almost twice Jae's size.

Ebdiel.

The Nefili stranger floated over her in silence. The moments passed like years. She kept breathing, savoring the air she had agreed to give up. To die in his waters.

Should she say sorry? Apologize on Pa's behalf? How little words must mean to a thousand-year-old stranger. A decade or two was hardly a blink to him. Surely, the grief for his son was still fresh as a bloody wound.

But he must be merciful, at least a little, or he would have let her drown.

At last, his voice reached her. "*You are his daughter. The mortal who killed my son.*" His voice was dull and indifferent, like the passing of time itself.

No point in lying, or in painting the truth to seem sweet and rosy. "Yeah."

"*You'd give your life for him?*"

In spite of it all, she wanted to roll her eyes. *No. I thought I'd let myself drown for the hell of it.* "Yeah."

Ebdiel circled around the dome of air. "*You are young. My son was about your age when he was killed.*"

Two Nefilium could have an immortal child. A Nefili and a human's child . . . a witch or a warlock would have power, but someday, death would come for them.

No wonder warlocks were rare. What must it be like to watch their own children die, then walk this earth without them for evermore?

Jae thought of Sterling and his brothers. If he found out about her, would their deathless father demand her life as a price for his sons? Or would he care at all?

"*Your father was the one I wanted. The last of the men I wished to c laim.*"

Fury set her alight. "Well, you can't kill him, and I'm the only one left in our family." All her life, it had been just the two of them. "So I'm your only choice. Just . . . just kill me, please. Let the ghosts rest in peace so my pa can go free. I'm tired. I'm *done.*"

"*I can't kill you,*" he said. His tone was unemotional, lifeless, as if he were stating a simple fact.

Jae went tense. *The mark.* Did it extend to her as well? And if it did, then how on earth was she supposed to set him free?

"I want my pa to go free," she said. "If the mark is protecting me too, then I—"

"*No.*" He glided closer to her. His head nearly broke through the air dome, and his murky gray eyes seemed to stare right into her soul. It was like gazing at a face carved out of stone. "*I cannot take a man's child. I have lived through that pain. I have carried it for years. Never does it lessen. It burns, and it burns. This curse . . . will not bring back my son.*"

"It's me now, or Pa when . . . I don't know . . . when he's grown old and his heart stops."

And he deserved freedom—for however long he had left. Not a life bound on a lakeshore, fast asleep until he died—a strangled soul in a thin, tethered body.

She thought she heard Ebdiel sigh. "*I cannot remove the curse I have placed, I can only alter it.*"

Make up your damn mind already.

He motioned to her wrist. "*Hold out your hand.*"

What was he going to do? Sever her hand? Would that be a quicker death than drowning?

She'd already drowned once today. Perhaps this would be a mercy. If it was . . . she'd take it.

Jae knelt before the Nefili man and slipped her hand into the cold waters outside the air bubble. She waited for the sting of the blade.

But the sting didn't come.

Only shock.

Then, her entire body went numb.

Ebdiel's blade slid down the length of her forearm. The weapon cut deep—had it reached bone? She couldn't see the wound itself, but she did see the cloud of blood rising from the wound, disappearing into the water above.

So much blood.

"*It is done.*"

The waters crashed over her, and Ebdiel vanished into the deep.

———————

Her shirt was turning red.

Soaked in lakewater and her own blood, Jae broke through the surface. Someone was crying—raw, guttural. Pa.

"Pa!" she cried. Her legs kicked furiously, desperate to stay afloat. She shoved her bleeding arm against her chest, fighting to keep paddling with her free arm, her only hand. "Gryff!"

Only after she'd called for them did she remember that it was useless. Both of them were tied up. Until she reached the shore and cut them loose, no one could help her.

The water pulled at her body. Even if Ebdiel had set her free, the lake seemed loath to follow suit. The waters were calm, but the fog in her head was getting thicker.

The ghosts were nowhere to be seen. They'd simply passed *on.* Onto the place Jae had been certain she'd reach just a few moments ago.

Kick. Push. Swim.

She'd never been much of a swimmer.

The will to move left her. She went slack. The waters swallowed her head.

Go up.

She kicked again. Jae met the air once more, gulped it down, and began to paddle back to the shore with one arm. The lake grabbed at her, grasping like a thousand greedy hands, but onward she kicked.

Closer, closer, closer. She kept swimming, but the numbness in her muscles and the fire in her wrist threatened to stop her.

She swam until she was in the shallows, close enough to the land that her feet could touch the lakebed. When she began to trudge toward the shoreline, she shoved her bloody forearm against her chest and drew her soaking shirt around it.

Her eyes fluttered shut. The rush in her head was like a rainstorm. Briefly, the feeling seemed to leave her knees, but she forced herself to take another step. Another. The feeling returned, and she opened her eyes. The water was up to her ankles, now.

And then, an old, familiar voice called out her name. "Jae?"

There was so much uncertainty in it. It was as if he didn't quite believe his own eyes.

But they weren't tricking him. "Pa!" she cried back. She opened her eyes, though the world was starting to appear hazy. "Pa! I'm coming!"

Jae half-ran, half-stumbled in the direction of the stone spire. It was close. There, kneeling, shivering like it was the middle of the coldest December, was Pa.

When she clumsily staggered up to him, she fell. Pa might have cried her name again, but her head was spinning. She was fragile—glass, falling, about to break. How much blood had she lost?

Jae pushed herself up, careful to keep her wounded arm pressed to her chest. The world around her was beginning to blur. *Knife. Rope.*

She pulled the knife from her boot and crawled up to the rope. She was in a stupor as she sawed, though her eyelids were getting heavy as iron. There was a ringing in her ears, now, drowning out the sound of the breeze, the water lapping at the shoreline, and Pa, who may have started screaming at her.

But her blade was good to her. The fibers snapped beneath it, yielding swiftly to her knife. And when the last bit of rope broke, Jae collapsed onto her side.

Then she saw him coming. Pa was rushing to her aid, swift as an arrow.

She smiled. How good it was—to see him awake, to see him free. She'd won.

Years of lonely roads, bloody hands, and hauling thieves to their cells had led her to this. And he was here at last. Who'd have thought it? Somehow, her unshakable faith had not failed her.

Jae couldn't hear what he was saying—couldn't comprehend it, at least. The sharp, flaming pain in her wrist was lessening, now, and gradually turning into a dull ache. Shoving her wrist closer to her chest, she found she couldn't fight the heaviness falling over her.

She shut her eyes.

Maybe Ebdiel hadn't actually meant for her to live.

The soft mud cradled her body. Everything around her was black, and though she could barely feel her own limbs, now, she still had her thoughts.

I did it.

Pa's free.

This was better than drowning. The pain really wasn't so bad, now . . .

Then an arm wrapped around her—one she'd know in pure darkness, after a thousand years. He pulled her close, like when she'd been a little thing and he'd been shielding her from the thunderstorms, from the bad men—nothing in this world could hurt her when he was there.

She let herself stiffen, then went limp.

He had her.

It was alright now.

Pa was talking to her. Haziness had turned the whole world into a snippet of a dream, but at last, she could make out what he said. *"Jae, Jae. Stay awake. Stay with me. Jae . . ."*

For the third time that night, she braced herself for death.

But for the first time, she was not afraid.

Chapter 42

"*Wake up, kid. Pull through.*"

Gryff. Jae tried to open her mouth, but something had sealed her lips, and with them, her eyelids. They were somewhere very cold.

"*She'll pull through. I know it.*"

Pa!

His voice was frail. Once it had been hearty, full of life, but years of going unused had made it wither. Still, if he was well enough to be up, to be *speaking,* then that was more than enough to be grateful for.

But it still wasn't enough to rouse her. Her limbs were weak, and though she felt cloth binding her wound, the gash burned. She couldn't force her eyes open and spring upward, ready to face the world once more. Already, she felt herself slipping back into the darkness, and all she could do was pray that she wouldn't sink so deep into it again.

Before she faded back into a slumber, Pa's voice said, *"Remind me how she got caught up with you, again?"*

––––––––––

It had been ages since Jae had had a pleasant dream. Most nights, she found herself falling into a purely dark and silent oblivion. Other nights, nightmares of ghosts and gunshots painted her mind red and silver.

But now, the air seemed to hold her like a pair of tender arms, and the only thing that filled her was the notion that here, there was no harm that could come to her. Crystal clear were her surroundings. If she'd known better, she might have even thought she'd awakened . . . but the skin on her left arm was smooth, with no sign of a wound or scar, so this had to be a dream.

Right?

Jae stood outside the cabin she'd shared with Pa as a girl. Thick grass carpeted the ground, and although the air was almost autumn-cool, flowers sprouted in the green. Above her was the brightest night sky she'd ever seen—there were so many stars filling it that she couldn't pick out the constellations she knew among them.

The stars tugged on her—a gentle tug. It was the softest touch of a current that wouldn't drown her. Instead, it would carry her somewhere full of warmth. She held up a hand and tried to count the stars between the gaps of her outstretched fingers. It was almost funny to feel so small.

Nearby, there was a woman standing in the grass. Bright-eyed, she was, with a few streaks of gray in her dark hair, garbed in a frock the color of cornflowers. She looked a little bit like Jae, but mostly like a stranger. Yet Jae knew her at once.

"Hey, Ma."

She'd spent countless hours picturing her mother, letting their imaginary conversations unfold, growing so familiar with them that sometimes she forgot they weren't real.

Ma came closer to Jae, and they stood a breadth apart. Ma raised a hand as if to touch Jae's shoulder, but she pulled it away at the last second and held her palm to her own chest. "Dear girl. It didn't hurt much, did it?"

"Oh, it hurt." Jae forced out a chuckle. Even now, it seemed important to try and brush it off. "But not anymore."

"You're braver than I ever was. You got that from your father, no doubt."

Jae tipped her chin up to the stars. Giddiness began coursing through her, and she felt as though she were on a ledge high above a deep lake, in that split second before diving in or turning back.

. . . Perhaps this wasn't a dream at all.

"Have you been watching me?" she asked. "All this time?"

"Some of the time," said Ma.

So Ma had seen all the ugly parts of her. She knew that Jae had blood on her hands. "I'm sorry. If I ain't what you hoped."

Ma said nothing, but Jae couldn't bring herself to meet her eyes. What would it be like to watch the others? Would looking on as they faltered, unable to reach them, be the price for peace?

No.

She couldn't do that. Not yet.

"I want to go back."

"He's waiting for you, isn't he?"

He. Jae didn't know if Ma meant Pa or Halston—but both of those were right.

"I'm heading back for them."

Ma only smiled. "I understand. I'll see you another time, Jae."

All the warmth and comfort in those stars begged her to stay. She could have gone to them, let herself fade and become a light.

It ain't my time, she bid them, and with that fond farewell, they seemed to wave back at her. *Ain't my time.*

———————

The next thing Jae heard was Gryff and Pa bickering.

"I still don't see how you managed to lose track of her."

"She was on watch and snuck off. I had to go and find her after that."

"You're *kidding* me, right?"

"She ran away! What on earth was I supposed to do?"

"I don't know. Keep an eye on her, maybe."

"Keep an *eye* on her?" snarled Gryff. "She's damn capable of takin' care of herself. Made that very clear to me from the get-go."

"You said you found her in the woods! You didn't try getting her out of there?"

"Oh, believe me, I tried. It was those ghosts of yours that stopped me. Besides, I could be ten times bigger and I reckon I still couldn't have stopped her. She's made of somethin' different."

"That's true." Pa let out a sigh. "She certainly is."

Jae's eyes weren't open, but in that moment, she pictured herself watching them from overhead. There they were, staring at one another with a look of newfound understanding, and there she was, a motionless log with a bound-up forearm.

"Forgive me," Pa said. "I ain't seen her in years. I was sure I'd lose her."

"Nothin' to forgive," Gryff said, and Jae barely caught it at all. "I understand."

––––––––––

The water came up to her knees. It had soaked through the legs of her pants, but Jae hardly cared. The sky was the exact color of the sea. She heard the squalls of what might have been birds, but there was nothing to see but *blue*.

Seeing Ma had not been a dream, she was sure. Those stars had been far too clear. But this was a dream, and Jae knew it.

On her lips, she tasted salt. There wasn't much to see here—it might've been the quietest place she'd ever come across. The water was still, stretching far past where she could see, motionless save for the ripples caused by her presence. For once in her life, she wasn't craving movement, and she wasn't itching to race out of here, onto the next plain or dash into a nearby thicket. She didn't want to run, or hide. She just wanted to *be*.

To think that all this time, I could've been chasing peace.

Someday, she'd reach it. Right now, there was work to be done, and a world to see.

Jae bid the shallow sea goodbye and felt herself sinking back outside her head.

––––––––––

The birdsong was the sweetest sound she'd ever heard.

There was a dull ache in her arm, and the ground was firm and solid under her back. Her body was heavy, still, but a far cry from how it felt when she was struggling to cross the lakeshore. Soreness stiffened her arms and legs, but nothing so strong that it would keep her from moving.

Jae kept her eyes closed for a minute—just to listen for a while, without having to face what came next. She wouldn't deny herself the peace, no matter how brief it was. She'd grant herself this one gift. Enjoy it a little longer.

She was somewhere warm.

And she had lived.

Oh, stars and skies above, she had *lived!*

The laugh started welling up in the deepest part of her. She couldn't stop it as it left her mouth. At last, she opened her eyes and faced the world around her.

She lay inside a cave . . . more of a canopy of stone, really, all covered in vines and moss, about three yards wide on all sides. The ground was a little damp, but it was still better shelter than she could have hoped for. She was still dressed in her clothes from the lake, but by now, they were dry. Her jacket was gone and her sleeves were pushed up, leaving her arms bare, and her boots sat together off to the side. Bandages circled her left forearm, and she bit her lip when she raised it. There was a faintly painful tingle in her wrist.

"I knew it. I *knew* you'd wake up laughing."

Jae froze. "Pa?"

He stooped under the low, rocky roof and knelt before her. Never had Jae seen so much pride shining in his eyes. "Look at you. You're a fighter if I ever saw one."

He was real. He was *there*. His face, once round, was now thin, with prominent cheekbones and a much sharper jaw. There was a pale white scar on his forehead that hadn't been there when they'd parted. He'd lost the brawn he once had from ages of splitting wood and hefting saddles, and now his frame was narrow, almost wiry.

But he was *alive*.

When he embraced her, she let her tears fall. "That bastard *got* me."

His hand stroked her matted hair. "Any other time, I'd ask you not to swear, but you're right."

"But I lived." Through her tears, she laughed again. "I did it."

"Yes, Jae," Pa whispered against the top of her head. "You did it."

They stayed that way a long time.

And nothing else mattered. There were no more ghosts to haunt either of them. At last, at long last . . . they could go on.

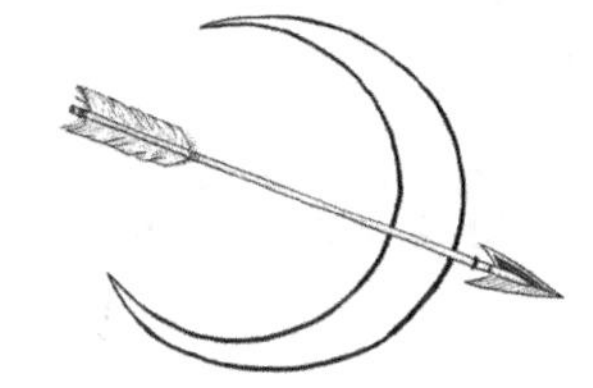

Chapter 43

The Drifter had not died, but death was whispering in his ear. Long ago, he'd given up on trying to end it. The casket was tight, and he could barely move at all, let alone free himself from the bonds. He'd started by smashing his head against the lid, but that had been to no avail. Then, he'd hoped he'd run out of air, that his breathing would cease . . . but the magic in the cloth protected him.

The damn cloth. The wretched, cursed cloth.

His thoughts had become a blur, and then, they'd turned to nothing. Over time, he'd learned to drown them out.

Soon, all he knew was darkness, and that was the closest he could ever come to release.

So time went on.

And on, and on.

The Drifter felt nothing when the earth around him began to stir, though perhaps some silent part of him was annoyed that his rest had been disturbed. When the casket began to shake, he felt it being hoisted into the empty space above . . . and a faint sense of curiosity pricked at him. He'd forgotten that he was in a casket at all, that he'd been buried in . . .

Where was he, again?

The lid came off, and the Drifter faced a different sort of darkness. But this one was comforting, because there were a million stars to pin it back.

And above him, staring down . . . was a face.

The Drifter kept gazing at that face. It plucked a familiar chord somewhere within him. He knew this face, he just wasn't sure from where. Yellow eyes, gray skin, a pair of dull horns sprouting from its head. Monstrous, but . . . benevolent.

The creature was smiling. "Let me help you out there."

The Drifter wasn't sure if he wanted help. He wasn't sure he wanted anything other than that complete, predictable, restful darkness . . . but he tolerated the creature removing the chains from his body.

"Can you walk?" the creature asked. He offered the Drifter a hand.

The Drifter took the creature's hand. Slowly, he stood and stepped out of the coffin. All around them were trees. The sky was black, peppered with stars, and the earth was springy under their feet.

The Drifter knew he'd been in this place before, but he could not recall what had happened here.

Nearby, a straight path of hardened stone cut across the ground beneath the dark canopy of branches. The Drifter blinked at the path. Like everything else he saw, it looked familiar, and he was faintly aware that he was supposed to start walking down that path. For some reason.

"I found out you were here," the creature said. "It was time I returned the favor."

"What favor?" The Drifter coughed after he spoke. There seemed to be a layer of dust coating his throat.

The creature looked puzzled. "Don't you remember?"

"No."

The Drifter began digging through his memory, but all he found was a blur of light and color, things he might have dreamed, faces he may have only imagined. He wanted to remember this creature. He had a kind face. But though he tried, the Drifter could recollect nothing.

"You saved me." The creature motioned to the expanse of trees behind them. "Long ago, you freed me from my tethers."

"I did?"

"You did."

The Drifter had no words for him, but at last, he managed, "Thank you."

"Go," said the creature. "Live your life. Don't let it go to waste."

What life?

And really, what did he have to thank the creature for? For digging him out of his own grave, taking that blissful darkness away from him? For returning him to this strange, foreign world?

What was he?

He was no one.

He was nothing.

The creature kept staring at the Drifter, as though he were waiting for something. *I have nothing more to say to you. You should go.* But the Drifter didn't say so out loud. Though a part of him longed to return to the unchanging darkness, there was only kindness in the creature's eyes. A gentle kindness, without condition, that expected nothing in return.

The stone path seemed to beckon to him. The Drifter felt a slight tug somewhere inside him, as though an invisible thread was sewn to the path and looped around his heart, drawing him to it. He took one step, then another. Both feet were on the path.

He looked forward, down this strange, flat road of stone, leading into the thick shadows beyond.

He didn't know why, but somewhere, far past the stirrings of his mind . . . he felt he had to keep going.

Although the Drifter was nothing, he had nothing else to do, and nowhere else to be.

So the Drifter headed down the path.

Chapter 44

Early that morning, the land became steep, almost mountainous. The road rose and fell between large black boulders, the trees sprouting on slopes of precipitous land. Flint said that they were getting close to the caldera, where Telin lay at the bottom. The sky was overcast.

In the afternoon, Flint led them off the trail. Halston and the others spent a few moments gazing into the shadowy woods, which seemed to emanate a sickly air, as if to fend off anyone who entertained the thought of venturing into them. But Flint insisted that he knew the way, that he'd marked a safe trail with cairns and marks etched into dead trees. They passed one of his stone piles, and a crude X he'd hacked into the bone-dry stump of a dead ponderosa, and thus far, the woods remained quiet but heedful. The land knew they were here, and a part of Halston hoped that if they respected it, then it would not send misfortune their way.

Before long, Flint led them to rest in a small meadow about a half mile from one of his cairns. The skeleton of a deer lay in the lush green grass, and there was a bough of pale orange flowers blooming through the socket of its eye.

Halston sat down at the edge of the meadow in the shade of the pines, just before the grasses and wildflowers gave way to leaf litter and topsoil. His heart jumped when he thought he saw the outline of a slender, dark-haired woman in the corner of his eye, and he turned to speak, half-ready to shout Jae's name.

But when he turned, there was nothing there.

A spirit of the woods? A ghost? A figment of his mind? Halston snorted. Perhaps he was starting to lose it.

He closed his eyes. His heart twisted when he recalled the sight of Jem, how he hadn't even seen the bullet coming, how it had destroyed all of his hopes for a second life in no time flat. He envisioned those bodies lying bloody on the forest floor, men whose names he didn't even know. All dead now, for the life of a stranger. And he pictured those new-made revenants just before they vanished through the portal. Six left. Then there was the warlock, and that man with the cloak and knife.

Are they from our realm?

He knew there were men who had disliked his father, had questioned his abilities as a lord and a leader, but he'd been just thirteen when they'd fled their realm. Hodge had been *twelve*. What vengeance could someone hope to satisfy by slaughtering Joad Harney's sons?

Somebody tapped him on the shoulder. Halston opened his eyes and came face-to-face with his brother.

Hodge's expression was stern, and briefly, Halston scarcely recognized him. He looked less like Halston's brother and more like a stranger who had come across them in the woods.

"Listen," Hodge said, sitting on the grass beside him. "I . . . I *wanted* to say I'm sorry for that spat we got into back there. But the thing is . . . I ain't sure I'm sorry. I mean, I'm sorry for hurting you, but I ain't sorry I had to do it."

Halston sighed. "I know what you mean."

"I don't get it." Hodge scratched his temple, then brushed a lock of black hair out of his eyes. "Who could it be? We've riled up a bunch of bankers and money chargers over the years, but nobody who could . . ." He waved a hand. ". . . do *this.*"

Halston pressed a hand to his temple. "What if it's Sterling's father?"

It would make sense. Sterling had been the son of a Nefili man and a human woman. Halston had overheard him mention it a time or two. But whenever he spoke of his father, anger had found its way into his voice. 'Good for 'nothin,' Sterling had called him. He'd said that his father was rarely around, always meandering off into the woods while his mother had waited for him longingly at the window each day.

"Maybe," Hodge said. "But Sterling always made it sound like he wouldn't have given a damn if any of his sons died. Besides, how would he know it was us?"

Halston shrugged. "He's powerful. Maybe that's just another one of his abilities."

Damn this. Damn all of it. He closed his eyes, wondering how long it would take for the warlock and the revenants to reappear. Ultimately, it didn't matter who he was, or what he wanted with them.

What mattered was making sure that nobody else took any more blows for them.

Halston kept his voice low when he said, "Hodge. I think we need to leave."

"No," Hodge said quickly. "We're going to Telin first."

"Hodge—"

"Flint says we'll get there by *tonight*. The sooner we fix our conduit, the better. I ain't turning back now."

"If they come back, I'm not letting the others *die* for us." Halston closed his eyes again, unable to stop the image of Tsashin, Lorelin, and Flint's fresh bodies shuddering back into life, staggering forward as mindless, soulless revenants. "I don't know what the warlock wants, but it certainly isn't anything the others can give him." Then, Halston placed one hand on his brother's shoulder. "I don't want to fight you again. But I know I can't stop you from following me, if I leave."

Hodge smiled sadly. "We're in this together, then?"

"Of course we are," Halston said, returning the smile. "Like always." Perhaps, he thought, he'd been foolish to try and have it any other way.

"Have you forgotten that I'm right here?" Lorelin came striding over to them, with a piercing, stubborn look in her eyes. Tsashin walked next to her, though Flint still sat on the other side of the meadow, looking off into the trees.

"Gods above," Lorelin said with a snort, "sometimes I feel like you two don't even realize how *loud* you are. Anyway, you're crazy if you think I'm letting you two abandon us."

"Lorelin—" Halston started.

She just cut him off, quickly snapping her fingers together, as if she were catching his voice like a moth. "Don't you remember? When I first joined you, we all made an agreement that we'd look out for one another. This doesn't change a thing."

"I don't want him going after you!" Halston blurted out. "And I don't want the revenants *killing you* because you stood in their way!"

Lorelin just gave him a wild grin. "Then I'll just have to gun them down first."

"You don't understand." He noticed that his hands had started to shake, then he balled them into fists, hoping nobody had seen it. "We got lucky last night. There's a chance we'll—"

"If it counts for anything," Tsashin said, tilting her head up to meet his eye, "I have faith in you. I have faith in *all* of us."

Halston hadn't realized he'd been making a face, but Hodge said, "Gods, Hal. I know that look. You only get it when you're about to make a martyr of yourself."

Halston tensed up. "If they come again," he began, "and we can't take them down, I'm going with them. I'm gonna do whatever they ask of me."

"No," said Hodge.

Halston just frowned at him. "Hodge, cut it out. I won't let them take you away, but if they won't rest until they have me, then—"

"No. You ain't making that choice, Hal. Because you won't have to. I'm gunning every last one of those suckers down."

"I—"

"Do I need to repeat myself? Listen. We fought tooth and nail to get here, and odds be damned, *luck* be damned, we're *all* leaving the Outlands alive."

That fierce determination . . . Halston wanted it. But if Hodge could summon it, then so could he.

If, for nothing else, he could do it for his gang. And he would carry it with him all the way to Telin and back.

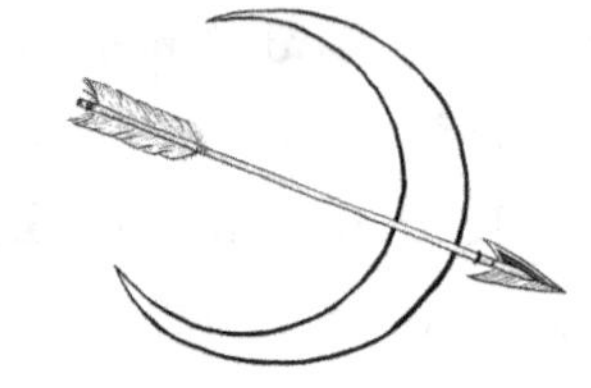

Chapter 45

The night was the warmest Jae had felt since they'd entered the Outlands. They'd dug a small pit and gotten a fire going, and the sparks chased one another into the open air. The sky was clear and the moon was bright, and its light trickled down and made the pines glimmer, and for once, this forest did not seem so strange and frightening. It was like being back in the woods Jae had known as a girl, vast, open, full of adventures to be had.

For a long time, she'd felt that she may have somehow lost that sense of wonder forever. But now, it was back, however small it was.

She sat outside the little cave with Gryff and Pa, feasting on pine nuts they'd foraged earlier. Pa had let her help shell them, but he'd made her stay put when Gryff ventured into the woods to go and find them. He said the longer she stayed put and kept her wound clean, the faster it would heal. All day, he had not left her side.

"How long was I asleep?" she asked.

"Three days," Gryff replied. "We branded your wound shut."

"Did he cut me to the bone?"

"Close, but not quite."

Jae shuddered and thanked her lucky stars that she'd been out cold when they'd branded it.

"We'll have to keep an eye on your arm," Pa said, pointing to her bandages. "If we see redness spreading, we'll have to act quickly."

Pa had always had a working knowledge of healing. A Ranger had to know his way around common ailments that befell men in the mountains. Snakebites, broken bones, things of that sort. While she trusted that Pa had done exactly what she'd needed for her wound, she still wished Lorelin were here.

Jae missed her. She missed *all* of them.

Pa gestured to Gryff. "Gryff told me everything while you were asleep. Seems you've been . . ."

He didn't finish his sentence. Jae forced out a soft laugh. "Up to no good?"

Pa smiled. "I wasn't going to say that."

"S'true though," Gryff said with a snort, though Jae heard a bark of laughter in his voice.

"I've . . ." Jae tapped her fingers against her knee, trying to figure out exactly how to phrase it. "Well . . . you always had good stories for me, Pa. I reckon I can return the favor, now."

Gryff stood. "I'll give you two a minute. I could still go for a few more nuts, anyway."

Jae nodded. Gryff disappeared back in the direction of the pinon grove.

Pa sat quietly by her side in the shade. Years later . . . here they were.

It seemed an eternity, and at the same time, like nothing at all. The last he'd seen her, she'd been a frightened girl, clinging to the shadows. Now . . . well, she wasn't quite sure what she was now.

But Pa?

He was just the same.

"Did Gryff tell you everything?" she asked.

"Just about." He tipped his chin in the direction Gryff had gone off. "He's a fine fellow. I mean, if you were gonna get wrapped up with a band of outlaws . . . I guess I'm glad it's this one."

Heat rose into Jae's cheeks. "I ain't proud of everything I've done with them, Pa. But I'm so glad I met them. I wouldn't trade them for a thing. Even if it makes me . . ." She bit her lip, searching for the right words. ". . . well, a crook. And I hope you're not . . ." She almost didn't finish the thought, but she made herself say it. ". . . ashamed of me."

Pa touched her shoulder. "Jae. Of *course* I ain't ashamed of you. There are lucky men, there are blessed men, and then there's me. Somehow, I wound up with a daughter like you. I reckon it doesn't matter if I live another twenty years or fifty. I can't ever thank you enough for finding me."

Jae wasn't looking at him anymore. His tone was nothing but sincere, but she still caught herself studying the ground, counting the pine needles.

Pa was silent for a while. "Look here," he finally said. "Lawmen, outlaws, everyone in between . . . there ain't such a thing as a simple man. Folks are . . . complicated. I learned that quick in my Rangering days."

Jae nodded slowly. Somehow, even as a bounty hunter, it had taken her a while to learn the same thing. Some folks were rotten. Some just *did* rotten things.

"They arrested us." She was still facing the ground.

"I know. Gryff told me."

"And they'll do it again if they catch us. But Halston . . ." She pressed her forehead to her knees.

Pa didn't say anything after that. He just kept a tender hand on her shoulder.

Jae thought of the ghosts. She wondered if they'd found some peace, wherever they were. "You never told me about the lake."

"I know, Jae," he replied, barely above a whisper. "And I should have told you. Sometimes, a man is too frightened to think straight. Ain't till after the fact that it hits him—that he did wrong. Worse than wrong."

Jae swallowed. "They told me you were discharged. After the fight."

"I was." He took in a long breath, closing his eyes. "I'd never seen anything like it. Amon . . . he could move the water as if it were a part of him. He brought it from the lake in giant waves. He'd use it to knock us down, and then he'd have his robbers finish the men off. We were outnumbered. Fifteen men to a gang of forty. I thought I'd go deaf from the sound of gunfire.

"By the time I got a shot at Amon, most of my men were wounded, if not already dead. I thought the battle was over, that the fight was lost. I thought we'd all die if we stayed there, and I ran. I left my men behind.

"I regretted it as soon as I came to my senses. The Rangers didn't care whether or not I was sorry. I made a vow to stay with my men, and I broke it.

"I still regret it, but the ghosts ain't the worst of it. The worst of it is what Ebdiel did to *you*, Jae." He pressed three fingers to his temple. "When we saw them in the woods that day . . . I knew what they wanted with me, and I didn't blame them in the least. I deserved what I had coming to me. My only fear was that they'd take you, too."

Jae's heart stung at that. She thought back to how he'd hidden her in the trees before charging downhill to face that horde of vengeful souls.

Pa held his wrist out before them. "I got this mark from a Nefili man in my younger days. I found him half-dead in the forest. He'd nearly bled out, and he gave this to me in exchange for saving his life."

Jae squinted at the mark. It was so small that she couldn't even remember whether or not she'd ever noticed it before. It was at the base of Pa's wrist, about the size of a pebble. "It looks like a burn scar. From a cigarette." Certainly not like a gift from an immortal, magical being.

"I wish I'd never found him. I wish I'd never taken his mark," Pa said softly. He pinched the bridge of his nose. Jae thought he might cry, and it broke her heart to see it. "Who am I?" Pa whispered as his hand left his face. "It's my job to protect *you.*"

"You *did,* Pa. Those ghosts might've taken me, too, if you hadn't—"

"*Ebdiel,*" Pa muttered the name with scorn. "He's lucky I don't swim back down there for him."

"He spared me," Jae said. And to Pa's amazement, she told him how Ebdiel had allowed her to live because he could not bear to put another man through the pain he'd once suffered.

Pa said nothing, but she sensed a thousand different thoughts spinning behind his eyes. Jae just shook her head. "He doesn't matter. He got my arm. He swam off. I lived. He can't hurt me anymore."

She wasn't lying to Pa *or* herself. Ebdiel could live till the ends of time or die tomorrow morning, and it wouldn't change a thing. She'd lived, she'd gotten Pa out, and she was *here.* That was all that mattered.

"I meant to tell you about Lake Arania someday," said Pa. "I knew that you'd understand when you were older. I told myself that when you weren't a little girl anymore, I'd tell you all the . . . uglier truths."

Jae wrung her hands. He hadn't lied to her, really. He'd kept things from her, but . . . she'd kept things from a lot of other people. For worse reasons. "I've got some ugly truths for you, too."

So there, under tangled branches and a ceiling of stars, Jae told her pa about what she'd become. A bounty hunter, and then a friend to a band of outlaws. She told him that she'd shed blood, about the anger she'd carried inside her all this time.

As she spoke, Pa said nothing, but nodded in understanding. Occasionally, he'd raise an eyebrow or blink in surprise, but for the most part, he just let her tell the story. And Jae told it in full, rough edges and all.

Sterling came into the tale. Pierce, Argus, Jem. The time she'd spent trapped in the cellar with Halston, the burning barn, and how nothing was the same after that night. She told him how Lorelin had escaped her groom-to-be, how she could patch up anyone's wound in a pinch and still manage to laugh the whole way through. Then she described Hodge and his trick shots, his humor, how he'd throw himself into a storm to save them all. She spoke of Tsashin, and her stories, and her too-gentle heart.

When she talked about Halston, she was careful not to get carried away. If she didn't watch herself, she'd talk about him all night. She didn't mention all the moments they'd shared . . . but she told Pa about the conduit, his quest for silver, for a place where he could open the portal, the mother and sister he'd left behind. The brother he'd lost.

There were things she didn't say. She didn't tell Pa about the night on the train, or by the pond, or the first evening they were free from Sterling.

But she did tell Pa about herself.

She told him that she didn't quite like all the parts of herself, but maybe someday soon, they'd stop threatening to trip her up all the time. They'd never go away. That much was for sure. But she could learn to leap or tiptoe around them. Maybe she'd even learn to thank some of them.

At the end of it all, Pa said, "All that to find me?"

"Of course I did all that. You'd do the same for me." *Hell, you'd do* worse *for me.*

She nibbled her lip, hoping to get some of her nerves to quiet down. Here she was, by Pa's side at long last and telling him that she'd fallen in with wanted robbers. He wasn't angry. Had she expected him to be angry? She wasn't sure.

"It's a lot. I know it," she said. "But they're good, Pa. And they're . . ."

Pa offered her a soft smile. "They're what?"

It was then she spoke a truth she'd known for a while now. She just hadn't found the courage to speak it aloud. "They're my family. I mean . . . you are, too. But . . . if I don't find them, I feel like I'll waste the rest of my life away. The regret will drive me mad. All I'll ever do is *wonder.*

"It's the craziest thing. I thought I was gonna walk away from them. So that I could find you."

Pa grinned. "Well, you found me."

"I can't leave them now. I've gotta go back for them." She fought the urge to hide her face in her hands. "But I can't leave you either, Pa."

Here they were.

Pa was silent for a moment. Was he wondering if he was about to lose her again? "This Halston fellow," Pa said slowly. "He sounds . . . very fond of you."

Fond of her.

Yes, that was true.

It was then she told him what she'd denied knowing for weeks, up until the night at the lake.

And though she felt like speaking it might make her heart cave in on itself, she said it anyway. "I love him, Pa."

She thought it might be easier saying it the second time, but it wasn't. The truth had a terrible habit of showing itself too late.

She'd never been afraid to tell Pa what she was thinking, but when a stretch of silence followed her admission, worry stirred inside her chest.

Pa tilted his head. "He's been kind to you?"

"Nothing but."

Then, Pa said, "Does Telin show up on your map?"

"Sure does. Checked a while ago. It ain't far from here, either."

Pa pulled her close to him. "In that case, I'm going with you. And we're finding them."

Jae almost drew back in shock. "Pa! You can't! I mean, it might be—"

Oh, damn it all. She couldn't leave Pa. She couldn't leave Halston and the others. And she couldn't put Pa in harm's way. Not when she'd feared she'd never again see him alive.

"Sure I can." He smirked in a self-satisfied way. "I was a damn good Ranger, remember? Whatever it is your friends are up against, I imagine it ain't anything worse than what I've seen before."

Should she argue? "Pa. I . . . I can't let anything hurt you."

"Jae." He gave her shoulder another squeeze. "You don't have to worry about me. And if you trust these folks, then that's good enough for me. Wherever they are, whatever you have to do . . . I'll go with you. And I'll do what I can."

This was just like him, wasn't it? Waking from a cursed sleep and jumping back into the fight headfirst. There wasn't a thing on this earth that could douse his fire.

"Pa," she said, struggling to fight the tears that came. "You don't have to."

What he said next was no surprise.

With that brave and ageless smile of his, Pa said, "You raised me from the dead, Jae. It's the least I can do for you."

Chapter 46

That day, they traveled to Telin in sullen quiet, treading through the shadowy woods. Halston's thoughts were restless. He kept thinking he saw things lurking in the trees—faces peering down through the scraggly branches, leaning out from behind thick trunks and bramble-covered bushes, but each time he turned his head for a closer look, all he saw was a still and silent wood.

Jae was gone. Gryff was gone. Jem was really and truly gone, and the ghosts of the men from Levi's village were haunting Halston in his place.

Every time he closed his eyes, he saw the newly dead men sprawled on the ground, then twitching madly as the masked man raised them back to what only a madman could call life.

Halston kept expecting Jem to reappear, to emerge from the thin air and hoot about how close they were, then tell them a story about his life. But he was . . . elsewhere.

I hope you're somewhere better than this world, Halston bid him silently, and he hoped that his words would drift across all the space they had to, to wherever Jem was now. *I hope you've found your peace, Jem.*

Flint hadn't spoken to them beyond mentioning that they were getting closer. As he led the way, Halston wanted to approach him, to tell him once again how sorry they were for what they'd brought upon Levi's village, but what did it matter?

Nothing would change it.

If the warlock came, they would fight. They would fill the revenants with the adamite bullets. At least they'd managed to scare them off last time, but if their pursuers caught them off-guard in the woods, what then?

All throughout the day, he kept catching himself whispering into the woods. *"Show yourself. Get back here. Let's finish this now."*

After the sun went down, he stared at the unwavering darkness, one hand by his holster, braced for some sort of release. The first bullet in his cylinder was an adamite one.

Maybe the next fight would end his life, but at least he wouldn't be running anymore. Still, if he had to fall when they came, he hoped with all his strength that he could bring the warlock and the revenants down with him. Hodge would live. Lorelin and Tsashin and Flint would live. They'd be free.

"Get out here," he whispered. *"Get out here and finish this with me."*

Still, the woods replied with nothing but an empty sigh, indifferent to all that passed through them.

A few hours into nightfall, they reached a new part of the woods. Gradually, the trees began to change, and soon there were no more pines. No live ones, anyway. Instead, dead, blackened trees rose from the earth like an army of gaunt giants. Their barren arms reached for the sky, not a speck of green amongst them. They resembled mourners. Halston could almost hear them weeping. Maybe he was imagining it, but the ground felt warm, even through his boots.

"There must've been a wildfire here," he said to no one in particular. Though something told him that the source of this fire hadn't been a natural one.

They trekked across the scorched ground, skirting around ashy logs and brittle stumps. Soon enough, they came to a massive curve of dark rock, framed by several dozen burnt trees. They looked so fragile, like a man could topple them with a single finger. Below them was the caldera.

It was enormous. Halston could scarcely make out its other side. He guessed it was at least two miles in diameter, and at least a half-mile deep.

Halston looked down into the caldera, then squinted. Where was Rogue's palace? He made out several stairways leading down from the edge of the forest and into the crater, all crudely hewn from its rough, black stone. Knobby arches and boulders were strewn about the bottom of the caldera, but Halston couldn't make out anything resembling a *palace*, like Flint had described.

"It's underground," Flint said.

"Hmm?"

"Telin. The palace itself is underground." He motioned for Lorelin and Tsashin to come closer. "Listen here. Until we're out of here, keep quiet unless somebody else speaks to you, and do as I say. She might toy with you. For her, it's all in good fun. But so long as you don't anger her, she won't hurt you."

The air was growing heavy, and as Halston breathed it in, it tasted stale in his mouth. Halston thought he could smell something burning—hot copper or singed meat.

He narrowed his eyes as something caught his gaze. Through

the blackened bark of one tree, he could still make out its texture. Not jagged lines, like a proper pine. No. The bark was marked with swirling, round patterns. Dozens of them. Almond shapes with smaller, darker circles in the center.

Eyes.

The eyes widened at him, then blinked away.

Before Halston could open his mouth, the tree fell apart.

Chunks of wood scattered around them like exploding earth. The pieces struck the ground, then joined back together in the forms of feet, legs, chests, heads. And teeth. Rows and rows of teeth. In the tree's place stood a rank of monstrous soldiers.

The bud of a shout caught in Halston's throat, but he couldn't make a sound. Dumbly, he tried to reach for his gun, but the soldiers were already closing in. Their dense armor was textured like the blackened trees. Bits of charred twigs and moss clung to their necks and cheeks. Their eyes were dull, textured like firm treebark. Helmets covered the top halves of their faces, leaving their gaping jaws bare.

The monsters trudged forth in silence, all of them bearing weapons—thick clubs and meaty spears with jagged edges.

One of them rooted its gaze to Flint, who stood with his hands in the air, shoulders tense, stance broad. The creature's lips arched into a cruel smile. It was close enough that Halston could finally make out its gaunt, skull-like face.

"It's good to see you, Barrow. Did you find the waterstone?" Its voice was scratchy, heavy, as if it was suffering from a combination of a parched throat and deep hunger.

"Yes," Flint said flatly.

"With only a scratch to show for it? A mighty feat, indeed." The monster began ogling at the others, squawking with something that might have been delight. "Do they come for a challenge?"

"Yes," Flint said with enviable clarity.

The monsters tittered. "And who will be their champion?"

Flint glanced back at his companions. His expression was unreadable.

"I will," Halston said at last.

Each of the monsters smiled, beaming with unmistakable amusement. They chattered

amongst themselves in their own tongue, then their leader spoke again. "Very well, then. Shall we lead the way? We'd hate to miss your champion's triumph."

They were led, then, at spearpoint, over the caldera's ledge to one of the stairways. The steps were steep, and just wide enough for everyone to walk with a monster at each side of them.

They began their descent into the caldera. Halston stood at the front of their line, Flint just behind him. He tried not to look at the guards on the long climb down. They stank faintly of decay.

The stairs brought them to the bottom of the caldera. Halston could see now that every stairway led to a large, rectangular pit in the stone, each one surrounded by strange, chalky runes. Underneath, there was Telin. What were they about to march into?

Another guard emerged from the hole at the end of their stairway, this one sporting a helmet with curved horns and a stave with a spearhead on either end. It spoke to the other monsters in their language, then tersely nodded and motioned for them to follow him downward.

This was it.

Before they ventured down the last flight of stairs and into Telin, Flint whispered to Halston, "Don't look in the mirrors."

Halston looked over his shoulder at Flint. "What?"

Flint didn't repeat himself. The monsters were leering at all of them, now. Flint pressed his lips together—a signal that to say anything else would be unwise.

Mutely, they passed through a torch-lined tunnel, then a cavern riddled with cracks, and spent ages trekking around a deep chasm before finally entering an enormous, empty hallway.

Carved pictures covered the towering walls. Halston tried to study the images in the scanty torchlight. He could make out suns and moons and stars, monsters with wings and spear-like teeth, fighters brandishing blades and shields. Inscriptions framed the images, runes similar to those etched on the archway outside. He wished that he could read them.

Surely these icons had endured thousands of seasons, stayed behind while a hundred ages came and went past in the world above. The forest's age was a blink in the eyes of this hall.

Soon, up ahead, the pictures gave way to flat, reflective walls. *The mirrors.* Halston urged himself to look straight ahead, focusing on one of the guard's charred helmets.

Behind him, there was a scream.

"Tsashin!" Hodge cried.

Halston spun around. Tsashin lay on the floor, arms splayed out at her sides, eyes shut. She looked just as she had when they'd dug her out of the ground, right before she'd cried out and leapt out of her coffin.

Everything around him seemed to freeze. No. Gods above, not Tsashin . . .

Hodge knelt beside her and gathered her small body in his arms. He pressed two fingers to the skin beneath her jaw. "She's okay." His voice wavered between shaky breaths. Tears glinted in his eyes. He kept holding onto her.

The words left Halston's mouth before he could stop them. "What happened?"

"She faced one of her worst fears in the mirror," one of the monsters said slowly, its tone rancid with disdain. "Too much for her, it seems."

"She'll be fine," Flint assured them. "She'll wake up soon."

Searing anger shot through Halston's entire body. Why hadn't Flint warned them sooner? The mirrors hung over them like looming enemies, taunting them before delivering the death blow. Halston kept focusing on Tsashin, who still lay limp in Hodge's arms.

What would he see if *he* beheld the mirrors?

"We must make haste," one guard said. "Our lady waits for you."

"I ain't leaving her!" Hodge fired back. He hugged Tsashin closer to his chest.

"Would you rather *we* looked after her?" one of the monsters purred.

Hodge only glared at them, then stood, raising Tsashin from the floor. For a moment, she stirred in his arms, then her body slackened once more. "I'll carry her."

"If you insist. It's all the same to us," the monsters said, then gestured with their spears for them to hurry. "Now then. This way."

When the hall of mirrors ended, they stepped onto the edge of a large, rectangular pit in the floor. Long, misshapen steps rose on all sides of them. The floor was a rough stretch of stone—darker than the night sky itself. Stone the earth had spit up, molten and red, and hardened into masses of glimmering black.

The beasts had brought them to the center of a cavernous great hall. Along the rim of the rectangular pit, Halston noticed multiple entrances, and he guessed they led off to other winding hallways and corridors throughout Rogue's palace. Halston faced the ceiling, which stretched at least a mile overhead, feeling as though he'd found himself in the belly of some great and ancient beast. Suddenly, Halston wasn't sure if they were nestled somewhere deep inside the earth, or above it. A thin slash in the ceiling revealed stars burning in the far-off void. They shed some light on the enormous room—just a hint, but far better than nothing.

Flint led them forward, the guards flanking their sides. Before them, crouching at the end of the pit and on top of the final step, where a throne should have been, was a woman. She sat with her knees drawn to her chest, her hands clasped together as though she were praying.

Her body was frail, almost childlike, and there was scarcely any flesh padding her bones. Heaps of feathery cloth and ornaments of teeth and bone cradled her limbs. Dark tresses of hair cascaded over her chest.

As they ambled closer to her, she remained motionless, so still that it was almost unnerving. Soon, they were near enough that Halston could make out the shackles binding her thin wrists. The chains trailed up to the stone wall, tacked somewhere Halston could not see, and although they didn't look any different from ordinary iron, Halston was sure they must have been fashioned from something otherworldly to keep her bound here.

Her head turned. When she grinned—teeth glinting through a red, soft-edged stain on her mouth—Halston fought against every urge inside him to shrink away from her.

Flint had said she was a witch . . . but that couldn't be true. Sterling was a warlock, but in life, he'd had the face and form of an ordinary man.

Nobody could mistake this being for a human woman.

Her golden eyes were rimmed with dark circles, and when Halston looked upon them, they burned as if he were staring at the sun. Ashen splotches of rot stippled her face, but the rest of her skin glimmered. It was translucent. Through it, Halston could make out her skull.

Her thin lips stretched into a mirthless grin. "Hello, Flint. The waterstone, please." Despite her deathly appearance, her voice was steady and plain. If he'd closed his eyes, Halston could have believed that it came from an ordinary woman.

Flint fished around in his pack, then removed a rectangular stone the color of seawater. Halston wondered how he'd come by it, whether it was from a living man or the depths of a tomb. Flint paced up to the witch, set the stone on the ground before her, then retreated back to the rest of the company.

Rogue let out a murmur of approval, then her thin hand reached out to settle on the jewel. Halston could see every one of her bones through the skin of her fingers. After she'd inspected it, the gemstone disappeared, and Rogue tilted her chin up at the gang, eyeing them like a wolf watching prey from a shadowy hideaway.

"I thought you preferred to work alone, Flint," she said slowly.

"They've come to seek one of your treasures, my lady." Flint held his head high as he spoke, dignified, as if he were speaking to an equal.

"Well, don't tell me so yourself. Which of them will bargain with me?"

Halston stood, summoning all his strength to keep from shaking. Once, he'd seen his father standing at the prow of his ship, motionless and firm, looking as though nothing he faced could possibly deter him. Halston tried to do the same.

"We've come for a conduit. Half of an adamite knife, with Alfirian runes on the blade."

"Oh, yes." Her indifferent gaze passed over him. "I remember the blade."

"We've heard you are willing to trade."

She looked back at him with a dull stare.

"Name your price," said Halston. "I'll take any challenge you give me."

Halston did not receive an answer. Rogue's attention lingered on Hodge, who was still cradling Tsashin.

Rogue stared at her with a look of pure contempt. "Fragile thing. Usually they only *scream* at what they see. They almost never collapse."

One of the monsters began to chortle. "Seems a bit daft to carry around all that deadweight, ah? What do you say, boy? We could toss her to the riverbeasts out back. *That* could be our trade instead."

Hodge looked to the monster. Slowly, he took a few steps toward Lorelin. Without so much as a whisper, he passed Tsashin's sleeping form to Lorelin. Then, he dove toward the monster. A sharp crack sounded as he slammed it against the wall of the pit, pinning the beast by his shoulders. The monster dropped its spear. Terror roared through Halston's veins.

Flint darted for Hodge, seized his arms, and pried him off the fiendish creature. The monster was only cackling as Hodge bellowed every obscenity he knew.

"I *like* this one!" the beast hooted, sprawled out on the floor, shaking with its demoniacal laughter.

Halston was ready for a fight. Would bullets even harm an enemy like this? He thought of the adamite bullets in his pistol and wondered if these monsters were undead, if adamite alone could finish them off.

But the monsters didn't move. They merely sneered amongst themselves, entirely unbothered.

Rogue, however, was different. She faced them all with an unnerving stare. Halston looked away from her dour, fiery eyes.

"You should have left my guard alone," she said slowly.

"I'm sorry," said Hodge, though Halston knew that he was hardly concerned about sounding sincere.

Her dark glare jumped back and forth between Halston and Hodge, then her red mouth curled into a smile. "Halston and Hodge Harney. You seem to leave a trail of death behind you, don't you? First your enemies, but now, innocents. Men who hadn't the faintest idea that your presence would bring about the end of your lives . . . and that poor ghost who was traveling with you. He won't be returning from undeath now, will he?"

Halston would not turn away from her. He didn't know what game this witch was playing, but he wouldn't cower, wouldn't give in.

"You should know what happened to your father," she said slowly. "The beasts came and devoured him. He was long dead, of course, but they swallowed his bones with ease."

Halston took a step back.

"His death was not quick, if that was what you'd hoped for. An instant of pain endures far longer in a collapsing mind. Like your brother. His lungs burned as he sank, and the riverbed tore his flesh. Do you remember his shredded face?"

The next moment passed too quickly for Halston to register.

Because a moment earlier, the space at his feet had been empty. Now, there lay the body of Elias.

It was exactly as Halston had seen it that night. Bloated, nearly unrecognizable, vegetation clinging to his limbs and sodden clothes. Mouth half-open. Eyes blackened.

Halston closed his eyes and hoped with all his strength that the sight would be gone when he opened them. It couldn't be real.

But he'd seen it.

"*You could have stopped it,*" Rogue reminded him. "The weight of failure is heavy, is it not?"

Her voice tempted him to tear off his own ears.

But Halston reminded himself that he could not give her that satisfaction. Elias wasn't really here. They'd buried him. He'd been there.

Halston forced his eyes open and heaved out a sigh of relief when he found that his brother's body no longer lay on the floor. Hodge stood next to Tsashin's sleeping figure, staring down at the empty space. All the color had drained from his face. He'd seen the apparition, too.

Halston had to fight to keep his voice steady. "I'm sorry. For what my brother did to your guard. But *please*, grant me the challenge. Tell me what you'd have me do."

She smiled again. "I admire men with the will to make demands of witches."

Halston would make demands of a thousand witches if it meant returning to his world. To Lia, to his mother, to his home.

Rogue returned her focus to Hodge. "There is a yearning in you. A powerful one. You wish to return to your world. The Second Realm. Your mother waits for you there, but the monsters still devour your people. You still think of that darkness blanketing your home, don't you?" She bared her teeth like a canine. "I know why it came. If you knew who sent it . . . My. I imagine your knees would tremble."

Halston fell still.

Somehow, this witch knew about his world, his father's death, and . . . that someone had *sent* the darkness?

Halston had always thought that a monster had brought it on, one of the many terrors running rampant through his realm. Could this be true?

"Faithless fool," Rogue said to Halston. "Of course it's true."

Halston suddenly felt faint. The things she'd said were almost enough to make him falter—to push his mind away from what he was here to do.

"If I *do* give you a challenge," Rogue said, one hand lingering beside her mouth, "you must brace yourself for darkness. For things that may be worse than what you witnessed when you fled your own world. Are you ready for that?"

Hodge was staring at Halston instead of the witch. Blood coated his mouth and chin. Had he bit his lip in his attempt to strangle the monster? Right now, he looked so much younger than he really was—Halston recalled how he'd looked when they'd escaped the darkness swallowing their world, eyes wide as saucers. He was still only a boy.

Don't do it, Hodge's eyes seemed to say.

I'll be alright, he thought, willing it to enter Hodge's mind.

"I'm ready," Halston said.

Rogue hesitated, then, looking almost perplexed. Halston wondered if the contenders who entered Telin were usually so eager.

"'I've one in mind," she said at last. "You wish to return to your home world? Then crossing through another world will be your task."

Halston didn't follow.

"It's simple enough," she continued. "There is a pathway you will follow. Do not stray from it. You will speak your name when you arrive at the *gates*. When you have done so, you will re-enter this world. Then, I'll give you your half of the blade."

"The gates?"

"You will know them when you see them."

Halston swallowed hard and nodded.

"You may *only* take the clothes on your back. No weapons," she said.

Halston removed the pack from his shoulders, set it on the ground, then dropped his gun on top of it. He bent down and retrieved his half of the knife from the pack. He picked it up and he walked over to Hodge.

Without a sound, Hodge took it from him, and Halston whispered, *"Use it well."*

He turned from his brother to face Rogue. She gave him an approving nod, then said, "You will not need food or drink in this world, nor will you age. It may feel as if years have passed when you reach the end of it. Decades, perhaps. Are you ready for that?"

The answer shouldn't have come as easily as it did.

"Yes."

Before she sent him on, the last thing Halston was aware of was Hodge and Lorelin crying his name, a whirlwind of light and color circling around him, and for the faintest moment, an overpowering hope, one that cast all of his fears aside.

———

The Drifter came to his senses in a world of stars and sand.

He pushed himself upright. Starlight cast its glow on the surrounding dunes, which stretched farther than he could see. Beside him lay a path of smooth stone, arrow-straight, running far, far ahead.

This was his path.

At the end of it, years or miles ahead, were the gates.

My name is Halston Harney, he reminded himself. *I took a challenge from a witch called Rogue. I'm here to find the gates and speak my name.*

And, with the slimmest whisper of courage, Halston took his first steps on the path.

Chapter 47

Jae had never imagined that her first journey after Pa's rescue would look like this.

The day's hike carried them through the woods and into a steeper part of the land, and at dusk, they reached a fire-scorched portion of the forest. Jae's eyes repeatedly flitted to her map, checking their path, counting down the miles to Telin. Every time, she mouthed the word, its shape strange and unfamiliar on her lips.

Telin.

Now, it was less than a mile away.

While they were moving over the fire-touched land, Pa raised a hand to halt them. "Look here." He knelt to the earth, tracing a finger over the pock-marked ground. "Boot tracks. Fresh."

Jae drew in a full breath. Maybe they belonged to another pack of travelers, but a quiet part of her hoped that perhaps the others were close by.

As they moved on, watching the stars take over the twilit sky, Jae wondered if this was how prey felt, right before the death-bite.

"You ever dealt with a witch before, Ven?" Gryff asked.

"A time or two," Pa replied. "Though I can't say I've ever dealt with one who could grant wishes. Ain't ever run into anyone *that* powerful."

Jae and Gryff had heeded Flint's warning and passed it onto Pa—how Rogue conjured up obstacles for the travelers entering her palace for the first time. She thanked the Wandering God that Pa and Gryff were there with her, because after braving a storm-bird, ghosts, and a Nefilium water lord . . . perhaps they *could* make it through whatever came their way.

And she prayed that Halston and the others waited for them at the end.

Somewhere along the way up, Pa lost the tracks they'd been following . . . perhaps they'd been scattered by the wind. Still, Jae had her map, and she knew that they were headed in the right direction.

The ground seemed to be pulsing beneath their feet. Under the layer of stones and soot, she sensed something vibrant—something ready to lurch out and swallow them at any moment now.

They kept scaling the sloping earth. Jae's legs were beginning to cramp from their ascent, but she pressed on. Upward they moved, past droves of burnt trees, over unyielding earth, until it stopped in a curved, wide-spread arc.

Beneath it was the caldera. It wasn't what Jae had expected. Upon her first glance, the stony hollow was enormous but unremarkable, not frightening in the least. But then she sensed the hunger lurking under the earth, and no amount of ignoring it would make it go away. It lingered. It waited.

Stairways scattered around the carter led to the bottom, and Jae did her best to take in all of them. They all seemed equally steep, and all were empty.

"Think it matters?" she murmured, her gaze jumping to the nearest one.

"Whatever gets us down the fastest," Gryff answered. "But be ready for anything that might jump out at us."

Duly noted, though Jae had been ready for things to jump out as soon as they'd entered the burnt part of the wood.

They took to the stairway. Slowly, they began their descent into Telin. As they moved, Jae squinted. It was getting darker, difficult to make out what lay below, but she could see that each of the many stairways led into its own rectangular hole in the fine-grained rock. She wondered what the palace halls would look like when they stepped into their pit.

Around halfway down, Jae was practically shaking from the climb. These were the steepest stairs she'd ever climbed down, and it was almost impossible to keep a steady pace. They crept toward the bottom gradually as they could, but the thought of doing anything but running as fast as they could was killing her. Time was racing, but one false step would send them plummeting.

Jae kept her focus on her path, but it was hard not to let her attention shift to the large, black boulders strewn across the slope. Perhaps her mind was playing games with her, but she swore she saw a few that resembled burnt corpses.

When they were just a few yards away from the entrance, fear started toying with her mind. It was the same heat that had overpowered her outside of Dolorosa, when she'd been certain that the ghost of Argus would come for her. Beyond the first few steps plunging into the darkness, she couldn't see what waited for them in their path.

But somehow, the notion that her gang was waiting down there for her overpowered her fear.

There was nowhere worth going but forward—right into the beast's mouth.

Nobody spoke, but Jae exchanged a terse look with Gryff and Pa. There was a world of pure trust in their eyes, and it filled her with hope. It was time.

She'd been so tense that she hadn't felt Pa placing his hands on her shoulders. And when he whispered, it was with a softness that she hadn't heard since she was small.

"Jae," he said slowly. "You don't have to go in there. We can turn back now."

This didn't surprise her. Not in the slightest. But she'd had her answer ready long before they'd come here.

"I have to, Pa."

His mouth curved upward, but his eyes were sad. "Let's get going, then."

The steps led them down about ten more yards, then leveled out into a wide, dim tunnel.

The three of them broke into a run, their footsteps echoing off the stone walls. No one spoke, and they kept their hands ready to draw their weapons. Jae's wound was tender under her bandages, and she prayed that it wouldn't start bleeding again. At least she could still shoot.

It took everything in Jae not to shout Halston's name.

Jae had never seen a place so empty. It wasn't like Nestor's Caverns, where the stone, untouched by time, had been allowed to grow and spiral into spikes and shafts the way it pleased. This tunnel was pin-straight, and the stone walls were too smooth. Too perfect. There were torches mounted on the walls every several yards or so, and Jae thanked the Wandering God that they had some light. The tunnel was nowhere close to bright, but she could see all she needed to.

They hurried onward. It was far too easy to picture the walls collapsing in, the ceiling breaking apart, raining down and crushing them all. She could no longer breathe deeply. The scanty air entered her chest in thin, stale huffs. Dizziness threatened to make her stumble.

Keep going.

Jae swore she heard noises here and there—a faint growl from somewhere nearby, a clipped laugh, a muffled shriek. Was this magic, or was her mind playing tricks on her?

They'd come too far. She wouldn't let her terror hold her captive. Instead, she moved faster.

They've got to be close, she told herself. Even if it wasn't true, she had no choice but to believe it wholehcartedly.

At last, the tunnel broadened into a massive, cavernous room. The ceiling curved high above them, and the walls were full of cracks so thick it was a wonder they didn't collapse on them. There was a dark strip trailing down the center of the floor. That must have been the continuing path. They took off down the shaded line of stone, and nobody dared to stray from its borders.

But they'd barely started coursing through the cavern when Jae glimpsed motion in the corner of her eye.

A dark shape flitted out from one of the cracks in the walls, then zipped downward, scurrying toward the floor. Two more followed it. Five more, six, and then Jae lost count. The creatures overflowed from the rifts in the rock, a thousand feet joining together in a sickening patter. The meager light glinted off their sleek bodies, and through the shadows, Jae could make out curved tails and barbed stingers.

Scorpions.

They sprinted down the hall, fast as their muscles would allow. The scorpions were beginning to reach the ground, now, and the creatures barreled toward them, legs scrambling, stingers twitching.

A fire blazed in Jae's skull. She wouldn't dare waste a moment getting a closer look at them, but most of the creatures were the size of pigs. Their stingers were bigger than some knives she'd seen. Which would kill them first—the stabbing stingers, or the venom that would then shoot through their veins?

The monsters came in droves. Already, the creatures flooded the floor, bustling toward the three intruders. If they kept coming, there would be nowhere to run—they'd either have to gun the beasts down or leap over them.

Pa and Gryff opened fire on the monsters. Bursts of inky blood exploded from the mass, and their sleek bodies shuddered and crumpled. Jae followed suit, drew her pistol, and killed two scorpions. A third. Three shots left and precious little time to reload.

They kept racing down the path, but the scorpions kept on coming, and they were just as fast.

When Jae's heart was about ready to burst, the path ended. A chasm some two yards across opened before them, stretching to somewhere far beyond their sight to their left and right. On the other side, the path continued.

They'd have to jump. Jae wasn't sure if a sting from one of the monsters would be much better than falling to her death, but they at least had a chance of leaping over the gorge.

Gasping, she looked over her shoulder. The scorpions were still gaining on them, but they were in the lead.

The chasm was closer, closer . . .

A dark shape fell from the ceiling, then cut off their path. Jae skittered back on her heels. A scorpion half the size of the horse had landed in front of them, and it was close enough that Jae could make out all eight of its golden eyes perfectly. Behind them, the smaller beasts swarmed over the path.

Surrounded.

Jae drew her gun and fired. The giant scorpion jerked to the side, and the bullet barely skimmed its tail. The creature let out a piercing cry and flung itself in her direction.

Jae jumped to the left. Something broke under her foot with a sickening crunch. She'd stepped on one of the smaller ones. She leapt away, not bothering to check if her weight had crushed the life out of it. The huge one still had its sight set on her. A shot from Gryff or Pa grazed its back, but the great arachnid hardly seemed to notice.

The head. She had to get it in the head.

But before she could aim, the monster came for her, faster than an arrow. The scorpion swept out a claw and hit her, knocking her off her feet, and her head struck the floor. Pa cried her name. Stars spun when she opened her eyes. For a second, all her limbs might as well have been made of lead. She could barely move.

Clarity returned to her too late. She'd dropped her gun in the fall. She lay there, helplessly caged by the monster's legs. There was nowhere for her to move her arms.

Writhing, unable to look where her foot would strike, Jae kicked upward. The beast shook a little at the impact, just barely, but it bought her enough time to free her right arm.

The scorpion's head lashed out. Before its fangs could nip her nose, Jae closed her hand around one of its pincers. With all her strength, she pushed the head away from her own. Its screeches were like dull blades in Jae's ears. Its jaws shook, and she let go of the pincer, braced to kick it again.

A shadow fell over them. Something swung out of the air and slammed into the scorpion's head. The monster roared like hell, and

Jae threw her arms up, practically clawing at the ground. In one desperate shove, she slid out from under the beast.

Jae sprung to her feet. The creature darted away from Gryff. Its tail started pulsing madly, and Jae dodged each blow, barely missing the stinger each time.

Her gun lay about two yards away. Clumsily, she jumped for it, then kicked aside two smaller scorpions in her way. She bent down and seized her gun, and the giant scorpion's stinger cut the hem of her jacket.

Without a second thought, Jae shot it in the mouth.

A burbling screech escaped the monster, and it wobbled on its feet, raising its head toward the ceiling. Jae cursed and shot at it again. Blood erupted from its face and rained blue spatters on her clothes.

The movements of its still-twitching body put her in a trance. For a couple seconds, her feet stayed bolted to the floor, and she stared at the corpse.

Then, her instincts kicked in, and all of them ran.

Jae wasn't sure she'd ever really known what it meant to *run* until then.

Thousands of quick feet skittered on the path behind them. The wisps of their motion prodded Jae's legs, and she braced herself to feel the nip of their pincers at any second. They were nearing the gorge, now.

Gryff leapt first, then Pa.

Jae reached the edge of the chasm, and with a surge of blind, maddened faith, leapt into the air.

Both feet struck the ground. She faltered briefly, but kept herself from falling. They'd made it! Sweet gods above, they'd made it!

On she ran, Gryff at her right, Pa at her left. Behind them, the scorpions were gathering on the ledge as if waiting for them to turn around and come back.

In another time, Jae might have smirked at that, but she wouldn't let herself be grateful just yet. She dared not guess what might lie ahead.

Still, they kept running.

Chapter 48

After they'd leapt over the chasm, they ran until the path widened, and a constant roar filled the corridor. Jae ran faster, braced for some new horror to show itself. But as they raced forth, the tunnel widened to reveal a gaping cavern up ahead. The roar mingled with the sound of water dripping onto stone. A river?

The three of them hurried to the end of the tunnel. Mist kissed their faces as they entered the edge of the chamber ahead. The domed ceiling was so high it made Jae's stomach lurch. It was then they found the source of the roar: a waterfall, flowing freely from somewhere up high and into a river that rippled and sloshed through the belly of the cavern. Above the river was a stone bridge. No rails.

Jae swallowed hard, wondering what sort of monstrosity might appear if they stepped onto the bridge. The river wasn't wide, but there was no landing spot on the other side, save for the end of the bridge. Even if there was a spot for them to jump to, they'd be cutting it close.

"Stay behind me," Pa said slowly, then began leading them across the bridge, knife in hand. Jae and Gryff followed him, walking in a line, and Jae kept one hand near her hip, though having her gun hardly made her feel better.

The surface of the bridge was slick, and so narrow that the slightest shift in her balance would send her tumbling into the rapids.

She pushed that thought away. Instead, she imagined the others waiting at the end of the next corridor. Hodge would laugh, Lorelin's embrace would practically crush her, Tsashin's smile would be sweet as the summer rain. And Halston . . .

Halston.

They could stay awake the whole night, and the next ten nights, and she reckoned she'd still not be finished with all she had to say. And if she lived through this, never again would she hold her tongue so long.

"*Jae!*" Gryff shouted.

She glimpsed it too late. A clawed hand with flesh the color of rotting wood closed around her ankle. It yanked.

Down she went.

Jae flailed, reaching for something to cling to, but her hands only caught the empty air. Her body struck the river's surface. Water covered her legs, torso, her arms and shoulders. Then, she was no longer breathing.

Before the panic could set in, the world around her slipped away.

Suddenly, she was completely dry.

She was somewhere warm, standing in a shaft of sunlight.

Jae blinked several times. Where was she? When had she come here? Jae paced around the room, the wooden floor creaking under her feet, waiting to hear another voice. The space was small, with a single window, a desk covered in papers, and a chair on either side. Through the thin walls, she could hear the wind whistling faintly from outside. There was one door at the far end of the room, but when she jiggled the knob, she found that it was locked.

Sitting unclaimed on the desk was a small badge in the shape of a star. She made out the words *County Sheriff,* the engraving slightly tarnished.

"Hello?" she called out. She received no answer.

Jae rubbed her eyes. Her heart raced faster as she tried to remember when she'd come to this office. The days, the *weeks* before this, were a muddled blur. She smacked her lips. Her mouth was dry as dust. Had she been walking through the desert before this?

What was she even doing? Was she supposed to meet somebody here?

Jae paced up to a small, murky window. Through the dusty glass, she could make out a gallows against a backdrop of rolling desert. A body dangled from the noose.

Jae pressed her head to the glass for a closer look. The body swayed on the rope, turning very slowly in a circle. The rope twisted, and then, Jae saw the victim's face.

And she leapt away from the window.

Not a single thought entered her mind. There was only heat—fierce, roaring heat, coursing through her veins.

A banknote lay on the desk in front of her. One hundred crowns, in her name. A bounty, paid in full, for the capture of Halston Harney.

A scream tore out of her throat.

She leapt away from the window, then raced around the perimeter of the room. A cry was already shaking her, but she reached for the doorknob and shook it furiously. She had to escape this place. Wipe it away. Forever.

She'd done this to him.

She'd killed Halston Harney.

Trying to keep from shaking, she slid down the wall and collapsed to her knees. She dug her fingers into her hair, then covered her face with her hands. What had happened? Who had brought her here?

Who had strung that noose around Halston's neck?

Jae tried to think back to the moments leading up to this, but the first thought that came to mind was that night they'd walked to the Banderra border and found the old piano in the plains. How their song had filled the night. The laughter, spilling over in her chest, had made her new.

And then she recalled how they'd walked along the banks of the lily pond, in the company of a million stars.

The ravine, the stormbird, Gryff saving them both before they'd shared a quiet night.

After that, they'd returned to the woods, and Jae had faced the ghosts and Ebdiel. Though she'd almost bled out, Pa had saved her, and then, she'd told him about all she'd done, all she'd become.

It was time, she'd told him, for her to go to Telin and find Halston.

And here they were.

There was nothing to worry about, because Halston was still alive. None of this was real.

At the realization, the sheriff's office shattered like thin glass. A million shards broke away, carried off by some invisible force.

Jae found herself kicking to stay afloat. The imaginary world had fallen away. She'd returned to the water, and now, her lungs were flaming. Air—she had to breathe. Around her, circling savagely in the water, wraithlike monsters gazed at her with beaming yellow eyes. Not unlike the shifter, they resembled gaunt skeletons with gray skin pulled taut over their frames, with long fingers ending in pointed claws.

They moved with a swift fury. Did they know that their trick hadn't worked? Surely, they must. But she wasn't afraid. She'd sunk in deeper waters, climbed out, dazed and bleeding, and lived.

One of the creatures grasped at her calf. Jae kicked it right in the chest, and it lurched away, letting out a burbling yelp. Another swam out from behind her, and Jae cried out when she felt its fingers graze her bare neck. Immediately, she felt dry again, and she caught the briefest glimpse of the Mescan desert before her. Murrietta's Rock loomed like a giant in the distance.

"This ain't real!" she screamed, though she felt her lungs might shrivel into nothing as she cried out. At once, the image vanished, and she was thrashing in the deep water again.

She'd broken the spell they'd cast over her. They'd fought their way into her mind, and she'd driven them out. Maybe it was nonsense, but she was certain that the memory of those waiting for her—of Pa and Halston and the rest—had kept her alive.

There was *nothing* they could take from her.

Nothing she wouldn't go down fighting for, at least.

Jae kicked her way to the surface, dodging more swipes from the creatures' boney fingers and claws. Finally, her arm broke through the surface. Her hand found the bridge, folding over the slippery stone, and she poked her head out and gulped down a long, precious breath. Then, a pair of massive hands grabbed her waist. Gryff raised her from the water like she weighed less than nothing. He lowered her back onto the bridge, and as she struggled to sit upright, she glanced over her shoulder. Before they braced themselves to start running into the next tunnel, she glimpsed one of the gray, monstrous hands slip back into the current.

Jae smirked. *Nice try.*

"Jae!" Pa knelt beside her and threw his arms around her. She clung to him for a moment, her sopping braids dripping water onto his sleeves. "Are you alright?"

"I'm fine," she breathed out. "I'm fine. But we've gotta go."

Pa nodded, then helped her to her feet. The path waited for them ahead.

On and on they ran.

They sprinted till at last they reached a point in the hallway where the path split into two separate tunnels. There was no need to ponder which way to go.

Because just as they'd stumbled upon the fork, a startled scream came from the right.

And Jae was sprinting down the path before she knew it. *"Lorelin!"*

Her answer came through a harsh chorus of shouting. "Jae?" And the way she said it nearly broke Jae's heart. *Jae? Jae, you're alive?*

I'm alive, Lor. I'm here. I'm coming.

At last, at long last, she'd found them . . . and if Jae Oldridge had any say in it, she was never going to leave them again.

Chapter 49

Hodge could barely breathe.

He stood at the spot where Halston had stepped into the other world, staring helplessly, waiting for his brother to return. This couldn't be real. He was dreaming and he was going to wake up.

He hurried back to where Lorelin was waiting with Tsashin. Her eyes were still closed, but Hodge couldn't tell if she was conscious or not. She was shivering wildly, and as he came closer, he made out beads of sweat on her skin. Flint hadn't budged from where he stood, and though the room was hot, he'd tugged his duster jacket tight around his shoulders as though trying to block out a chill.

Hodge briefly wondered why Flint had stayed behind. He'd finished his errand. He'd upheld the offer he'd made them.

Hodge turned to Rogue.

How unassuming she looked, chained up like that. It was almost easy to forget that she was still the mistress of this place, and that if they crossed her, she would manifest their worst fears before their eyes. Maybe she wouldn't even stop there. For all

Hodge knew, she could cast him into some unknown realm at her next whim.

Hodge tried to steady his pounding heart, to no avail. Was *any* of this real? Was Halston's entry into another world just another trick, an illusion she'd created to distract them? Was Halston actually somewhere else? Hell, he might even still be in this room.

Rogue was staring at them with a keen look on her face.

Hodge almost spoke to her, tempted to ask *where,* exactly, Halston had gone, but he stopped himself. If he crossed her again, who knew what she'd say, what she'd conjure up for him?

Instead, her lip curled back when she looked down on him. "They're on their way," was all she said.

"What?"

She turned to her troop of monsters and said, "You may watch. It's been eons since I've had a proper fight within my halls." She looked happier than a bride.

The monsters roared with delight.

Footsteps pounded on the floor, echoing in the hallway leading to where they stood. Heavy, uninterrupted.

Time seemed to creep into a crawl. Hodge stood still and waited, facing the opening of the hallway, not daring to let his sight leave it. He didn't even blink.

And together, their enemies came running from the shadows, six dull-eyed corpses tearing in their direction.

Boundless, blazing hatred flared inside Hodge. Their hunters had found them. The remaining revenants had returned, and now, they were racing alongside that strange man in the cloak. His knife was at the ready.

Hodge waited for the ground to start lurching, to crack open chasms for them to fall into. But as he narrowed his eyes at the dark gap leading into that hallway, there was no sign of the masked warlock. A faint spark of hope sprang up inside of Hodge, but he forced himself to keep it tame.

Hodge drew both pistols. Earlier, he'd chambered six adamite pistols in the right one, six lead in the left.

It was time.

Rogue's monstrous guards began to scale the walls, practically roaring with laughter as they scampered up to the ceiling like spiders, then hung from the stone like bats, eager to guzzle the scene below like sweet wine.

The cloaked man hurried down the steps and into the pit, and the revenants followed him. They moved faster than Hodge had first recalled, though he'd only caught glimpses of Captain Crane's revenants moving back at Fort Marksdale. Hodge had expected that they'd be sluggish, that decay would make them clumsy, but that couldn't have been further from what he saw. They had a fluidity to their movements, like animals—like predators. Mindless beings with nothing to lose and no conscience to hold them back.

Hodge fired at one revenant, and at once, its body burst into dust. He looked over his shoulder at Lorelin and shouted, "Protect Tsashin!"

Hodge caught sight of Flint, then, who seemed to have come out of his half-trance. But he still had not moved from his spot. Perhaps he was regretting that now. They didn't exchange words, but somehow, Hodge understood the look Flint gave him perfectly. Hodge recognized a silent '*shoot well*' when he saw one.

And then, Flint disappeared.

Hodge's gaze ran across the long steps descending into the pit, though over the clamor of footsteps he couldn't distinguish Flint's.

Though Hodge couldn't blame him for leaving, he couldn't keep the anger from swelling in his chest. Now, it was him and Lorelin against the rest.

Now, more than ever, he'd have to shoot carefully. Lorelin guarded Tsashin toward the other end of the rectangle, just beneath the ledge where Rogue sat in her chains. Somehow, he'd have to gun them all down before they reached the girls.

Hodge dashed backward from the charging horde, then took out another one of the revenants. A villager—a round-faced, wide-eyed boy who couldn't have been any older than Tsashin. As it burst into a puff of ash, Hodge remembered who they were. They weren't really his enemies—they were pawns the warlock had brought back to life.

"Stop!" shouted a muffled voice.

The cloaked man. That strange strip of cloth over his mouth had softened his words. Hodge's focus leapt to the man. He took in his broad figure, that big hood shading his face, that strangely beautiful knife he was wielding . . .

Before Hodge could dodge it, one of the villagers—a brawny fellow who could have easily been mistaken for a bear if he wore a fur cloak—took a massive stride in his direction and grabbed his left wrist. Hodge shouted. The revenant's grip was so strong, he was shocked that he didn't hear his own bones crack when it squeezed. Captain Crane took his other arm, his clutch not half as strong, but just as unyielding.

Hodge struggled against their grasps. The two other revenants— tall, freckled, auburn-haired villagers that were almost certainly brothers—trudged forth, one on either side of the cloaked man, who approached Hodge with a gently raised hand.

"I didn't want a struggle this time," he said, though the cloth over his mouth and his heavy breathing stifled his words. "Please. Come with me now, and there will be no need for a fight."

Hodge hadn't dropped his guns. If he could just get these revenants to let go of his arms, he could end this.

He recalled Halston telling him how familiar the cloaked man had seemed, how he couldn't quite place it. Hodge stopped struggling for a moment as he tried to take in the man's face, but there was little he could see. "Who are you?"

The cloaked man pulled down the cloth hiding his face, revealing a salt-and-pepper beard and a somber, frowning mouth, and Hodge reeled back in shock.

Lothar.

This was who'd been helping the warlock all this time?

Hodge hadn't seen Lothar since he was a boy. Though Hodge hadn't known him well, he'd been his father's friend. His daughter, Ingrid, and Lia had been as close as sisters themselves. Lothar had once had an easy, almost musical laugh. Hodge remembered that when they found Ingrid's shredded body in the field, Lia had wept for days.

Hodge felt glass shattering in his chest.

What did *Lothar* want with him?

"Lothar?" Hodge said, fighting to keep the combination of anger and sheer confusion from his tone. "What's happening?"

"The Source," was all Lothar said. "We need you. You must take your father's place."

Hodge would have asked him to clarify, but there was no need for that.

A gunshot echoed off the walls of the great hall, and Captain Crane's revenant burst into dust. Hodge watched the bits of his body scattering, disbanding, then becoming nothing. Hodge lost his sight for a moment, coughing as the ashy bits of Captain Crane clouded his eyes. He blinked rapidly, and the other revenant let go of his arm.

Lothar's voice shouted something incoherent. Hodge stumbled around for a moment, trying to regain control of his senses.

When he'd finally blinked most of the dust out of his eyes, Hodge turned to see Lothar swatting at the empty air with his knife, like he was trying to bat away a wasp. The revenants lumbered around them, arms flailing.

The bear-like revenant thrust itself forward, then someone cried out. Flint appeared from thin air, the revenant's hands on his shoulders.

"*Flint!*" Hodge cried.

His power, Hodge thought as Flint grunted and struggled against the revenant's grasp. *It doesn't work if someone's touching him.*

Lothar and the auburn-haired revenants recollected themselves and lunged in Hodge's direction, Flint and his attacker forgotten. Hodge dodged sideways, darting out of their reach, and shot at the enormous revenant's leg.

Flint stumbled forth when its body became ash, and though Hodge couldn't see him any longer, he shouted, "*Thank you!*"

Hodge said nothing in answer. His head was spinning.

You must take your father's place.

The cackles raining down from the monsters on the upper walls weren't helping matters.

Lorelin fired twice at the two revenants heading in her direction. She missed both times.

"Don't shoot again!" Hodge yelled, bolting back into the revenants' path.

One revenant spun in his direction, and its blank, lifeless eyes chilled him to the bone. The revenant struck Hodge with its foot, nearly knocking him off his balance, then the revenant seized his shirt and flung him to the ground. Hodge slammed into the floor, and the impact knocked every bit of wind right out of him and made him lose both guns. Rogue's laughter almost shook the room.

Then, another shot blasted from behind. Lorelin had fired. The revenant who had thrown Hodge down shattered, and as its body burst apart, Hodge thought he saw a look of horror in the other's eyes. His heart twisted. Even in this state, did some part of their human minds remain?

Hodge jumped back to his feet. He snatched one pistol off the floor. Then the other.

"Stop this!" Lothar shouted, hurrying in front of the final revenant, waving his arms and blocking Hodge's shot at the last revenant. "Hodge!"

You must take your father's place.

Flint had made himself invisible again, and Hodge wasn't sure where he'd gone. Hodge looked back at Tsashin and Lorelin, who was standing with her feet braced in a firm stance, gun in hand, aimed at Lothar.

Somebody else cried out.

Chills prickled down Hodge's neck. Footsteps sounded from inside one of the hallways leading into the great hall. They were almost here. If there was a new throng of revenants about to emerge, his adamite bullet supply wouldn't suffice. Hodge braced himself to begin firing, but instead . . .

"Lorelin!" a voice cried from inside the corridor.

Hodge blinked, trying to make sense of what he'd just heard. Had he imagined it?

"Jae!" Lorelin yelped.

Jae came dashing out of the hallway and into the room. A man was with her. Hodge had never seen him before, yet he knew him at once. He shared Jae's chestnut hair, angular jaw, and keen brows . . . and he had that same self-assured look in his eyes that Hodge had come to know all too well.

Jae's father was here. She'd finally found him.

Jae ran along the side of the pit, then bounded down the steps, cutting off Lothar's path before he could move further toward the others. He lurched backward, then Jae slammed her heel against his shin. The knife tumbled out of his grasp. He wavered for a second, and Jae seized him by the shoulders, then tackled him to the ground. Lothar shouted as Jae slammed his head against the floor. The red-haired revenant reeled back from the two of them, giving Hodge just enough of an opening to shoot him in the chest. With that, the final revenant crumbled away, returned to dust.

Jae hopped away from Lothar, whose eyes fluttered open for a moment, then closed again. She hadn't killed him, and he hadn't blacked out. Hodge heard him groan, but he didn't rise to his feet. Surely, he'd regain clarity and stand to fight once more, but for now, Jae had bought them time. Still bent over Lothar's slackened figure, she shouted, "Watch out!"

Hodge looked to where she was pointing.

His stomach dropped.

The masked warlock jumped down the stairs and into the pit, then began striding directly toward Hodge.

Hodge's fear slipped away for a second, overcome by his resolve. The warlock had just put himself right in his line of fire. Without a second thought, Hodge raised his left pistol and shot . . .

The bullet struck right where the man's heart should have been.

And yet, the warlock did not fall.

Hodge shuffled backward. The man was getting closer. This couldn't be. He hadn't missed—the bullet hole in his chest was plain as day. He cocked again, shot again, and this time, the bullet hit the warlock's throat.

Once again, it tore through his high collar and left a smoking, gaping hole.

And the warlock did not fall.

Before Hodge could aim at his wavering form once again, his

attention jumped to the heavy footsteps ringing out from the hall. And then a large, hulking, glorious figure came bolting out of the entryway.

"Gryff!"

The Azmarian hurried into the great hall with a sharp fury in his eyes. Inky blood coated his face, but he didn't seem to notice it. He moved, whiplike, with his gun at the ready. With a roar like a battle cry, Gryff leapt into the pit, aimed for the masked man.

Gryff struck the warlock with the butt of his rifle. It let out a thunderous crack as it hit him squarely on the head. The man came crashing down on the floor. As soon as his form lay slackened, Hodge shot it.

Once. Twice. The man's body jolted with each strike, but still, the man pushed himself up on his forearms and faced Hodge. Hodge was trembling with shock.

The bastard wouldn't die!

It was boldness, or madness, or both that forced Hodge's body in the man's direction. He let out a strangled cry and threw himself forth.

Then, the ground vanished from under his feet.

"Hodge!" three strangled voices screamed his name. Hodge lost control of his senses for a moment as he fell. Beneath him, the ground kept sinking, vibrating, shaking him wildly until at last it leveled out.

Cursing, Hodge pushed himself up. The warlock had isolated himself and Hodge in a square shaft around three yards wide on all sides, so deep that the voices tangling up above seemed a mile away. There was no climbing out of here.

Hodge's pistols lay between his body and the warlock's feet. The warlock's jacket hung limp from his arms, his hands raised. In that position, he looked like a scarecrow.

With all the swiftness he could muster, Hodge jumped to his feet and leapt for his guns. He glimpsed the chamber of the first one as he picked it up—lead bullets. He fired another shot into the warlock's stomach as he dove for his second gun. There was no blood. The warlock didn't even flinch.

"What *are* you?" Hodge shouted.

"Come with me," was all the warlock said. His voice was chilling . . . but it wasn't *threatening*. It didn't carry the same menace that Sterling had whenever he threatened to whip Halston bloody or have his cronies pummel Hodge into the ground. There wasn't a hint of anger in it, or desperation, or even a note of warning. Simply, all he did was *speak*. And it terrified Hodge.

Could he be some type of revenant? Hodge doubted it. None of the other revenants spoke, but perhaps adamite could still take his enemy's life. Two adamite bullets were left in his gun, and he was going shoot both of them through the warlock's skull.

The pistol rested firmly in his grasp, and he was putting every bit of faith he still had in this next shot.

Hodge was about to take aim when the ground sank again. Just a foot or two this time, but enough to throw him off balance.

Hodge landed on his knees. He hardly noticed the pain that shot up his thighs.

Hodge's blood roared through him. Driven by instinct and rage, he threw himself at the warlock.

The warlock did not try to fight him. His body was impossibly light. Hodge brought him down by the shoulders, pinning him to the floor with ease.

If the adamite bullets didn't work, he at least had to know *why*.

He jammed the muzzle of his gun to the forehead of the mask and fired.

Shock roiled up Hodge's arm. There was a bullet hole in the

metal, ragged at the edges, which meant there should have been a gaping hole in the warlock's head. Not a drop of blood.

Desperately, he reached out, grasped the edge of the warlock's mask, and yanked with all his strength. The strap snapped, and Hodge cast the mask to the side.

It was the longest moment of Hodge's life.

And the sight below would brand itself into his memory like a burning scar.

He lay there, propped on one forearm, right hand clutching his gun so hard it hurt. Yes—he'd shot the man in the mask.

But there was no blood. No flesh.

Hodge stared down at a bare and motionless skull. In the center of its head, gunsmoke curled from the bullet hole.

Disbelief turned him to solid ice.

The man in the mask wasn't a man at all.

But as Hodge stared down, he felt the being shift under his weight. Moving. Alive.

The warlock was undead.

So why could he speak, and why hadn't the adamite killed him?

The skull-faced being under him shifted slightly, then the walls of the pit rumbled around them. Hodge leapt up, lost his balance, and hit the ground hard. Three pillars of stone sprang from the walls of the hollow and crossed over his body, trapping him in the corner of the trench.

The warlock approached Hodge, then reached for a strange stone talisman hanging from his neck. Hodge tried not to shake, to keep the fear from showing on his face, but he couldn't shake the feeling that he was staring at the face of death itself.

The warlock's jaw didn't move when he spoke, but Hodge had heard his voice all the same.

"You may continue trying to shoot, but nothing will come of it.

All this can end," he said. "All this can end if you come with me. No harm will come to your brother."

For weeks, they'd been running. Men had died in their stead and risen, lifeless, to chase them down.

His enemy could not be killed. Unless he complied, Hodge knew that there was no getting out of this pit alive.

So through gritted teeth, Hodge uttered his reply: "Do it."

The world around him slipped away, fading faster than he could grasp. His body went numb. The others were still calling his name. The pang of regret nearly killed him—he hadn't known it would be so quick, hadn't been offered a chance to say goodbye.

But Hodge was too frightened to cry.

Chapter 50

Salt air stung Hodge's eyes. Feeling returned to his limbs, and sight to his eyes. Above, the sky was murky gray, and the air carried the softness that only came with the dawn. There was grass under his back.

Hodge squeezed the grip of his pistol. Slowly, he sat up.

Moisture glistened on the grass. He stood to look down on the waves crashing against the cliffs. For miles, they stretched on, disappearing past the horizon. To the island's end. Beyond that, the rest of the Second Realm waited.

His world.

He was home.

Behind him, the stony voice of the masked revenant said, "You may have a moment here, if you like. It is all the same to me. Your uncle waits for us."

Hodge whirled around and fingered his gun, on instinct alone. Two adamite bullets chambered, but he'd forgotten that against this enemy, they'd do him no good.

The revenant had slipped his mask back on, hiding his skeletal face once more. Hodge wasn't sure which was more frightening: the bleak, dull metal with those bolts and thin eye slits, or the bone face behind it. Hodge thought of the bare, dry bones that surely hid beneath his leather gloves and baggy clothes.

"You cannot kill me," said the skeletal being. "I drew blood from my offspring in exchange for eternity."

"Who *are* you?"

"I'm called the Vagrant."

A strange sense of calm overcame Hodge, then. "How did we get here?"

"The timestone," said the Vagrant, motioning to the pendant hanging from his neck. "This cost me another one of my sons. I can leave and enter worlds as I please."

Without silver. Without a conduit.

"We can return, if you wish," the Vagrant went on. "But only if your brother will come in your place."

"Never," Hodge snapped, then spat at the Vagrant's boots.

The Vagrant ignored that. "Alright, then. It can be you. As I said, it doesn't matter to me, but the ritual requires one who shares your blood."

Your uncle waits for us.

Hodge suddenly felt faint. He tried to picture his uncle's face, but it was difficult. As a boy, he'd scarcely seen his uncle at all. All he remembered were his father's vague frustrations with his brother, but they were always short lived.

Uncle Dain.

"So my uncle sent you after us?" Hodge asked. The disbelief twisted like a knife inside of him.

"Indeed."

"Why ain't he here, then?" Hodge spat. "Why can't he just kill himself or something?"

"The Rite demands a sacrifice," the Vagrant said, without a hint of feeling. "One must draw blood from his own kin."

For a few moments, Hodge stood there, shoulders rising and falling with each staggering breath he drew.

He was about to die.

He saw no other way.

Somebody else came traipsing up the hill to join them, his cloak flapping in the gentle breeze. Lothar.

Should Hodge kill him? He had nothing left to lose. If he was to be a sacrifice anyway, then there was no reason he shouldn't fire a bullet right through Lothar's eye.

He met Lothar's gaze for the first time since coming here. In his pale eyes, Hodge swore he saw the ghost of Ingrid.

He'd never forget how Lia had cried the day they'd found Ingrid's remains. He wondered if Lothar's sobs had been much the same.

Hodge's hand closed into a fist, then relaxed. He couldn't kill Lothar. Even though the eyes staring back at him belonged to a man leading Hodge to his own slaughter, he couldn't bring himself to believe that he was a traitor.

He was a part of this world, too. This realm had become a feeding ground for monsters, and they'd feasted on Lothar's daughter.

Lothar would never see her again, but perhaps the pain—a pain Hodge had come to know when he saw Elias lying bloated in the river—had led Lothar here. All he'd wanted was to protect his world.

"Please," Lothar said to the Vagrant, voice trembling. "Can Hodge and I have a moment? Please."

"It doesn't matter to me." The Vagrant sounded almost reasonable when he spoke. He walked in the direction of the cliffs.

For a minute, they just looked at one another. Lothar looked so much older than Hodge remembered. It was like decades had passed since the last time Hodge had seen him instead of several years.

"It's been you," Hodge snapped. "This whole time. You've been using your powers to track us, haven't you?"

Hodge still remembered that Lothar had been one of the best hunters on their island when he was a boy. He could track any animal, no matter how far it had strayed from the party. Never had it crossed his mind that Lothar could do the same for people, for *him*.

Even if he *could* . . . why would he *want* to?

Lothar neither admitted nor denied it. "Your father," he started, sounding almost ready to cry, "wanted to find another way. Your uncle wanted us to perform the Rite at once. It divided our whole crew—some of the men feared that a civil war might break out when we returned. And Joad . . . he would have told everyone. Your uncle demanded that we keep it a secret. Didn't want the islanders in hysterics, he said."

That was the day their father had returned from his voyage, looking more somber than Hodge had ever seen. He hadn't told any of them what they'd found far from the shore. The next day, the darkness had come, and he'd jumped to his own death.

Was this all some dream? Some other apparition brought on by Rogue? A second punishment for Hodge's insolence?

"What do you mean?" asked Hodge.

"On the voyage," Lothar began, "we found the Source."

Hodge could scarcely believe what he was hearing. At last, they'd discovered it? The Source of the monsters mercilessly, savagely destroying their world?

All this time, there'd been an end in sight, and Hodge hadn't even known. "What is it?"

"Across the sea . . . we found an ancient god, who'd been left there by some forgotten force. The father of the monsters.

"He promised that it would cease, that he would return his children to another realm, if we performed a sacrificial Rite, and he demanded that one of your father's kin pay the price for it.

"Joad . . . he wanted to make it known, insisted that his people deserved the truth: that we'd found the Source, but he wished to find a way to close it without shedding any blood."

Hodge curled his hand into a fist. "If it's gotta be someone from our bloodline, why can't Dain just give himself up?"

"I told you. The Rite demands that he draw blood from his own kin." Lothar shut his eyes, and Hodge could almost see the memory unfolding in Lothar's mind himself. "Your father refused. He believed that there had to be another option, some other way we could close the Source. But your uncle refused to wait. He . . . he wanted it to be quick. Painless. He ordered a warlock to cast that spell to put your family to sleep. From there, he'd take Joad, and . . ." His voice trailed off. "None of us knew what Dain had been planning. By the time Joad leapt, it was too late. He . . . he must have thought it was another one of the monsters. That there was no escape for him."

Hodge forced every muscle in his body to go rigid. It was all he could do to keep himself from shaking uncontrollably, then doubling over with fury.

His father had never known about his brother's treachery, and he'd taken his own life for *nothing*.

Hodge had no words for Dain. For the coward—the damned coward!

Because if the Rite demanded slaughtering one's kin, that meant that his father had had a chance to spill his own brother's blood, and he'd passed it on. Dain hadn't had the same backbone. And Hodge's father had still paid the price for it.

"I wanted it to end, Hodge," Lothar said finally, and the tears poured freely down his cheeks. "How many others had to die while we wasted our time searching for another solution? One that might have never come at all? How many more bodies, mangled by the fangs? I think of Ingrid every day, Hodge. I never heard her screams in life, but they plague me in all my dreams."

"So I'm gonna be a *sacrifice* to this god?" Hodge looked to the sea.

"There was no other way, Hodge."

"Save it. I don't wanna hear it. So, it's me or Halston?"

Lothar's face was hesitant. Maybe he was searching for the right thing to say. He might have even been looking for some morsel of comfort to offer Hodge, but they both must have known that there could be none.

"Yes, it's you or Halston. Or Elias."

Hodge couldn't stop the bitter, furious laugh that escaped him. "Elias is *dead*."

Lothar's mouth parted. "Dead? How?"

"He drowned a couple years ago."

"Hodge, I'm . . ."

Hodge snorted. Here Lothar was, about to haul him away to his own death, offering condolences for the loss of his brother.

The Vagrant was still waiting for them, back turned, motionless as a lone mountain. Who was this living corpse? Why was he working for Dain?

His uncle wasn't even *here*. If he was going to send Hodge away like a lamb to the slaughter, then he owed it to at least look Hodge in the eye and hear him speak.

"What does he want?" Hodge asked without looking away from the Vagrant. "Why the hell is he working for my uncle?"

"He seeks a vein of magic ore," Lothar replied. "And your uncle has promised him a vyrship to aid his search in exchange for your capture."

Hodge glared at Lothar. "How stupid can you *be?*"

"I'm so sorry, Hodge," Lothar said in a hushed voice. "I really am."

"No," Hodge said slowly. "*I'm* sorry, Lothar."

Hodge kicked him fiercely in the stomach. Lothar doubled over, hands flying to his face. Hodge lunged to Lothar's side, then seized him. Tightly, he wedged a forearm under Lothar's chin, and pressed the muzzle of his gun to his temple with his other hand.

"Don't move, and don't speak," Hodge hissed. Lothar went tense and silent in his arms. Hodge looked to the Vagrant, who was waiting at the cliffside, facing the sea.

"Vagrant!" he shouted. "Get over here!"

When the Vagrant spied Lothar in Hodge's arms, he hustled toward them, moving more quickly than Hodge had seen before.

Hodge spoke as fast as he could. "Can I make you a deal?"

The Vagrant studied them for a moment, utterly impassive. "What is it?" And maybe it was just Hodge's restless mind, but he swore that he heard a hint of fear in the Vagrant's voice. Whatever this being actually wanted, it seemed he needed Lothar to live for it.

Oh, he'd gone mad. He was bargaining with a lost soul, but he'd grasp at all the straws he could, now.

"Give me *six months*," Hodge said. "Six months to find another way to close the Source, to banish the monsters from this world. One without this *Rite*."

"We have you *now*, Hodge," the Vagrant said dully.

"Not for long." Hodge gritted his teeth and pressed the gun against Lothar's head once more. "Either you let me go, or he goes down first. And then . . ." He swallowed, then made himself speak again. "I'll follow him."

"You would take your own life?" the Vagrant asked, sounding more curious than alarmed.

"I will. And my uncle will never find Halston without Lothar. And without us, he'll never give you his ship."

At first, the Vagrant made no reply, then, "That is a monumental task, Hodge Harney."

"I don't care. I'm going to find a way. If I don't, then you can take me with you. But if you don't let me go free, we'll both be dead in a minute."

Hodge watched a dismal future—the one where he'd become a sacrifice—unfold in his mind, clear and vibrant as if he'd already lived it. Would it be quick? Or would the Rite demand a slow death, so he could drown in his own regret as he waited to take his last breath?

It didn't matter.

Because it would be him, and not Halston, or Lia.

"There will be more death if I let you do this," said the Vagrant. "If you do not give up your life, the monsters will continue to ravage this world."

"There will be death either way."

Hodge could feel Lothar's labored breathing against his chest. Guilt rippled through him, and it was almost strong enough to force him to release his father's old friend. Maybe Hodge was just as monstrous as the Vagrant himself. But if this is what it took to protect Halston and Lia, he'd be as monstrous as he needed.

A moment of silence. Then, "Six months, Halston Harney. No more, no less. As soon as they have passed, we will seek you again."

He extended one skeletal hand, and when Hodge shook it, he could have sworn he felt death itself run its cold fingers down his spine.

When the Vagrant released his grip, Hodge let go of Lothar, who then fell to his knees, gasping.

Before he left them behind, Hodge was certain that a wave of pity and remorse washed over Lothar's face.

But he did not look back for long.

He flew over the land, treading over the lush, vibrant grass, leaving Lothar and the Vagrant far behind him. All around him, the sound of the crashing waves and gulls traveled through the air, and he breathed in the smell of salt that years of desert and pine had nearly caused him to forget.

Hodge was not familiar with this island. It must have been enormous. There was no end in sight to the land, and he hadn't a clue where he was running.

But he had to carry out his father's wish. If there was a way to close the Source, one that didn't demand the sacrificial Rite . . . he would find it. He hadn't any idea where to begin, but for Halston, he could do it.

For his father. For Lia and Elias and his mother. For his gang, who waited for him a world away. As Hodge ran, he thought of them standing in Rogue's grand hall, gazing down at the pit into which he'd disappeared. Would they know where he'd gone? Would they think he was dead?

In that case, Hodge thought with a humorless smile, *I'll just have to come back from the dead.*

And for their sake—for all the miles they'd wandered, for the dawns that had greeted them and the dusks that had bid them goodbye, for the wounds they'd taken, for all these wild, reckless years . . .

For his brother, and for his gang, he would try.

Hodge was running blind, lost, entirely alone and without a plan.

But he was *home.*

And for now, he was free.

Chapter 51

It was decades or days into the Drifter's journey when he arrived at a pair of gates.

Slowly, the forest around the path had disappeared, giving way to a vast ocean of clouds that floated for an eternity on either side of the stone path, sweeping out beneath the dark and endless sky. The Drifter didn't bother trying to look into them to see if anything lay beneath the clouds or if a single step would send him plummeting through empty air.

It didn't matter. *Nothing* mattered.

The gates rose high, and their silver spires pointed to an immeasurably large expanse of sky, a sky that would make gods feel insubstantial. It was not black, rather a muted, stormy blue with undertones of silver.

And the *stars*.

The stars beckoned to him as they basked in one another's radiance, like a commune of souls content with an afterlife of stillness to adorn the face of eternity.

The path was different here. It wasn't the same flat, dull stone he'd first stepped onto, when the creature had freed him from his own tomb. This part of the path shone like rippling water. It seemed as though he ought to sink in it—like at any moment the magic would fade, the illusion over, and the silent waters would swallow him. On either side, the blanket of thick clouds continued.

What did they hide? What waited at the edge of this world?

When the Drifter turned his back to the immense gates, all he felt was a small but powerful sense of panic.

He hadn't slept or eaten in ages, but weariness and hunger were sensations he recalled only vaguely. Time had passed. He couldn't say how much. But he had changed.

All he'd known—in a lifetime in this world—was walking and darkness, darkness and walking.

But he'd reached the end of the road.

What was there to do from here?

He was alone. Really and truly alone.

It might please him to die.

After all, it couldn't be much different than coming to the end of the road. It would probably be quieter. There wouldn't be any-thing to look at. He'd miss the company of the stars . . . then again, he couldn't say for certain there'd be none in whatever came next.

How *did* one die here, exactly?

He didn't know, and the thought frustrated him. Vaguely, he re-called slaying a monster some time ago, but perhaps that was just a delusion. He wouldn't kill another one, if it came. He would let it devour him whole.

The Drifter sat down, sitting on the path with his back to the gates. He faced the burning stars and thought about speaking to them, but they likely had a language of their own, and his tongue was weak and useless from ages of silence.

A feeling of dullness surfaced within him. He longed to be made of something again, to have muscles that strained and skin that weathered with age, to have eyes that burned without blinking and bones that shook from the cold. Again, perhaps he was deluding himself into imagining that he'd ever been that way. Had he ever been anything other than a forgotten snippet of this world?

Did every living thing come to this? A point where they wanted nothing but to surrender their minds in exchange for peace?

The Drifter examined his body. He wore clothes. Yes, he remembered what clothes were. He knew what a knife was, and blood, and sleep.

Maybe he *could* sleep here. There was a heavy ache inside him, but maybe he could drown it in a dream, if not in death. Yes, he remembered dreams. He used to dream and make the whole world disappear. Perhaps he could return to the darkness he'd known in that casket.

He lay down on the road, then rolled over onto his side. Something dug into his hip.

The Drifter reached into his pocket. Inside it was a lump of wood.

No, not just a lump of wood. At once, he knew it was a bird. He remembered birds, flapping through blue skies. Birds, who sang to signal daylight. Robins, sparrows, cardinals. Jays. Blue jays.

Jae.

The ache vanished.

He leapt to his feet.

Jae. Hodge. Gryff and Lorelin and Tsashin. Flint. They were waiting for him a world away.

The gates!

The challenge!

From so long ago!

The end of the road didn't mean death. It meant victory.

And for the first time since he'd been unearthed from his grave, Halston Harney ran.

"Halston!" he cried up at the gates. "Halston Harney!"

And—just as he'd wished—the world around him disappeared.

Chapter 52

Halston's feet struck a floor of stone. The strange world that had become his life slipped away like vapor into the void, and now, he stood beside a gathering of people he had not seen in . . .

How much time had passed?

He stood at the edge of the stone pit in the great hall on one of the long, flat steps. Above him, Rogue still reclined on her pedestal with the chains hanging from her thin wrists. Far overhead, stars twinkled through the opening in the ceiling.

Halston blinked. He looked down at his hands, only vaguely aware of a slight pain in his body. This body, which suddenly felt foreign to him.

He mouthed his own name. *Halston Harney.* He barely recognized it.

He'd spent what felt like decades trekking across that world. He'd fought a monster in the desert, then sought refuge with a strange old man and a kindly weaver. She'd gifted him the cloth that had, at once, been his salvation and his torment. He'd freed a creature from the hunters, and then those same hunters had buried him alive.

Then the creature had returned and saved him, and now, his warning was already haunting Halston. *Live your life. Don't let it go to waste.*

How was his skin still smooth? How did he have the strength to remain standing? How had he not turned to dust as soon as he fell through that portal? So much time had passed.

But here, he realized quickly . . . hardly any time had passed at all.

The challenge was over.

They'd get their knife back, now. Gryff was here, and surely, the silver was still in his knapsack. They'd return to that spot by the Shroud, where the veil was thin enough to cut through.

They were going home.

And though it seemed he hadn't been there in centuries . . . he longed for it just the same.

Halston studied the faces of everyone in the room. Before him, standing with bloodied faces, mouths agape, were his gang. They were trembling, as though they'd just barely limped away from a battlefield. In the center of the floor was a square hole, a deep crater. He was fairly certain it had not been there before.

Lorelin's eyes shone with tears, and she knelt beside Tsashin, who was no longer unconscious, but the heartbroken look in her brown eyes made her look distant and unaware. Flint and Gryff just looked stunned. Behind them stood a man Halston hadn't met.

Halston rose, got to one foot, then the other. He had to say something. Tell Hodge that he'd done it, that he'd spoken his name at the gates.

. . . Hodge.

Where *was* Hodge?

As Halston spun around, gaze darting all over the room for his brother, the silence was deafening.

Something was wrong.

Rogue's eyes were piercing through Halston. She was seething, like a serpent braced to strike.

"You broke the rules," she said plainly, the thin veneer of disinterestedness in her tone barely holding back her rage.

"No, I didn't."

"You did. I told you that you could take *only* the clothes on your back." She frowned. "It seems you brought a token in your pocket?"

Halston lifted a hand to his pocket. There, he touched the lump of the wooden bird Jae had carved for him. A gift from eons ago. The very thing that had caused him to recall his name at all.

Without it, he would not have won the challenge.

Rogue began grinding her teeth. Halston was certain that her jaw would unhinge and a torrent of darkness would flood the room, taking them all with it forever.

A high note rang out on the stone floor. Halston looked down.

Half the blade was at his feet. The tip of the knife sparkled like a sea of diamonds. Here, there was enough light that he could make out the inscription on the flat of the blade.

They had the conduit.

They had the silver.

They'd found a place where the veil was thin enough to sever.

They had everything they needed.

Halston could go home to his broken world.

"Well done, Halston," Rogue said, the heat in her voice replaced by a strange chill. "The conduit is yours. Though you owe a great deal of thanks to *her,*" she went on, tipping her chin toward a figure standing at the edge of her grand hall.

The one person in this room Halston hadn't dared look upon, yet. If he did, he feared he might fall apart.

But he couldn't stand it any longer.

When that cursed realm he'd crossed had faded away, the first thought to surface in his mind had been of her face. As the gates had vanished from his sight, all he'd wanted was to see her again.

Jae.

Jae, I remember you.

Running from the cellar while the fires blazed behind. Lying at his side in the company of a hundred million stars. Her head beneath his chin, his arms gathered around her, in those first few seconds of freedom, when Sterling Byrd lay dead.

How on earth could he have forgotten her at all?

At last, Halston looked upon her. Jae Oldridge, kneeling on the stone, waiting for him far across the room. There was blood on her face, hair clinging to her damp forehead. Her clothes were sopping wet. One of her eyes had blackened. He could tell she was trying to hide it, but her arms were trembling.

In all his life, both here and on that near-eternal road, she was the most beautiful thing he had ever seen.

And now, he was going to run to her, and nothing would stop him.

It was then that Rogue flicked her hand, and something seemed to strike Jae down. Halston didn't see what it was, but a pained scream escaped her lips. Jae collapsed forward, breaking her fall with both hands.

"*No!*" Halston screamed.

He ran to her, his head burning with fear and rage. He waited to see blood raining down her chest, to watch her body shudder into lifelessness.

No, this couldn't be.

He'd take another challenge. He'd beg—no, he'd *demand* that

Rogue give him another. He'd walk down that road again, face a thousand more monsters, let them bury him another thousand years, if only Jae got to *live*.

That scream only could have come from somebody on death's door.

Halston braced himself to watch death close her eyes for good. Instead, her skin began to glow. No, it wasn't glowing. She resembled a ghost, or the Wydrian memories, a rainbow cast on the sky just before it faded away.

"A wanderer, this one is." Rogue's voice rose with a teasing lilt. There was no evil in it, and that made it all the more vile. "I know your desire to see the world, little one. So I will let your lover make your wish come true as his consequence. He broke the rules. He should not have succeeded. But he did, all because of you.

"So, my will be done. Every night, you will fall asleep in one place. Every morning, you will wake in another. Imagine all the beauty you will see. Every day, a new corner of the world. It's all you ever wanted, is it not?"

No.

Halston jumped for Jae. A wall of fire could have blazed between their bodies. It would not have stopped him.

He tried to throw his arms around her, but they passed through empty air. Already, nearly all of her was gone. Gone somewhere far away.

Torn from him.

But part of her essence remained—some echo of Jae's soul was still in this room—and before every last trace of her was gone, he caught a whisper from her lips.

"I will love you till the winds fall silent."

And then, every part of her was gone.

Time drudged on. Halston waited where she'd stood, willing her to return, to cling to him as he'd tried to latch onto her. To keep her in his arms and never let her go again.

This wasn't supposed to happen. He'd won the challenge. She was supposed to be by his side, now.

Where was she?

Gods above, where had Rogue put her?

He closed his eyes. At once, he regretted it. The memories of an eternity on the road smothered him. The darkness, covering him. He'd been buried. They'd thrown him into that hole *alive*.

Footsteps came from behind Halston. The only stranger in the room came to join him in staring helplessly at the spot where Jae had disappeared. When Halston got a closer look at his face, he knew this man at once.

This was Jae's father. Ven Oldridge.

Ven's body shook, and his dark eyes shone with a fury Halston had never seen in another before. Only a madman would have stepped in Rogue's direction so assuredly, but Ven Oldridge did.

As he darted in Rogue's direction, an apparition appeared in his path. The ghost of a pale man in a Ranger's uniform manifested before him, gazing at him with a look of utter hatred.

Ven cried out, then a force—invisible as the wind—struck him down. Ven cursed as he fell to his knees. Tremors rattled him. Lorelin leapt to his aid, trying to calm the spasms with soft words and gentle hands. The vision of the ghost had disappeared.

Halston should have moved—helped him as well. But he was paying tribute to nonsense, to the thought that by rooting himself in the spot where Jae had disappeared, she would come back. If he stayed here long enough, she'd reappear, and at last he'd take her hand and lead her out of this place for good.

"Where did you put her?" He spun around to face Rogue, balling his hands into fists. "And where's Hodge?"

Her eyelids dropped slightly. "Your brother returned to your home world. You missed quite the spectacle while you were gone. He went with that warlock . . . It's a shame you were not here to go in his stead."

Halston tried to slow his breathing, then looked to the gap in the ceiling. *You should have been here,* the stars seemed to whisper down to him.

But he'd left.

He'd crossed through another world, and in that coffin, enveloped by earth and time, he'd forgotten his brother.

Hodge, who had not left his side in years, was lost.

"Not to worry," Rogue purred. "He is still alive. For now." She stretched out her neck, briefly glancing at the aperture in the far-off ceiling. "As for your lover . . . if you want her back so badly, then go and find her."

If every bit of hope had drained from him, if Halston had nothing left to lose . . . he would have thrown the conduit at her face. He doubted that a simple knife would even cut a witch this powerful . . . but the storm raging inside him was enough to tempt him.

Rogue merely regarded him with a snarl. "You wouldn't be the first man to dream of cleaving my skull in two. And if you tried, you wouldn't be the first man to leave my domain with each heartbeat sending a wave of fire through your veins and the feeling of daggers in your throat every time you tried to speak. Now take your prize before I reconsider."

Halston finally picked the blade up off the floor. It felt strange in his hand. It was like holding starlight, or a memory he'd forgotten.

He fought to keep his expression unreadable. Inside, he was screaming.

Hodge was gone. Jae was gone. And they'd slipped from him before he could even say goodbye.

"You have ten minutes," Rogue crooned, inclining her chin, "to leave. Take your spoils, leave my halls, and do not let me see you again, or my guards will feast on your bones. Go."

———————

The night was over.

Perhaps the netherworld, the forgotten road, had claimed more of his mind than Halston had first assumed. Right now, he couldn't speak. Not yet. Words seemed simple, almost foolish, after what he'd seen.

My name is Halston Harney. He'd recalled it at the gate, but now it seemed likely that he would soon forget it again.

He felt a stranger to his own body.

It was as if he'd stepped into a painting he'd glimpsed once as a child, and now, he was walking through a world he'd only spent seconds perusing before. What was his time alive compared to the time he'd spent walking down that road? Holed up in that desert house? And, at last, the time he'd spent buried, bound, and undying?

In his pack, he had a conduit—a full one, ready. On Gryff's back, there were several dozen pounds of silver. He knew the spot in the Shroud where the veil was thin . . .

He had all he needed to return to his realm.

Hodge.

Rogue had said he was alive.

And though he'd been away for what felt like ages, the notion of Hodge being lost—trapped in the clutches of the warlock who'd pursued them—shattered something inside Halston.

He'd done what was necessary. He had taken that challenge to get their conduit back.

And yet, he'd failed his brother, and he'd failed Jae.

They mounted the stairs and began making their way back to the forest above in silence. Halston didn't spare a single glance back. If he could help it, he would never look upon Telin again.

Unless, by some cosmic chance, he came across a power that could overcome Rogue's. Then, he would destroy this place.

They reached the summit of the stairway, and Halston took the first step back into the burnt woods. Though he wasn't sure where they were going, he moved more quickly than the others. The sooner he put as much distance as possible between the gang and Telin, the better. Everyone stepped steadily behind him, save Lorelin, who jogged to catch up to his side.

"Lorelin," Halston said, ready for the truth. "What happened?"

Lorelin did not look at Halston while she replied. Her sea-green eyes kept studying the ground, as did Gryff, Ven, Tsashin . . . and Flint. *Flint.* Why was Flint still with them?

"They came while you were gone," she said, nearly inaudibly. "The warlock. The revenants. Someone named Lothar."

Lothar.

Halston dug through his trove of memories and found a face from his childhood. Lothar. The father of his sister's dearest friend, his father's own confidant.

Lothar.

What on earth could Lothar want with his brother?

"Hodge." Despair rose inside Halston like water ready to break through a dam.

Tears welled in her eyes. "We didn't see what happened. We'd killed all the revenants, but Lothar . . . he kept shouting at Hodge to stop. That there didn't need to be a fight. Then the warlock came. He dug Hodge down into that pit, and we were calling for him, and then . . . they all disappeared. They were there for a moment, and then they weren't. And then you came back."

Lothar. Why him? He had no vengeance to claim, no reason to chase the sons of Joad Harney, his friend, to the ends of the earth and back.

"Why?" Halston asked, though perhaps there was no answer that could satisfy him. "Why Hodge?"

"Something about a source," Lorelin said, though her voice was starting to break. "He said that Hodge needed to take your father's place."

The Source.

Halston stopped walking. The others froze in their tracks, looking upon him with woeful stares. Even the tar-black trees seemed to be peering right at him.

The Source of the monsters. The darkness that had claimed his father, fated to take them all. That hollow look on his father's face when he returned from that voyage . . .

Hodge was alive. Lia was still out there, and so was his mother. Before he returned to them, Halston had to find a way to shield their world for good. Portal or not, the monsters would plague their home until the Source was closed.

And he didn't yet understand why . . . but Lothar had come here for a reason. Somehow, he and Hodge were tied to the Source.

Halston began pacing in circles over the dark, scorched ground, trying to unearth those impossibly hazy memories of the world he'd been born into. They'd been only children when the monsters first appeared, and still just boys when they'd come to the First Realm.

He didn't know what they could do to get Hodge back, to find Jae, to defeat the monsters . . . but there had to be an answer. And, gods help him, he could find it.

The uncertainty felt larger than the sky itself, but Halston wasn't afraid of it. Right now, the only thing he was afraid of was surrender.

He would find them. All the time he'd spent a universe away had not been enough to shatter the bonds between each of them, and nothing short of death could break them now.

Tsashin nudged Halston on the shoulder and offered him a shred of hope. "I know where we can go for help."

Halston tilted his head. "Where?"

A veil of sorrow dimmed her face, but it wasn't quite enough to smother the hope that was also there.

"My family," she said. "I remember where they are now."

Lorelin raised her eyebrows. "*What?*"

"The mirror," Tsashin said in a hushed voice. "I . . . I saw them. It showed me *everything*."

Somebody else tapped Halston on the shoulder. He turned to meet the gaze of Ven Oldridge.

"You're Halston," he said. His grief-stricken eyes sent another spear of pain through Halston's chest.

Halston. Yes, he was Halston. He was Halston Harney, and he was nineteen years old. He'd come from the Second Realm and worked as a cowhand before he'd become an outlaw. He had a sister he had not seen in ages. One of his brothers was dead, and the other was alive. "Yes."

He waited for Ven to curse his name. Halston would deserve it if he did. But all he said was:

"Thank you, son. For looking after her." He drew in a breath. Tears glimmered in the corners of his eyes. "She told me all about you. And I'll make you a deal right now. I'll help *you* find her, if you help *me* find her."

Halston forced a small smile and nodded.

The sky was beginning to lighten. Halston wondered if the sun was rising at the same time for Jae or Hodge.

Halston felt someone take his hand. He met Lorelin's eyes, and somehow, she managed to smile at him.

On his left, he felt Tsashin's presence, and then she whispered, "They'll be alright. I can feel it."

Despite it all, Halston willed himself to believe it.

Perhaps they hadn't a clue where they were headed next. Halston wasn't sure, exactly, what faith felt like. But as they stood there, impossibly small, just grains of sand in the desert of the world . . . he was fairly certain that this was it.

And so they faced the rising sun, braced for the dawn that would come.

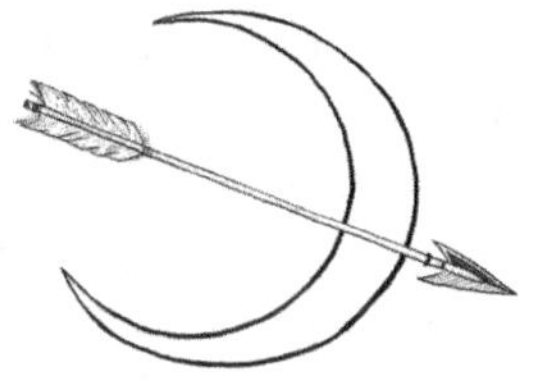

Epilogue

*J*ae hadn't spoken yet.

It wasn't because she'd been unable. It was because the second she'd found herself in this new place, she'd screamed until she lost her voice.

In those first few minutes, she hadn't even opened her eyes to look. She'd just shouted until her throat felt as though it might start bleeding. When her scream ended with a crack in her voice, she sank to her knees.

Open your eyes, she thought. *Stop it. Shouting out loud will do you no good. Look around at where you are.*

And finally, she listened to herself.

She looked around at where she stood.

Jae was in a field of dawn-touched gold. All around her, stretching for miles and miles, was a sea of wheat. Above, the sky was a brilliant, cloudless blue. She breathed in deeply and found that the air smelled crisp and new.

She still had her pack. Jae unslung it, and dug her arm deep inside, feeling around for . . . *yes.*

She still had it.

Jae flipped open the compass in her hand. Pa's compass. Each time she'd stared down at it in these past years, it had reminded her that he was still out there, waiting for her. That someday, she'd see him again. She'd believed it with her whole being, and finally, it had come true.

Perhaps, she thought, she could do it again.

So then, she closed her eyes and made for herself a new belief.

I don't know what sort of curse I'm under, what kind of magic this is. But I'm going to find a way out of it. I'll break it. And then, I'm going to find them again.

And though she couldn't speak above a whisper, she said every one of their names out loud.

'Pa' and 'Halston' left her lips lastly.

Then, Jae shut her pack. She didn't pocket her compass yet. *Which way do I go?*

Jae glanced at the thin strip of sunlight rising in the east and decided that was as good a place as any to start.

Acknowledgements

Hi there. Sorry about that cliffhanger. (I'm not actually sorry.)

Hoo boy.

I committed a grandiose indie author faux-paus by taking almost three years to crank out this book. That said, *Sons of Vagrants and Lords* is a project that emerged from three incredibly dynamic years of my life. These three years have been full of changes for me. Positive changes, but changes all the same. It took a while to get there, but at long last, the second chapter of Jae and Halston's story has been told.

And it couldn't have happened without some very special people.

Thank you to Lina Amarego for the chapter headers, and to Franziska Haase for the incredible cover. I am still in awe of your talents!

To Taylor, Maria, Abby, and Christina: thank you so much for being such fantastic critique partners. Without fail, you guys have let me bounce ideas off you, and this book couldn't have taken on its final form without your input. Thank you for helping it get there, and for being fantastic lifelong friends (and a fantastic sister) as well.

Thank you so much to Cameron and Josiah at JD Book Services. Thank you to Cameron for thorough (and hilarious) editing and feedback, and to Josiah for helping this series get to where it is now. You both have been such a pleasure to work with these past few years. I'm truly lucky to have worked on this project with you both.

To all my friends who have supported me on this journey (you know who you are): thank you for all the laughter, tears, and everything in between. You are my Harney gang.

And to Mom, Dad, Christina (sucker gets to be in here twice), and Sia: thank you for your unconditional love and support. I could not ask for a better family than y'all. I love you guys to the moon and back.